Praise for *The Troublemaker Next Door*

A *Publishers Weekly* Top 10 Romance for Spring

"Filled with strong-willed characters and a reluctant love affair. The love scenes…will make readers sweat. Readers will get caught up in this story and feel like they have a front-row seat to all the antics."

—*RT Rook Reviews*, 4.5 stars, Top Pick! Gold

"The first in Harte's McCauley Brothers series… [is] a winner. The story is fast-paced, with countless spicy scenes that will make readers hungry for the next installment."

—*Booklist*

WITHDRAWN

"Ms. Harte kicks off a new series, Nora Roberts style except with a lot more erotic heat. Ms. Harte is hands down one of the best erotic sex scene writers I've ever read."

—*La Crimson Femme*

"*The Troublemaker Next Door* is definitely a character-driven romance. There is humor, laughter, emotional connections, and a hero and heroine who strike delightful sparks off of the other. It's a fast, easy read with a lot to enjoy."

—*Long and Short Reviews*

Praise for *How to Handle a Heartbreaker*

"The second installment of the McCauley Brothers series is just as tantalizing as the first. The characters are inspiring and endearing, and some of the scenes are liable to bring readers to tears. The emotions presented are raw, only soothed by the passion ignited by the two main characters."

—*RT Book Reviews*, 4.5 stars

"The McCauley brothers are at it again. Harte's new adult romance is funny, addicting, and full of hot sex scenes, leaving readers eager for the next McCauley novel."

—*Booklist*

What readers are saying about Marie Harte's McCauley Brothers series

"*The Troublemaker Next Door* was a great, easy, panty-dropping sexy read. I can't wait to read the other books in this series."

—Nancy

"This book really blew away every expectation I had and I can't wait to read about the rest of the McCauley Brothers."

—Carrie S.

What to Do with a Bad Boy

MARIE HARTE

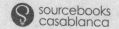

sourcebooks
casablanca

Published by Sourcebooks Casablanca, an imprint of Sourcebooks, Inc.
P.O. Box 4410, Naperville, Illinois 60567-4410
(630) 961-3900
Fax: (630) 961-2168
www.sourcebooks.com

Printed and bound in Canada.
WC 10 9 8 7 6 5 4 3 2 1

To DT and RC. I love you.

And to the Minions, who've helped me spread the good word about my books. You guys rock.

Chapter 1

FINALLY. ALL WAS AS IT SHOULD BE. MICHAEL McCauley nodded to himself as he glanced around his parents' dining room table.

James and Beth McCauley—his parents—were back together again. Happy, smiling, and doting on Colin, Mike's pride and joy. Or, as his brothers called the boy, Mike's little clone.

Colin grinned and exposed a missing front tooth. One that had cost Mike five friggin' bucks. The tooth fairy had definitely succumbed to inflation. Then again, it was a first tooth. With any luck, he could get away with leaving quarters under his six-year-old's pillow in the near future. That bottom tooth looked suspiciously loose.

"Thank you, Grandma." Colin took the extra roll from Mike's mother and smothered it in butter and jelly, ignoring his vegetables in favor of bad carbs and sugar.

Terrific. "Mom, no more. Okay? Colin needs to finish his broccoli."

She frowned at him. So of course, his father frowned at him as well. In an attempt to suck up to his wife, James would do anything and everything to stay out of the doghouse.

"Jesus, boy. It's just a roll. Ease up."

"Yeah, Dad. Ease up." Colin smirked.

James winked at his grandson.

"*Colin.* Dad," Mike growled. When his mother turned to

help Colin cut his steak, Mike leaned closer to his dad and whispered, "Laying it on a bit thick, aren't you, old man?"

James shrugged. "Hey, I learned my lesson. When your mother's happy, I'm happy."

Nice that his father had learned that after thirty-six years of marriage. Mike considered himself a fast learner. After three dates with Lea, he'd known how to please his girl.

Pressure balled in his chest at the thought of her name.

He coughed to hide the pain building inside him and drank his water. *Shit.* He hated being like this, an emotional basket case. But he turned a little nutty this time of year, no matter how much he tried not to. Thank God he'd learned to hide his feelings, or his mother would be all over his ass to share.

"Del said hi," Colin said around a mouthful of dough. "Her daddy's really big. Just like Grandpa."

Mike started. "Del?"

His mother talked over him. "Isn't he, though? Liam is just a big sweetie." Beth smiled, prompting James to scowl. "Oh, stop, James. So we had coffee a few times. Liam is a very nice man. He said encouraging things about you, you know."

His father's scowl faded. "Oh?"

"Yep. Said you were so in love with me, you couldn't help acting like a fool."

Back when his father had been separated from his mother, Mike had worried they might never get their acts together. He breathed a sigh of relief when his mother's sly grin soon appeared on his father's face. Mike didn't have the energy to go to work day after day and watch his father turn back into a shell of a man.

And having seen his mother cry… He never wanted to witness that again either.

"Well, Liam was smart about one thing. He knew better than to lay his hands on my woman." James pulled her close for a kiss.

"Ew, Grandpa. Gross." Colin made a face.

"Yeah, Dad. Really? I'm trying to eat here." Secretly, Mike reveled in his parents acting lovesick. It had been too long since they'd engaged in playful banter. Yet the clear affection showed him how much he was missing as a single dad. It didn't help, either, that his brothers had all recently found love, making Mike the odd man out. Everything was changing, and he didn't like it. At all.

He pushed around his mashed potatoes and focused on what mattered—the here and now. Turning to Colin, he asked, "Since when are you and Del hanging out?"

Delilah Webster. His sexy nemesis and constant headache, though she'd captured Colin's admiration easily enough. Mike didn't like the woman. Not her sexy tattoos, her brow ring, the stud in her nose, the funky way she wore her ash-blond hair, or those wolf-gray eyes that seemed to stare through him. *So not my type.* The woman and her mouthy attitude totally put his back up.

Colin frowned. "When Uncle Cam watched me, we went bowling. And Vanessa and Del were there."

He could see Vanessa ignoring his wishes to keep the woman away from Colin. Now pregnant and engaged to his youngest brother, she had a way about her that didn't invite question. But Cam knew better.

"Vanessa shouldn't have—"

"Ahem." His father frowned at Mike and shook his head. Then he turned to Colin. "Did you have fun?"

Colin grinned. "Yeah. Del has big muscles and her arms are so cool. I want arms like that."

Sleeves of tattoos. On a *woman*. Mike did his best to convince himself she turned him off.

"J.T. came too, and he's huge." Colin had stars in his eyes. *Damn Del.* "As big as Daddy."

"J.T.?" Beth asked.

"Her brother," Mike muttered, not pleased at all. He'd known as soon as he'd met the guy that Colin would idolize him. The resemblance to a certain celebrity, one of Colin's favorite people, didn't help matters.

"I'll bet he might be as big as your dad, but he's not as strong," Beth said gently. For his sake or Colin's?

"He's a wrestler, Grandma."

Mike sighed. "No, son. That's The Rock you're thinking of. Del's brother is someone else." J.T.—the big bastard—had tried screwing with Mike not long ago. Unfortunately, Mike hadn't gotten the fight he was still itching to finish. With J.T. *or* Del.

"He's fuckin' awesome." Colin beamed.

The table fell silent.

Mike met his mother's stunned gaze, but his father continued to eat and question the boy, so he figured he hadn't heard what he thought he had. She shrugged and returned to her dinner as well.

After a few moments, he chimed in. "Colin, tell us about your field trip coming up. You're not going to the zoo, are you?" Seattle's Woodland Park Zoo had always been one of Colin's favorite places to go.

"Nope. We're visiting the Reptile Pit." Colin waxed on about his upcoming visit to the Pit, a popular place that taught kids about reptiles.

Enthused that his son liked school and showed signs of being as gifted with academia as his grandma, Mike encouraged him with questions.

"Yeah, Dad. I'm going to sit next to Brian when they bring the snakes out. He likes them too. Maybe you can come. They need chaperones."

"I'll try." But the timing would be tough. He was right in the middle of a massive remodel that was behind schedule due to some screwups courtesy of the homeowners. He hated being behind.

"Do you get to handle the snakes?" James asked.

"Ew. How about lizards instead? Maybe some cute little frogs," Beth suggested.

Colin smirked. "Grandma, don't be such a girl."

For all that Colin loved his grandmother and crushed on Del, he still had a bias against girls. Not that Mike could blame him. His mother's recent matchmaking efforts had nearly driven him insane with the opposite sex. Now that she had her hands full dealing with his father, he could ease back into—

"Pass the fucking potatoes, Dad." Colin waited.

"*What?*"

His mother dropped her fork. His father choked on his drink.

Colin blinked innocently. "Pass the potatoes?" The mischief in his blue-eyed gaze was straight-up Brody— another troublesome brother too busy playing house with his girlfriend to come to Sunday night dinner. "Did I say something wrong, Dad?"

"Oh hell no. We're not playing Ubie's game." Ubie— Colin's nickname for his Uncle Brody.

"Mike," Beth warned.

"Where did you hear that word? The F-word." Mike had said his share of choice phrases. He worked in construction with his father, for God's sake. Swearing was a McCauley way of life. But the F-bomb… From his six-year-old?

"Um, well…"

"It was Del. Wasn't it?" The woman plagued him, even on a Sunday with his family.

"No."

Mike knew that tone. "Tell the truth."

A mulish frown settled over his son's face. "J.T. said he wanted some fucking nachos. So Del told him to get his own. Then she told him to 'mind his damn mouth because of the kid.' She nodded at me. I'm the kid, Dad." Colin glowed.

"I get that."

"So it wasn't Del. I *told* you."

The little smart-ass. "Watch your tone, boy. And your mouth."

"Well, if that ain't familiar," James said in a low voice. "Déjà vu, eh, son?"

His mother coughed to hide a laugh.

Mike narrowed his eyes at his old man. "You know, I remember getting my butt handed to me the first time I said 'damn' at this very table." Trust his folks to turn on him when they'd been the ones hammering him with manners for the first eighteen years of his life.

"Pass the damn potatoes, please." Colin held out his plate.

"Colin." Mike glared. "We don't curse, and we don't use bad words at the table. Especially when you don't even know half of what you're saying. One more smart remark and you're going to bed early tonight. Understand?"

Colin heeded the warning. Finally. "Yes, Dad."

"Try again. How do you ask for the potatoes?"

In an exceedingly polite voice, Colin asked, "Dad, would you *please* pass the mashed potatoes?"

"Sure thing." Mike pushed them next to the boy and knew he couldn't avoid it any longer. Time to talk to Del again. He squelched any sense of anticipation, knowing the time had come to put a stop to his son's growing attraction to the female mechanic draped in piercings and tattoos.

And this time, Mike wasn't going to play nice.

—∿∿—

"Oh my God. Dale, get in here." Delilah Webster stared in dismay at the chaos that had become her office.

The new guy popped his head in the door, snapping gum and doing his best impression of bored. He didn't fool Del. She could see him sweating, and he refused to make eye contact.

"Who the hell did this?" She waved around at the once-neat stacks of papers now scattering her desk. "You know the rules."

He nodded while remaining a fair distance away, in the doorway. "Um, yeah. No one touches your office."

"Well?" She planted her hands on her hips, so she'd keep them free and clear of the twerp's neck.

"I swear, it wasn't my fault. I tried to get him to go away, nicely. He said he needed some paper to draw—"

"*J.T.*" she bellowed, knowing who was at fault.

Dale vanished like a ghost, and her brother ambled in from the garage door. The automotive repair shop that her father had started over thirty years ago now ran smoothly, courtesy of her administrative skills. Though she could turn a wrench and diagnose problems almost as well as her father, Del's true strengths lay in her ability to organize the idiots around the place.

She hired and fired without a problem. Some called her a bitch. So what? She got things done, people were paid, and they had clients out the ass. Something Liam Webster liked to brag about to all his buddies down at the pool hall.

Unlike Del and her father, her older brother's talents had gone in another direction. A temperamental artist with no respect for *her professional space*.

"Yo, Del. What's up?" He strolled into the office like he owned it, and her blood boiled.

"What the fuck, J.T.? This is not your personal playground."

He tsked. "Language. Really, little sister. Is that any way to talk to the man who just designed the hood for your client's fancy wheels?" He waved a piece of paper at her. "I was in the garage with Johnny when your rich dude came by. He saw my tats and wanted something like my skull on the hood." He pointed toward the classic '67 Chevy Camaro sitting in the garage. "I mean, I thought for sure he'd go for standard stripes. But the guy has a creative streak I thought you'd appreciate."

"That's if we can translate your artwork the way he wants it. I don't suppose you told him you're a tattoo artist, not my painter?"

"Well, no. But this isn't going to be anything Lou can't handle."

"It better not be," she muttered and ripped the paper out of his hands. She took a hard look at it, noting the lines of the design, and grunted.

J.T. laughed. "You sound just like Dad. Where is he, by the way?" He shot her a sly glance. "Still sniffing after that fine Beth McCauley?"

Del stiffened at mention of the dreaded M-word—McCauley. "No. She's living her happily-ever-after with her husband and four annoying sons in Queen Anne." Ritzy Queen Anne—away from the south side. Rainer Avenue was going through a transition from lower income to upscale, but she liked the garage on the rough side. Kept all the hipsters out.

"The sons might be annoying, but she's got a cute grandkid. I like Colin."

She gave a reluctant smile. "Yeah. He sucked at bowling, but he's a funny guy." Truth be told, when she'd first met Colin McCauley last year, she'd been taken by the six-year-old's sweet disposition and the mischief brimming in his bright blue eyes. Someday he'd grow up to be a real heartbreaker. He'd watched as she'd fixed the flat tire for his sitter, then asked her a million questions while she worked.

Del didn't have kids, but she liked them. Unfortunately, her many tats and piercings often put them off. But not Colin. He'd been in awe of her full sleeves, the colorful work her brother had created.

"Colin's the only one I like." She paused. "And maybe the women around him, but they're not McCauleys, technically." Not yet. She liked Maddie, Abby, and even the icy Vanessa. The trio had embraced Del with a sureness she still didn't understand. They acted as if they truly liked her, and Del had never had much in the way of female friends. Well, not counting her cousin Rena.

"So these women…" J.T. leaned a shoulder against

the wall. "You think they'll stick to the McCauleys? Because Vanessa was fine as shit." At her look, he amended, "Ah, I find her rather attractive."

She snorted. "*Rather*. Gimme a break. Besides, she's pregnant. I think her fiancé might mind you trying to hook up with his baby's mama."

"Bummer."

"Don't even start on the others. They're all taken."

"Well, not *all*, Del," he answered way too nicely. "From what I remember, that big hunk o' love, Mike McCauley—Colin's daddy—he's single. Isn't he?"

"Shut up." She did her best not to blush, recalling all too easily her last altercation with Mike. The ass. She'd caught him here in the office with her father. She thought he'd come to mess with her again. The guy had a bias against sugar, and sue her, the one and only time she'd baby-sat Colin, it had been Valentine's Day and they'd shared some chocolate. Big deal. But not according to Mike.

After lashing out at him, she'd learned he hadn't come to bash her, only to talk to her father. Embarrassing enough. Then the galoot had taken her aside and threatened to *kiss* her. In front of everyone. She snorted. As if she wanted any part of him touching her. The jerk.

She ignored the flare of heat that always accompanied thoughts of said jerk and started straightening up her desk.

"Oh, you *like* him." J.T. snickered. Six feet and four inches of adolescent humor. The gift that just kept on giving.

"Don't you have a job? Away from here?"

He shrugged. "It's after four. I'm taking the evening off. Got a date with Gina."

"Big boobs?"

"Big ass. You're thinking of Tina."

"Oh, right." With J.T., if it wasn't one girl it was another. He spent more time getting a piece of tail than she did behind her desk. How he had time for his successful career she didn't know. "So when are you settling down and giving dad grandkids?"

"Please. I'm in my prime."

"You're old. Thirty-two."

"Shit. That's young. Forty is the new twenty."

"You mean thirty." She read the magazines.

"Whatever. Point is, with a body this fine, it would be selfish not to share the love. But you. So pitiful. So ugly. You should find a man and get married, stat."

"Pick me," Johnny yelled from the garage.

"No, me," Sam argued.

Foley growled. "She's mine, dickwads. Get your own girl."

J.T. grinned at her while the guys yelled at one another in the garage—which echoed. With her luck, her father would walk into the conversation.

She glared at her brother. "You're such a dick."

"I know." He chuckled, then closed both doors to the office. "But you know I'm right."

"Please. I'm beautiful." Maybe not beautiful, but Del had never hurt for male attention. She knew she intimidated most people with her looks and attitude, but that had never stopped men from checking out her ass when they didn't think she was looking. "Besides, I'm not into marriage."

His gaze softened. "You should be. You have a lot to offer a guy."

"I know. I like to offer *all sorts* of things," she said with a mock leer.

He flinched. "Ouch. Please, no details or my ears will start bleeding."

She laughed, wishing she could take the idea of marriage seriously. She ignored the urge to rub the scar on her arm now covered by a dragon's claw. "You don't want to hear me get ugly, quit trying to marry me off. There's no one I'm even remotely interested in." Mike's face flashed across her mind's eye. "If anyone's going first down that road, it's you. I'm still Dad's baby girl." She batted her eyes. "I'm too young to get married."

"You're twenty-eight and you work too hard. Get a life. Go hang out with your new gal pals. Get laid, get your nails painted. Be a girl, for God's sake."

She barely resisted the urge to throw a wrench at his head. "If you don't leave in the next four seconds, I will kick your—"

The door to the hallway bounced open.

"—mother-fucking ass."

Mike McCauley stood in the doorway, glowering like a demon. How everyone thought he was the nice McCauley amazed her, because she saw nothing nice or saintly about him.

"And here's my answer," he growled in a deep voice that set her on edge.

J.T. grinned at them and wiggled his brows.

She flushed and hated that she felt discomfited. "Who the hell invited you here?"

Mike entered and closed the door behind him. He wore faded jeans and a T-shirt under a denim shirt and Down vest. His scuffed work boots and rough hands attested to the fact that he didn't staple papers for a living. From what she knew, he and his father owned a construction company, one her father wanted to hire to do some work on the garage.

Over her dead body.

At thoughts of dead bodies, she noted the anger in Mike's gorgeous face. Just like his son, he had "ladykiller" written all over him. Short black hair, bright blue eyes, a square jaw, and full, firm lips. He made her feel small and had as much, if not more, muscle than J.T. God, his hand could probably span her entire face. Big hands, big feet, big… She jerked her gaze up from where it had been wandering, mortified that he raised a brow, having seen her study.

Burying her embarrassment behind the attitude she'd honed from years of practice, she growled back at him, "I'm running a business. I don't have time for McCauley theatrics. What do you want?"

"I want to know why my son asked me to pass the fucking potatoes last night." He crossed massive arms over his broad chest. "Something he said about bowling with you two nimrods told me you might have something to do with his mouth."

J.T. laughed then coughed when Mike frowned at him. "Oh, er. Well, I have to get back to work."

"Don't you mean Tina?" she asked nastily.

He winked. "Gina. Yeah. Don't mess with my sister, Mike, or I'll hurt you. And for some weird reason, I like you. Later, sis." Before he left, he gave a less-than-subtle nod to Mike and grinned.

Once he'd gone, the office felt oppressive under the silence and their dueling scowls.

"Well?" Mike asked.

She didn't like him towering over her desk. Over *her*. She rose to her feet and wondered if standing on her chair to gain a height advantage would seem too juvenile. "Well what? J.T. and I met Vanessa and Cam for a game of bowling. Colin was there. We might have let a few words slip, but it was an accident." Through the door, a loud curse sounded. "I work in a garage. We're not having a tea party, McCauley. Grow a set of stones and deal."

"Mike."

"What?"

He took a step closer, and she had a hard time looking away from his eyes. Man, she'd never seen a blue so…blue. "My name is Mike."

"Mike." She licked her lips, not liking the sudden dryness. To her consternation, his gaze fixed on her mouth. "So, uh, get over it."

"Right." Mike took a deep breath, then let it out and stepped back. "Quit cursing around my kid."

"I'll try." For once he hadn't ordered her to stop seeing Colin. "I don't know when I'll be seeing him again, so it probably doesn't matter."

Mike shrugged. "Abby's putting together a celebration party Wednesday night, for her new book deal, I think. She'll probably invite you."

Actually, Abby had sent the invitation via email that morning. "Oh. You're going?"

"Yeah." That handsome smile he so seldom wore appeared, showing a dimple in his left cheek. "But I know how I scare you, so I don't figure I'll see you Wednesday night. Don't worry, I'll tell Colin you were busy."

"Scare me? *You?*" She huffed. "In your dreams,

Mike." She moved around the desk to poke him in his rock-solid chest. "I'll be there Wednesday. Try not to be more of an ass than you can help. I mean, your kid will be there. Don't want to show Colin what you're really made of."

He leaned down, so that his nose was all but touching hers. "Sweetheart, you couldn't handle what I'm really made of."

Stupid Del wanted to drag his stubborn mouth closer for the kiss she could all but taste. From the look in his eyes, he wanted the same. Mike might not like her much, but the man wanted her. She could feel the chemistry between them, and it burned.

Self-preservation reared its head, and she ducked under him and hustled to the door leading to the hall. She opened it and waited. "Don't let it hit you in the ass, *Mike*."

He chuckled as he sauntered to join her. "You'll watch what you say around Colin?"

"Yep. When I see him Wednesday night, I promise to call you a buttwipe instead of an asshole. Fair?"

He sighed. "Guess it'll have to do. For now." To her shock, he dragged a rough finger down her exposed neck. "Nice hair, by the way. I like the braids pulled back. Shows off your pretty neck. No tats here, sweetness?"

She didn't know what to say, frozen by the combustible lust and confusion drowning her system.

He stared into her eyes again, gave a satisfied smile, then left.

She watched his fine ass leave the building, heard a few choice remarks from the guys in the garage who also watched him leave, and yelled at them to get back to work. Then she slammed into her office and plopped her butt in her chair, staring without seeing at the mess on her desk.

She rubbed her neck over the spot he'd touched and tried to be madder about what he'd done. What he'd called her.

Sweetness?

Chapter 2

WEDNESDAY NIGHT APPROACHED WITH A SUDDENNESS that left her head spinning. Del hadn't liked the onset of nerves, her indecisiveness over what to wear, or her second thoughts about skipping the party. Mike had practically dared her to show, and she could no more refuse to meet him halfway than she could stop breathing.

She scowled at the front of Mike's house as she parked and tried to stop fixating on the man.

A glance down at her jeans and red button-down shirt convinced her she'd fit in tonight. Hell, she'd even pulled her hair back into a normal ponytail, nothing weird about it today. Then she grew annoyed that she'd even tried to be more *normal*. It was Abby's party, after all, and the woman would either like her or not. Since she'd never expressed any issue with Del's appearance before, why the heck did Del feel the need to change herself now?

She unfastened the sleeves of her shirt and rolled them back until they rested at mid-forearm. Pleased to see her tattoos and knowing they, as well as her piercings, would likely set her apart in this suburban whitebread party, she pulled herself together, exited, and locked her car.

Right next door to Mike's place, the home Abby shared with her roommates, Maddie and Vanessa, might as well have had a white picket fence around it. Colored a slate blue with white trim, complete with Craftsman-style columns and a homey wooden porch to protect against the weather, the two-story house looked like something out of a magazine. So did the evening sky, turning a darker indigo, complete with wispy white clouds. Thankfully the weather remained clear though crisp. A typical spring Seattle day, minus the rain.

She forced herself to walk calmly up the sidewalk to the front door, like she belonged to the festive group she could hear inside. No cigarette butts on the sidewalk, no trash or weird smells in this neighborhood. Hell, there were flowers in bloom in a pot next to the welcome mat. Hello, Mayberry. Yet underneath her scorn, she made a note to pick up some pansies tomorrow. They'd dress up her place nicely.

Before she could knock, the door opened.

"Del!" Colin grabbed her hand and yanked her inside.

Still cute as a button, he grinned at her, exposing a missing front tooth. He wore a pair of jeans and a handsome blue sweater, and she wondered if Mike had had to fight the kid to make him wear nice clothes.

Chatter, laughter, and the low hum of rock music filled the warm home crowded with people.

Del had been by before, when Abby had strong-armed her into attending a book club. To support her new friend—a novelty at that—Del had attended. And had fun.

They had another meeting scheduled next week, and Del planned to be there.

A glance around showed most of the usual suspects. The dark-haired McCauleys—Flynn, Cameron, and Mike—lingered in the living room near the fireplace.

She ignored the flutter in her belly when her gaze caught Mike's, and she looked away, noting Abby's fair-haired boyfriend by her side. Brody Singer. Or, as Colin called him, Ubie. Though Brody wasn't exactly a McCauley in name, the clan had pseudo-adopted him a long time ago, and everyone considered him part of the family.

Abby laughed at something Brody said while Maddie and Vanessa floated around a bunch of people Del didn't know. Abby, short, stacked, and dark-haired, clung to Brody's arm while she nodded at something some guy said. Maddie fluttered around Flynn, the excitable red-head witty and mouthy, all at the same time. Flynn, her fiancé, was a trip. A funny, handsome guy who managed to be likeable, approachable, and truly enamored of his fiancée.

Vanessa, the cool blond who said whatever the hell she wanted without a filter, moved next to Cameron and reached to hold his hand. Del smiled, because Vanessa didn't seem like the lovey-dovey type, and the action brought a huge grin to Cam's face. Of all the McCauleys, she liked him best. He didn't try to overwhelm with charm, and his low-key attitude made him that much easier to like.

Unlike his oldest brother, now scowling at her and Colin, who'd refused to relinquish her hand.

"Oh, Del. Welcome," Beth McCauley said as she approached. Del blinked and fought the flush rising to her cheeks. Somehow, around Mike's mom, she felt small, worthless. As if the woman's class smothered all that Del had accomplished in life.

"Hey, Beth." She refused to call the woman Mrs. McCauley. Especially since her own father had once taken Beth out on a date.

The big guy right behind her had to be the husband. James, she remembered her dad calling him. She could see where Mike had inherited his brawn. James looked like he still benched anvils, and the guy had to be in his fifties, or nearer her dad's age.

"So this is Del," James boomed. Then he grinned, and she saw that McCauley charm clear as day. "The woman Colin plans to marry."

Colin whipped his hand from Del's and glared. "Grandpa."

Del patted him on the shoulder. "He's just teasing, dude. We all know how much you hate girls."

"Oh." Colin's anger deflated. "Sure. Do you want a soda?"

"I'm good. Thought I'd say hey to Abby though."

"Okay." Colin dragged her away from his grandparents before she could say good-bye to Beth or James and brought her directly in front of Abby.

"Del." Abby beamed then threw her arms around her, as Del had feared she would. Talk about a hugger. "I'm so glad you came." Abby had no problem showing affection. Behind her, Brody smirked.

"Uh, yeah." She peeled herself away. "You invited me."

"True, but I thought you might be too busy. Plus there's the book club next week." Abby frowned. "Coming tonight does not get you out of attending next week, you know."

"Damn."

"Damn," Colin repeated with cheer.

"Shi—oot. Colin, I'm already in trouble with your dad," Del confessed. "Don't repeat that."

He nodded.

Brody added, "Remember what we've talked about, kid. Never get caught."

"Nice." Del shook her head.

Abby sighed.

Colin grinned. "Right. Oh, there's Brian. Bye, Del." The boy took off like a shot, heading for a little redheaded boy playing with action figures by the kitchen table.

The house had one long, wide hall that made a clear path from the entryway through to the back kitchen door and was now filled with guests. In the living room to her left, more people milled about…near Mike, who continued to watch her. Did he think she'd steal the silver if he looked away?

She smiled at him through her teeth and took comfort in his dark frown.

"Don't mind Colin," Abby was saying. "Brian's his best friend. I invited him to keep Colin company."

She looked away from Mike and accepted the beer Brody handed her. "Nice crowd."

"Yeah. The McCauleys, of course. Robin and Kim." Abby's friends, a lesbian couple Del really liked, because they didn't take crap from anyone and had more than held their own with her during the last book club. "A few ladies from my romance writers group, their husbands, and a few friends of Brody's. Friends of mine too."

"Distant friends," Brody corrected.

Abby ignored him. "They're going to be helping me with research on my next book." Abby winked at Del. "Interested?"

"In his friends?"

Brody sighed. "Leave her alone. Although I'm glad you're trying to ease my mind, Del is perfectly capable of hooking up by herself."

Del took a drag of her beer. "Thanks, Brody. Good to know you think I'm capable of snagging my own man."

"Exactly." Brody's smile grew wider. "And speaking of men…"

"So." Mike's deep voice reverberated from behind her. "You came."

"Aren't you observant." Her pulse raced as he moved next to her to join the conversation. "I came to congratulate Abby." She frowned at the woman. "For what, exactly? This is a party about a new contract?"

Abby nodded, her eyes dark with pleasure. "The bidding war for my series ended. I'm no longer stinking poor! Now I'm straight-up middle-class!"

Brody grinned. "Yep. My girl can now afford to buy me a ring when she proposes. Hoo-ee."

"Idiot." Abby smacked him as he swooped down for a kiss.

They made a cute couple. Hell, so did Flynn and Maddie. Even Cam and Vanessa looked right together.

"So, Mike, where's your plus-one?" she asked, knowing it would set him off. She hadn't forgotten Abby and the girls gossiping about Mike the last time they'd gotten together. Something about his mother constantly trying to set him up.

As predicted, Mike's mouth flattened. "He's over there with Brian."

She followed his glance to Colin. "Uh-huh. Not that woman with your mom, the one who keeps eyeballing you?"

He followed her glance to his mother and the woman with her and moaned. "Oh hell. Not again. Abby, I thought I told you not to invite any single women."

What am I? Chopped liver? Brody caught her eye and raised a pale brow, apparently thinking the same.

Abby tried unsuccessfully to hide a smile. "Hey, don't blame me. I threw a party, but Beth wanted to bring a few people. The more the merrier, I say."

"Dude." Brody shook his head at Mike. "Maybe if you'd pretend to like people, Bitsy would ease up. You need a social life."

"Bitsy?" Del asked, fascinated by the turn in discussion. Mike didn't date?

"Oh, he calls Beth Bitsy and James Pop. Always has," Abby explained.

"Right." Whatever. Why didn't Mike date?

"I like people. Well, the ones who aren't desperate and clingy," Mike muttered.

"What's wrong, Mike? Problem finding a woman who doesn't mind your macho attitude?" Del took a few munchies from the tray Maddie offered as she breezed by with a smile. The evening was turning out to be more entertaining than she'd thought.

"No, the problem is fending off my mother's idea of what constitutes my ideal woman," Mike said, his voice like the rumble of a purring engine. "Christ, I'm thirty-four. I can find my own dates."

"Apparently not," Brody disagreed. "Oh look. They're coming this way."

Del had no intention of leaving. Neither did Abby or Brody.

"Hell."

Beth McCauley approached with a pretty brunette by her side. Like her sons, Beth had short dark hair, now frosted with silver. But where Mike's eyes were blue, like his father's, Beth's were green. She was beautiful now and must have been a stunner when younger. Trim, lively, and with a magnetic personality, the woman had attracted Del's dad without effort.

Too bad she didn't seem to like Del much.

Like clockwork, Beth's smile cooled when she noted Del. "Everyone, I'd like you to meet my new neighbor, Grace. Grace recently moved in with Nadine, and I thought it would be nice if she met some of our friends." Beth made introductions.

"Hi." Del nodded at the woman, whose eyes widened when she caught sight of Del's brightly colored wrists.

"Hello." The woman had yet to blink.

"So, Grace," Abby said. "Where did you move from?"

"Oh, um, Walla Walla." She tore her gaze from Del's tats and smiled shyly at Mike. "I'm very happy to be in Seattle, though."

"She moved here to help Nadine, her mother." Beth nodded. "She has a son about Colin's age. I thought it would be nice if they played together."

Del hadn't seen another boy at the party besides Brian.

"Is he here?" Mike asked.

"No," Grace answered. "My mother took him to the movies today. I was home doing chores when Beth came by. I hope you don't mind," she said to Abby, yet her gaze slid back to Mike.

Del noted the way he avoided looking at Grace and couldn't help feeling glad about it. A guy like Mike would chew up a shy woman and spit her out. What the hell was Beth thinking trying to set Mike up with this chick?

"No problem." Abby smiled. "Did you try any of those mini quiches? They're amazing."

Del watched them interact, conscious of Beth's scrutiny. After a few moments, she excused herself to use the restroom. When she returned, she saw Mike, Grace, and Beth by themselves, talking like old friends. Apparently his unease had disappeared in her absence.

Another twenty minutes and she'd bail, she decided. That way she'd seem supportive to Abby, and not like she was running away or bothered by the timid rabbit clinging to Mike. Because she wasn't.

She deliberately went into the kitchen, away from the crowd, and noted Maddie and Vanessa talking quietly in the corner. When they spotted her, they motioned her over.

She joined them. "What's up?"

"Did you see the way Beth keeps throwing women at Mike?" Maddie frowned.

"Women? I just saw Grace, and Beth was hardly throwing her at him." More like launching a desperation grenade.

Vanessa snorted. "No, that's Beth throwing at her finest. She may be smooth about it, but trust me, that woman's a predator."

"You'd know," Maddie taunted.

"Yep, I would. Mike's been signaling to Cam and Flynn to rescue him, but the guys are giving him a taste of his own medicine."

Ignoring a sense of relief, Del shrugged. "Oh?"

"Yeah. A week and a half ago, Mike had a fight with Cam to get Cam to make up with me."

"Because he knocked her up then ditched her," Maddie explained.

"Cam?" Del glanced back at him and Flynn grinning at Mike. "That Cam?"

"I know, right? The smooth-talking gentleman kind of freaked when he found out I was pregnant." Vanessa sighed. "But he's been making up for it ever since. What a guy."

Maddie rolled her eyes. "Anyway, Mike punched him around a little. As in, a fistfight."

"Oh." Impressive. "So why does Flynn want to screw with him?"

"Because he's Flynn." Maddie grinned. "My man figures Mike needs a little roughing up. He dates a little, but he hasn't seriously committed to anyone since Lea. And she died over six years ago."

Del hated to ask, but curiosity pressured her. "When Colin was born, right?"

"Yeah." Vanessa rubbed her belly. "I can't imagine that. I mean, now that I'm getting used to the idea of giving birth to my own little genius, I can't even think of not being around to see her grow up."

"That's got to be hard."

"Poor Mike." Maddie shook her head. "He deserves someone special, don't you think?"

Del opened her mouth to respond when she noticed their intense scrutiny turned on *her*. "Wait a minute."

"I've seen the way he ogles you." Vanessa tapped her chin in thought. "He has a definite fascination with your ass."

"Please, stop."

"Yeah, and he has an issue with you," Maddie agreed. "He's nice to everyone. But not you."

"You both realize you're becoming like Beth. Meddling in her son's life."

"Someone's got to. He's totally hot, available, and Colin's so cute. He needs a woman in his life."

"Lame excuse. The kid has all of you. And Beth." Del didn't like their continued focus on her. "Hey, I'm just here to congratulate Abby. And for the free food."

"Yep." Vanessa watched her like a hungry shark.

"Cut it out. You're making me nervous."

"Oh look. He's coming this way."

Del ignored the way Vanessa watched her, as if waiting for her to make a break for it. "I can't stay long," she felt the need to say. "I actually do have an early day ahead of me. And today was rough. So much paperwork."

"I hear you." Vanessa nodded. "I just went through the tax crunch. Audits out the ass. I'm tired."

"And pregnant," Maddie noted.

"Gee, thanks for the reminder. I almost forgot," Vanessa said drily. As a successful CPA now tied to Cam, a rich investor, she'd soon have money coming out her ears.

Del should be so fortunate. Most of what she made she put back into the family business. Her savings had grown slowly over the years, but she had a long way to go before she'd be financially comfortable.

A glance around this house reminded her again of her differences from the McCauleys. She wasn't poor, but she sure the hell couldn't afford to live in Queen Anne. This place had to be worth close to three quarters of a million dollars, if not more. A big-ass house, in this location?

"Get me the fuck out of here. Jesus," Mike hissed from behind her.

"And you complain about *my* mouth?" Amused at his frustration, she turned to make room for him in their little group.

"Look, I need an out, like yesterday. Mom promised Grace I'd show her around town this weekend, after going to *her place* tomorrow night for dinner. The woman isn't even pretending not to go along with it."

"So tell her no." Del felt for him. A little.

"I tried." He sighed. God, he really was a nice guy. "But she's quiet, kind of shy, and I feel like a monster for saying no to just dinner. She's new to the area. It's got to be hard to make friends. It's not her fault my mother's throwing me at her."

Del snorted. "You have no problem telling *me* to kiss your ass. Just tell her you're busy or something."

"Yeah, Mike," Vanessa said. "You seem to have no problem being rude to Del."

He ran a hand through his cropped hair, and Del did her best not to stare at his thick arms showcased by his sweater. One thing Del could say for Beth and James. They made really, *really* good-looking kids.

"Del won't cry if I look at her wrong."

"You got that right."

He stared at her, then gave her a calculating grin.

"What?" She felt on edge.

"I bet you have something at your place you need fixed."

"Huh?"

"Maddie, would you keep an eye on Colin for me?"

"Sure." Maddie nodded.

"Colin?" Del was confused.

"I need an out, and going next door isn't going to work. Mom was already pushing me to show Grace my place."

"Oh, right." Vanessa brightened. "The old leaky pipe excuse. Except unlike Flynn and Brody, you're no plumber. So what? She can fix her own car. Maybe she has a problem with her drywall or something? A leaky window?"

Mike snapped his fingers. "That's it. It's cold out, and if the window keeps letting all the cold air in, she'll get sick. Then who'll abuse people at her garage if she's at home coughing up a lung?"

"Okay, stop." Del put a hand up. "What the hell are you people talking about?"

Mike caught her gaze and trapped it. "Look, I need a favor."

"That's rich, coming from you." The man had ripped her a new one for giving his kid candy, then messed with her at her own place of business.

"I have to get away from here before my mother promises Grace my next born child. You take me out of here on an emergency, and I'll owe you."

The thought of Mike McCauley in her debt was tempting. "So you want me to take you away from this magnificent party? Away from your family and friends because you're afraid of that femme fatale?"

As one, the group turned to spot Grace beaming at something James and Beth said. Beth laughed, and James appeared enchanted. Del and her friends looked back at Mike.

"Hell, yes." He groaned. "I mean, it's bad enough with just her. I'm already committed to bringing Colin over tomorrow to meet her kid. If they become friends, I'm in big trouble."

Del looked from him to the others and sighed. "I know I'm going to regret this."

"Perfect. Be right back." He darted away to his mother's side while James and Grace spoke. Grace, Del noted, watched Mike with more than a friendly attitude. The woman looked man-hungry.

"Just think," Vanessa mused. "You have Mike in your clutches. Draw out the favor. He's a terrific contractor, you know. Man can fix anything. You've got to have something at home needing help."

"You want me to take him home with me?" Del hadn't thought to actually go through with the farce. Just drive him somewhere and drop him off.

"Why not?" Vanessa's sly gaze warned her to tread warily. "Unless you're afraid to be alone with him in private?"

She huffed. "Get real." Shit. Now she'd *have* to take him home or Vanessa would think her afraid of Mike. Because knowing Vanessa, the evil woman would weasel details of the evening out of Mike at some point.

"Great. So it's settled." Maddie dusted her hands together. "I'll make your excuses to Abby. Now go save Mike. He needs it." She leaned closer. "I don't like the way Grace is manipulating him. It's sneaky."

Del agreed, though she hated to side with Mike. "Fine. But he's not the only one who owes me. You two do too."

Vanessa frowned. "How am I roped into this?"

"By extension. You're carrying a McCauley and seem to be attached to the one I like, so you're in."

"You don't like Flynn?" Maddie blinked.

"I should have said like *best*. Flynn and Brody are tolerable, but Cam makes it a point to be polite."

"Oh." Maddie looked disappointed.

Vanessa grinned. "She has good taste. Go forth and prosper, tattooed one."

"You are one weird chick, Vanessa."

Vanessa laughed and prodded her to follow Mike.

Calling herself an idiot for helping the lug, she joined him by the front door. "I should say good-bye to Colin. I don't want to hurt his feelings."

"Later. Come on." Mike yanked her outside with him. "When I get home, I'll tell him you saved the day. You're already his favorite person. Trust me." He walked with a long stride to her car and stood waiting.

Knowing she had only herself to blame for caving in to her new obnoxious friends, she unlocked the door and slid inside. Before she second-guessed herself, she unlocked his door.

The car wasn't small, but with Mike filling the passenger seat, she might as well have been driving a Mini Cooper.

He shot her a devastating smile that truly revved her engine. "Where to?"

Oh man. That mouth should be illegal. No way she was taking him home. Screw Vanessa and her dare. "How about a beer? After tonight, I could use one."

"You're on." He continued to smile, a charming expression he'd never before used on her. And thank God. Because right now, she wanted to drop her pants, spread her legs, and agree to any frickin' thing he wanted that had to do with sex.

What the hell had she done to deserve this?

Chapter 3

WHAT THE HELL HAD HE DONE TO DESERVE THIS?

His mother's less-than-subtle matchmaking attempt and Grace Meadows's inability to ignore a gentle "not interested" had been bad enough. His mother had all but thrown him to the wolves—or lambs, in Grace's case. Mike had no problem with nice, but Grace's passive-aggressive manipulation made him uncomfortable.

Not like Del. Subtle was not in her vocabulary, and he respected that.

He kept his smile in place, doing his best not to read into the strange look she shot him. A combination of panic and…lust?

One could only hope.

He'd had time to admit it to himself. As much as the woman annoyed him, she turned him on like crazy. He had to work not to adjust himself in his seat and call attention to the erection she caused simply by being near. Hell, the woman breathed and he wanted to bend her over. It was more than time to put an end to his fascination.

Focus, moron. "So. Where we headed?"

She swore under her breath, started her car, and drove.

After a few moments, she answered, "Look. I saved your bacon. I promise not to hurt you in any way, shape, or form. So sit back and enjoy the ride."

"Touchy. Fine. Whatever," he added when her lips tightened.

She turned on the radio, and they drove with classic rock blaring between them. Through Queen Anne and past downtown. They ended up on the south side, at what looked like a run-down Mexican restaurant but turned out to be a dive bar with a bustling business.

"Welcome to Ray's," she muttered as she parked in the back.

"Yeah? 'Cause the sign said Mazatlan."

"Ray bought it ten years ago. It's Ray's."

A place only the locals would frequent. Mike had palpitations just from looking at the back entrance. The structure seemed sound but run-down, and the local color screamed biker bar. That or *Degenerates R Us*. The smirk on Del's face as she waited for his reaction warned him not to fail this test.

"Great. Let's go." He got out of the car and locked it before closing it. A shame if her sexy GTO was broken into while she did him a favor. Then again, she'd chosen this dump. He hadn't been to a place this rough in years, since before Colin.

They passed some bikers who paid them no mind, as well as a few bigger guys with tats who waved at Del but gave him the stink eye.

"Nice friends."

They skirted a guy making out with a woman against the hood of his truck, his hand snaking under her skirt and making no bones about grabbing her ass…and other parts…in public.

"Yeah, we're a friendly bunch here." She rolled her eyes at the couple, and Mike did his best not to superimpose his and Del's faces over the amorous pair.

Jesus, he needed to get laid. Too bad he didn't have

it in him to seek his regular hookups. Contrary to what his family thought, he was no saint. Mike had needs, and a few female friends wanted what he did—no-strings-attached sex. But for the past few months, he'd wanted something more. What, he had no idea. He had no plan to marry again—ever. He loved his family, his kid, his job. But with his brothers all hooking up, it made him feel weird. Dissatisfaction with his personal life reared its head every time he thought about a particular snotty mechanic.

Following Del into what he anticipated to be a real hole-in-the-wall, Mike was pleasantly surprised. The place didn't stink of more than beer and burgers. It was no palace, but the scarred wooden floors, mass of oc-cupied tables, and crowded bar looked well-kept. The waitresses and bartenders wore black shirts with their job titles emblazoned across the chest. They all sported piercings, wore their hair dark, colored, or were bald, and seemed to complement the alternative-rock music pumping through the speakers at either corner of the bar.

He glanced at a Goth chick holding a bottle-filled tray even he'd have a problem lifting. Tribal tattoos covered half her face. "Didn't know your sister worked here."

"Ha ha. Funny." Del guided him toward a far corner, where a few tables remained empty. She sat and pushed one of the menus on the table toward him. "By the way, you're buying."

Pleased to work off his debt, he nodded. "Whatever you want, sweetness."

"Quit calling me sweetness, jackass."

"I thought you weren't going to curse." He bit his lip to keep from laughing when she glared at him. She really was beautiful, in an unconventional way. Her ire just made her that much more attractive.

"Okay, buttwipe." She tried but couldn't seem to stem her laughter. "Geez. I wish you could have seen the panic on your face over that dishwater-*bland* neighbor. Really? She scared you?"

"Not her. My mother." He looked away from Del, mostly because he wanted to keep staring at her. She wore a subtle liner around her eyes, making her lashes that much richer. The gray in her gaze seemed to look right through him. Eyes like diamonds. The comparison bothered him, because he didn't think of women in terms of pretty words. He liked women, loved sex, but left his deep emotions at the door when engaging with them on a personal level. He didn't wax poetic about their eyes or wonder why he felt so drawn to them.

Not since Lea.

"Ah, Beth McCauley." Del nodded and glanced at her menu. "I get you. She's not someone I'd mess with either."

He grunted. Del might not be his type, but she had a head on her shoulders. "Yeah, Mom is great. I love her, but she's become a major pain in my ass. Just because my brothers shacked up, she's after me to do the same. Been there, done that. Didn't take."

She glanced up at him and frowned. "I thought your wife passed away."

"She did. Didn't take," he repeated with a frown of his own. He didn't want to talk about Lea.

"Didn't you like her?"

He studied his menu as if he needed to pass a test on it. "I fucking loved her. She died. I have Colin. End of story."

Instead of letting it go, Del snorted.

He snapped his gaze to hers. "What does that mean?"

"End of story. Right. You have baggage, dude."

"First off, don't call me dude. And second, I have no baggage. I am what you see." He shrugged.

"An annoyingly sure-of-himself father to one cute kid, and ringleader of three obnoxious younger brothers?"

"There is that. No, I was talking about the fact that I'm a handsome, successful, amazingly skilled general contractor and carpenter. One who scares you shitless."

She dropped her menu. "Where the hell do you get that?"

The waitress chose that moment to join them. "What'll you have? Oh, hey, Del."

"Lara. Rena here?"

"Nah. She called and said she had something keeping her. She'll be working tomorrow instead. Sue traded with her."

"Oh."

"Rena?" Mike asked.

"My cousin." Del glared daggers at him. "Lara, bring me tonight's special. And a Deschutes brew."

"Gotcha." The waitress snapped her gum. "What about you, handsome?"

Mike raised a brow at Del, and she blew out a breath, in annoyance, most likely. "What she's having. But add a plate of nachos and substitute a Heineken for the Deschutes."

"Right-o." Lara nodded and left them.

"Your cousin works here?" he asked.

She nodded but remained silent, staring at him as if trying to figure him out. Good luck to her, because he had no idea how *her* brain worked.

"So."

"So," she repeated, not making mention of the verbal dare he'd thrown in her lap.

The little coward. Actually, not so little. She had to be close to six feet, because she towered over Abby and had an inch or two on Vanessa. To Mike, however, she'd stand at the perfect height.

Lea had been petite, and it had always been a challenge to get her in the right spot for a kiss.

Del sighed. "Now what did I do?"

"Huh?"

"You're scowling at me."

He coughed to hide his confusion. "Oh. Sorry. Just thinking about something else."

"Yeah. Okay." As if she didn't believe him.

Unlike most women he knew, Del didn't try to make him feel better or placate him with nonsense or flattery. He didn't know why, but he found her attitude kind of refreshing. *So* different than Grace had been. "Fine. I'll just ask." A personal question that had been on his mind for a while, and since she had no problem asking about his dead wife… "J.T.'s your brother?"

She grinned. "Took you long enough."

"Well?" J.T. looked African American, or at least part. He had lighter skin, but no way was the big guy straight-up Irish.

"My dad met and married J.T.'s mom way before he met mine. She died. Then Liam went on a bender and met my mom. Knocked her up, she had me, then she died a few years later."

"Oh. Sorry."

She shrugged. "Life is what it is."

Interesting. "So you and J.T. are actually half-brother and -sister."

"Aren't you quick? My turn. Brody's not a McCauley with that blond hair and a last name of Singer, but you call him your brother. What's up with that?" She accepted the beer Lara brought and took a sip, the head settling over her full upper lip.

She licked it off, and he had a tough time stifling a groan. *Brody, she asked about Brody.* He took a healthy swallow of his own beer, nearly consuming half the bottle. "He moved in with us when he was five, never left. The little shit can lie, cheat, and rob you blind. We never let him deal when playing cards. But he's family. Like Flynn's twin, annoying as that sometimes is." He smiled. "Colin calls him Ubie— short for Uncle Brody."

"Right. Ubie." She nodded. "You guys all seem pretty tight."

"Yeah. How about you and your family?"

"Just me, Dad, and J.T. For all that J.T. can be a pain, he's cool. He did my tats." She held out her forearms and pushed back her sleeves.

Mike took a hard look at them and noted the beauty of the design. He ran a finger down one particular drawing, a dragon breathing fire with huge claws, and had to work to appear unaffected. He felt smooth skin, then scarring underneath and peered closer, but she moved her arm back.

The wary look she gave him did something to his insides, made him want to step back and tread lightly. Odd. He searched for something to say and found it in a memory. "Is that your bitchin' ass?"

Her tension eased and she smirked. "Yep."

Back when they'd first met bowling with his brothers and the girls, she'd distracted him with a story about Colin mentioning her *bitchin' ass*—the dragon tattoo her brother had done for her, during which she and J.T. had cursed at each other, hence the name. The distraction had worked, because he'd bowled like he was all thumbs. That and he hadn't been able to stop himself from staring at her all night, thoroughly ruining his concentration.

"Nice. Your brother's annoying, but he has skills."

"So he likes to brag." She huffed at a lock of hair that had escaped her ponytail, a long section of blond bangs.

"Is your hair really that color?" He wanted to know. Shades of gold, light and dark, mingled to create a halo for a fallen angel. Or a demon, he thought, the comparison apt.

"Lot of personal questions you're asking, McCauley."

"So what? You have nothing to hide, right? Unless you're actually a brunette."

"Whatever. No, I'm a blond. This hair is as real as it gets."

The ungentlemanly urge to ask if she would prove it by removing her panties struck him mute. He cleared his throat, damning his sexual drive for choosing today to demand to be noticed.

"Mine too. Naturally dark." He winked. "I know you were dying to ask."

"Please. There's nothing about you I want to know."

"Liar."

This banter he liked. No more anxious expression, no glints of vulnerability in the woman he wanted to slam up against a wall and fuck. It wouldn't be smart—at all—but he was coming to believe it was necessary for his peace of mind. And other parts...

"Go ahead," he prodded, instigating. "Ask what you want to know, Del."

"*You* asked *me* for a favor. All because you were too scared of that little woman your mother brought for you. I can't tell if you're a big pussy or just a momma's boy."

He liked her taking off the kid gloves. "I respect women. I don't like hurting feelings, and I take exception to being called a momma's boy. I love my mother. But I won't roll over for her and beg on command."

She raised a brow in that annoying way that drew attention to her sexy-as-hell brow piercing.

"Really." He scowled.

"Uh-huh."

"Anyone ever tell you you're annoying?"

Lara arrived in time to overhear and laughed. "All the time, handsome."

"Thanks, Lara." Del shook her head.

"Here you go, guys. A lot of food. More beer?"

"No thanks," Del answered. "I'm driving."

Mike nodded. "Hit me."

"I'd like to," Del muttered.

He grinned. "Sweetness, there's a lot you want to do to me, but hitting ain't on the list."

Lara cracked up as she left them, and he watched a delightful blush settle over Del's features.

"I come in here a lot, so watch what you say."

"Or what?" he dared.

"Or I'll sic *him* on you." She pointed to the far corner at the biggest guy in the place, a bouncer, by the look of his shirt that read *Bouncer*. The guy waved back at her. "Earl doesn't fight like Cam."

"You heard about that? Had to be Maddie." Flynn's girl was gorgeous and fun but liked to talk.

"Vanessa, actually."

The big mouth. Beautiful, annoying, and apparently chatty.

"Earl and I are friends."

"Lovers?"

"*Friends*," she emphasized. "He's like another big brother. All I have to do is look annoyed and he'll be all over your ass."

He kicked back after eating a few nachos. "Oh, now I see."

"See what?"

"You're scared. Afraid you like me more than you should, so you're going to get your bodyguard to rough me up. 'S okay. You don't have to be worried." He deliberately gentled his voice, more than amused when she glowered at him. "I'll never do anything you don't want me to." And his brothers said he didn't know how to charm women.

"You're an ass, you know that?"

"I know you want a look at my ass. Ask me nice and I might give you a peek."

She shoved a fry in her mouth and chewed with ferocity. "Say what you want, Mike. But we both know *you* want *me*."

Truth time. "I do."

She opened her mouth, then closed it. "You do?"

"Didn't know your voice could get that high."

"Shut up. Explain that."

"Should I shut up or talk? I'm confused."

She glared at him.

Unfortunately, she hadn't been kidding about Earl, because the big guy was suddenly standing at their table. "Problem, Del?"

Before Del could answer, Mike cut in. "The lady and I are talking. She's fine."

"Del?" Earl asked, frowning at Mike.

An itch to fight beckoned, a need to siphon off the growing lust and confusion in him that came from possessive feelings about a woman he had no business feeling possessive about. Anger built. Could the guy not see Mike was talking to her?

She smiled. "I'm fine, Earl. Just—"

"Why don't you take a hike, no-neck?" Mike growled at the bouncer.

She blinked at him in shock. "Whoa. Simmer down. Earl's a friend. Earl, Mike's fine. Just screwing with you."

"You sure you're good? 'Cause I don't mind taking this dickhead outside and pounding some manners into him."

Before Mike could launch himself out of his seat and take the guy up on the invitation, Del latched onto his arm. "*No.* No. We're good. Right, Mike?" The plea in her soft gray eyes hit him hard, right in the gut.

For a moment, he just stared at her, bemused at the need to soothe her when moments ago he'd been doing his level best to rile her. Then he eased back into his chair. "We're good." He stroked her hand over his arm, taken with the warmth growing through his entire body. From the contact, heat filled him, centering yet again between his legs.

"Great." Earl gave him one more look, then turned on his heel and left.

After a moment, Del squeezed his arm with a pinch.

"Ow."

"What the hell was that?"

"What?" He had a hard time looking away from her face, those full lips, high cheekbones, and expressively furious eyes.

"You go from Colin's dad—a nice guy afraid to hurt the neighbor's feelings—to pounding-on-your-chest *He-Man*? Did you really want to fight Earl? He could wipe the floor with you."

"I don't think so." He unconsciously flexed, needing another go at the gym where he normally worked through his frustrations. That or on the heavy bag in his garage.

"Well, maybe not." She grew quiet as she stared at him. "But I don't want you roughing up my friends."

"Ah, sorry." He drank the rest of his beer and accepted the next one Lara dropped off with a beaming grin. "Been a long day, you know?" He dug into his food, pleased when Del did the same with hers. "So...back to you wanting me."

She groaned.

"I'm thinking we should try it once. Get it out of our systems." The answer to his current dilemma. He only wanted her because he hadn't had her. Had to be the reason he obsessed over her all the time.

"What about Colin?" she asked.

"He's a little young for you, don't you think?"

"You are *so* annoying." She stabbed her fork into a fry, and he was glad his hands remained on his side of the table. "I meant, Colin and I are friends. He'll be hurt when you annoy the piss out of me and we're no longer speaking. Again."

"Please. That annoyance is a defense mechanism. Everyone loves me."

"Earl doesn't."

"Everyone worth knowing," he countered. "I consider you a decent person."

"Gee, thanks."

"Colin loves you. The girls seem to think you're okay. And yeah, you're sexy as hell. Why don't we—"

The rest of what he'd been about to say was lost when a large hand settled over his shoulder. Déjà vu. Time to deal with Earl once and for all.

"Oh hell." Del sighed. "Jim, what do you want?"

Jim? "He really wants to remove his hand before I do it for him," Mike muttered.

"I saw this guy bothering you. Earl let him off, but we don't like it."

Mike noticed four guys, none of them as large as him, standing off to the right. He hadn't gotten a bead on Jim yet, but the man had a large hand. No telling how muscular he might be.

Not waiting for Jim to throw the first punch, Mike yanked the man's hand from his shoulder and stood at the same time. He moved a few steps away from the table—away from Del—toward an unoccupied section of the bar. If everything went to hell, he didn't want to do more than damage Jim and maybe a table or two.

A subtle glance around him showed them the center of attention. Earl just smirked at him from the corner where he'd been standing, coming no closer.

Now face-to-face with Jim, Mike saw that his

opponent stood an inch or two shorter than himself. Mike had a lot more muscle, but Jim had a look in his eyes that told Mike he was no pushover. A street fighter, one who'd play dirty. The guy wore jeans, a T-shirt advertising a strip club, and had definite bruises on that hairy hand.

Mike glanced at Del, who stared back at him with a hint of worry. It annoyed him she didn't think he could handle himself. He hadn't bulked up over the years just by carrying lumber.

Doing his mother proud, he tried to be nice. "Now, Jim, we can do this the hard way, or you can apologize and leave us alone. Del and I were talking."

Del stood from the table and stepped away. "Come on, Jim. I'm here with my friend. Back off."

"Friend." Jim snorted. "Yeah, right. Never seen this guy before. Some fancy schmuck."

Mike raised a brow. "Fancy?" He glanced down at himself. "It's called a sweater."

Jim sneered. "What are you doing down here, rich guy? Slumming?"

Mike fought the urge to laugh. "You realize I'm here with Del, right? So if I'm slumming, then you're insulting her, not me. Not to mention the rest of the bar."

Jim frowned. "What?"

"Never mind. Look, it's obvious you want a fight. Why don't we take this outside so no one gets hurt and—" He saw the guy winding back, readying to throw down. So when Jim threw the first punch, Mike easily dodged it. Then he punched back, a blow right to Jim's solar plexus, which had the guy sucking wind, fast.

Not willing to let Jim take charge and possibly

damage the bar, or God forbid wind up hurting Del, Mike grabbed the guy and took him to the floor, relishing the fact that he was finally able to put his workouts at the gym to good use.

He had Jim in an arm lock, the force wrenching the bastard's shoulder down while Mike yanked Jim's arm across his back, effectively using his leverage to shove Jim's face against the dirty floor. The bastard cried out in pain when Mike overextended the arm even farther, to stop him from trying to fight back.

"You done ruining my night?" *You prick.*

"Mike, you win. Let him go." Del didn't sound pleased.

No victory kiss for him. Hell. "Why? So he can try to sucker punch me again?" At least the guy's backup hadn't lent a hand. Mike had been so focused on this dickhead he hadn't paid enough attention to the other guys. Earl and a twin behemoth appeared behind him, looking less than pleased. "Nice you finally showed up."

"I'm sorry. I'm sorry," Jim said in a shrill voice. "You're *breaking my arm.*"

"Not yet. But you lay a hand on me again and I will," Mike threatened, hoping he'd made his point. He didn't want to get jumped walking out of the bar by any of Jim's wussy friends.

"Sorry. Swear, sorry," Jim was panting. "Never again. My bad."

Ah. Message received.

Mike eased up and stood, then rotated his own shoulders. Adrenaline buzzed, and he wanted a fight like nobody's business. Sometimes when he worked out, a few mixed martial arts fighters used him on the mats to train.

Mike had perfected wrestling down to a science, and he could always be counted on to give a good workout.

Earl reached down and gently helped Jim to his feet. "Hell, Jim. This is twice in one week. You need to stop with the tequila." With a last glare at Mike, the bouncer and his monster friend walked away.

The small crowd around them dispersed, with the rough-looking group giving him subtle nods of encouragement and a few grins.

Del sat back in her seat with a huff. "Happy now?"

"What the hell did I do?" He sat too, then downed the rest of his beer. Before he could ask, Lara swept by to collect the empties and bring him a fresh one. "Thanks, honey."

"Anytime," the woman practically purred.

Del shot her a glare, which soothed his ego. "You made us the center of attention. Didn't I tell you I come in here a lot?"

"Hold on. Would you rather I let that weak asshole pound me into the ground? Then all your buddies would pity you for being with a loser." He shrugged and started in on the special, a burger loaded with fixings, cheese, and an ungodly amount of bacon. He could feel his arteries hardening as he ate, and he moaned. "This is freakin' amazing."

"I know," she said glumly, then took a bite. She talked while eating, which he for some reason found charming. She didn't seem to be trying to impress him, and her distance made him want her more. "Look, Jim's an ass. His wife left him and he drinks too much. I'm nice."

"Oh?"

"I mean I listen. That's it. So he's a bit protective."

"Like Earl. And all the other guys giving me the eye."

She chewed, swallowed, then drank some water Lara had dropped off earlier. "I'm a staple here. Been coming into Ray's for years. Hell, before I was legal. And J.T. has done half the ink on these guys. We're like family."

"Aw, and you brought me to meet the folks. Del, I'm touched."

"In the head." She frowned. "I'm just saying… Never mind. Eat. You earned it."

"I'm buying, so I might as well." He grinned at her. "What do they have for dessert?" What he wanted wasn't on the menu. But maybe if he played his cards right, he could taste a little bit of Del and be satisfied. Because anything more than a slap and tickle wasn't in the cards.

And never would be.

Chapter 4

DEL WITNESSED THE MAN CONSUME VAST AMOUNTS OF food and beer. Mike was a big guy, no question, but he didn't seem to have an ounce of fat on him. A big surprise considering how much he'd put away.

Dear God, watching him deal with Jim had been a thing of beauty. She hadn't been lying when she'd said Ray's was like a family. The guys and girls looked tough. A few had done time at one point in their lives or another, but they were good people. Her kind of people. Not debutantes and soccer moms living it up on the hill.

So how had Mike in his nice jeans, soft sweater, and smooth looks won over most of her friends with one small show of strength?

Maybe the speed and ease with which he'd done it, or the fact that he'd fought and then let Earl and John take Jim away, no mess, no fuss. She'd noticed how he'd stepped away from the table to engage Jim. Had even tried to let Jim back out of the altercation. Like that would ever happen.

"Why are you looking at me like that?" Mike asked as he finished the best chocolate chip cookies ever made. Lara had a recipe that knocked Mrs. Fields on her ass.

"Like what?" She pushed around her fries, her appetite having deserted her.

"Like you either want to kill me or…"

"Or what?"

He frowned. "Ah, forget it. I'm done. We can go, if you want."

"You sure? I think Ray might have a few more cows out back. Jesus, you eat a lot."

"Again, I'm paying. I'd think you'd complain less."

"You'd think."

He paid their tab, leaving Lara a generous tip, apparently.

"Hey, Mike. You come back anytime, sugar. Ask for me." Lara winked at him.

"Will do. Thanks." He nodded, then waited for Del to precede him.

When she walked in front of him, he put a hand on the small of her back. She had yet to put her jacket back on, and she felt that hand all the way to her toes. Damn him.

"Del." Earl nodded at her. To Mike he just grunted.

Mike grunted back.

Guys. So predictable, and still she didn't understand half of what motivated them.

Once out in the parking lot, a gust of wind froze her in place. Typical spring in Seattle—what felt like late-autumn anywhere else. She shoved her arms into her jacket and hurried to the car. Mike followed her without a coat, just that sweater. It was a cable-knit, but still.

"Aren't you cold?" She circled around to the driver side door.

"Didn't you see all I ate in there? Gave myself an extra layer of fat to protect me from the weather." He chuckled, and that dimple—the one that stole her ability to reason like a mature adult—tempted her to do something stupid.

She wrestled with the decision of how to handle Mike

McCauley. She didn't like him, except she kind of did. He could be a jerk, a pushy bully. And a genuinely nice person who had the cutest son ever. No way he was the ogre she wanted him to be.

Mike tugged the handle of the car. "You know, sweetness, that whole cold weather discussion? Yeah, I was kidding. I'm freezing. You going to unlock the car or what?"

"Big baby. And quit calling me sweetness." She circled the car to unlock his door. He closed in on her instead of moving back so she could open it. *Hell.* She could feel his breath on her neck and did her best not to shiver. "You want to back up and give me some space?"

"You have plenty of space. You're little."

"Please. I'm tall. You're just a giant." She turned. Big mistake. Because it put her in his arms, a hairsbreadth from his fine chest and those glorious muscles he'd used to incapacitate Jim in seconds. Jim had been drunk, yes, but he was a mean drunk and a decent fighter.

Mike had taken him down with little effort. So strong. Bad-ass. Just her type.

"You're not that big," Mike said in a low voice. "Just right for—"

She cut him off by dragging his neck down and plastering her mouth to his. For a moment, he remained still, and she wondered if she'd made a huge mistake. Handsome, sexy, probably rich Mike McCauley wouldn't want some cool chick like Del. He'd be after a Suzie-homemaker like his moth—

He kissed her back, taking charge of the embrace. Mike put his hands on her head to hold her in place while he kissed the ever-living breath out of her. She'd never felt so surrounded before. Del had dated larger men, but Mike dwarfed her. So big, so hot, so *damn sexy*.

He tasted like chocolate chip cookies, and that sweetness made her melt. He knew how to use his lips and tongue to maximum advantage. When he leaned in to her, she thanked her stars she hadn't zipped up her jacket. He pressed his chest against her breasts, and she sagged against the car, weak with desire.

He pulled back to look at her. His eyes had darkened to a sapphire blue. His lips were slick, his mouth taut, a furious hunger on his face. "I knew you'd be like this."

Before she could ask what "this" meant, he dug his fingers into her hair, holding her in place while he angled her chin up and dove in for a second kiss. He ravaged her mouth as she lost track of everything but the feel of Mike against her.

Nothing but need consumed her while he enveloped her in a blaze of arousal that obliterated sense. She had to get closer, had to touch him. But when she tried to move, he tightened his grip and held her in place.

Lord, but his dominance turned her on. She moaned and bucked, needing more. She managed to find his waist, and when she moved her hands under his sweater and ran her fingers over his T-shirt-covered abs, he growled and closed the miniscule gap between them.

He ground his pelvis against hers, and she trembled, understanding that Mike was big *all over*.

A horn blared. "Get a room." Someone laughed. More coarse talk.

She didn't care, until she grew lightheaded from a lack of oxygen.

Mike finally stopped the kiss and pulled back, letting

go of her hair, his body still rock hard against hers. They panted, catching their breath.

She just stood there against the car, pinned by his muscular body like a butterfly to a mounting board. *Mounting*… Not a great word to think of with the hunk of maleness trying to fit into her every nook and cranny. And God, did she want him to.

"Shit." He blew out a breath and leaned his forehead against hers. When she shifted under him, he groaned. "No, wait. Don't do that."

Elated that he'd been as affected by their kiss as she had, she suddenly realized that was not a good thing. Mike really wasn't her type. He came from a different class of people. She liked his kid, and a sexual relationship might have consequences that would hurt Colin. Besides, she had no idea what Mike thought of her as a person. Del was *so* done being used for nothing more than her body…unless *she* was the one setting the rules.

She just wished more than her brain would get the hint. Her nipples stood on end, her panties needed to be changed, and her entire body felt like one giant, exposed nerve. All from Mike McCauley. Talk about bad luck.

A few moments more, then they parted. Mike moved back, and she firmed her knees and stood straight, backing away from him to move to her side of the car. They stared at each other over the roof.

She said, "That was a mistake," at the same time he growled, "We need to do that again."

They considered each other in silence, then in mutual unspoken agreement moved into the car. She started the engine and drove him back to his house with only the radio breaking the silence between them. She parked and waited.

He didn't look at her, just stared through the windshield. "Hate to break it to you, sweetness, but that kind of chemistry is impossible to ignore. Come see me when you grow a pair." He stepped out of the car, with her gaping at him, then shut the door quietly behind him.

She watched the arrogant jerk walk to his front door and disappear inside.

"Grow a pair?" The nerve. She shot down the street, fuming, cursing, and…confused—because she wanted to turn the car around and continue where they'd left off.

With Mike McCauley.

What were the odds she'd be in lust with a man completely wrong for her? Del had been a lot of things. Vulnerable, scared, stupid. But now she co-owned her own business, had family who loved her, and friends she actually liked. Starting something that would only end in heartache made no sense for a smart, independent chick like herself.

She pulled into her driveway and parked in her garage, a sweet spot she'd paid extra for to protect her pride and joy. After letting herself into the townhome she shared with her cousin, she went straight to the kitchen and poured herself a tall glass of water.

She downed it in one gulp and poured another.

"Wow. Must have been some night."

She shrieked as she spun around, holding the glass out like a weapon.

"You going to stab me with a drinking glass?" Rena asked, amused.

"God. Put a bell on or something, would you?" she snapped. Her cousin had a bad habit of sneaking around on silent feet. Always had. Del should have known better than to think she might be alone on a Wednesday night.

Rena never went out. The woman was more a homebody than Del.

With cocoa-brown skin, laughing brown eyes, and the prettiest corkscrew light brown curls, Rena could have modeled for the hair salon where she worked. Instead, she continued to cut, dry, curl, and style her way to owning the business. Which explained her lack of a social life.

"So what happened to you to make you so jumpy?"

"I thought you were working tonight, but you weren't at Ray's." Her cousin put in extra hours at the bar to make ends meet while she continued to save money for her salon.

"I was scheduled, but Jenny needed a haircut. Her kids too. So I switched with Sue. I'm on tomorrow." Their neighbor Jenny was sweet…and broke with four kids and two baby daddies who didn't believe in child support. Del and Rena did what they could to help her, because Jenny worked harder than anyone Del had ever met.

"Oh." Good thing Rena had been busy, because if the blabbermouth had witnessed that kiss in the parking lot, she'd never let Del hear the end of it.

"So. Your jumpiness. What's up?"

"Nothing. Long day."

"Uh-huh." Rena followed her into the living room and sat with her on the couch. The house wasn't designer by any means. Not nearly as nice as Abby, Maddie, and Vanessa's pad. But it felt like home. A plushy couch and love seat, a scarred but functional coffee table covered in hair magazines and the occasional *Popular Mechanic*, as well as a few of Rena's romance books. And boy, had her cousin chewed her out for not inviting her to go along to the last book club. Apparently Rena had a thing for Abby's novels.

"So how was the party?"

Del shrugged. "Okay, I guess."

"What did you do?"

"Hung around. Chatted. And yes, you can come next week to the book club."

Rena squealed. "So awesome. I can't believe you fixed Abigail D. Chatterly's car."

"First of all, it was her tire. And her name's Abby Dunn."

"You know her real name. Man, that is so cool."

Del rolled her eyes. "She's a person, Rena. Just a writer. Not a pro wrestler."

"*Riiiight.* Because wrestlers are *real* celebrities. You're so weird." Rena paused while Del took another sip of water. "J.T. came by earlier."

Del swallowed a groan.

"Told me all about your friends—the McCauleys." Rena's eyes sparkled.

"Please. Stop right there."

"So about this Mike guy…"

"I'm so tired. I think I'll crash early."

"Talk. Come on. You know I have no life. Clearly you need to confess that you pulled him into a closet and did him right there at Abigail D. Chatterly's party."

Del blushed, remembering how much she'd wished she and Mike could have done more.

Rena's eyes widened. "Oh my God. You *did not* do him at that party. Did you?"

"No. Geez. Get your mind out of the gutter."

"Can't help that you put me there. So what's with the blush? Tell me."

Del sighed, related the night's events, in detail, then confessed her dark, dirty secret. That she'd liked when Mike had kissed her and thought about doing it again. And again. And maybe one more time, just to get her stupid craving for the not-so-nice guy out of the way for good.

Thursday night, Mike found himself entertained while he and Colin spent time at Grace's house. Nadine, her mother, had gone out to a movie with her good friend, Beth McCauley. Clever of his mother, to clear the way for Mike and Grace to do...what? Chitchat? Have sex? Smile and kiss?

Just the thought of the word *kiss* had him recalling how sweet Del had been. How incredibly arousing to touch and taste her. Digging his hands into her silky hair, holding her tight while he took and gave—

"This okay?" Grace interrupted his thoughts with a smile. She handed him a glass of lemonade.

"Perfect." No beer for him tonight, not when he had to focus on surviving this arranged dinner with his mother's idea of the new Mrs. Mike McCauley.

She nodded to the sounds of boys playing in the living room. "I think they're getting along pretty well."

Mike thought it too early to tell. Colin could get along with just about anyone, but piss him off one too many times and suffer his wrath. In a lot of ways, Colin reminded him of Cam. Smart, conniving, and once riled, nearly impossible to settle down. Then again, he was a con man with that obvious charm. A lot like Brody. Or Flynn, for that matter. But when he smiled and gave all of himself, he was like a chip off the old block. Loyal, a friend for life.

Yeah, he was biased. But he had the best kid in the world. Too bad Lea hadn't been alive long enough to see him blossom into his own little person. But with family helping to mold the boy, Colin had turned out more than okay. Mike knew he had it pretty good, having such a close-knit family. They could drive him nuts—like his mother with her need to fix him up—but they loved him and his son without reserve.

He glanced at Grace, conceding his mother had at least set him up with a woman he'd normally find attractive. Maybe it was the time of year, his missing Lea more than he normally did, or his run-ins with friggin' Del that had him off his game, but he didn't feel even a spark of lust for his host. At least she wasn't giving off any "do-me" vibes. She'd been nothing but pleasant since his arrival.

He must have imagined her friendliness the other day as meaning more than it did. After all, she was new to the area and trying to stay on his mother's good side.

"So you work with your dad?" she asked.

He nodded. "McCauley Co. Construction. MCC."

"How long have you been doing that?" She moved with economy, flitting around the kitchen preparing dinner. She stirred the spaghetti sauce, and the aroma of stuffed shells smelled heavenly. The oven timer showed another five minutes before it finished. Thank God. Mike's stomach threatened to eat itself if he didn't soon get something for dinner.

He knew he should have eaten before coming over. But it had been another long day on MCC's latest remodel. He loved having too much work as opposed to not enough, but hell, he needed to recharge.

"Mike?"

"Sorry. Shells smell amazing. I'm finding it hard to do more than fantasize about dinner."

She smiled, and he again asked himself why he'd prefer someone like Del over Grace. Grace had a kid. Del had an annoying older brother. Grace had a demure personality and a smaller frame, the kind of body he was naturally drawn to. Del reminded him of an Amazon with the build to prove it. Nothing shy or remote about her. Yet since their kiss he couldn't stop thinking about her. A kiss *she'd* initiated.

God.

"…enrolled in second grade. Have you had any problems with the school?"

He plugged back into the conversation. "Nope. Great elementary. All the teachers are terrific. Colin loves his teacher, Ms. Sheffer. She's amazing with the kids."

"Yeah, Dad," Colin yelled from the other room, apparently paying close attention to the conversation.

Normally Colin ignored him in favor of his friends. Were he and Noah getting along?

"Keep playing while you can," Mike encouraged. "We're going to eat soon."

Grace nodded and started preparing the salad.

No ignoring Colin's dramatic sigh. Uh-oh. Things with Noah must not be working out.

Hoping his son could try to enjoy himself at least, Mike gave Grace a wide smile. "Are you sure I can't help?" She'd refused the first time he'd asked.

"Actually, you can rinse and cut the tomatoes."

He hated tomatoes. In a sauce, fine, but by themselves? Still, he rinsed them and cut them into the salad anyway.

"So you have three brothers?" she asked.

"Yeah. I'm the oldest."

"I'm an only child. My mother kind of obsesses over my life."

"I get that."

She smiled. "I like your mom."

"She's great…until you're a single dad and all your brothers have paired up." He swallowed a snort of derision. "I love her, but she's a handful."

"Tell me about it." Her empathy eased some of the tension he'd been carrying. Grace was turning out to be all right. Maybe he and she could be friends. Heck, if all went well, and it kept his mother off his back, they could even possibly…date?

An image of Del's snarling face, of her description of Grace as a dishwater-bland neighbor, came to mind. Not nice, yet accurate. He tamped down a sigh.

"I hope you didn't feel like you had to invite us over," Mike apologized. "My mom can be a little pushy."

"Heck, it's my pleasure, Mike."

She patted him on the back, her hand lingering a little longer than he liked. Or was he being too sensitive again? Christ. He was acting like Cam—Mr. Feelings.

"Yeah, well, thanks for dinner."

"No problem. Thanks for the flowers."

His mother had picked them up and insisted he give them to Grace. Now Grace probably thought he'd gone out of his way to impress her, when he'd brought along a bottle of wine all on his own. Mike might not look sophisticated—at all—but he knew what he liked.

He ignored the memory of *liking* Del and concentrated on Grace. "So how long are you here for?"

"Until I get on my feet again." Grace pulled the shells out of the oven when it beeped and set the pan on top of the stove. "I recently divorced my husband."

"Sorry to hear that."

"I'm not." She snorted. "He was cheating on me with his secretary." She flushed. "But we moved on, Noah and me. When my mother told me she was having some problems with her legs, it seemed the perfect solution to move out here to help. We won't stay forever, but for a while until we find a place we like." She paused. "I'm a paralegal. I'm sure I can find work here."

"In Seattle? I'd be surprised if you can't."

She gave him a relieved laugh. They chatted about little boys and day care expenses. Before he knew it, they all sat at the dining table. Mike found himself eating his salad and enjoying her company. Too bad Colin had a stubborn look on his face, one that promised trouble if Mike didn't figure out what the heck had crawled up his son's tush and died.

"You know, Grace, I think I will have some wine after all."

She beamed at him, and Colin's glower darkened.

Colin didn't know why they'd been forced to come over here. Noah was annoying. Only seven, a year older than Colin, and he acted like he knew everything. According to the fathead, Noah's mom was great, his

grandma amazing, and his dad could do things that even
Superman couldn't. Yeah, right. If his dad was so great,
where was he? Colin would have asked, but Dad had
been pretty clear about the rules. If he didn't behave, no
TV or evening treats until the weekend. And Colin had
a thing about popcorn. He loved it. Could eat it all day
every day. All the time. No popcorn or cartoons at night
and he'd die.

So he tolerated Noah's bragging and lame-o toy col-
lection. No aliens or monsters in the boy's room at all.
Just Legos and paper airplane stuff and coloring junk.
Bo-ring.

"I think you're so lucky to have your family close,"
Mrs. Meadows was saying to his dad. She had that funny
look on her face, the one lots of ladies used when they
liked him. Girls. So gross.

Ubie had called it the *Look of Longing* and told Colin
to avoid it if girls tried using it on him. Too much Look
of Longing and his dad might get snared in a kissing
trap. The worst.

"Mmm. Fat worms." Noah plunged his fork into
a shell and watched the cheese ooze out of it. Along
with the spaghetti sauce, the fork wound made the shell
look bloodied.

That, Colin appreciated. When he did the same and
laughed, his dad frowned.

"Boy, behave."

Colin resisted the urge to stick out his tongue. Dad
didn't play around. A spanking could be harsh. Besides,
Colin didn't like when Dad got mad and yelled. It
didn't happen often, but when it did, his dad's temper gave him a bellyache and made him cry. So after

taking a bite of super-spicy food, he pushed around the mushy gunk on his plate, pleased to see his dad doing the same, and drank his soda instead. Soda—the only good part of tonight.

Mrs. Meadows gave a high-pitched laugh and put her hand on Dad's arm. Colin wanted to smack her, but that for sure would get him in big trouble. Man. Why did they have to come here anyway? He wanted to hang out with Brian. Instead, they had to be at boring Noah's house with his grabby mom.

"Ow." He reached for his leg, not happy when Noah kicked him again. "Cut it out."

Noah smirked.

"Noah?" Mrs. Meadows said.

"What?"

"Everything okay?"

"Yep."

No. The kid is a pain and won't stop bugging me. He opened his mouth to retort, but the look on his dad's face had him snapping his mouth closed. He stubbornly picked through his soggy salad for the cucumbers, then finished his soda. "Can I please be excused?" he asked in the voice Ubie had taught him. The super-polite one that usually got him out of trouble.

His dad nodded.

Without being reminded, Colin took his plate to the sink.

"Why, what nice manners." Mrs. Meadows beamed at him.

Noah, he noted, had left his plate behind and darted into his bedroom without asking to leave the table. And no one said anything.

After another slow half hour spent staring at Noah's alarm clock, where he swore the minutes went backward a few times, his dad came to gather him to go home.

"Finally," he muttered.

"Colin." His dad dragged him to Mrs. Meadows. "Thanks for the meal, Grace."

"Thanks," Colin added when his dad squeezed his shoulder.

His dad let him go. "We'll have to return the favor some time when my schedule eases."

"It's a date." She smiled.

Colin saw red. A date? Dates led to marriage and stepparents. Brian's mom had gotten remarried, and Brian had told him all about how new moms and dads worked. But Colin's dad didn't date. He never planned to get married again either. Colin had heard Dad tell that to Grandpa when he didn't think Colin had been listening. At first, Colin had been upset. Because if Dad didn't date, he'd never get that little brother he was wanting. Or a puppy for that matter. Dad always said they weren't home enough for a dog.

But if Colin found his dad a new wife—to be Colin's new mom—*she* could be home enough for a puppy. Maybe she could get a brother for him too. Finding a mom had proven a real challenge. Most of the ladies who gave Dad the Look of Longing were gross. They giggled and blinked a lot.

He'd had hopes for his new friends next door. They were nice. Especially Abby. She looked so much like pictures of his mom. He'd thought that might make Dad happy. But it was just weird. Maddie and Vanessa weren't going to work, he could tell. Now Abby and

Ubie were getting married. Uncle Cam had picked Vanessa, and Uncle Flynn chose Maddie. Instead of a new mom, Colin now had aunts who treated him special and gave him presents for his birthday. He liked the extra presents and the hugs.

But no more chances to snag a mom from the neighbors.

When he'd met Del, he knew. *She* would be his new mom. She was so awesome. She had muscles and fixed cars. Her arms were so cool. She had dragons and skulls and flowers in all sorts of colors. An earring in her eyebrow and in her nose, and she wore neat clothes. Not girly dresses, but boots and jeans.

He liked everything about her, especially the way she talked to him like he mattered. Not like a way to get to his dad. He might be little, but he knew when ladies pretended to like him so they could talk to Dad. Not Del, though. He wasn't sure she even liked his dad, which was a worry for another day.

He knew she liked him, and she made him happy. He didn't even mind her being a girl. There was just something about her that excited him when she was near. Maybe because her brother looked just like his favorite wrestler ever. J.T. said funny stuff, cursed, and was just plain awesome.

"I'm tired, Dad," Colin prodded and grabbed his dad's hand.

"Me too, buddy. Let's go. But thank Noah, first."

Thanks for being a big butthead. "Thanks, Noah."

"Sure, Colin." Noah grinned. "Bye, Mr. McCauley."

What a butt kisser.

"Bye, Noah. Grace."

His dad bundled him into his jacket, grabbed his own,

then tugged him by the hand out the door. They walked right past Grandma and Grandpa's house and headed home the few blocks it took to reach their place.

"Did you have fun?"

Colin glanced up at familiar blue eyes. "No."

His dad raised a brow. "No?"

"I don't like Noah. He's a dork." Colin went for broke. "And I don't like Mrs. Meadows either. She's stinky."

His dad coughed. "I think that was her perfume."

"I didn't like it. I didn't like her food either. It was mushy. She's stinky," he said again, then added slyly, "Not like Del."

His dad started. "How does Del smell to you?"

He knew his dad kind of liked her. Mostly. When he wasn't yelling at her. "She smells good. Like a car or something."

"Yeah?"

"Yep. And she's nice. She doesn't give me fake smiles. She likes me."

His dad frowned. "Did Mrs. Meadows give you fake smiles?"

"No." He rushed on, "But she only wants Noah to have a friend. Besides, she wants to kiss you. I could tell."

"Oh, er, okay. Don't worry, son. I'm not into kissing girls—*any* girls. Not even your precious Del. So don't fret that your dad's getting a girlfriend. No way, no how." He ruffled Colin's hair. "Now how about we go get some burgers? I'm starved."

"Yes." Colin pumped a fist into the air. "You're the best."

"I know."

That comment about Colin's precious Del... Dad didn't understand. If Del was going to be Colin's new mom, she had to be friends with Dad first. It was time he got some advice on how to figure things out. He knew just who to talk to.

Chapter 5

FRIDAY NIGHT POKER. MIKE SAT WITH HIS BROTHERS around his kitchen table. With Colin sleeping over at Brian's, he had a night to himself. Since Del—the sexy coward—had yet to call him, he'd insisted his brothers stop succumbing to the new estrogen in their lives and show up for some brotherly bonding.

Surprised the dare had worked, he sat staring at two fours and did his best to pretend he held a full house.

"Raise you five." Brody upped the ante.

Cam frowned. "We didn't let you deal. No way you have anything of value in that hand."

Brody shook his head. He'd probably been born shuffling a full deck in the womb. The card sharp could deal better than any Vegas dealer, and he was impossible to catch in a cheat.

"Cut him some slack, Cam. My boy's been working hard today." Flynn tossed in his chips.

"Yep. Had to unclog a sink, install a new toilet, and handle the old lady who's always feeling up Flynn." Brody sighed. "The things I do for my partner."

Mike grinned. "Patty Haynes? Your octogenarian friend who shoves things down her sink so Flynn will…unclog her?"

"She's only seventy-eight, not eighty." Flynn scowled. "Shut it and play or fold. I'm not getting any younger."

"Or sexier, apparently," Cam mused. "Why do

you lead that poor woman on? Haven't you told her you're engaged?"

"Fuck off." Flynn included Brody in his dark glare. "And you, big mouth. Why don't you stop gossiping?"

Brody gave his best look of wounded innocence. "What did I say?"

Mike chuckled. He'd missed this. The camaraderie, the fun, the way Flynn told Brody to fuck off with his trademark sneer.

"You're in a good mood." Brody called and laid down his cards.

They all followed suit, then watched with resignation when Brody took the pot.

"Why can't I be in a good mood?" Mike asked and retrieved another beer for himself from the fridge. As he sat, he saw a knowing look pass between his brothers. "What?"

"So what did you think of Grace Meadows?" Cam asked.

"She was okay."

Brody smirked. "Not what I hear."

"Oh?"

"A little bird told me her food tastes terrible, her kid's an ass, and she's stinky."

"Colin." Mike grimaced. "When did he tell you that?"

"Today when we picked him up from school," Flynn answered for Brody. "Mom was busy, so we volunteered. He got a kick riding in the truck." The company truck of McSons Plumbing.

"Great. So what else did the little punk have to say?"

"Not much." Flynn looked way too enthused about the nothing he'd heard.

Cam leaned back in his chair and put his hands behind his head. Wearing dress slacks and a button-down shirt, he looked like a square peg in a room full of round holes. Mike glanced at Brody, Flynn, and himself—all wearing raggedy shirts and jeans.

Mr. GQ drawled, "What I want to know is why you brought flowers to a woman you're not interested in."

Brody and Flynn leaned closer and talked over each other. "Yeah why?" "Were they roses? Roses mean romance."

"Colin told you I brought her flowers too?" His boy had a big mouth. Time they had another talk about keeping information in-house. Between his kid and his mother, he had no secrets.

"Answer the question," Flynn ordered.

Mike glared. "I don't have to tell you idiots squat. But for the record, *Mom* bought those stupid flowers. I brought a nice wine, one of your leftovers, Cam."

"Well, at least we know it was of good quality."

Flynn snickered.

Mike took a deep breath and let it out slowly. "My point is I went over to be nice to Mom's new neighbor. Wasn't my idea to invite myself, trust me."

"Oh, Bitsy still trying to set you up?" Brody asked.

"Yeah. Woman shows no sign of slowing down." Which totally sucked and wouldn't have been an issue if Lea had been here.

Damn. She kept popping into his memory lately. A melancholy settled over him, an image of his late wife's smiling eyes while she caressed her rounded belly, when she'd been pregnant with Colin, hitting him hard. In just a few days Lea would have turned thirty-four. He'd have to find some lilies to take to her grave...

"Yo, Mike?" Flynn snapped his fingers in front of Mike's face. "You okay?"

"Fine." He cleared his throat and took another swallow of beer, ignoring the concern he could feel from them. He tamped down the ragged wounds of Lea's passing. The way he always did when the memories swarmed. "Look. I have no interest whatsoever in Grace Meadows. She was nice. I did a favor for Mom, and that's it. Now if you're done playing twenty questions, I'd like to—"

"If it's not Grace that has your panties in a bunch, is it Del?" Brody asked.

Funny, Mike had thought the guy had more sense. He clenched his fist on the table. "*What?*"

"You know," Flynn said. "The tall, smokin' hot blond with those amazing tattoos? She has a way of staring right through you. Kind of sexy if you like women who can kick your ass."

"Which you obviously do," Cam added. "You pretend you don't, but then you watch her like a thirsting man in the desert."

"Oh, nice imagery, Cam." Brody clinked his Coke against Cam's bottle.

"Thanks."

"What is wrong with you people?" Mike snarled. They had to bring up Del. Just when he'd finally shoved thoughts of her to the back of his mind.

"So how did the rescue go?" Flynn pushed. "You know, when she took you away from Abby's party? What did you do?"

"Her?" Brody added with raised brows. "'Cause I'm thinking no way you had a home run that fast. Maybe

you slid into second. But you're not a stealthy guy.
You'd try aiming out of the ballpark, and with Del you
need a little finesse. Third base, max."

"If I understood even half of that, I'd probably pound
you." Mike rubbed his temples. "Del and I went out for
a beer and some food. That's it. She took me home."

"Oh come on." Cam frowned. "Even Flynn isn't buying that one."

"*Hey.*"

"To avoid any confusion," Mike spoke slowly,
flexing his fingers, and pleased his brothers showed
some sense by shutting the hell up, "Del and I had a
nice time. I'm not interested in Grace Meadows or
Mom's attempts at lame hookups. And the next fucker
who mentions me and *any* woman in the same sen-
tence again is getting a fist in the gut, then the face.
Repeatedly. Understand?"

Three violent nods, then the game continued around
a much tamer conversation about the Mariners' chances
against the A's next week. Brody and Flynn picked at
each other about their fiancées, and Cam continued to
pepper Mike about kid stuff.

"Cam, it's not that hard. You've been around Colin
since his diaper days. Relax. You have another, what?
Seven or eight months to get used to the idea?"

Cam flushed. "I know. It's just…she'll be my child.
It's different."

"She?" Brody asked. "You can't know the sex
already."

"Vanessa thinks it will be a girl."

Flynn nodded. "Ah. Of course. And since Vanessa is
never wrong, you're having a girl. Better keep a leash on

your daughter. If she's anything like her mother, you'll have your hands full."

Cam laughed. "No kidding."

Mike slapped him on the shoulder. "You'll do fine. But for God's sake, let the kid live a little. They say if you want them to have a great immune system, they need to be around dirt when they're little."

"What does that have to do with you?" Flynn snorted. "I swear, a guy spills one chip in this house, and you throw a hissy. Talk about OCD cleanliness."

Mike ignored him. "And you." He pointed at Brody. "Just tell us when you need us and we'll get your house up and running so Abby can move in. I know you have the money, so get a move on, dumbass. Why the stalling?"

Brody looked uncomfortable. "I just… I know you guys are busy. We can take our time."

"Brody." Cam sighed. "Vanessa and I are making the move to live together. And she's one tough woman."

"No kidding," Mike muttered, then held up his hands when Cam shot him a glare before continuing.

"It's scary, I admit. But if you're serious about a life with Abby, you might as well live together first. Then you'll really know what you're getting into."

Brody shrugged. "I guess. She seems so happy and sure. I just don't want to ruin things."

"By letting her see your bedhead?" Mike snorted. "Hell. She already tolerates your shortcomings. You're obnoxious, too loud, you cheat, and you're not nearly as slick about corrupting my kid as you should be," he ended in a low growl. "But somehow she still puts up with you. Quit being a pussy, get the renovations done, and don't give Abby any more time to possibly change her mind about you."

"Nice advice." Cam nodded and said to Brody, "I'd take it if I were you."

"What they said," Flynn agreed.

"I guess." Brody blew out a breath. "I can do this. I mean, I want to do this. I just don't think I could take it if she left me. Never having her around again would kill me."

They all grew quiet, and Mike forced himself to laugh. "No shit. You're almost as bad as Cam when it comes to feelings."

"Hey." Cam glared. "I might be a little sensitive—"

Flynn snorted. "A little?"

Cam continued, "But at least *I'm* not afraid of women. I would have told Grace I wasn't interested. And I don't argue with Del to cover an attraction. That's juvenile. Besides, Mike, she's a nice woman."

"Who could totally take him in a fight." Flynn rubbed his chin. "Oh yeah. I'd pay to see that."

Brody seemed to have shaken off his mood, because he grinned. "Shit yeah. Are you kidding? From what Cam said about her behemoth brother, you might not make it out alive if you screw with the Websters." Then, no doubt to rub salt in the wound, he added, "And I don't mean screw *literally*, you dirty-minded—"

"I warned you." Mike jumped from his chair, rounded the table, and knocked Brody to the floor before he could run. He had Brody in a headlock, choking and begging for help, before Flynn jumped on his back.

"Leave him alone, you big bully." Giving an evil laugh and trying to muscle under Mike's left arm, Flynn had nearly managed to pry Mike free from Brody's neck when Cam dove over Mike's back from the other side and plowed into Flynn.

"Ha. Take that, loser. For making fun of me."

Flynn coughed and knocked Cam back. "Hell yeah, I'll make fun of you and your vicious girlfriend. Where she can't see or hear me. She's scary, bro. You sure you want to attach yourself to her forever?"

Brody laughed under Mike. "Please. Pussy boy is a goner. Almost as bad as Mike is about Del," he ended in a wheeze as Mike tightened his arm around Brody's throat.

"Sorry. What's that, blondie? I couldn't quite hear you."

More scuffling. A chair overturned, then another, and Cam started swearing at Flynn. Considering the youngest normally refrained from any profanity, Flynn must have hit him where it counted.

Mike enjoyed the skirmish. He let Brody breathe, almost think he could win, then settled into another choke hold.

"Get off, motherfucker." Brody yanked at his arm as Mike laughed and muscled him flat onto the floor.

"And you said I have problems?"

Everyone froze at the sound of that husky female voice.

"I knocked, but apparently no one heard me over the brawling and the swearing," Del said from the open front door. "Is this a bad time?"

Mike and the others scrambled to their feet. "Del."

"Well, I'd best be going. Nice to see you, Del." Cam left through the back.

Flynn and Brody made hasty excuses and followed him out the door, leaving Mike and Del alone.

He wiped the sweat off his forehead with the shoulder of his grungy T-shirt, pleased when she watched the movement with eagle eyes.

She closed the front door behind her and nodded to the downed chairs. "What happened?"

"Nothing. Brotherly squabble." Over her.

"Great role model you are," she muttered. "Where's the kid? Thought I'd swing by to say hello to the scam artist."

He glanced over his shoulder at the kitchen and noted the time. Normally Colin would be in bed by nine on a Friday night. He glanced back at Del, noting her jeans, the clean but worn sweatshirt, and the braids at her temple blending into the length of hair he was dying to sink his fingers into again.

He walked toward her, gratified when her eyes narrowed.

"Don't even think of putting *me* in a headlock, buddy."

He stopped a few feet from her and smirked. "Oh, so *now* you recognize I can do some damage. Guess seeing me knock Jim on his ass didn't enlighten you to the fact that I'm not a huge wuss. But giving Brody a noogie convinces you I'm a tough guy?"

"Ha. What tough guy? Yeah, you're a wuss, just not when it comes to fighting."

"Oh?" He crossed his arms over his chest.

"Everyone acts like you're some kind of saint. Mr. Nice Guy. How was your dinner last night?" she asked, her voice bland. "Did you and Grace have fun?"

"We did, actually." Was that jealousy in her gaze?

"The food sucked, but she turned out to be a nice woman just wanting to meet new people."

Del snorted. "Yeah, right. Woman was man hungry. She's lulling you with big blue eyes and that pathetic helpless routine. I thought you were smarter than that."

"You're just jealous."

She growled at him, "You're an ass."

"Oh? At least I wasn't scared of that kiss in the parking lot." He buffed his nails on his chest then casually glanced at her, more than pleased to see her lips firmed into an unhappy line. The woman wanted him, but she didn't like it. *Hell. Join the club.*

"I wasn't scared." She huffed and walked around him, looking around his clean but—according to Maddie—boringly brown house. "So you never answered. Where's Colin?" She craned her head to look down the hallway.

Mike subtly moved closer, boxing her in. She could escape to the kitchen or out the back door. No going around him to the front. Through him? That was another story.

"Colin is sleeping over at his buddy Brian's house tonight." A broad grin curled his lips when she audibly swallowed. "Good timing, you finally growing a pair and showing up."

She licked her lips, and he barely contained a low growl. "Bull. I wasn't scared of you before. I was tired of dealing with McCauley nonsense."

"Oh?" He stepped closer, and she backed into the kitchen table, then stood firm.

"Yeah. I did you a favor. That was it." She glanced at his mouth and flushed, then planted her hands on her trim hips. "Your macho stunt the other night had those idiots ratting me out to my brother, who told my dad and the guys at work. Now they're all giving me crap about how my *date*"—she put in air quotes—"had a problem with his temper, and that I'm probably to blame."

"You are."

She opened her mouth and closed it. "First of all, it wasn't a date."

"Was to me."

"Second," she said, ignoring him, "my presence had nothing to do with your temper."

He wanted her. Bottom line, no matter where his head had been lately, his body had been living in a fantasy world with Del at its center. He dreamed about her. He jacked off to thoughts of her and had been since he'd first seen her. He knew if he didn't soon sate this craving, he'd lose his freaking mind.

Taking the lead with her, he closed the distance between them, lifted her in his arms, and kissed her while he walked them to the nearest wall. Then he pushed her against it and continued to taste her sweet lips.

Past the protest she started but never finished, through the warmth under her thin clothes, Mike consumed the woman never far from his thoughts. She tasted minty, like the candy he'd seen in her car. The feel of her took his breath away. She gripped his forearms, and he gentled the kiss, not wanting to push if the embrace wasn't welcome.

Her strong fingers yanked his shoulders closer, and he groaned, in lust with the feminine strength gripping him tight.

He left her mouth to trail kisses along her jaw to her

ear. He sucked on her neck, aroused anew when she lifted on her toes and arched away from the wall, her breasts straining against his chest. Del had a sizeable rack, and it took everything in him not to slam her back against the wall and fuck her raw.

He nipped her earlobe and jerked when her hands moved down his torso to his waist, then under his T-shirt. Her touch, over his naked skin, turned his cock from hard to rock-solid-ready to fuck.

"You're so hot," she whispered as she angled her head, giving him better access to her throat. "Full of muscle, no give." She raked her short nails over his abs, and he bucked uncontrollably.

He hadn't realized he'd planted his hands on her hips until he squeezed. But he wanted to feel more of her. He dragged his hands up her belly, over her rounded, firm breasts with their pointed nipples, to her neck, where he gentled his fingers around her throat. He put pressure there, angling her head to the side so he could let her know what she was in for. No games, no more teasing.

He whispered into her ear, "You don't want this, you need to leave, *now*. I'm done waiting. I want you. Gonna fuck you right here, right up against the wall." He slid a leg between hers and ground his knee against her clit. "Yes or no? Because I can't wait any longer."

Two days had been too long for her to come to her senses. Yet it had been much longer than that. He'd been waiting for months, since he'd first been out-bowled by the sexy rebel in boots and tight jeans.

She gasped when he sucked at her throat, then yanked him back by the hair to stare into his eyes, hers so light he swore they glowed. "I'm here, and I'm ready. What are you waiting for?"

The magic words. Not pausing a moment more, he kissed her hard—taking, not asking. Like before, she melted into his embrace, and he knew she liked him taking charge. With Del, he didn't temper his strength, because she pulled at him and squeezed, demanding more. Her legs wrapped around his waist, and he yanked off her sweatshirt in one move.

Then he ran his fingers through the smooth, golden strands of her hair. "I want to feel this over my cock while you suck me," he growled. "Later. After you come all over me the first time."

Her eyes glittered with lust. She seemed as into their encounter as he felt, if that were possible. Mike was lost to everything but Del. He shoved his face between her breasts and inhaled, taken with her musky scent. So sweet, not cloying, but pure.

He sucked her nipples through her lace bra. Nothing so standard as white cotton for his exotic playmate. Del wore black lace, through which he could see her rosy nipples. With a groan, he kissed both breasts until she squirmed and begged him to take her.

"Music to my ears," he murmured and unhooked the lace binding her beautiful breasts. Freed, they remained full, high, and so fucking amazing he could do nothing but stare.

"Come on, Mike. In me," she rasped and grabbed his hand, shoving it down the front of her pants.

He loved a woman not afraid of her sexuality, and Del's passion lit a fuse he was hard-pressed to ignore. He didn't want to scare her by being too rough. Yet her frenzy stirred him. Too much.

He yanked her hand away and delved into her jeans, past her underwear to the slick heat of her.

"Fuck," he swore as he slid a finger inside her. "So tight."

"Yes." She moaned and leaned her head back against the wall while he shoved his finger in and out of her, fucking her with his hand.

He rubbed her clit with the heel of his palm, his finger buried inside her, and she rode him with an urgency that showed she neared her end. Watching her, seeing her pleasure in his touch, aroused him past the point of no return. He prayed she wouldn't change her mind and tell him to stop, because God help him, he didn't know if he could.

He had to feel her come, to see her in climax, that beautiful release so close he could all but taste it.

Moaning, he leaned close and stole another kiss, mashed against her breasts and immersed in the minty taste of Del. She sucked on his tongue, raked her fingernails over his chest, and pinched his nipples.

He growled into her mouth, sensitive to her touch and needing more.

But her panting and frantic gyrations warned him to be patient. He pulled from her mouth and watched her seize in the most beautiful orgasm, her rosy lips parted on a cry, her breasts flushed, the nipples hard and full. Her flat belly contracted, and he stared from her face to his hand, buried beneath her jeans. He could feel the thin strip of hair on her mound, but her folds were nude, slick, and soft.

"I want to eat you up," he confessed. "To feel you come all over my mouth."

"Yeah," she sighed and pulled him close for another kiss. This one slower, but no less devastating.

"You move a little more and I'm going to come in my jeans. Not what I have planned for you."

She pulled back and blinked. "Oh. Sorry." She froze. "Um, not trying to be a tease or anything, but I didn't come prepared for this."

"Trust me, not what I was expecting either. But I'm not complaining."

She chuckled, and the movement tightened her body around his finger.

"You feel so fucking good." He slowly withdrew his hand, grazing her clit, and she shuddered.

"Holy shit. That was amazing." Del released his waist and let her legs down to stand. She pushed him back, and he stared at her, watching as she removed the rest of her clothing.

"You are without a doubt the sexiest woman I know." Trite, but damn it all if he wasn't being honest. Del's colorful arms matched the tribal marks over her belly and around her sides, no doubt meeting over her lower back. The artwork on her body only enhanced the play of muscle on her solid frame.

A real woman, not a stick-thin model, but a healthy female with tone and muscle most fitness instructors would envy.

"Man, I want those thighs wrapped around my head," he rasped and licked his lips.

"Yeah, about that." She moved closer and tore his T-shirt off him. "Christ, Mike. You are seriously ripped."

"Comes with the job."

"I know a lot of guys in construction. None of them look like you." She stared at him with admiration, and he felt ten feet tall. "I want you. All of you." She cupped him through his jeans, and he swore. "But I didn't bring anything. So unless you have a condom…"

He nodded. "I think I have some in the bedroom."

Her sultry smile grew. "Then what are we waiting for?" She walked away from him down the hall, toward his bedroom. Her fine ass swayed invitingly, and he stripped out of his jeans and underwear, praying he had more than one condom in his nightstand. Because he was going to need at least a few dozen to get this craving for her out of his blood. For sure.

Chapter 6

DEL DIDN'T KNOW WHERE HER EUPHORIC CONFIDENCE had come from, but after that earth-shattering orgasm, she felt as if she could rule the world. Had she known what she'd been missing, she would have jumped Mike months ago. *Oh my God, he really rang my bell.* A genuine encounter built on seeing to her pleasure first. A miracle in itself. But seeing Mike's bare chest… That alone would have made tonight worth it.

Before she reached his bed, large arms circled her, bringing her back to his hot body. She felt his cock along her backside, that huge monster slick and rubbing against her, showing her Mike had been far from unaffected.

"Condoms?" she asked, sounding as needy as she felt. Despite her orgasm, her desire hadn't abated. She wanted to feel him inside her on a level that unnerved her.

"Bedside drawer," he said against her ear as he kissed her. His soft breath, the large hands pressing against her belly, pulling her back against him, made her weak at the knees. "Oh yeah. I've had fantasies of bending you over. Fucking you so hard."

She panted, enthralled at the thought of big bad Mike McCauley having sexual thoughts about *her*. "Yeah? Did you touch yourself, thinking about taking me?"

He thrust against her ass and slid to the small of her back. Dear God. Mike was *huge*.

"You have no idea." Mike turned her head and kissed her lips, the carnal sensation of being overwhelmed stealing her breath. "Check the nightstand, Delilah."

She hated her name. But for some reason, Mike saying it like that turned her on even more.

Unsteadily, she hurried to the nightstand and found a few foil packets. *Thank God.* She held one in her hand and turned. And froze.

Mike stood without any clothes, and she had her first good look at him naked. He could have passed for a statue come to life. All muscle and sinew, that square jaw, blazing blue eyes, and glory be to Andretti, but she'd never seen a man better put together than Michael McCauley. A sprinkling of dark hair feathered over his chest and down his washboard abs, all leading to that thick cock beckoning her closer.

He held himself for her, stroking a few times, then growled, "Put it on me."

She ripped open the packet and walked to him. "You sure it will fit?"

"It better. Because I'm coming inside you in like two seconds. I've never been this hard in my life."

She suppressed a shiver and rolled the latex over him, captivated by the grimace of need on his face. "Yeah, you like that? My hands on your dick?"

"Yeah." He covered her hands with his, keeping her hold tight. "God, I want you."

"Mmm. Me too. But this time I want to come all over you."

She gasped when he lifted her in his arms and tossed her back on his huge bed. He blanketed her in seconds and nudged her legs apart. Ready to accept him and hoping she was slick enough it wouldn't hurt, she hadn't expected him to slow down, to stare into her eyes as he positioned himself at her entrance.

"Mike?"

"Watch me. See me enter you." He braced himself on his thick forearms and inched the head of his shaft inside her. She readied for his thick intrusion. Del hadn't been intimate with anyone in nearly a year, and before that she'd been pretty selective with her lovers.

He closed his eyes as he slowly pushed deeper. She traced his expression with her gaze, then with her hands as he thrust more and more of himself inside her. Becoming a part of her in a way she hadn't expected.

"Faster," she ordered and tried to urge him deeper. She wasn't sure she liked this slow taking, drawing it out. Emotion festered, a curious affection that would turn simple sex into too much more.

But Mike refused to be rushed. He opened his eyes and stared at her. "No. I'm running this show." He shocked her by pinning her arms above her head on the bed and continued to move inside her until he'd seated himself entirely, his fullness at first uncomfortable.

"Don't move," he said through his teeth. "I don't want to hurt you."

She felt stretched, too tight, and then her body started to ease around him. She wrapped her legs around his waist, imagining where he ended and she began, and a curious warmth unfurled deep inside her.

"You feel so good. All that snark and sass, that hot attitude. So fucking sexy," Mike rasped.

She met his gaze, overpowered by the stark lust on his face. "Take me."

"Oh Delilah, I plan to." He grinned, and that warmth inside her grew.

Then the man moved. A slow retreat that eased the tightness inside her before he pushed forward again. This time he hit a spot inside her while he grazed her clit, and she squeezed him without realizing.

"Shit, Del. Do that again," Mike groaned. He started fucking her, in and out, his hands tight on her wrists, not allowing her to do anything but constrict her inner walls.

"More. All inside me," she encouraged, wanting to see him lose it. That precious control, that hold on his sexual energy. He'd made her lose her mind, and she wanted to return the favor.

"Yeah, all in you." He leaned down to kiss her, his strokes coming faster, going deeper. "Need to come so hard," he muttered as he took her. "So fucking hard, Del."

She met him thrust for thrust, pumping her hips as fast as he did. To her astonishment, she felt the rise to climax all over again. "Oh yes. Yes, Mike."

"That's it. All over me," he ordered. "Come, baby. Drench me." He kissed her again, then let go of one of her wrists to slide his hand between their bodies. He rubbed her breasts, her belly, then reached her pelvis and went lower.

"I said come," he demanded and pinched her clit hard enough it should have hurt.

Instead, the pain shot her into a shockingly brutal orgasm, and she screamed as she clenched him tight.

Mike grunted and removed his hand, then slammed into her twice more before he moaned her name and jerked, coming with force.

After a moment, he continued to pump while he rained kisses over her face, stealing her breath and her will in one last, final surge.

When Mike finally pulled back, she couldn't move. He withdrew and flopped next to her on the bed, breathing hard. They lay together, not speaking, for what felt like a long time.

"Am I dead?" he asked on a groan.

She chuckled. "That was going to be my question."

"Christ, Del. I think you about gave me a heart attack."

"Right back at you, Mr. Huge. Damn, Mike. You really have a big dick."

He said nothing for a moment, then he started laughing. Joining him in the moment, she embraced the joy and laughed as well. When they finished, she had to wipe tears from her eyes.

"That is probably the nicest thing you've ever said to me." Mike choked as he stemmed his mirth. "Jesus. I have a big dick. News at eleven."

"Shut up."

"Oh no. Not in my bed, missy." He rolled over her in a flash, pinning her down with that enviable strength. "Here, I rule."

"I concede you're stronger."

"And prettier." He kissed the side of her mouth.

"That's debatable."

"And smarter." He kissed her nose.

"Please."

"More polite." He kissed her forehead.

"You have me there."

"And…?"

"And what?" she said on a breath, not sure she should

be feeling aroused again. Not when she wanted to sleep for a week.

"And I'm an amazing lover. Go ahead. Tell the truth."

She tried to shrug but couldn't with his hands holding her down. Stupid that that still excited her, but his dominance flipped a switch she couldn't seem to turn off around him. "You're okay."

"Okay? You screamed as you came." He smirked. "Tightened that hot pussy around my cock." He nuzzled her neck, then lowered his kisses to her breasts. "And man, you have the nicest body. I mean, stellar."

"Mike." She wriggled. "You, um, that condom needs to go."

"True. I made a huge mess. For you."

"Thanks?"

He rolled off her and laughed again, heading for his adjoined bathroom. He returned clean and flaccid. Finally. But even soft, the man's girth and length were impressive.

"Like what you see?" he bragged.

"Yes, you're sexy. Happy now?"

"Not as happy as I was before." He joined her on the bed and muscled her to lie on top of him. Studying her with an odd look on his face, he shook his head. "I was positive I could get you out of my system once we fucked."

"Nice." That hurt. Not that she expected poetry, but he could at least be nice for a little while after that tremendous orgasm. So much for basking in the moment. She tried to move away, but he held her fast. "Mike," she warned, "let go."

"Not so fast. I wasn't finished. I was saying that I

thought once we fucked, we'd be done. But I'm as hungry for you now as I was before." He frowned. "What is it about you that's so freakishly sexy?"

"Freakishly?" Bewildered that his admission eased her hurt, she tried to glare at him. Except she found him equally fascinating. "You're not classically handsome." She traced his brow with a finger.

"Nope. You're not traditionally beautiful."

"Of course not. Stereotypes are boring."

"Yeah." He pulled her close for another kiss. Then he dragged her head back. "Your hair is so damn fine. Like silk." He ran it over his fingers. "How do you get it to be so soft?"

"I call it shampoo. You might want to try it sometime." Yet his own short hair felt like satin.

"Funny." He sniffed her collarbone and smiled.

"What?"

"Colin likes the way you smell."

The change in topic threw her. "Huh?"

"Yeah. Said you smell like a car."

"I do?"

He nodded. "I can catch the faint scent of oil, but it's buried under a wallop of hot woman."

"Flatterer."

"Yeah. That's me. Mr. Charming."

She chuckled and ran a hand over his square jaw, slightly rough with stubble. "Prince Charming, you mean."

"So you see me as a prince?"

"Don't sound hopeful. Basically, you're a pain in my ass. And no, not in the way you're thinking."

"Hoping."

"Dork." She snickered when he crossed his eyes. She

never would have imagined Mike as one to be fun in bed. Sexy, intense, *freakishly* good—yes. Funny? No. "So what was tonight about, really?"

"Wish to hell I knew." He blew out a breath and wound a strand of her hair around his finger. "You get to me. Why, I have no idea. You're obnoxious half the time, swear like a sailor, and scare most men."

"Sweet talker." She smiled through her teeth.

"But man, when I'm around you, I can't think of anything but getting inside you."

She blushed.

"Fuck, Del. Don't do that."

"What?"

"Be so sexy. That blush? Don't you know how hard you make me?" He arched his cock against her and to her shock, he felt semi-aroused again. "You look so tough, but then you have these moments of shyness."

"I do?" Odd, she hadn't known she showed that.

"Yeah. And those contrasts… I'm only human."

And a lot deeper than she would have thought. Mike seemed to see the real her, not the tough persona she presented to the world. What did that mean?

"Human? Or not so human? How can you be hard again?"

"I told you. It's you." He didn't sound happy about it, and for some reason, that made her feel better.

"Let me get this straight." She tapped her nails on his chest, noting the ragged edges that would never see a French manicure or be painted all girly red. "You think I'm obnoxious."

"Yeah."

"I scare you."

"Not me. Other men. You turn me on."

"Great. So I get you hard."

He groaned. "All the time. I'm tired. I mean, I'm beat. It was a long day, hell, a long week. I came so damn hard in that condom. But I want to make love to you again. Right now."

She started. *Make love?* "I should go."

"Scared?"

She stiffened. "Of you? Dream on."

He chuckled and stroked her back, and goose bumps followed the pleasure of his touch. "I don't want you scared, Delilah. I want you hot for me. I want to feel you come all over me, hear you moan my name when you're shuddering and dragging those sexy tits over my chest."

She trembled. "Mike." Damn it. How did he do it? How could he make her want him again so soon?

"So what do you say we play together? You and me? No drama, no ulterior motives, just you and me giving each other pleasure? You're not a notch on my bedpost. You can see I don't even *have* bedposts, and I'm too busy being a dad to Colin to date everyone in the neighborhood." He smirked. "Not even Grace Meadows. Love that jealousy, honey. It's cute on you."

"Fuck off."

He chuckled. "Man, that mouth gets me hard too. I can't wait for us to play with my favorite number, sixty-nine."

"Yeah? Try another number, because I don't know you all that well." It shocked her that she could lie with a straight face. Trouble was, he *did* scare her. And she *did* know him.

Mike didn't mess around. He wasn't a kiss-and-tell

type of guy. He loved his son and his family and would do anything for those he considered his. His company had an amazing reputation, and with the exception of Jim, she didn't know anyone who didn't like him. Even Earl had bragged about how her "dick of a boyfriend had put Jim on his ass but good"—high praise from Ray's best bouncer.

"Okay. What do you want to know?" Mike asked softly and continued to caress her back. He stared up at her with those intense blue eyes, and she fought the urge to succumb to temptation and fall into his arms.

"Er, well… You're not seeing anyone, are you?"

He snorted. "Yes, as a matter of fact, my girlfriend is hiding in the closet until you leave. No, dumbass, I'm single. I don't screw around. Can't stand infidelity, by the way."

"Me either." She frowned in case he was implying something, but he only nodded. "You aren't looking to get married?"

"Nope. You?"

"No."

"Good. Same page then."

"Um, I guess." She frowned. "So what is this? A one-shot deal or what?"

"Weren't you listening? I said I want to do this again."

"Tonight?"

He smiled at her. "Sure. Or tomorrow, or Sunday. Hell, maybe we'll really go for it and fuck on Tuesday—a *school* night."

She chuckled at his pretend daring. "Laugh it up, funny guy. I'm just trying to make sense of this."

He sighed and tugged her close for a hug. A hug?

"Well, when you figure out what *this* is, let me know."
He let her go, and she looked up so she could see his
face. "Del, let's have fun. You and me. We can fuck,
get this need out of our systems. And in the process, we
become better friends. What's so hard about it?"

"Nothing, I guess." But it all sounded too open to in-
terpretation. What did *better friends* mean to him? Hell,
to her? "I like you enough."

"Gee, thanks." He put his hands on her hips and
ground up against her. "I like you too."

"So we're fuck-buddies then?" She needed a label.
Labels made sense.

Mike didn't seem to like that one. He scowled. "Hell
no. That's too—"

"Crass for you, Mr. Sensitive?" She snorted. "Geez,
Mike. It was just sex."

He rolled her over and under him before she could
blink. "Yeah? Does this feel like just sex to you?" He
kissed her and rubbed his cock against her pussy, sliding
over her clit until she wanted to scream. "It's good. Too
good. Not normal."

"N-no. Not normal." She moaned. "What are you doing?"

"I have no fucking clue. All I know is if I don't get a
condom on in like two seconds, I'm coming inside you
without one." He stopped and stared down at her.

Much as she wanted him bare inside her, Del was
nothing if not intelligent. She took birth control, yet so
had Vanessa—now pregnant. No way in hell was Del
ready for kids. She didn't doubt Mike was clean of dis-
ease. Well…she mostly didn't doubt it.

"Yeah, we'll go slow. Condom. For now. Until we
know each other better." Mike moved off her to don a

condom and seconds later resumed his position. "But, Del, we're going to know each other better. We're friends and now lovers."

Labels. She could handle that. Not that she understood the distinction right now, but she wanted to feel him inside her. The rest could come later. "Yeah, yeah. Fine. Now fuck me."

He laughed then groaned as he pushed inside her. "Damn. You're killing me."

"I plan to if you don't get a move on. I'm not fragile, Mike. If I say fuck me, I mean, *fuck me.*"

Mr. Sensitive and Nice vanished in the heat of his blue-eyed glare. "You want a fuck? You got it, Delilah."

She shivered under that carnal stare, and then she moaned his name as he gave her exactly what she asked for. And what she didn't.

—∞—

The next morning, Mike stared out the back window of the kitchen, noting the promise of a clear blue sky. He couldn't believe he'd made love to Del all night long. Well, not without breaks. But still. He'd insisted she stay the night, and to his good fortune, she hadn't protested. Now the morning had arrived, when for sure the nosy neighbors—Abby, Maddie, or Vanessa—might spot her GTO near the house. But he didn't care.

He should have. The guys would be all over him. The girls would demand details, barging into his life as if born McCauleys. His mother would disapprove, naturally, because she still considered him her wounded chick who didn't know his ass from a decent woman.

Then again, he didn't think Del would like being called "decent." He grinned. Even the notion that his mother might interfere couldn't get him down.

How the hell had he succumbed so thoroughly? With so much pleasure?

Del appeared in the hallway, looking tired, haggard, and thoroughly pleasured. "Okay, hot stuff. I'm leaving. Unless you want to plant another hickey on me I'll have to explain to my father and/or brother?"

Her hair lay in waves around her head, her clothes once again covering up that sexy-as-hell frame.

Wearing only a pair of Seahawks pajama pants, he left the kitchen and his glass of orange juice and walked to grab her.

Before she could say anything else, he kissed her. She must have used his toothpaste, because she tasted minty. He pulled away and grimaced. "Ew." Too late, he realized *Ew* wasn't the thing to say after a kiss with a woman you'd just made love to all night long.

Del, as usual, did the opposite of what he'd expect. She didn't get mad or hurt over his insensitive comment. Instead, she wiped her hand over her mouth. "No kidding. Toothpaste and orange juice is a disgusting combination." She pushed out of his arms and found his glass, then downed it with a grimace.

"You okay?"

"Fine," she said on a sigh. Then she sauntered back to him, dragged his head down, and kissed him with a thoroughness that left him light-headed. "Much better. Juice-to-juice works. Juice-to-toothpaste? Not so much."

"Um." He licked his lips and kissed her back, until both of them seemed unsteady.

"Shit. I have to go."

"Okay." He didn't know what came next, only that something had to. "So, maybe… You want to come to dinner tomorrow?"

She paused. "Here?"

"No, in Paris."

"Smart-ass." But she smiled.

"Yeah, here. Colin and I could make you something. What do you like?"

"I like pizza."

He grimaced. "Something nutritious. Green is a good color. And I don't mean green jelly beans. I'm talking salad, spinach, broccoli, kale—"

"I'll just stop you right there." She held up a hand and squealed when he squeezed her tight. "Okay, okay. I'll come to dinner. But I'll bring dessert."

"Del."

"What? It won't be candy, I swear. What are you, the food police?"

"I'm the dad of a kid who goes off like a rocket when he's had too much sugar."

"Oh. Well, how about if I bring fruit or ice cream? That okay with you, Commandant?"

He grinned. "Now who's the smart-ass?" He gripped her butt, taken with her firmness. "Man, you should probably go before I forget myself and bend you over the couch. We didn't get to that yet. Or you blowing me."

"You mean, you didn't get to blow me yet," she corrected.

"That too." He sighed, wishing he wasn't hard again. Damn, but he was tired. In such a good way. "So tomorrow at six?"

"Sure. So you know, I like everything but onions. Yech."

"Colin's the same. I don't like tomatoes, so we'll do something without the stuff we don't like." And something he could cook. "How do burgers sound?"

"And fries."

He frowned.

"Potatoes are vegetables."

He just looked at her.

She groaned. "And yes, a salad. Happy now?"

He smiled. "I'm very, very happy, Del-i-lah." He loved that pink flush over her cheeks. "You are one tall drink of sex."

"That's drink of water. Get it right."

"I did. So tomorrow for dinner."

"We established that. I guess all the blood is rushing to the wrong head, eh?" She snickered.

Her joy was infectious, and he laughed with her. "Laugh it up, sexy." He cupped her head and kissed her, a soft peck that didn't linger but packed the emotion he didn't know how to handle. "I meant it before. Friends first."

She studied him, and he let her draw back, so that only their hands remained touching. "Friends, huh? I guess that means I should stop calling you an asswipe."

"That would be just super, Del." He gave her a too-wide grin, then tightened his fingers around hers in warning. "Remember, no cursing in front of the kid."

"How about kissing?" she asked. "Should we be hiding that we're doing the nasty?"

"I prefer to call it the bump and grind, but tomato, tomahto." He let her tug her hands away. "Around

Colin, we should probably keep things normal. He's already sensitive to dating and marrying with my horny brothers hooking up left and right."

"But we're not dating."

She seemed to want clarification, and he could have sworn they'd gone through this last night. "No. That's what you wanted, right?"

"Right." So why did she seem uncertain?

"Look, Del…" How to say this? "My wife, Lea, we were close. Closer than most people ever get. McCauleys love deep like that only once. I'm done with that kind of relationship."

"So now you just want to fuck and forget?" She didn't sound judgmental, just curious.

"Not forget. And not just fuck." He didn't understand what he wanted, to be honest. But one-night stands with Del didn't seem right. "I… Hell. I'm not into marriage and the whole ring thing. I'm being honest."

She sighed with what sounded like relief. "Good. Me neither."

He hadn't expected a declaration of love, but he didn't like hearing her agree with him. "Oh?"

"Yeah. Guys tend to get clingy when they know I'm not into forever. I think we want the same thing. Fun, no strings, no mess when we go our separate ways. Friends first and last, right?"

"That's exactly what I want." *Mostly.*

She hugged him, kissed him on the cheek, then cupped his face. "Fine. You're still a jerk though."

"You're still brutal."

They nodded. Her tentative smile brightened his own. "Okay then."

"Right." He walked her to the front door and opened it for her. Only to find Brody and Flynn on his doorstep. "Shit."

They stared from him to Del and grinned like twin Cheshire Cats. With no sign of stopping.

Del chuckled. "Oh yeah. You're going to have a great time explaining me. Later, Mike."

"Delilah." He laughed at the finger she shot behind her back at him before taking notice of his brothers again, who stood in his friggin' doorway and stared from him to Del with wide, *understanding* eyes.

He groaned.

Flynn's sly grin made it worse. "Get the coffee going, Brody. We have *lots* to talk about this morning."

Mike growled until he noticed the sweet smells coming from the bag Flynn held. "I'll tell you nothing."

"We can infer." Flynn nodded. Brody as well. "We're good at inferring."

"The best," Brody agreed. "Now tell us, is she mean in bed too? And if so, can you explain…in detail… with pictures?"

Chapter 7

Colin waited anxiously for his hero to return. According to Ubie, Operation Sampson was on track and moving smoothly. Colin didn't understand the name, but Ubie said it fit.

Whatever. Colin just wanted that puppy. The little brother too, and before next year would be great. Summertime might be pushing it, but he figured he could always dog-sit Hyde, Abby and Ubie's dog. He could practice being a dog owner and get paid while doing it, so when he had his own puppy he could buy it treats and know how to train it. He'd ask Abby for help on that, because Ubie was pretty pathetic when it came to disciplining Hyde. Everyone said so.

"Remember what I told you?" his dad asked.

"Yes." Colin took note of everything. Dad wore his nice jeans, a button-down shirt, the kind he wore to church—when they went—but no shoes. That wasn't too dressy. "Dad? I see your toes." Grandma wouldn't like that. Whenever they had company, they had to wear socks and shoes and clothes with no holes.

"Yeah, yeah. It's just Del." But he'd worn a hint of cologne.

Bingo. Ubie said cologne was always a good sign.

"Do I look okay?" Colin glanced down at his church pants and favorite sweater, the one with the green and blue stripes. He'd even taken a shower for the occasion. And it wasn't bath day.

His dad grinned, and Colin felt a wave of love for the man who gave the best hugs in the world. "You look amazing, champ. Almost better than me."

"Ha. I am better!" Colin leaped onto his dad's leg, trying to climb up his frame. But his dad was too hard to beat. Even his uncles had to gang up to get Dad down.

They wrestled until the doorbell rang.

"Come in," his dad yelled.

Del entered. "Really? Again? What is it with you? First you bully your brothers, now your kid?"

Colin moved out from under his father's huge arms and raced to Del. "Hey, Del." He tried to look normal, smoothing down his hair. After taking a deep breath, he let it out quietly, like Uncle Flynn had once shown him. *Be cool, man. Be cool.* "What's up?"

She grinned and ruffled his hair. "Nothing, C-Man. Just happy for the invite to free food." She held out a tub of ice cream. "Rocky Road okay?"

"My favorite." He grinned and out of the corner of his eye saw his dad roll his eyes. Colin turned to glare at him, and his dad pasted a fake smile on his face. Actually, mint chocolate chip was Colin's favorite, but for Del, he'd admit to anything to make her happy.

"Put it in the freezer before it melts, boy."

Colin darted away, and when he returned to the living room, he saw his dad run a hand over Del's shoulder. Hmm. Not quite kissing, but touching was good. Colin would keep an eye on them over dinner though, to make sure there was no rough stuff. If his dad started wrestling with Del, he didn't think she'd like it.

"You didn't bring J.T.?" Colin asked her, darting between her and his dad to lead her to the couch.

"J.T.?" His dad looked alarmed.

She shook her head. "He's working tonight. Had a special tattoo to do."

"Yeah? What?" his dad asked. "More prison tats for your friends at Ray's?"

Del glared at his dad.

Time for some interference. "A bitchin' ass?" Colin asked, staring at her dragon.

His dad groaned. "Colin."

"What?"

To Del, his dad said, "I blame you."

"As you should." Del chuckled. "No, Colin. No dragon. A three-headed dog, I think."

"Cerberus. I have him!" Colin raced from the room and returned with one of his favorite monsters—a dog with three heads. He put it in Del's lap. "Do you like dogs?"

"Yep."

Even better. "Do you have one?"

"Oh hell." His dad leaned back against the couch. No putting one over on Big Mike—as his grandpa liked to call him.

"No. But when I find the right dog, I'll know. He has to come with me to the garage and not make a mess."

"Good luck with that." His dad stretched out and stared at Del, a funny look on his face. "So you like dogs." Dad looked at Colin. "How about funky little boys? You like them too?"

Del grinned at him, and Colin just *knew* she was the one. "They're okay. I guess. For boys."

Colin paused. "What's wrong with boys?"

"What's wrong with girls?"

"Well, uh, they cry a lot. And they don't like fun stuff."

"I do."

"Yeah, but you're special." He leaned closer to her and whispered, "Even Dad thinks you're special. He's wearing cologne and his good jeans." He leaned back to see his dad frowning at him.

"What's that?"

Del shook her head. "Just Colin asking if I'd brought any candy. Which I didn't," she hurried to add.

A nice save. Just more proof that she'd make the best mom. He winked at her, then left her and Dad to talk. He still had a half hour more of video game play. Now time to let Dad work his magic, which according to Uncle Flynn he had little of. Colin crossed his fingers before turning his digital dinosaur loose on the innocent city in Wii land.

Del watched Mike, curious at the nervous butterflies taking up space in her stomach. It had been bad before she'd had sex with him. So she had a tiny crush? Any woman with a pulse would find Mike McCauley and the way he cared for his kid attractive. But knowing how he'd played her body like an instrument and made her *beg*…

She swallowed. "So."

"So." He smirked at her.

The jerk. "You been beating anyone else up lately? Maddie? Your mother? Grace?" Shoot. She hadn't meant to bring up the passive-aggressive neighbor again. He'd accuse her of being jealous.

Yep. There went that mocking grin that both turned her on and irked her to no end.

"Why, Delilah. You sound almost—"

"Don't say it."

"Jeal—" The oven timer beeped. "Saved by the bell."

"Jackass."

He frowned.

She glanced around for Colin, who'd darted off to his room. "Sorry. Butthead."

"I thought it was buttwipe."

"I wouldn't want to bore you with menial insults."

He chuckled. "You never bore me. That's for sure." Walking away from the living room into the kitchen, he moved with an unconscious grace.

Oh man, I have it bad. Coming over here was such a mistake. One stupid night of fucking and she was confusing attraction for something more. Hell, he'd straight up admitted he wasn't looking for forever. He still mourned his dead wife, now going on *six years*. A person couldn't compete with that. Not that she wanted to.

Annoyed at her train of thought, she followed Mike into the kitchen, appreciating the good smells. "I don't see any fries. Just salad."

"Easy there, Lady Death Wish. The fries are in the oven. Hold on." He left the kitchen to go outside, and she watched him fiddle with the grill.

He returned carrying a plate of mouthwatering burgers. "Angus beef, baby." He wiggled his brows. "Yeah, I have big meat."

A heartbeat of silence, then she had to say it. "That was just forced. Pathetic."

He sighed. "I know. I've been trying to come up with something about 'my meat' all day. I mean, hot dogs I could work with. My wiener? Sure. Patties? I dunno."

She laughed. "You're such an idiot."

"An idiot who took one for the team while you skated yesterday morning." He groaned. "You have no idea what it's like to go from heaven on earth"—he lowered his voice—"inside you, to dealing with Mario and Luigi." His brothers, the plumbers.

"Oh, now see, I get that. I've played my share of Mario Brothers games. That was clever."

"Thanks." He beamed and set the plate of burgers down on the table.

She liked the simple arrangement. Nice plates and silverware, complemented by paper napkins and plastic cups with superheroes on them. No candles or flowers in sight, just good old home-cooking.

"Want me to get Col—" she started.

"Colin," he boomed. "Get in here."

"I think I'm deaf." She touched her ear and crossed her eyes.

To her delight, Mike blushed. "Oh, sorry. I'm used to yelling for the boy."

"Wow. You are really red."

"Shut up. I'm trying to be polite."

"Obviously a stretch."

"Keep it up and I'll give you a noogie. See if I don't."

"Yeah?" Her eyes narrowed. "You touch one hair on my head, I'll make you suffer, buddy."

The light in his eyes drew her closer. "Promise?"

She shook her head. "I can't imagine how anyone thinks you're a nice guy."

"You wound me...Delilah."

"Quit calling me that."

"You liked it the other night." He moved closer and somehow had her in his arms and thoroughly kissed before she could blink. He set her back as fast.

"Y-you—" Before she could return a little sensual payback, Colin popped in the kitchen with a big grin.

"Hey, Dad." He sat down in front of the Spider-Man cup and pointed to the spot between him and Mike. "Del, you sit here. With me."

Del sat, glared at Mike, but said nothing to him.

Mike made a face at her behind Colin, and she had to work not to laugh at him. The big goof.

Dinner passed too quickly. The food was amazing, and she felt generous enough to compliment the chef on everything, even the salad. Colin behaved without fault, making the meal more than enjoyable. She couldn't put her finger on it, but the warmth, the belonging, felt natural. They joked and teased, and nothing felt awkward.

Until Colin mentioned his mother.

"My mom is thirty-four on May twelfth, Del. How old are you?"

As if a shutter had been pulled down over Mike, he lost all expression.

"Ah, I'm twenty-eight."

"I'm six." Colin darted a look at his dad but continued talking a mile a minute. "We're going to make Mom a cake. I never knew her."

"Oh." Could Mike look any more wooden?

"Colin," he said, sounding weary.

"And we'll eat it for her and everything," Colin continued. "But I can't go see her."

Mike frowned. Uh-oh. Not good. "We can talk about this later."

"But, Dad, Del's mom is dead too."

Del blinked. How had this been dumped into her lap? Both Mike and Colin looked at her.

"Um, yeah."

Mike's gaze softened. "That's right. I'm sorry."

"It was years ago." She'd come to terms with her mom's passing a long time ago. She glanced at Colin, saw him nod, then looked back at Mike, only to see him staring at her forearm. Where she was stroking the scar.

She forced herself to put her hands flat on the table.

"Yeah, but you knew your mom, right?" Colin pushed. "Mine died before I ever met her. Dad won't talk about her. Won't even let me go with him to see her."

Del didn't want to interfere, but she could see Mike struggling to hold on to his temper. Hoping to defuse the situation, she spoke quietly to Colin. "You know, sometimes when people leave us, they leave big holes in our hearts. Some people talk about those holes all the time, hoping words will close them up. Other people pretend the holes aren't there, so that maybe they'll heal if they aren't bothered with so much."

Colin frowned. "But my hole isn't there. I don't have a hole." He looked at his dad. "Not like Dad."

Mike coughed. "Colin, let's talk about this later, okay? I'm sure Del would much rather have some ice cream than think about her mom."

Del wanted to agree and change the subject, let things lie. But the stubborn part of her couldn't do it since she so clearly disagreed with how Mike handled his grief. "Not think about her? I think about her plenty. It's no biggie, Mike." Her father had wanted her to know her mother. Except he'd left out all the parts she'd unfortunately already known, and others J.T. had helpfully added—that her mother hadn't been the angel she'd appeared. Far from it.

"I want to think about Mommy too," Colin said, a hint of stubborn in the set of his jaw.

This must have been an argument they'd had before.

"You *should* think about her," Del said to soothe him. She didn't like the glint of tears in Colin's big blue eyes. "But—"

"But not now, when we have a guest for dinner," Mike said through his teeth.

"I just want to know her." A tear spilled over one cheek, and Del's heart broke for the boy.

"I can tell you something about my mom," she offered quickly. As she'd hoped, she diverted his attention.

"What?"

"She hated dirt. Anything greasy or grimy made her freak out." Especially when that grime happened to be her daughter.

"Really?" Colin wiped his nose on his sleeve.

Mike said softly, "Del, you don't have to—"

"Yep. I used to play with my dad's grease gun. He'd take me to the shop and let me help out. Well, where I couldn't get into much trouble. A lot of times J.T. would watch me."

"Where was your mom?" Colin asked.

Out fucking whatever rich guy offered her the most for her time. "Shopping, probably. She had a lot of stuff to do when I was little. I don't remember her much except for pictures. So my dad used to tell me stories." *Lies to make me feel better, until I found the letters...*

Colin turned to Mike. "Dad, why don't you tell me stories? Then I could remember her too."

Mike put a hand through his hair. "Since we apparently have to do this *now*, what do you want to know?"

Del sat quietly, not wanting to interrupt what had to be hard for him.

"Was she pretty?"

"Was she?" Del seconded.

Mike blinked at her, then gave her a ghost of a smile before turning to his son. "Well, she didn't have the colorful artwork Del has. But yeah. Heck, boy. You know what she looks like. You have a picture of her right by your bed."

"I heard she looks like Abby. That true?" Del asked.

Mike looked at her, but she couldn't read the expression in his eyes. "Yeah. A lot like Abby."

"Dad was going to marry Abby, probably. But Ubie got her first." Colin shrugged. "I like her as an aunt though."

"Colin." Mike's cheeks looked pink, and Del wondered if Colin's words had any truth to them. "I did *not* want to marry Abby. I never did and still don't." He glared at her.

"What? I didn't ask."

He turned his scowl back on Colin. "Abby looks like your mom, but she's not your mom. We talked about this."

"I know." Colin sat glumly.

"Jesus, Colin. This is totally not the time to be talking about your mother."

Del heard his hurt. Damn, talk about baggage. It had been six years since he'd buried his wife and he could barely talk about her. "What was her name?"

Mike continued to look at Colin. "Lea."

"Did she like burgers?"

"Did she, Dad?" Colin asked softly.

Mike cleared his throat. "No. She didn't like meat."

"At all?" Colin goggled.

"She liked fish and eggs. Kind of a loose vegetarian."

"Wow. Did she eat pizza?"

Del grinned. "It's not the end of the world if she didn't like pizza. Some really cool people hate pizza."

"Who?" Colin asked, suspicious.

She turned to Mike, who stared at her with a frown. "Well?" she asked, unable to come up with anyone cool who hated the best food on the planet. "Did she or not?"

"She liked pizza," he said slowly. "And vanilla ice cream."

"I like mint chocolate chip," Colin announced. "Rocky road, too," he hurried to add.

She had a feeling rocky road wasn't his favorite. "I like chocolate."

"Dad does too."

Del warmed. Stupid to feel good that she and he liked the same ice cream, something his dead wife hadn't. *And burgers, don't forget the meat. Oh God, I am truly going to hell competing with a dead woman.*

She took a long drink of lemonade and encouraged Colin to ask another question. The most important he could ask. "Mike, I think Colin needs to know what really matters."

"Oh?"

"Yeah. Who was Lea's favorite person in the world? Be honest. Colin can take it."

Mike stared at her for a moment, then reached across the table to grab her hand and gently squeeze. He let go and smiled, his grin banishing the sorrow swimming in his gaze. "Colin, I don't know if I should tell you this."

"Tell me, Dad. Please." Colin looked on the edge of his seat.

"Well, your mom was a pretty popular lady. Everyone liked her, and she had a ton of friends. But…it's you. You were her favorite. I mean, it was a close run with Brian, but…"

"Dad." Colin laughed. "She didn't even know Brian. He only moved here two years ago."

"Oh, right."

As if the mini-blowup hadn't happened, Colin changed the subject to the reptile excursion he planned to go on with his class and talked happily about Brian, his intention to pet and hold an actual snake, and added a hint or two about catching some frogs for an inside aquarium they really needed to buy.

Del stared down at her hand, where she still felt Mike's touch, then did her best to shrug off her weird feelings. Attraction worked. Lust made sense. Anything deeper was plain stupid.

They ended the dinner with ice cream and a promise from Del to bring J.T. the next time she came.

"Over my dead body," Mike murmured while she gave Colin a kiss on the cheek to say good-bye.

"I heard that."

"Heard what, Del?" Colin looked back and forth at them.

"Nothing," Mike growled. "Go brush your fangs, mutant."

Colin hissed and clawed his hands at his father, then raced down the hallway to the bathroom, where he proceeded to make loud gurgling noises while brushing.

"Nice technique." She stared after the boy, wondering why her heart should race now, of all times.

"Back at you." He pulled her into his arms and kissed her. Hard. "That…damn. I know it's stupid. I sometimes have a hard time dealing with Lea's passing. Next week is her birthday, and I get all fucked up about it."

"Nice mouth."

He swore again, and she forced a grin, not wanting him to see that his pain affected her. *Keep it light. Be a friend.*

"Yeah, yeah. Whatever, Saint Delilah." He grinned with her, the same dimple on his cheek that popped at her when Colin smiled.

"You two good? I mean, you aren't going to wrestle him into submission when I leave, are you?" she asked.

"I would, but I'm scared he'd take me down. He's tenacious."

"Wonder where he gets that from."

Mike stared at her.

"What?"

"He actually gets that from his mother."

"I, oh." What should she say to that?

"I know you lost your mom."

"Yeah."

"But you talk about her and it doesn't hurt?"

She reached for his hand and entwined their fingers, pleased when he gripped her back. "My mom's been gone for more than twenty years, Mike. It's different. Plus, we were never that close."

He stared at her forearm, but he didn't ask any questions about her relationship, for which she was grateful. "You think I should talk about Lea with him? Tell him stuff about her?"

"If he's asking, he wants to know. You loved her, right? And she loved him?"

He nodded.

"Then she'd want him to know her."

"I hadn't thought about it like that, but yeah." Mike sighed. "It's just...hard."

She refused to give in to the compassion burning in her chest, thinking about how difficult it must have been for him to lose someone he'd loved so much. "Yeah, well, suck it up, McCauley. Life's hard. As someone once told me, grow a pair."

He blinked at her and gaped. "What?"

"Solid advice, if you think about it. I mean, I came back, and then we fucked each other's brains out."

He slapped a hand over her mouth and carried her to the front door, away from the hallway. "Would you shut up? You and that F-word."

"Sorry, *Dad*."

He grimaced. "Del, please. Don't call me *Dad* or *Daddy*. Creeps me out."

"Oh, well. I get that. You being an actual dad and all." She grinned. "You can put me down now."

She loved that he could so easily physically maneuver her. And that he'd lost that wounded look in his eyes, his gaze now filled with lust as he regarded her.

"You ever been spanked?"

"I—what?"

"By anyone."

Immediately turned on by the thought of Mike doing the spanking, she shook her head.

"Didn't think so. You need it. Discipline, I mean." He kissed her hard and left her breathless. "Oh yeah. Next time we get together, I'm going to give you exactly what you need."

She felt him aroused and rock-hard against her. His entire body was like living steel, hot, unbending, yet molten when handled the right way.

"Yeah? Well I'll give you what you need too, studly. Don't think you can manage me."

"It's on, brat."

She glared. "Did you just call me a *brat*?"

"Did I stutter?"

"Dad," Colin yelled. "I'm done."

"Be right there."

They sure did yell a lot. Though annoyed by the big bully, she found the shouting match with his son charming.

So she did it too. "See you, Colin."

"Bye, Del," he shouted back.

"Just call us the Manners family," Mike muttered while she laughed. "Come on. I'll get your coat."

"I didn't bring one. I brought ice cream, remember?"

"Yeah, and don't think you're getting it back. Chocolate is my favorite."

"Mine too," she reminded him.

He frowned. "Well if you're going to have a hissy about it, I'll—"

"Excuse me? *Hissy?*"

"—bring you one when I see you next. Your place. Thursday night work?"

"Can't. I have book club Thursday. If I miss it, I'll never hear the end of it from Abby." Or Rena, who was salivating at the prospect of meeting the great Abigail D. Chatterly.

"Friday then. I'll bribe one of my brothers to babysit Colin." Mike pulled her close and rubbed against her. "I want you."

"Still? I'm impressed. Thought you'd worked me out of your system."

"Like you've done with me?" He snorted. "Try again."

"I still want you." She shrugged. "But then, my standards aren't that high."

"Bullshit. I asked around. You haven't been on a date in forever. I mean, you babysat my kid on Valentine's Day. Pathetic."

He kept her close, and she placed her hands on his chest to push him away. Except the feel of his muscle under her palms made her itch to continue touching him. "Yeah? Well at least I didn't go out on a date with *my mom*."

"Hey, I was trying to help her deal with my dad being an asshole," he said in a low voice. "All the while *your dad* was making moves on her."

She grinned and pinched his nipples, pleased when he hissed and ground his cock against her. "What can I say? We Websters are lethal."

"No shit." He took a deep breath and let it out, then set her far away from him. "Before I come in my pants, go home. Friday, your place."

"I have a roommate."

"Yeah, well I do too. I'm taking care of mine, take care of yours. Besides, I want to see your place."

"Why?" Did he want to see how she lived? If she was good enough? Just because she looked a little tough and worked in a rough part of town didn't mean she couldn't afford—

"Because I want to fuck you hard in that bed. Then you won't be able to dream without seeing me there." He pointed a finger at her. "The way I dream about *you* thanks to the way you took advantage of me Friday night. It's a real problem not being able to fall sleep with a hard-on."

She blinked, not having anticipated that answer. "Good. Serves you right."

"You're such a cruel woman. But I can deal. Friday. Your place. And if the roommate is there, she can watch."

"You really are a bad boy, aren't you, McCauley?"

His leer gave her the shivers. "You have no idea, Webster. No idea."

She left, seeing him in the doorway through the rearview as she tore down the street. Yet it wasn't the remembrance of his leer that stayed with her, but the sight of his grief over the monumental loss of his wife that crept into her thoughts when she'd least expect it.

Chapter 8

"WHICH ONE, DAD?"

Mike swallowed around the lump in his throat and pointed to the small rise to his right. He and Colin walked down the paved path and turned to the grassy grave that had been freshly tended and cleared of yard debris.

"Oh, that's nice. Look. It says her name. Lea McCauley."

They carried flowers for her—lilies from Mike, carnations from Colin.

Mike felt worse than awful. As he stared at his wife's tombstone, he saw bright gray eyes laughing at him. A vision of ash-blond hair and a sneer. Tattoos and steel-toed boots.

Ridding himself of thoughts of Del, he had to work to conjure a picture of Lea, not Abby, whom he'd seen just yesterday. He'd never had to work so hard to envision Lea before, and it scared him.

"Dad?" Colin gave him a worried look, clutching the carnations in his hand that he'd already accidentally smashed in the car. "Are you having a problem with the hole in your heart?"

It still amazed him how well Del had handled the concept of grief with his six-year-old. How simple an explanation, and how spot-on. "Yeah. I guess I am."

"Is that why you never talk about Mommy?"

Mike hadn't thought this would be so difficult.

Bringing Colin with him made sense. The boy had asked to come, and unlike last year, he seemed much more mature, able to handle seeing his mother's gravesite.

"I guess. I loved your mom a lot, and I miss her."

"Me too." Colin put his hand in Mike's, his hand so much smaller, frailer. Like Lea's had been.

"Okay." Mike took a deep breath and forced it out. *Don't cry, you big pussy. It's been six years already.* Yet seeing Colin so grown-up, yet still small, reminded him how fast time could fly. How little time any of them had with the ones they loved. Lea's death had not only deprived him of a wife, but his son of a wonderful mother. *Fuck. Get it together.*

Mike cleared his throat. "So. This is the part where you get to talk to her. I'll go over there, by the tree, where you can see me. But you get this time to talk to her by yourself."

"She's not there, Dad." Colin looked confused. "She's in heaven."

"Yes, she is." *God, Lea. You left us too soon. Look at what a wonderful boy you had.* "But here, it's like we can pretend she can hear us. I know she's not here, but it gives me peace to talk to her sometimes."

"Oh." Colin chewed his lip. "Can I talk to her now?"

Mike nodded. When Colin just looked at him, he stepped away. "I'll be over there." He placed the lilies he'd brought for her over her grave and walked away to the far tree to lean against it.

The weather had held off. Gloomy but not raining yet, the sky promised a bleak hump-day to break up the week. He watched Colin gesturing wildly, petals going this way and that before the boy realized he'd nearly demolished the flowers. He hurriedly placed them next to the lilies before talking again.

What could he be saying? Telling her about his field trip, most likely. Mike grunted, still not sure he could take the time to join Colin on his day. It would hurt the boy if he couldn't come, so Mike had to figure a way to take the extra time. He loved that his family was close to help out, but he hated always needing to rely on them. His parents had retired. He didn't want them raising his son. Yet he had to admit the babysitting support alone had been invaluable for years.

Colin ended his conversation and returned to Mike with a smile. So strange, seeing his son's joy in this place of sorrow. But knowing Colin was okay about it gave him a sense of ease as well.

"Your turn, Dad."

Mike glanced around, seeing no one with them on this late Wednesday afternoon. "I'll be right over there. Okay?"

"Yeah. I'm gonna look for ants and bugs."

Mike nodded. "Fine. Just don't hurt the tree." The great oak was like a bastion of life in this area of death. Mike liked seeing it there, reminding him life indeed went on.

"I won't, Dad. Vanessa told me I should never hurt trees or plants, because if they come to life, they might pull out my roots."

"Vanessa has a vivid imagination." He snorted. "But she's got a point. You get what you give."

"Yep. Karma."

"Karma?"

"Abby and Maddie were telling me all about it.

Karma. Like when some guy cut Maddie off in the car, she said he'd have car karma. And she put up three fingers at him." In a lower voice, Colin added, "But I know she really meant the middle one."

"Terrific. Then you understand." Car karma. Really?

He was putting off his own discussion, discomfited to think someone might watch him talking to a grave. His own son, yet it felt weird. Watching Colin scoot around the tree's base looking through grass for bugs, he let out a sigh and headed to Lea's side.

There, he hunkered down into a crouch and positioned himself to see both her headstone and his boy. "Happy birthday, honey."

The wind whispered against his face, a cool breeze with a hint of rain on the air.

"The big three-four. You should see Colin. He's getting so big, he's nearly as tall as you." An exaggeration, though with her small size, it wouldn't have taken much for anyone to tower over her. He made small talk, telling her about his parents' mess of a relationship, of them finally getting back together. And then he rounded to a subject needing address—with himself more than her. "So, something funny's happening to me. I met this chick." He cleared his throat, unsure yet needing to tell her. As much as he knew she didn't exist in the ground, talking to her like this gave him a sense of closeness he missed all the time. "This woman. She's nothing like you."

He pictured Del in his mind's eye, but this time everything about her faded but her gentle smile, the way she'd helped him talk to Colin and made sense of something he had a hard time putting into words.

"I don't worry about hurting her feelings. Or her.

She's a tough woman, and she's got muscles nearly as big as mine." An exaggeration, but Del's fit body really turned him on. "I… I like her a lot, Lea. I had sex with her," he confessed in a low voice, feeling a tinge of guilt he'd never before felt. He hadn't been a monk for six years, but none of his other partners had mattered to him like this.

The ground stared up at him, silent with condemnation. Especially because he kept seeing Del's face over Lea's. "I'm sorry, baby. I just…" He took a moment to compose himself. "I love you so much. I'm confused. Del's so… She's tough. She swears. Had Colin telling me to pass the fucking potatoes," he remembered on a surprising laugh. "But she was so great with him the other night. Had me talking about you for the first time in a long time. It hurt so much." But he'd felt better after. He rubbed his eyes to rid himself of that awful burning sensation.

"I…sometimes I forget your face. I know your smile, your scent, your touch. I have your picture in my dresser drawer. Always close. But, Lea, I'm afraid I'm forgetting you." An unconscionable sin against the woman who'd sacrificed her own life for her baby. No one had known her heart couldn't take the strain of giving birth, or that she'd bleed so damn much. A freak thing, then she was gone. And he'd been alone.

The pain of that moment of loss stole his breath away, so he kept it tucked inside, not wanting to relive it. "Does that make me weak, Lea? That I don't want to feel bad anymore?" His family had gone along with his wishes not to talk about her all those years ago. That silence had allowed him to recover, to be the strong father Colin needed. The years passed, and he kept that grief buried, stirring guilt because he couldn't think of her without pain.

"I think I'm going to see Del again. You'd like her." Lea had never had a bad word to say about anyone. The sweet woman had sometimes driven him insane with her kindness. But she'd made him a better man. "I like her. I like her a lot. But never more than I loved you." *Loved?* Since when did his feelings become past tense? "Love, baby. I love you."

Instead of giving him solace, his pledge felt hollow. He could love her all he liked. She couldn't love him back. And he was still alone.

He glanced at Colin, who waved and smiled.

"He's such a great kid. Smart, conniving—that's Brody's fault. Charming, athletic. I love him so much. Thanks for Colin." He patted the grass. "You did good with that one. I'm just sorry you only got to hold him that one time."

One glorious moment, when she lit up with love, her hair in disarray, her face blotchy, tears streaming down her face. Yet he'd never seen her look more beautiful as she'd gazed at their son with love. She'd handed him to Mike, who took the small bundle with shaking hands.

Then the nurses had nudged him aside, rushing to her when she seized in pain. It felt like forever but had been seconds as she just faded away.

Like she'd begun to fade from his memories. One moment in time, she'd been all he could think, fantasize, wonder about. Lately, she seemed foggy, like a remnant of a dream. Now when he thought of a dark-haired, petite woman with a nice smile and deep brown eyes, his thoughts flew to Abby, Brody's fiancée.

"Brody had a thing for you, you know," he admitted the truth out loud, more comfortable talking about his family than her. "He's totally into Abby though. She looks a lot like you. At first it was weird, but I never felt anything for her. And she's a very different person than you. Brody is over the moon for her. The punk." He laughed. "She writes those books you used to love. Oh, and Flynn fell for Abby's friend, Maddie. She's gorgeous, and she knows it. She keeps him in line, has a heart of gold." He sighed. "Even Cam, that pretentious little jerk, found someone to tolerate him. Vanessa seems cold and aloof, but she's sweet. Not that I'd tell her that, but I know she's good for Cam. Lightens him up. She's having his baby. So if you can, put in a good word. No one's said anything, but they worry about her. Especially with how you left us."

He didn't know how Cam would handle Vanessa in harm's way, and he didn't want to think about it. One senseless death in the McCauley family was one too many. "Yeah, keep an eye out for Vanessa, Lea." He stood and brushed his hands on his jeans. "Maybe I'm getting all moody because everyone's hooking up but me. And maybe it's because I miss you more during this time of year. I don't know." He sighed. "Well, happy birthday. Hope you're still living it up in the clouds. I know you're watching over us." He paused. "I miss you."

Then he walked to Colin and took him by the hand. They left the cemetery for the truck, both of them quiet while the wind blew and the drops began to fall.

Mike worked like a demon the next day, glad his father had taken the hint and left him alone. All the guys ignored him, as they had all week, for which he was profoundly grateful. After dealing with bullshit delays on permits for their next project, he'd returned from the city building department and worked through lunch and all through the day, doing much of the sanding and flooring he normally left to Jess.

"Okay, boy. It's quitting time." His father slapped a pair of leather gloves together and loomed over him while he finished cutting a replacement piece of flooring.

"I'm almost done."

"Mike, you've been slaving all week without breaks." His dad grew quiet. "I know it's tough this time of year."

Normally Mike would tell his dad, nicely, to mind his own fucking business. But yesterday had helped him cope. "Just about finished."

"Put the wood down, son."

"I said I'm almost done," he growled.

"Now," his father growled back.

Annoyed, Mike put down the piece he'd been cutting and turned off the saw. Then he stood. "Well?"

"So how are things?"

"You want to make polite conversation? *Here?*"

"Answer the fucking question."

"I'm fucking great. Thanks," he snarled. What the hell?

"Yeah? Great with Grace?"

Baffled at the direction of the conversation, Mike stared at his father. "Grace? What does she have to do with anything?"

"Nothing, apparently. Your mother owes me money." His dad grinned.

"Have you been drinking?"

James laughed. Mike took after him in a lot of ways. Tall, broad-shouldered, muscular, and with a creative streak he expressed best by building things. Though James McCauley acted like he was a blue-collar schmoe, he too crafted woodwork with real skill, a talent he'd rounded and brought out in his oldest son.

"Dad, you okay?"

"I'm not the one everyone's worried about."

Mike hated being pitied. He glared. "Well, everyone can quit worrying about me and deal with their own crap. A lot of weddings and babies being planned. Not my bag. My kid is six going on forty, but I got it covered. I don't need fucking *concern*."

"Nope. Not when you've got a great little lady like Del Webster hanging around." His father smirked.

Hell. No doubt Brody and Flynn had been gossiping. His brothers were worse than hens with all their clucking.

"Not sure what you mean." Mike unplugged the saw and started gathering up his things. He'd lock up and get gone. He checked the time. Nearing six. His mother was probably ready to make dinner. He would have been fine putting his boy in the school's aftercare program, but his mother wouldn't hear of her grandson being tended to by strangers—strangers who only taught the kid for six and a half hours every day.

"They told me at Sunday dinner, but I thought I'd wait and see if you brought it up."

Mike remained silent. The key to dealing with his parents—avoid potential verbal minefields whenever possible.

"So the boys told me she came over Friday night."

Don't confirm or deny.

"Left Saturday morning looking a little rumpled." More silence. "Colin said she came to dinner Sunday night too."

Mike blew out an exasperated breath. "What? You're pimping my kid for information now?"

"Hey, he'll talk. For a few dollars, you can get a lot out of him."

"Dad."

"Come on, Mike. I worry about you."

"Yeah, well, don't. I'm a grown man capable of inviting a woman to dinner."

"But you didn't invite Grace. You invited Del."

"So? Colin loves her."

"Uh-huh. You had her over for Colin."

The innuendo was impossible to miss. "What?" he snapped. "We had burgers. She brought ice cream. We ate. She left. But you'd know that, since you put the thumbscrews to your grandson already."

"Strawberry cupcakes, and he sang like a canary."

Mike smothered an unwanted grin. Colin's sweet tooth was his known downfall. "Dad, what's your point?"

"Nothing." Great. Now his dad looked uncomfortable. "Hell. Look, Mike. Your mother wanted me to—"

"I *knew* it."

"She's worried. You always get weird around Lea's birthday. But, son, it's been six years. We know you miss her. You'll always miss her. But don't you think it's time to start living again?"

Mike started. "I *am* living. What the hell? Since when are you Mr. Emotional?"

James frowned. "I know. I blame your mother for this. Well, her and that shrink she insists we still need to see. Thing is, I kind of agree with her. You're a young man. Lost your wife too soon. We all loved her. She was a special girl."

Mike nodded, relieved not to feel the urge to cry. He'd used up a lot of useless tears last night in bed. Now he just felt tired instead of sad when he thought of all he'd missed with Lea.

His father continued. "There are other women out there. Grace is—"

"Not my type."

"Really? Because seems to me the last women you dated all had that short, stacked kind of build. You seem to like them small."

"Shit, Dad. Do we really have to talk about my taste in women here?"

"Not at all. We could go home and talk at my house." *With your mother* went unsaid.

"What do you want me to say? Because I'll say anything to get you to stop talking."

"Not nice, boy," his father growled. "But fine. I'll be blunt."

"Thank God."

"Stop being a pussy and make a move on Del."

"Thought I'd already made it," Mike said with snark.

His father slapped him in the back of the head, a move he normally reserved for Flynn and Brody.

"Hey."

"Smart-ass. I'm not talking about sex. Invite her to dinner again. Take her out to a movie. I like her."

"Huh?"

"Your mother isn't sure about her. But I like her. More, I like her for *you*. She's not someone you can walk all over when you want to move on. Woman'll make you work to get her."

Already had her, he wanted to say, but didn't want to put Del out there like that, well, more than he already had.

"You know what I mean," his father added, no doubt reading his mind. "Point is, Colin really likes her. Boy has a good head on his shoulders when it comes to people. He's just like me."

"Yeah? Well he doesn't like Grace Meadows much."

"Hmm." His father rubbed his chin. "Have to see about that. I'm afraid your mom is pretty taken with her. The fact that Grace has a kid of her own is a huge plus."

"For Mom, maybe. Look, she's only got a few more months before she's a grandma again. Knowing Vanessa, the kid will come early. Can't you distract Mom for me?"

"Sorry, son. You're on your own. I'm barely in her good graces again. I'm not screwing it up. No way, no how. She wanted me to talk to you; I talked. Now when you see her again, tell her what you told me. Well, not about shacking up with Del."

"I never said that." He hoped to hell he wasn't as red as he felt. Why did his family have to fixate on him when they had so many other things to worry about? Like his brothers, a baby, therapy. "Dad, Del and I are friends. We're a little more than casual, but that's it. I'm not getting married again. Period. So can you get Mom off my ass about it? At least get her to stop trying to fix me up. No more arranged dates. *Please.*"

His father clapped him on the back. "I feel for you. I do. I'll try my best, but she's pretty focused on you lately. You're not the only one who was hit hard when Lea died, you know. Your mother lost the girl she'd been wanting for a long time when Lea passed. Think on that."

James helped him lock up, then they drove together back to Mike's parents' house, where Colin waited.

Mike had no more stepped in the door when Colin latched onto him with a death grip. "Help me, Dad," Colin whispered.

Then Mike spotted the small boy in the living room sitting with Grace, Nadine, and his mother around a coffee table filled with treats. That Colin wasn't stuffing his face full of mini-cakes spoke volumes.

Noah waved. "Hi, Mr. McCauley."

"Call him Mike, honey," Beth corrected.

Mike frowned, not wanting any more familiarity with Grace or her family. "Hello, Grace, Nadine. Hey, Noah."

Grace smiled. He tried to see some hint of trickery but noticed nothing more than a woman sandwiched between her mother and his. To his way of thinking, another pawn played between two conniving, masterful queens.

"Hi, Mike. Long day, huh?" Grace asked.

"Long week." He shot a glare at his father, who wisely smiled but said nothing. "That's nice you could come for a visit, Mrs. Meadows."

Nadine Meadows smiled. An older version of Grace, she had a pretty smile and a softly rounded figure. If Grace followed her mother's example, she'd age exceedingly well. "Oh, we're just stopping by to get Beth. I mean, Grace is."

"We're on our way to Abby's," his mother explained.

"Abby's?"

"Abby's book club, Dad." Colin still hadn't released his grip on Mike's leg. "I think we should go too. *Del's* going to be there," he said in a loud voice.

Christ. Just what Mike didn't need. His father smirked. His mother frowned, and Grace and Nadine looked puzzled.

"You met her at Abby's party last week," his mother explained. "The girl with the weird hair and tattoos?"

"Her hair isn't weird," Mike defended, then wished he hadn't when all three women sent questioning looks his way. "She's just…different." He swallowed a groan. "Come on, Colin. We have to go."

Grace waved. "Nice to see you again, Mike. Bye."

"Bye, Mike," Noah parroted.

Mr. McCauley, his inner voice growled. "Yeah. Have fun tonight." Grace, his mother, and Del. In a small space. Man, talk about a good night to go out to dinner. He pulled Colin with him and left as quickly as he could without appearing to run. "We're doing dinner out tonight."

"Oh man. I wanted to see Del."

Me too. Mike scowled at the useless need he couldn't seem to help. "Yeah, well, too many girls next door could be a problem. What if Grace decides to stop by?"

Colin grimaced. *I feel you, boy. I do.* "Oh. Yeah. Let's eat somewhere far away."

"Just what I was thinking."

An hour later, while Colin played in the arcade after consuming the crappiest pizza known to man, Mike wished he'd brought along a pack of Tums to combat the riot of pepperoni fighting with the greasy cheese in his belly. Imagining Del making mincemeat of Grace didn't help either, because Beth would be watching it all and taking mental notes. Then Mike would get the brunt of the rundown from his mother, Abby, Maddie, and no doubt Vanessa. That's *after* Del ripped him a new one for some infraction he'd have caused just by existing.

At the thought, he perked up. Maybe if Grace annoyed Del as much he thought she might, Del would storm over to his place to complain. His neighbors would see her there, comment of course to anyone who cared enough to listen, but at the end of the day, he'd have Del in his arms. They could have sex and be friendly. No deeper emotion necessary, and he'd get this gnawing hunger for the woman out of his system again. A win-win any way he looked at it.

Even his sour stomach and the sounds of children whining and crying couldn't take away his good mood.

He plunked a coin into an air hockey machine and waved his son over. "Here, Colin. Best out of three, and the betting is open."

Colin grinned. "Great. When I win, I get to ask Del over for dinner again."

Mike nodded. "I win, you not only clean your room, but your bathroom too."

"Awesome."

"Perfect."

Mike lost game one, then game two. By game three, he'd been thoroughly trounced. And he couldn't have been happier.

Chapter 9

DEL ARRIVED AT ABBY'S WITH AN EXCITED RENA chattering behind her. She noted a larger crowd than she'd expected and swore under her breath when she saw Grace sitting next to Beth in the girls' living room. Following her gaze, Vanessa leaned closer to murmur, "An unexpected—and uninvited—guest. But what can you do? Abby's future mother-in-law brought her. Hell, she'll be mine too."

Del liked that Vanessa didn't seem to like Grace. It made her feel better for succumbing to that bane emotion Mike too easily brought out in her—jealousy. Because really, what the hell did she have to be jealous about? Mike didn't belong to her. No more than she belonged to him. If she wanted, she could go out and get laid by any number of guys down at Ray's. She wondered if Mike knew how lucky he was she'd let him have her.

"Interesting expression. A kind of glare-dare," Abby mused. "Hey, Del."

Del nodded, then winced as the hand digging into her waist clenched harder. "Ah, yeah. Thanks for the invite." She pulled Rena's fingers free and yanked her cousin around to meet Abby. "Abby, this is my cousin, Rena. She's your—"

"*Biggest fan.* Oh my God. I love your books," Rena squealed then hugged Abby. Hard.

Abby disappeared, enveloped by Rena's strong arms, and let out an *oomph*. Vanessa smirked. Del wanted to sink through the floor when Beth frowned at the commotion.

"Ah, nice to meet you," came Abby's muffled response. Rena let her go, and to Del's relief, Abby laughed. "Wow. It's *really* nice to meet *you*." She pulled Rena with her and introduced her to the rest of the group. "See, Kim? Rena actually reads my books. She *likes* them."

Kim and her life partner Robin laughed and made fun while engaging Rena in conversation. Del looked around and spotted two sisters she'd met at the last book club. May and June. Or April and July. She couldn't remember which. Maddie joined Abby with the others. Del turned to the pair she'd been leaving for last—Beth and Grace.

So much for having a fun time tonight. Especially since the only seat open was right next to Grace.

The woman in question waved and patted the seat next to her on the couch. "Hey, Del. Come on over."

Under her breath, Vanessa hummed the death march.

"Funny."

Vanessa snickered and shoved Maddie, her cousin, aside to make room on the floor. Rena, the traitor, hadn't looked back once to see how Del fared, smitten with her idol—an author of those romance books her cousin gobbled up like candy.

With a forced smile, she made her way over to Grace and Beth. "Hey."

"Hi."

Beth nodded and smiled politely. "Hello, Del."

"I'm gonna grab some food. Be right back." With any luck, someone would nab her seat before she returned. Del took her time in the kitchen filling her plate, amused to see a gluten- and sugar-free section on the table for Vanessa. The thought reminded her of Mike's wife, Lea, and her intolerance for good old meat.

Del took an extra helping of wings and grabbed a sugar-laden soda, then returned to the living room. To her relief, Vanessa had claimed the spot next to Grace.

When Vanessa saw her staring, she raised a brow in that arrogant way of hers. Even dressed down in sweatpants and a *Say Yes to Organic* T-shirt, her golden hair pulled back in a pristine ponytail, the woman looked like a model. "You got a problem with the pregnant lady taking your seat, Del?"

Robin shook her head. "She's really milking this baby thing."

"No kidding." Kim frowned. "Del, you sit right next to me."

"On the floor?" Del snorted. "Gee, Kim. Thanks for moving over."

Robin chuckled. "Ain't my woman sweet?"

The others laughed before buckling down into a discussion about Abby's latest heartthrob, a Marine hero, and the female doctor who puts him in his place. At least Abby wrote about strong women. Del chanced a glance at Grace.

"Right, Del?" Abby asked loudly, frowning.

"What did I do?" She took a drink of soda, not intimidated in the slightest to be at the center of the group's focus.

"You aren't paying attention."

"To *meeee*," Maddie whined, and everyone laughed. "Sorry, Abs. You're getting a little diva-ish."

"Pot calling kettle. Hello," Vanessa interjected.

"That's not what I meant." Abby scowled. "Del, put down the chicken wing and tell me what you thought of the book."

Rena grinned. "*I'd* tell you, Abby, but then, I'm just a guest. Not a regular, like my cousin."

Everyone glanced from her to Rena. Just like Del and J.T., the obvious skin color differences tended to throw people.

Not Vanessa, who dove right in with, "So what gives with you two? Adoption? Different dads? Moms? What?"

Abby turned red. "Vanessa."

Beth sighed. "Really, Vanessa."

Del and Rena cracked up, and Rena explained, "My mom and J.T's mom were sisters. Technically we're step-cousins, I guess. No actual blood relation."

"Wish I could say the same." Maddie pointed at Vanessa. "Vanessa's mom and mine are sisters."

The conversation flowed away from Del and Rena to bad baby names. It seemed Vanessa was an expert about what she refused to consider. Anything on the popular list had to go.

"Ahem." Abby stood up. "Back to the book discussion? I'm serious. This is going to help me with my current project."

"So why not tell us about that?" Del offered.

The wicked grin Abby sent her had her rethinking the idea. "Great idea, Del. My latest story revolves around a female mechanic and the man who broke her heart."

"Oh hell." She'd already dealt once with Abby's

research the last time they'd met at her shop. Apparently, Abby hadn't changed her mind about her character's profession. Wonderful.

Beth grinned, and Del saw the charm everyone else normally interacted with. "Go on, Abby."

Abby paused, and Maddie elbowed her. "Yeah, Abs. Do tell."

"Abby, please?" Rena begged with puppy dog eyes. No one could resist the eyes. Abby couldn't either.

"Well, see, there's this tough woman who's really not that tough at all. She just seems tough."

Everyone looked at Del, and she scowled. "This is *not* about me."

Beth's smile faded. Grace didn't look too pleased either, but when everyone began talking about Mike, whom Abby had modeled the hero on, and dropped Del from the conversation, Del finally relaxed.

"Oh my gosh, Beth. Mike is so amazing," Maddie gushed. "It's hard to believe he's been alone for so long."

"I raised good boys," Beth said with pride. And she had. Del wished she could dislike the woman more, but she had a nice family and a stamp of approval from Liam. Her father could be a horse's ass, but he understood people. He liked what he knew of Beth McCauley. Too bad Beth seemed to hate Del.

"Well, Flynn's *my* favorite." Maddie beamed.

Abby shook her head and teased, "Brody is hands-down superior. No offense, guys."

"Personally, I'm taken with James. And he's taken with me," Beth teased back.

Considering how unhappy the woman had been with James not so long ago, Del enjoyed knowing Beth had found her own happily-ever-after with her bear of a spouse.

Rena, damn her, would not shut up. "Abby, when is this book coming out?"

Abby shot Del a grin. "As soon as I can get Mike to give me an interview, I figure I can pound this book out in a few months. It's due to release in the winter of next year."

"I can't wait." Rena shot Del a smug look. "Tell me more about the hero."

"Yes, he sounds awfully familiar," Beth said dryly.

"He does, doesn't he?" Grace added with a chuckle. "I don't know Mike that well, but he's been *super* nice to me."

Super, Del wanted to repeat and shake her imaginary pom-poms, but didn't. She felt enough like a moron as the inspiration for Abby's book. Acknowledging jealousy that shouldn't exist annoyed the crap out of her. Del didn't do relationships or envy—not over men. So why this weirdness about Mike?

"He's been nice to Noah," Grace added.

"Who's Noah?" Rena asked.

Vanessa answered, "Her son. He's how old?"

"Seven, going on eight pretty soon." Grace smiled. "He and Colin seem to get on really well. It's so great to have friendly neighbors."

Neighbors? She lived next to Beth, not Mike. *Gah. Who cares? Not my problem.*

Instead, Del concentrated on Abby's discussion, which eventually circled back to her book club pick. Del added a little to the conversation. She'd read some of the story before her cousin had snatched the book out of her hands and refused to give it back. Even now the suck-up held it to Abby to sign.

Del glared. "You know, Rena, that's my book."

"Not anymore." Rena clutched the signed copy to her chest. "Thanks, Abby. This is *so* great. You'll sign my other ones?"

"Sure." Abby grinned, no doubt basking in Rena's obvious adulation. "See, Del? This is how you should act. Like you like me."

Del rolled her eyes.

"*I* like you." Grace laughed, a tinkling sound. "I'm sure Del is just teasing."

Like Del needed Grace to make excuses for her. She opened her mouth to retort and saw the daggers Rena shot her. She clamped her lips shut, then took a deep breath before saying, "Abby knows I like her just fine."

Abby frowned. "Of course I do. Del loves my work."

"I wouldn't go that far," Del muttered, and Vanessa snickered.

Maddie coughed to hide her laughter. "Don't worry about Abby, Del. It's all Brody's fault. He's so in love with her it's making her head swell."

"Not sure that's possible. It was already pretty big to begin with when I met her." Del didn't think she'd said that loud enough for anyone but Maddie to hear, but Vanessa laughed so hard she started coughing.

"Oh God. Now that was funny. Good one."

Del sighed. "I need a beer." She took the opportunity to dart into the kitchen to root around for a beer. She found one in the back of the fridge. No telling how old it was, but she didn't care.

She pulled it out, uncapped it, and had taken a deep drag of it when Grace entered the kitchen. More awesomeness Del could have done without.

Grace gave Del an overfriendly grin. "Hey, Del. I just wanted to say how great it was to see you again."

"Ah, sure."

"I wouldn't put too much stock in Abby's characters or anything. Not like she's actually basing her lovers on you and Mike." The too-bright smile warned Del to tread warily.

"O-kay?"

"Mike's a single dad. Clearly he's more concerned with his son than hooking up with anyone."

"Clearly." *Those twelve hours of sex last week must have been an aberration.*

"Well, you and he aren't exactly the same type. You seem much tougher and more independent than a man like Mike would go for. I mean, you're so strong. Your muscles are almost bigger than Mike's." She laughed as if teasing and daring Del to laugh with her.

Oh, Grace was good. Light and airy, nothing said that could be construed as really insulting. Just those little digs that would chip away at a woman with less self-esteem.

Behind Grace, Vanessa arrived to stand in the mouth of the kitchen, taking in the show.

To Del's joy, Grace wasn't done. "I'm sorry," Grace said with a blush. Real or feigned? "I didn't mean to imply you might be manly or gay or anything. I *totally* think you're straight. If you were gay, that would be fine too though."

So great to have Grace's permission to be homosexual.

The gabby woman continued, "Your tattoos and muscles are *totally* feminine, at least, to me. You're tough, but in a womanly way. I hear a lot of guys *totally* like tattoos on women nowadays."

Three "totallys." Del wanted to turn it into a drinking game, a sip for each one. She took another drink of beer, then deliberately wiped her mouth on the back of her colored forearm, playing up her differences to get the greatest effect. "Thanks, Grace. That means a lot, coming from you."

Grace half-smiled, as if not sure what that meant.

"For the record, I have no problem with anything anyone thinks of me. I like me, and that's all that matters."

Grace frowned. "I like you too."

Del snorted. "Sure you do. Look, I'm just fine with my appearance. You don't have to tell me not to worry about Mike. He'll be damn lucky to have me again."

Grace's lips flattened.

"But you try your best. He's a stud in bed, by the way. And, honey, he ain't all that nice, so don't think batting your eyes and whimpering is gonna have him inside you with that monster cock any sooner."

Grace gasped and fled, brushing by Vanessa. A moment later, Del heard the front door open and shut, then the silence in the other room that gradually filled with noise again.

"Too much?" she asked casually.

Vanessa grinned. "Not enough. What a little bitch."

"Uh-huh." Del stood there, not sure what to do now. Should she go? Stay? Track Grace down and punch her in the face just because it would feel good?

Vanessa watched her. "So are you going to nurse that thing in here all night or what?"

With a shrug, Del followed Vanessa back into the living room with her beer. "Did you follow Grace into the kitchen to save me?"

"No, to save her. Too bad I was too late." But Vanessa didn't look upset at all.

When Del sat back down, Beth looked from her to Vanessa. "What happened to Grace? She flew out of here without a word."

Vanessa answered before Del could. "Ate something that didn't agree with her, I guess. Sometimes you need to learn when to fight your battles. I mean, I don't do gluten for a reason."

"Oh." Beth sighed. "I guess I should see if she's all right, since we came together. Abby, thanks for having me." Beth said her good-byes, polite even to Del, and left.

The moment the door closed, the group turned to Del.

"What?" She scowled. Why didn't they look to big-mouthed Vanessa for answers?

Robin and Kim glanced at each other, then back at her. "What did you say to her?" Robin wanted to know.

"'Cause that woman had her claws out from the time you walked through the door," Kim added.

"Even I saw it," June agreed.

"Saw what?" Abby asked.

"God, Abby. Get a clue." Maddie shook her head. "The woman was clearly jealous."

"What did you say to her, cuz?" Rena asked, smirking. "'Cause if I know you, and I do, it wasn't pretty."

Vanessa chuckled. "Oh, it wasn't. It was a thing of beauty."

The room quieted.

"You can't tell Beth," Del blurted. "She already hates me."

"Yep, she does," Vanessa agreed.

"She does not," Abby snapped.

"Vanessa." Maddie shook her head. "She likes you, Del. Mostly."

"So what did you say, Del?" Rena prodded.

Del was going to have a firm talk with her cousin when they got home. The girl did *not* know when to leave well enough alone.

Vanessa answered with amusement, "Basically, Grace called Del masculine, gay, and told her not to worry that Abby was in any way, shape, or form intimating that Del and Mike would be a good couple."

"Really? That's not very nice." Abby frowned.

"Then Del took a manly swig of beer, wiped her mouth on the back of her arm—"

Rena groaned. "Del, really? I want to come back here."

"You're invited, Rena. Del too," Abby said without hesitation.

Good to know at least Abby had her back. Del hadn't missed her cousin's glare.

Rena shook her head. "I'll watch her more closely next time, Abby. I swear."

"Oh, come on, Rena." Del frowned. "The woman was baiting me. What was I supposed to do?"

"Exactly as you did." Vanessa nodded. "So after Grace calls Del a man, Del answers back that she's already had Mike once, and he'd be lucky to have her *again*."

"You go, Del." Robin held up a hand for a high-five.

Del groaned but leaned forward to slap it anyway.

"Then she added that Mike's a stud in bed, and Grace being all wimpy isn't—and I quote—'gonna have him inside you with that monster cock any sooner.'"

Silence. Then Del got a standing ovation.

Even from Abby. "Oh wow. Can I use that line?"

Del laughed with them, but inside she wondered if she'd just shot herself in the foot. Because Grace would either narc her out to Beth, or Beth would find out Del was doing Mike and warn her son away as fast as she could spit. Despite being a lady, Beth McCauley could no doubt spit with the best of them. She had four strapping sons and that big-ass husband after all.

Somewhere, the death march sounded again, this time for Del's sex life.

———※———

Beth hurried after Grace, not sure what had put a burr under her saddle. Except she did know. Beth slowed, not at all as clueless as her family would believe. Oh, she'd heard the others talk about Mike's fixation on Del. Colin was already in love with the woman.

Despite Del's odd dress and liberal use of jewelry all over the place, she'd been nothing but pleasant whenever she was around Beth. She treated Colin like a treasure, and for that alone Beth liked the guarded woman. However, when it came to Mike's heart, Beth wouldn't—couldn't—go easy.

Besides feeling as if she'd lost her own child when Lea passed, Beth had been crushed to see Mike's desolation during that difficult time. Of all her sons, she worried for him the most. He'd given up on love when he lost his precious Lea, and he hadn't come out of his shell since. He helped everyone needing it. Always did for others and gave his son all the love he deserved. But Mike took nothing for himself.

She'd thought, perhaps, that Abby, with her likeness to Lea, might break his lonely streak. But he hadn't been interested, and then Abby had lost her heart to Brody. Maddie and Vanessa might have been contenders, except Mike never looked at a woman as more than casual entertainment, and Flynn and Cam had clearly staked their claims.

Poor Mike worried her.

Grace seemed ideal for her eldest, and Beth hurried after her. Grace was a mother, a dutiful daughter, both pretty and kind. Her son though... Noah could be a handful, but what son wasn't at one time or another?

Beth had seen nothing shy of wonderful in the woman, and she had high hopes Mike might see the same. Except he seemed to have eyes only for Delilah Webster—Lea McCauley's polar opposite.

"Grace. Oh Grace." Beth hurried and caught Grace just as she neared the front step of Nadine's walkway. "Honey, are you okay? You left pretty suddenly."

Grace turned, spotted Beth, and a tear trickled down her cheek.

Alarmed, Beth caught her in her arms and lowered them both to the step to sit. "What's wrong?"

Grace hurriedly wiped her eyes. Even crying, she seemed sweet. God, she reminded Beth of Lea with that look of injured purity. "I'm so sorry. I said some terrible things to Del, and I didn't even mean to. Somehow I called her too manly or something, when I was only trying to make her feel better." Grace looked so remorseful.

The poor thing. "Everyone makes mistakes. I'm sure she'd forgive you if you apologized."

"I would, but I don't want her to think I'm poking my nose where it doesn't belong." Grace sighed. "I had no idea she and Mike were an item."

Beth frowned, not pleased to have her suspicions confirmed. "Oh?"

"Abby made it sound like she was modeling her characters off Del and Mike, and I thought Del might feel embarrassed about all the attention. Instead I put my foot in my mouth."

Beth hugged her. "I'm sure Del can hold her own." Could Liam's girl not see she'd hurt Grace's feelings? "Want me to talk to her?"

"I—probably not. I should apologize myself, shouldn't I?"

"Don't you worry a thing about it. I'm sure Del was just being Del." Gruff and sarcastic, like her father, but not as soft. Odd to think of Liam as the easy Webster to deal with. "I'll talk to her and Mike and get this sorted out." She held up a hand. "But don't worry. I'll keep you out of it. I'll just dig around as the concerned mother. I did see you storm out of book club."

"I guess." Grace sniffed. "I should go check on Mom."

"Okay. I'll see you tomorrow for lunch?"

Grace gave a watery smile. "Sure. Mom and I would love it."

Beth watched her go inside the house, then decided to make a phone call to her son. She'd get to the bottom of his situation with Del, then see how she felt about it. She'd already let Mike hide his heart for way too long. Now that she'd almost lost her husband—partly due to her own stubbornness, but still—she understood how every second counted. She hated that Mike seemed to have forgotten that fact, especially after all he'd been through. It was time she reminded him.

She entered her house and smiled at her husband. "A mother knows best."

He turned from the TV. "Beth?"

"Nothing, dear. Where's the phone?"

Chapter 10

MIKE GRIMACED AS HE PULLED INTO DEL'S DRIVEWAY for their Friday night date. Oddly enough, thinking the word *date* didn't send him into a panic or make him want to flee like it did with most women wanting more. He and Del knew the score, and he appreciated her honesty. Almost as much as he appreciated how incredibly fine the woman was without clothes.

Trying to calm himself down, he glanced around and didn't see her car. She must have stashed her precious GTO in the garage. In this neighborhood, he'd have done the same. Not that it was all that bad, but he'd seen a few sets of bars on windows.

He parked and got out, prepared to deal with one of the *many* women currently making his life miserable. At least with Del, a happy ending waited on the other side of her bedroom door. His mother… He'd deal with her later. And tonight, he didn't even want to think about Grace Meadows.

He knocked on the door of the two-story town house, noting its run-down yet cared for exterior. She could use a new coat of paint, some minor repair work on the door and the tilted window boxes under the first-floor window. The home had a charm about it, though, from the pretty pansies in the ceramic pot by the door to the cheery welcome mat under his feet.

Del answered after the third knock. She cracked the door open and peered at him through the gap. "Oh, it's you."

"Nice greeting. You should write for Hallmark."

She chuckled and opened the door a fraction more. "So about tonight—"

He pushed the door open and walked inside before she could keep him from entering. After his mother's phone call, he'd had a feeling the night wouldn't go as smoothly as he'd hoped. Not unless he fixed things before they went to hell.

"Come right on in," she muttered and closed and locked the door behind him.

He looked around, noting the worn but comfortable furniture, the myriad books and magazines organized into stacks all over the living room, the sectioned-off kitchen, and hallway leading to the rest of the first floor with the stairway to his left, right by the entryway.

"What's down there?" He nodded toward the darkened hall.

She sighed. "My bedroom. Rena has the upstairs."

"She's here?" He hadn't thought Del would take him up on the offer of her cousin watching, but he was more than game. Because if she thought her cousin being around would throw him off, she didn't know Mike.

"No, she's out with some friends tonight." She frowned. "So get that hopeful look off your face."

Rena was pretty, but she was no Del. "Not sure what you're implying."

"Yeah, right."

"Let's talk about you." He paused, ready to put his game into play. "And my mother. And *Grace*." And the earful he'd gotten.

She blinked innocently. "What?"

"Do you know how long I had to listen to my mom

yammering about my responsibilities as a good neighbor and inviting kind of guy? About how I should be nicer to Grace because *some people*"—he glared at her—"didn't understand a joke? Because I know all about being a single parent, and that in this day and age, it's so hard and terrifying to make new friends...*blah blah blah*? What the hell did you say to Grace, anyway?"

"Not much."

She looked guilty. He knew Del well enough to understand she'd never deliberately hurt someone. Grace had obviously said something to put her back up. No way Del would just verbally attack the woman for no reason. But his mother had implied Del had been too sensitive about some innocent remarks. He was dying to know what the hell had gone on at Abby's book club.

"Why did Grace collapse in tears in front of her house after her talk with you at the party?"

Del stared. "How do you know she did that?"

"My mom found her and had to console her. Then *I* had to hear about it."

"Jesus. Tell me you aren't buying that. Collapsed? Really? *This* is the woman you want to tie yourself to? A woman who resorts to crocodile tears to suck up to your mom?"

He swore he heard a hint of jealousy, and he wanted to puff up with satisfaction. "I never said I wanted to tie myself to her." *To anyone*, he reminded himself as he once again unconsciously imprinted Del's image into his tomorrow. She was just so incredibly sexy. Her hair hung around her face, silky strands caressing her sharp cheekbones. She wore a gray long-sleeved T-shirt that emphasized the brightness of her eyes and a pair of lightweight cotton pants, showcasing her long, toned legs. Legs he soon planned to have wrapped round his head while he made her really, really happy.

"You want to know what she said?"

"Uh-huh." He subtly stalked her until she backed into the wall.

She flushed. "Quit moving in on me."

"Make me." He planted his hands on either side of her head, gratified to see her rapid breathing, her gaze settling on his mouth. It had been nearly a week without her, and he was dying to feel her around him again, to sense that connection and relive the powerful orgasm that had rocked his world.

"You're being very immature about this." She sniffed.

He leaned close and nipped at her throat, smiling at her soft moan. "I'm waiting." He leaned back to watch her.

"Fine. She basically called me a man, said my muscles were too big, implied I was a lesbian, then told me not to worry about Abby basing her book on you and me being a couple, because we're too different to ever get along like that."

He frowned. "We're not that different."

"*That's* the part that bothers you?" She huffed. "But me being manly and gay is okay?"

"What?" He didn't like the thought of anyone making snap judgments about him and Del. Who the hell did Grace think she was, anyway? He and Del suited perfectly. Not that they'd ever intended anything more permanent. But they *could*—that was the point.

Del blew out a breath, one that landed on his cheek with warmth and the hint of chocolate. "Forget it."

"No way. She said all that? So what did you tell her?" This had to be good.

"You really want to know?"

"I asked, didn't I?"

She smirked, and he went from semi-hard to full-out erect. "That you'd be lucky to have me *again*. And that all her simpering and wimpiness wouldn't get your monster cock inside her anytime soon."

He blinked. "No shit?"

"No shit."

He couldn't contain a grin. "You really said that? About my monster cock? To Grace Meadows?"

"We were in the kitchen when she went all passive-aggressive nasty on me. I hate her type. You want to call me a lesbian, say it to my face. And for the record, I see nothing wrong with being gay."

"Me neither." His heart skipped a beat. "I don't suppose you have any girlfriends you want to call over...?"

She groaned but couldn't seem to stop herself from laughing. She had a gorgeous smile.

Time to get right down to it. Mike traced her chin with a finger, captivated by her soft skin. "Now. To the matter at hand."

Her smile faded. "Matter?"

"Not only did we make plans for a Friday-night date, which made the week drag, but I had the added frustration of dealing with my mother. Cruel and unusual, to say the least, that I was forced to suffer for my *girlfriend's*"—he used air quotes—"overly sensitive temperament."

"Overly sensitive, my ass," she growled. "Wait. Girlfriend?"

Her frown and that tone pushed him past patience. He kissed her, taking possession of her mouth. He licked and teased his way into her good graces, gratified as all get-out when she clutched his neck and kissed him back. As hungry for him as he was for her, and damn, but that set him off.

She ravaged his mouth, but he was in charge. He didn't want to come yet. Mike broke the kiss, panting, and pushed her shoulders against the wall. He held her there, loving the fact that she tried to move but couldn't.

"You're really strong." She swallowed.

He groaned, wanting her to swallow *him*. "And really hard."

"I can feel it." She rubbed her pelvis against him like a cat.

He teethed her throat, and she arched her neck, giving him better access. He sucked, not too hard, but enough to remind her who was in charge.

Apparently she liked his dominance, because she responded when he took control. Heavy moaning, increased air intake, her desperation to get closer…

For years he'd fantasized about rougher sex with a partner. But for one reason or another the opportunity hadn't materialized. With Del, he didn't think she'd mind. He didn't fear hurting her with a small show of strength. The woman handled *him* on a regular basis. God, he wanted to let loose for once.

"You mind a little rough handling?" he asked, staring into her eyes as he waited.

She grinned, a mean smirk that made him ache to tame her. "I doubt you can handle me, but by all means try."

"You're itching for a spanking, aren't you?"

Her breathing hitched, and he thought he'd found one of her kinks. One to match his.

"Go ahead. Try it."

"I won't hurt you, sweetness. Not much anyway."

She tried to glare at him, but her desire was impossible to miss. "Do your worst."

"Oh, I plan on it." He pulled her from the wall and hefted her over his shoulder in a fireman's carry. She yelped once but didn't protest again, and he walked them down the hallway to her bedroom.

Done in lavender and white with accents of deeper purple, her room looked both modern and eclectic. A lot like Del. The area was mostly neat, save for those odd piles of her things stationed around the room. She had a sense of neatness mixed with a cluttered chaos that charmed him without meaning to.

His attention focused on her spindle-board bed and stayed there. He'd have no problem tying her down. He couldn't wait.

Mike tossed her onto the bed. "Don't move."

To his surprise, she didn't balk at the order and watched, frozen, while he stripped to nothing and took out a few condom packets from his pants pocket, placing them on the bed stand.

She licked her lips, and he held himself out to her. "Lick me."

She raised a brow.

"Now."

"Make me." She stuck her tongue out at him, and he grinned.

In seconds he stripped her naked and kissed his way down her belly to the thin strip of blond hair over her mound. "You look so fucking sweet. Let's see if you taste as good as I've imagined." He didn't wait for a response but prodded her thighs wider and clamped his mouth over her.

A responsible adult would have discussed safe sex with her again before licking her pussy, but Mike damn well knew the woman wouldn't chance her health on a one-night stand. Not without being smart about it. And he couldn't wait any longer, not with her naked and splayed out on the bed before him.

She tasted like flowers, a lavender scent that went straight to his head. Had to be a lotion or soap, but now the scent was intrinsically linked to Del. He opened his mouth wider to take her all in, and he licked and stroked her clit, lapping up her cream.

"Mike. Yeah, baby. That's so good." She clutched his head with strong hands, encouraging him with those rough fingers. "I'm so close," she moaned on a breath.

So he pulled away.

"Wait. No, come back."

"Not yet." He sat up on his knees and reached over to grab a condom. Waiting to take her wasn't going to happen. Not this first time, but he'd make their initial go worth remembering.

She watched him roll the rubber over his cock, then gripped him tight. "You're so thick. I want to feel you inside me again."

His eyes nearly crossed, and he hurried to pull her hand away. "*You* want? Uh-uh." He scooted to the head-board and put his back to it. Then he grabbed her and manhandled her belly down, in paddle position, over his lap. Awkward with his erection, but he managed.

"Hey, what are you…" She ended on a moan when he stroked her ass.

"Bad girls who need discipline get spanked."

"Mike."

He swatted her ass, and she jerked. He spread her legs wider and shoved a finger in her pussy, keeping it there while her body clamped hard on him. Jesus, he needed to be inside her. "You're so wet. You want this, don't you?"

She buried her face in her crossed arms on the bed. Strewn across his lap, she dangled at the edge, her breasts almost clearing the mattress. Mike cupped her and toyed with her nipples, still keeping that one finger inside her.

"Oh God. Do it again." She wriggled her ass, and he smiled.

"You're a bad girl, aren't you?" He needed to fuck her in the worst way.

"Yeah, I am."

"Tell me all the bad things you did." He withdrew his finger from her and sucked it, loving her taste. "You taste so good."

"Oh man. Did you just lick your finger?" She tried to push up, to look at him, and he planted his hand on her back and shoved her back down, her belly to the bed. She lay perpendicular to him, which wouldn't work if he planned on taking her any time soon. But in this position at least, he couldn't forget himself and "accidentally" thrust inside her while he played.

He spanked her again, harder this time. A rapid succession of forceful pats that had her panting and crying his name. He thrust his finger back inside her, then added another. "Damn, you're wet. And tight. I'm dying to be inside you."

"So what are you waiting for?" she rasped.

"So bossy." He grinned despite his iron-hard cock. He smacked her a few more times, then unable to bear any more, eased her off his lap and left her face down on the bed to circle around toward her feet. The bed stood at the perfect height for pleasure. Grabbing her by the ankles, he dragged her across it, so that the V of her thighs met his erection.

"Mike, please."

"Tell me what you want." He palmed her reddened cheeks and toyed with her slick folds, edging his thumbs close to her pussy before backing away.

"Don't tease," she whispered. "Oh God. I'm going to come."

"Not without me you don't." He spread her thighs wider and positioned the tip of himself at her entrance. "Want me to come in?"

"*Yes*. Fuck. Now."

He entered her slowly, putting just the head inside her. Then he spanked her.

She jolted. "Mike, yes. Yes, again."

He pushed more and spanked her while he entered her. To his incredible satisfaction, she cried out, "Mike, yes. *Fuck, yes*," and clutched the bed sheets, coming hard while he pumped and swatted her ass.

He couldn't wait any longer. "I'm gonna ride you so hard." Taking her from behind, staring down at the beautiful artwork over her sides and lower back, her forearms, hastened his need. He thrust himself balls-deep inside her and rested only a brief moment before withdrawing, then pushed forward again.

He slammed into her, encouraged by her throaty

moans and the way she raised her ass to allow better penetration.

Mike took her like he owned her, and in that moment, he did. He gripped her hips tight as his orgasm neared. "Oh yeah. I'm coming. So hard."

"In me. All in me," she whispered and pushed back against him.

He felt surrounded by her, welcomed inside that taut warmth. He tightened his hold on her hips and rammed harder, going as deep as possible as he reached his end and yelled out. He spasmed, shaking as he jetted inside the condom, wishing against sense that nothing separated them. No rubber, no rules. Just him and her, together.

The orgasm left him light-headed, and when he caught his breath, he eased his hold on her and kissed a path along her spine to her shoulders. He pushed aside her golden hair and kissed his way to her cheek. "You feel so good around me," he admitted in a throaty voice.

"You too." She squeezed him with inner muscles, and he moaned and leaned up, propped on his hands. "Oh, that's nice."

"Shit, yeah." He glanced to where they joined and grimaced at the marks on her skin. "I left fingerprints on you. Sorry, Del."

"I'm not," she rasped. "Oh man, that was hot."

"I told you I wanted to bend you over. And let's face it, you really did need a spanking." He swore as he withdrew. "Be right back."

He left to dispose of the condom in her bathroom trash and returned to see her lying naked, on her back, in the center of the bed. Not content to leave her alone, he joined her and covered her with his body, levering his weight on his elbows.

"You'll crush me."

"Quit your whining." He kissed her on the lips, loving her scent. "You need a blanket, and I'm volunteering for the position."

"Mmm." She opened her mouth, allowing his lazy kisses that felt like so much more than just sex. He would have been more worried if he could think past the pleasure still filtering its way throughout his body.

"I taste me on your lips."

"Yeah. Sweet as sugar."

She chuckled against his mouth, and he broke the kiss to watch her.

So fucking beautiful. He sighed. "So I guess we should have the safe sex talk now. You know. Before you blow me."

She snorted. "Little late for that, huh? I mean, you had breakfast, lunch, and dinner just seconds ago at Café Between My Legs."

He chuckled. "Yeah, I did." He licked his lips, pleased when she followed the movement, her eyes narrowing into diamond-bright slits. "And we're gonna go again, because I missed dessert."

"Maybe." At his look, she huffed. "Yeah, yeah. I know, you earned it. Especially after dealing with your mom."

He grimaced. "Having sex here, Delilah. Don't mention that woman right now, okay?"

She snickered. "Big bad Mike. Embarrassed about fucking and…" She made a face. "Okay, I'm with you.

'Cause now I'm seeing your mom in my head and it's squicking me out too."

"Yeah."

They stared at each other, then Mike leaned down to kiss her again. He *had* to.

She responded as if made for him, and the notion unnerved him. He broke the kiss, more than aware of her rounded breasts and pointed nipples grazing his chest, like little beacons of arousal.

He needed more time to recover, but kissing and rubbing against her were doing the trick, because his dick was no longer soft. Semi-hard and growing longer.

"So about this safe sex," she mumbled between kisses. "I haven't been with anyone but you in a long time."

"How long?" He kissed his way across her cheek to her throat. She had the sexiest neck. Long and creamy, so smooth.

"A year, okay?"

He leaned up, blinking in surprise, noted her blush, and felt something inside him give. An odd flutter in his belly that he quickly attributed to unquenchable lust. "If you've been celibate, it's because you wanted to be." He believed that wholeheartedly.

Her blush grew brighter, and he stared, enchanted.

"Why are you looking at me like that?"

"Your cheeks are pink. I just spanked and fucked you, and *now* you're blushing. You are too cute." He laughed when she smacked his chest.

"Fuck you."

"Oh, baby, I'm going to. Just let me get my second wind again." He rubbed against her, skin-to-skin, and grew harder. "I haven't had sex without a condom in over six years. And yes, I know this because Colin's my measuring stick."

This time she grimaced. "Okay, no mom or kid talk while screwing."

"Making love," he corrected, just to annoy her.

She rolled her eyes. "Whatever, Casanova. You were saying…?"

"I'm saying I always use protection. And it's been like six months since I last got laid. I'd like to say four, but that one instance of heavy petting didn't really count, because I ended up jacking myself off when my partner got hers."

"Great to know." She frowned at him.

"What? You asked. I'm being honest. She's a woman I know, a friend who only wants sex. She's careful, I'm careful. It works."

"Then why are you here with me, McCauley?" That mean tone had him rising up on his hands, to remind her of his growing erection against her.

"Because I can't get your wolf eyes out of my head."

"Wolf eyes?" Said eyes widened. "Really?"

He groaned and rubbed against her, more than hard again. "Figures you'd take that as a compliment."

"Wolves are cool."

"I know." He continued thrusting against her mound, then her belly. "They're resilient, powerful, and have big teeth. I'm hoping you'll take into consideration that my monster cock is not a chew toy." He chuckled at the glare she shot him. "Now come on, baby. I sucked you off. You can do me, can't you?"

"Maybe. What's it worth to you?"

"To see your mouth around my cock?" Just saying that excited him. "What do you want?"

"Hmm. Bargaining. Now this I like," she said with a sly undertone.

"Fuck. When you get all mean like that, you get me so hard."

She watched him, looking for what, he didn't know. "Mike?"

He stopped the teasing, because her tone had grown serious. "Yeah?"

"I can trust you on this, right? Like, if I go down on you, and you come, I'm not going to get anything."

She looked so vulnerable, and his heart did another one of those somersaults he had a hard time understanding. He lowered his face to hers and kissed her tenderly, feeling... *No. Not feeling.* Just being protective of a friend.

"Honey, my safety is the one thing I don't play around with. I have Colin relying on me to be clean as a whistle. Not to kill the mood, but at some point I have to go home and kiss my son with this mouth. Trust me when I say safety is a priority with me."

She relaxed. "Me too."

"I know. I trust you, Del."

She watched him with a darkening gaze. "You're a good dad."

"Yeah. And a better lover."

"So you say." Then she yanked him down by the hair and nipped his lower lip. "Prove it."

Chapter 11

DEL COULDN'T BELIEVE SHE WAS GOING TO DO THIS, but she wanted to taste Mike in the worst way. She was no angel, and she'd had her fair share of sex after her rebellious teen years, but only with men she found worthy of her, which limited the number considerably. To her, a blow job was more intimate than regular sex. Trust was a huge deal to Del. Mike might annoy her on occasion and royally piss her off, but she believed he'd never try to hurt her in any physical way. Emotionally…she had no doubt she'd end up taking a fist to the heart. But not today, and not now.

"Prove it?" he growled and kissed her hard, a punishing mashing of his mouth that turned her on like crazy. And the bastard knew it. She liked spankings, a bit of rough play. With Mike's size, he gave *rough* all new meaning. But that faith in him remained. She understood, instinctively, Mike was a protector.

"Yeah. Prove it," she repeated, then hissed when his lips found her nipples and sucked her so hard she thought she'd come from that alone. His fingers refused to remain still. Between his lips and his hands that found all her sweet spots, she was teetering on the verge of an orgasm all too soon.

"N-no. Supposed to make you come first," she rasped and arched up when he shoved two fingers deep inside her, rubbing against that spot that set her the hell off.

"Yes, oh God. Yes, again." She cried out and came hard, squeezing his fingers inside her, wishing he'd given her more.

Opening eyes she hadn't realized she'd closed, she saw him staring at her, his face drawn, his body still and hard as stone.

"You are fucking beautiful when you come," he confessed before he kissed her.

The desperate, rough embrace she expected didn't come. Instead, the kiss was whisper-light, a breath of affection from his lips to hers. He continued to kiss her—her lips, her cheeks, her forehead. He removed his fingers from inside her, and she felt bereft until he stroked her belly, her breasts, her hair.

She felt the tenderness, awash in pleasure and an afterglow that seriously scared the hell out of her. Raunchy sex could be dirty and oh-so-good. But this climax had been all for *her*, unselfish, thorough in execution that didn't stop as he eased her down. Had she ever been so taken care of, so…cherished?

"M-Mike?" How had their tryst segued from her blowing him to…this? Whatever this was?

"Hmm?" He had a dreamy look on his face as he petted her, yet that cock of his remained full and hot against her.

She cleared her throat, determined to take charge of what should have been a dirty coupling but instead was turning into something else.

"What?" he asked as he focused on her face.

"My turn." She shimmied out from under him, aware she got free because he let her, then shoved him onto his back.

"I want to see," he complained. "I can't if I'm flat on my back."

"Good point." She wanted him so turned on he couldn't think. The way she'd just been. She needed that control, because without it, she felt…dependent. On him for pleasure, for ease. For the gift of his smile. *Gah. Get off the love train, sister. This is about fucking for fun. Nothing deeper.*

Mike sat up against her headboard, then propped a few pillows behind his back. "So my back won't get bruised from your spindles."

"So weak. Go ahead…*Nancy*."

He laughed. "Nice one."

"I might have overheard your father the other day. Plus, Vanessa likes to taunt Cam with that."

"So what do you have to taunt me with?" he asked. "'Cause *Nancy* doesn't hurt like you think it should."

She licked her lips, and his humor faded, replaced by a look of intensity. She winked. "Does that hurt?" She licked her lips again and moaned, and he blew out an uneven breath.

"Witch."

"That's me. Now spread your legs."

He did so without any further encouragement.

"You're plenty big." She crawled between his thighs, taking her time, and heard his mumbled swearing. "Big cock, big balls. Like the rest of you."

He groaned when she breathed over his bobbing shaft. "You're going to draw this out, aren't you?"

"Hell yeah."

He leaned his head back. "If you must…"

"Shut up. Better yet, why don't you hold on to the bed frame, so you're not tempted to lose control."

"Please." He snorted. "I can take…anything…" he trailed as she kissed her way up the insides of his thighs. His muscles contracted, those powerful legs tense.

"Take anything…?" She licked the spot on his leg right next to his sac and watched him shudder.

"*Fuck*. Just do it."

"My motto, right up there with the big swoosh."

He groaned, and she laughed.

Then she lost her humor, needing to see him crumble, the way she had. "You're going to *beg me* to finish you."

"I'm ready to beg now," he muttered. "I beg you…stop yapping and get to suck—*ing*."

She took him into her mouth and bore down, accepting him to the back of her throat without gagging. A handy skill she'd learned in high school, when she'd been determined to be the queen of something. Obviously not books or school, but Queen of Easy had come to her without too much trouble, sad to say.

It worked on Mike now, for which she was grateful. He moaned her name and pumped his hips, and she tasted a small spurt of seed. The big guy wanted her like crazy. After giving her such a treat before, he'd more than earned his happy time.

She leaned down farther and cupped his balls in her hand while she moved her lips over him, slowly. Then she raised her ass in the air, knowing it was like waving a red flag at the particular bull readying to unload in her mouth.

"Fuck. Baby, that is so good." He swore when she stroked him with her tongue. Right at the sensitive point under the head of his crown. "Oh shit. Del, I'm not gonna last. Fuck."

He seemed to have devolved into a one-word vocabulary. And all because of her.

She liked the power, liked knowing she held him, literally, in the palm of her hand. But more than that, she liked the intimacy between them. This open contact neither of them had had in a long time.

Del pulled back and looked up at him, disconcerted to see him staring at her with that funny look on his face. When he caught her gaze, he let go of the bed with one arm, showcasing a mouthwatering array of muscle, and brought his huge hand to her head.

Instead of shoving her back down over him, he cupped her cheek.

Affection again, a clear messing of what should have been nothing more than a hot fuck between willing friends with benefits.

Alarmed yet oddly touched, she closed her eyes, blocking out his expression, and started moving faster. She took less of him between her lips, the shallow drags a result of her speed. She used her hands to make up for his lack of full penetration. But he was so large, she couldn't move so fast over him and not choke.

He tried to resist, she could tell, as his hand stroked her cheek. But it didn't take long before his fingers tangled in her hair, urging her for more.

"So fucking hot. Yeah, eat me up. Suck my cock. So tight."

He gripped her hair hard enough to hurt, and the bite of pain aroused her all over again.

"Oh fuck, Del. Touch yourself. Come hard, when I'm pouring into your mouth," he ordered in a harsh voice. "Yeah, oh yeah. Coming so hard in you."

She gripped his balls tighter, and he swore so loud she feared the neighbors might hear. Then he jerked inside her mouth, and she released his sac to fondle herself as she swallowed him. He came for a long time, and had she not known better, she wouldn't have thought they'd climaxed at all just moments ago. But damn if his release didn't push her own. She came one final time while she swallowed the sweet yet salty taste of her lover's seed.

Once she could think again, she eased off Mike's slowly softening erection.

She licked her lips clean of him, not surprised when he stared at her in shock, breathing hard.

"Good, hmm?"

"Fuck me, but I think you blew my mind." He sounded hoarse, his eyes wide and wild and so dark blue they looked black.

"Told you." She pretended she didn't feel more than smug about his orgasm. It wasn't that *she*—not another woman—had satisfied him. Or that she'd taken his wildness and that huge cock and had given him mindless ecstasy.

"You did. You totally did." He continued to pant while he watched her. Then, quick as lightning, he snatched her from between his legs and hugged her so tight she squeaked.

"Mike."

"Anything you want." He eased back to stare at her, his breathing slowing. "Seriously. You can have my house, my job, my kid, but the next time you do that, my mouth is buried in your pussy. That way when I die and go to heaven, I'll be surrounded by all of you."

She laughed. "Gee. I get your house, your job, *and* Colin? What a deal."

"And me. Don't forget I get to be the one licking you up again. I mean, *wow*. I gotta say. I'm still going to dream about someday coming inside your pussy, but now it'll be a tie for remembering your mouth. You were right. You totally schooled me."

"That's right. I did."

He flattened her under him in a heartbeat and kissed her until she couldn't breathe. When he leaned up, his eyes gleamed. "But don't forget I had you begging when I spanked you. I'm thinking next time I'm in you, we have you tied up so you can't move. Hmm. I'd *love* to see you bound. How'd you like that?"

One of her favorite kinks, but only with someone she totally trusted. Like Mike.

When she nodded, his eyes narrowed. "So three orgasms for you, and it's only," he paused to look at her clock. "Ten? Shit. I have another two hours before my glass slippers break."

"That's when your carriage turns back into a pumpkin, you mean." Such a guy. Obviously princesses weren't on the menu at the McCauley household.

"Whatever. So what are we going to do for *two hours*?"

She groaned at the spark of devilry in his gaze. "Two orgasms is one more than most guys can handle in a day. I don't want to break you."

"Aw, scared, Delilah? Is mighty Sampson too strong for you?" He made a muscle.

"Idiot."

He snickered then eased back off her. "So I'm here

'til midnight. And I'm thinking we won't be dressed until I go."

"Oh you do, do you?"

"This isn't going to embarrass you, is it?"

"How so?"

"Well, when your cousin comes back, my *monster cock* will no doubt be buried inside you again. And you know, she'll hear you crying out my name and begging me to finish you. You okay with that?"

"Dream on, Conan." She eyed his arms. Not a bad likeness, and truth be told, she liked the idea of him getting her hot enough to beg. "How are you so buff anyway?"

He settled on his back, and she became his blanket this time. She liked being on top. It gave her the feeling of being bigger, when she knew darn well she wasn't. "I work out a lot. I'm a big guy anyway, but I was into wrestling as a kid. Then I kept at it, because I liked it."

"You still wrestle?"

"I hit the gym. Got a heavy bag in my garage that helps me de-stress. It's either that or punch Flynn, and Maddie put a stop to that."

She grinned.

"The gym is great, because the mixed martial arts guys like to use me to train with. Keeps me in fighting shape. Go ahead, baby, touch. You know you want to."

"Arrogant much?"

He smirked. "Well, seeing as how you're touching me, I'm not far from wrong, am I?"

She swallowed a swear, because no way would she not take advantage of feeling every ripple and tendon on his incredible body.

"But don't worry, I'm as fascinated with your fine ass as you are with mine."

"Yeah, it is fine."

"Honey, I know. I've been dying to get my hands on you forever. But now I can't just stop at hands. Like, my mouth and tongue and cock…"

She grinned. "Quite the vocabulary, McCauley."

"Fuck yeah, *Webster*." He sneered. "Now let's keep touching while we play twenty questions. The one who comes first owes the other one a foot massage."

"Ew. No way I'm touching those giant whales on the ends of your legs. Besides, that's not a fair contest. I'm a chick. We have stamina. You're most likely done until next month." Laying it on a bit thick, but she liked challenging him.

Mike knew his worth, and that confidence gave him a whole layer of sexy he didn't even need. "Oh, game on, Delilah. We'll bet for something else then."

"Bring it, MC."

"MC?"

She grinned. "Monster Cock."

When he flushed, then tried to hide it with a grin, she laughed at him and pointed out his other assets. One way or the other, she planned on getting a bite of that tight ass before he left tonight.

And then the betting really got started.

———

Mike had never been so sexually sated in his life. He didn't remember what he said to Cam and Vanessa when he returned, but they laughed at him and left soon after, so he didn't care.

The next morning passed into afternoon in blessed peace. Colin had swimming lessons and a birthday party to attend. Del planned on joining them Sunday evening for dinner, one she had to prepare since she'd lost their bet.

He smiled at Colin and nodded, wondering what she'd make for dinner.

At her place. With Rena and J.T. And maybe her father in attendance.

He sobered as he realized the full ramifications of their bet. The sex had been beyond explosive. Thinking about it wasn't a good idea, because just the notion of Del and a bed got him hard with the memory of her taste. That lavender candle his mother insisted on burning was as bad, because the scent reminded him of Del.

Hell, everything reminded him of Del. Not good, especially since they were just friends. He still had a wife to mourn. Half of Lea's birthday cake sat in the fridge at home. Yet he had a difficult time holding on to his grief lately, and he didn't know how to feel about that. On the one hand, it had been six fucking years. Everyone wanted him to move on. But now…he thought he might be ready to.

What would that mean for him? For Colin?

Going to Del's house, surrounded by her family and friends, taking his son…it would send the wrong message. It was too soon.

"Too soon for what?" he muttered, watching Colin weave in and out of his friends to score a goal at the indoor soccer party. He'd have to remember that for Colin's birthday, because Colin showed no signs of being disinterested in anything to do with his favorite sport.

"Wow. He's good." Belinda Daniels, Brian's mother, appeared beside him. "He still as fixated as he was last season?"

Mike groaned, and Belinda laughed. "Yeah, Brian too." She jerked her head at her husband. "Ryan's planning to coach this year. Do you want to get Colin on his team?"

"Are you kidding? Why would I even think of separating Colin from his best friend? That would be like putting salt on the table without pepper. Crazy talk."

She laughed again, and he thanked his stars that he actually liked Belinda. She and Ryan made a solid, dependable couple, and they had accepted Colin like he was one of their own. The way Mike treated Brian. A good kid. Not like the smarmy boy he saw entering the sports complex with Grace behind him.

He groaned again, this time meaning it.

"Oh. Sorry." Belinda grinned. "I mean, I'm not. I think Grace likes you."

"How would you know?"

"It's all over the neighborhood. Sexy single mom. Sexy single dad."

He wondered if somehow his mother had gotten to Belinda. It was like *Invasion of the Body Snatchers*, starring Beth McCauley. "*Et tu*, Belinda?"

"Come on, Mike. You need to get out and live a little. All the women in the neighborhood are mooning over you."

He hated that he liked that fact. Del would have a field day taking him down to size over his ego. "Nah. They just see a guy who likes kids, has a job, and isn't living with his mother."

"There is that."

"So of course I'm a catch." He winked. "Then there's the McCauley charm."

Ryan joined them. "Oh God. Not the charm again."

Mike grinned and forced himself to keep his smile in place when Grace approached. As he watched her, he wondered if maybe he was looking at her all wrong. If things with Del might be progressing too fast, perhaps Grace was the hand brake he needed to slow things down.

He nodded to himself as she made small talk with Ryan and Belinda. Noah joined Brian and Colin, and unlike the last time they'd all been together, this time Colin seemed to take to the boy.

Again, memories of Beth McCauley's nagging to be nice to new neighbors intruded on his thoughts. Being the new kid seriously sucked. He knew he'd had things easy growing up, because after finally settling in their neighborhood, they'd only moved that one time, from the house next to his current one into the one his parents now lived in. And the move hadn't necessitated a school transition. He still saw guys he'd once gone to elementary school with. No having to make new friends and adapt to a new place.

Grace turned to him with a smile. "Hey, Mike. You look happy."

Sexually satisfied down to the bone. His heart went trippy at thoughts of the woman who'd inspired such pleasure, and he didn't like the fact that he'd started missing her the moment he left her townhome last night. For a friend, she felt awfully more than that. If that made sense.

Fuck. Now I'm talking about feelings to myself.

He turned to Grace and, before he could talk himself out of it, asked her if she wanted to go on a tour of Seattle the following night—the same night he was supposed to go to Del's. He could get his mother to watch Colin, and Nadine could take care of Noah. While Grace nodded with a smiling yes and his friends looked on with amused support, another part of him wanted to smack himself for complicating things.

No, not complicating, making sense. Taking a step back. No more Del with every thought and breath. Time to concentrate on being a single, *unattached* father doing a favor for his mother, to help out a friend. He'd go on a non-date with Grace. And he'd make sure she knew it was nothing but neighborly support. Somehow.

Not like he owed Del any explanations. They weren't dating.

He continued to talk himself out of his weird attachment to Del as the day wore on. Grace, fortunately, took his proposed meeting as he'd meant it. She seemed to have no problem with his carefully worded invitation to tour the city. With *a neighbor*. A *friend*. Period.

Once he and Colin left the party, he wondered if he should text Del or call her, then decided he'd man up and call her. No wimping out and texting because it would be easier to bail on her without hearing her sexy voice. He was no Nancy.

After he and Colin entered the truck, he dialed her, a part of him hoping to get her voice mail.

"Yo."

Figured she'd answer. "Hey, sweet cheeks. It's me," he said gruffly, remembering how he'd handled her "sweet cheeks" just last night.

"Oh, hi, Mike." Her voice softened, the way it did lately when she talked to him.

Some weird part of him felt guilty for dodging tomorrow, but hell, it wasn't anything, really. Just a stupid bet for dinner.

He wasn't a dick and wanted to be up front with her. No sense in hiding anything, especially since he wasn't planning to date Grace and Del at the same time. *Not a date with Grace. And not like I'm dating Del either.*

"Mike?"

"Oh. Sorry." A glance in the rearview showed Colin waving, no doubt wondering why the hell they weren't driving. "Just wanted to let you know we can't do tomorrow."

A pause. "Oh?"

"Yeah." He had a hard time getting the words out and felt like an ass. *Man up, dickless.* "I promised Grace I'd show her the city for my mom." Not a complete truth, but the gist was there. Mostly. "And with her schedule, tomorrow—"

"Okay."

He frowned, having expected more of a problem on her part. "I mean, we can do the dinner another time, right?"

"Oh sure. No biggie."

She sounded way too chipper on the phone. Maybe she hadn't wanted him to come over, and that bet had forced it on her. Stupid for him to have been thinking about her all damn day when she apparently didn't want him there. Now he felt glad he'd made up that part about needing to schedule the thing with Grace for tomorrow.

"Yeah. Just wanted to let you know. *Delilah.*"

"Thanks for calling. *McCauley.*"

Frustrated and annoyed, because his irritation with the woman made no fucking sense, he mumbled a hasty good-bye and disconnected before Colin begged to talk to his favorite person—who wasn't his father.

"Dad? What about tomorrow night?"

Realizing he'd now have to break it to Colin that they wouldn't be seeing Del or J.T., Mike did himself a favor and ran through Colin's favorite drive-through for an ice cream sundae before breaking the news.

The kid took it like a champ, especially since Mike made it clear Colin would be staying with Grandma and Grandpa while he showed Grace around.

As he drove them home and tucked Colin into bed later, he wondered what the hell he'd been thinking to turn down a fun dinner with Del in favor of a night with Grace.

A vision of Del's smile, her laughing gray eyes, danced in front of him. The thought of her kiss still made him weak in the knees. With resolution, he opened the fridge, pulled out the remainder of Lea's cake, and took a huge piece.

Despite it tasting way too sweet, the way she'd always liked it, he forced himself to eat every bite of the orange frosted chocolate cake before moving into the garage to work himself into a good lather.

His hands ached by the time he'd finished hitting the bag, and he could feel a film of tooth decay and sugar working its way into his enamel, but he no longer let himself feel disappointed Del hadn't insisted he come over tomorrow, or that she didn't seem to care about him hanging out with Grace.

He brushed his teeth and got ready for bed. Before he moved under the covers, he took Lea's picture out of his dresser drawer and lingered over her features—her bright brown eyes, her dark hair that feathered over her face, caught in the soft wind that had blown over them that day. He stood behind her in the picture, holding her, laughing and happy and whole. A lifetime ago.

Yet the pain he normally felt when he looked at the photograph seemed muted, not as sharp, and he slowly tucked the picture away, not sure what the hell was happening to him. He crossed back to his bed, feeling lost.

"I love you, Lea," he said as he slid under the covers, wishing the words didn't sound so empty. Who did he want to hear them? Her, or himself? So that he'd remember what should have been his first and last thought of each day?

As he tried to settle into sleep, he had to work to flush Del's image from his mind, determined not to dream about her for once. He was stronger than that.

He woke the next morning with Del's name on his breath and her taste on his lips.

So not how he'd planned to start the day.

Chapter 12

DEL SMILED THROUGH HER TEETH AT J.T. WHILE HE made yet another remark about her dry chicken. Yeah, she'd overcooked it. But the ass didn't have to call her out in front of her cousin and father, did he? She was coming to hate hosting family dinners. Ever since Liam had found out how Beth spent her Sundays with her family, her father insisted they had to get together once a week to grow tighter as a clan. Friggin' McCauleys...

"I mean, I can't even cut it with my knife." Her brother sawed away at the yard bird while she did her best to ignore him.

Next to her, Rena piped in with a cheery voice, "I'm just glad I didn't have to cook tonight. Thanks, Del." She chased down a bite of chicken with her iced tea.

For not jumping on the hater wagon, Del wanted to give her a big hug. But then Rambling Rena, the queen of talking too much, said, "I don't understand why Mike didn't come to dinner tonight. Why did he bail again? Something about helping out his mom?"

Her father and brother looked at her.

"What?" She wished Rena would stop reading into everything. Tonight wasn't even a date, just a bet gone sideways. "I'm not his keeper." *Or someone who can hold his interest, apparently.* To her horror, a rush of inadequacy struck her mute, the pain of his dismissal burning a hole into her heart. His girlfriend? Ha. She'd been right. He hadn't socked her Friday night. Instead, he'd waited a day to rip her world apart. Treating their sex— what he'd called *making love*—like it meant nothing.

Rejection. Such a familiar friend. She dug into her meal, pretending she hadn't completely lost her appetite, and wanted to pound something. *Shit.* Even the asparagus had turned soggy.

Rena continued, "So he's out with Grace, right? A favor for his mom, you said?"

J.T. frowned. "Hold on. You guys are hooking up, then he ditches you for that loser chick?"

Before Del could ask, Rena explained, "I told them about book club."

By *them*, she obviously meant both her brother and father, because Liam looked none too pleased either.

"Del? Is this true? You're seeing Mike McCauley?"

"Fuck, Dad. I'm twenty-eight years old. My love life is none of your business."

"Watch your tone, Delilah." Liam frowned.

"Yeah," J.T. repeated.

To her brother, she flipped the bird and retorted, "Sure thing, Jethro."

J.T. flushed, hating when she called him by his first name, a name which normally never failed to amuse her.

Rena broke into Del's secret pity party. "Um, I think maybe you guys are jumping to conclusions. Mike is a nice guy. Right, Del?"

Eager to put the topic of Mike behind her, Del nodded. "Yeah. Tonight was a casual dinner at best. End of story."

"Casual…with his kid in tow?" J.T. asked.

She ignored him. "Mike said he had to take Grace around for his mom." Which she just *knew* wasn't the whole truth.

Liam's frown eased. "Oh, well."

"'Oh, well'?" J.T. wore a scowl like a thundercloud. "The dick stood up your daughter, and you don't care?"

"J.T., it's not like that. I lost a bet and agreed to make him dinner. It's no biggie." She told herself to listen and take heart. She'd had amazing sex. Period. Why make more of it than there was? Hell, they'd never committed to anything more than orgasms anyway. Fun friends.

Yeah? Then why did he refer to me as his girlfriend? Because he did.

She so wished she could forget about that, but whenever she remembered their time together, she found herself thinking about his tenderness as much as his freakishly hot body. That soft smile full of gentle affection, the laughter they'd shared…

"So you're telling me it doesn't bother you that you went out and bought all this food and McCauley isn't even here to enjoy it? Well, the not-so-rubbery parts of this chicken?"

She lost it without meaning to. Del tossed her plate of chicken, soggy asparagus, and limp salad at her brother's face. "Fuck off. I'm going to Ray's. *Don't* follow me."

Del didn't wait to see if he obeyed. She left the kitchen, grabbed her keys, and darted to her favorite bar. A terrific place for losers to congregate on a Sunday evening.

As usual, the place had its share of patrons who never seemed to go home. She nodded to Earl as she entered.

"Where's your friend?"

She stopped and swung around to gape at him. Earl never asked after more than her family or the shop. He'd never once been interested in any guy she'd brought by, though admittedly there had been fewer to comment on the past years.

"Are you talking about Mike?"

"Big muscles, dark hair, put Jim on his ass. Him, yeah."

She swore under her breath. "He's fine. I guess."

Earl shrugged. "Good."

She left him staring after her and headed to the bar, where Lara sat laughing with one of the bartenders.

Del crooked her finger at him. "Yo, Scotty. Give me whatever's cheapest on tap."

"You got it, sexy." Scotty winked and fetched her a beer.

Unfortunately, another patron called him over, so Scotty handed her drink to Lara, who delivered it with a question Del hadn't wanted to hear again so soon. "Where's your big, hunky friend?"

Del took a healthy drink before answering with patience, "He's busy."

Lara raised a brow. "Oh?"

"We're not attached at the hip." Del wanted to guzzle her beer and down three more before she could take a breath. But she'd never been one to drown her sorrows in alcohol, so she paced herself.

"Maybe not," Lara said. "But he sure looked like he wanted to be attached to some part of you." Her eyes widened at something over Del's shoulder, then they crinkled when she smiled. "Hey there, sexy, what can I get for you?"

Del's palms sweated and her heart raced. Had Mike sought her out here? She refused to turn around and find out, so her stomach dropped as she had her second huge disappointment for the weekend when J.T. answered, "I'll have a Coke. I'm driving."

She dropped her head on the bar and groaned. "Leave me alone."

"Come on, Del. What's up?" He thanked Lara for the drink then pulled Del with him to a side table. She'd barely managed to grab her beer before she was sitting across from him.

"J.T., go away."

"No."

She raised her head. "What is your problem?"

"You. Rena agrees. You're acting weird lately."

"Bullshit."

"Yeah, you're full of it. Since when do you storm out of the house from a little teasing?"

"I worked hard on dinner. You might actually try appreciating it instead of jerking me around." *Mike, you asshole. I prepared that dinner for* you.

"You can tell me, sis. Is McCauley fucking with you?"

If only. "Nope." *Not anymore. He blew his chance when he took out Wimpy Woman.* "Look, I appreciate you looking out for me. I do. But I don't need your help. There's no problem, nothing to worry about. Mike and I are just fine. We're not tight, but we're not enemies. Tonight was no big deal."

He frowned but nodded. "Okay. You want a ride home?"

She huffed. "It's one beer, and you'll notice I'm drinking slow. Go on home, Nancy." Damn. She thought about Mike again. "I'm going to hang here. We're going to have a full week, because I've got a meeting with our wiring guy and two high-end clients Wednesday, and I have a lot of prep work to do. So let me enjoy the end of my weekend, okay?"

"Fine, fine." He sipped his soda, making no move to leave her alone.

"You're still here."

"I know. Thought I'd hang out for a while. That cool with you?"

In his own way, her bozo of a big brother was trying to help. Lord love him, but he really was a great guy when he wasn't acting like an ass. "Fine." Then she frowned. "Say, this isn't because you're trying to avoid Gina, is it?"

"Nope." He drank some more. "Not exactly."

"J.T." She sighed. "What did you do now?"

"I blame you. You kept calling her Tina, and when Gina and I were… Well, I was having a fine time. Until I called her Tina in the heat of things. Now she won't take my calls."

She choked on her beer. "You're calling her?" J.T. never called after his one-nighter girlfriends.

At her look of shock, he winced. "I forgot my favorite belt at her place, okay? I want it back."

Del shook her head. "Such a player. You are *so* gonna get your heart handed to you one of these days."

"Like you, you mean? And don't even try denying it. Rena and I both know you better than you know yourself. You like the big dude, casual and all."

"I do not." Not anymore.

"Yeah, you do. And for once, he's a decent guy. Maybe. I'm not sure, because you won't tell me what he's done."

"Nothing," she growled. "Now leave me alone."

"Fine." He opened his mouth to say something when

Big Daddy Kane blared from his back pocket. He shot her a grin. "It's hip-hop '80s week. Cut me some slack." He pulled out his phone and frowned at the number. "I have to take this."

"Problem?"

"Nah. Be right back." He left her sitting over her beer, wondering why the hell she'd let Mike McCauley into her loop. Into her body, she totally understood. The man was built, handsome, and hung. What wasn't to like? But why had she let him inside the emotional fortress she'd spent so long building?

Hadn't Penelope Webster done enough damage twenty-odd years ago? Del rubbed the scar on her arm, remembering a past better kept buried. Just what she didn't need, memories of her mother's rejection on the heels of Mike's. Yet as much as she wanted to be pissed as hell at him, she knew they had nothing together but incredible sex. She might very well have imagined all that closeness and shared emotional intimacy Friday night. Once again confusing reality with what she wanted to be real.

She glanced across the room at her brother's scowling face while he listened to what must have been bad news on the phone. "When will we learn?" She sighed. "Mike had his fill of me, and Tina—or Gina?—finished with J.T. Forget her and move on, bro."

If only life were that simple.

—*∿∿*—

Colin glanced around, making sure his grandma was occupied with Nadine Meadows and Noah while he pretended to go to the bathroom, closeting himself in the spare bath.

He clutched the cell phone tight and whispered into it, "He's not back yet." Colin didn't know what to do. So far, the plan Ubie and J.T. had come up with to get his dad together with Del hadn't worked. Even worse, his dad had gone out with Grace while Colin was forced to hang around the most annoying person on the planet.

"What's the situation?" J.T. asked, his voice low and grumbly, like Colin's dad's.

"I'm stuck here with Noah. Dad is out with Grace." He didn't like calling her Mrs. Meadows, because he didn't like her. "I heard Grandma and the older Mrs. Meadows"—Nadine, whom he *did* like—"talking about what a good couple they make. Then Grandma said how nice it was Dad asked her out, and without her telling him to. I don't get it. I thought Dad did this as a favor for Grandma?"

"You got me, kid. Shit." J.T. swore a few more times, and Colin committed the neat phrases to memory. "Look, keep your ears open. You tell me or Brody what's up, okay? Something's not kosher."

"What?"

"Did your dad say or do anything weird? Did he wear his nice pants and cologne, like the last time he met with Del?"

Colin had relayed that information to Ubie, who'd shared with J.T. "No," Colin said with relief. "He wore regular clothes and didn't seem happy about tonight." Colin bit his lip, then blurted, "I think he misses Del and wishes we'd have come there for dinner."

"Well, only good thing I can tell you is you missed some God-awful chicken. Can your dad cook?"

"Yep. He makes great hot dogs."

"Good. With any luck, you won't starve through the teen years."

"Huh?"

"Nothing. You did good calling me. Keep your eyes and ears open. You're spy number one, right?"

"Yeah." So exciting, this mission of his.

"I'll talk to Brody. Don't worry. We'll get to the bottom of this." J.T. paused. "So you feeling better about your mom?"

Colin had confessed his feelings to J.T. a few days ago after secretly borrowing Uncle Cam's phone. "Yeah. Dad answers my questions if I ask. And he doesn't get mad or anything."

"Good. So... That picture of her? It still in his dresser?"

Colin frowned. J.T. seemed very interested in pictures of Mom. "I think so. But it's not on the dresser like it was last year." Usually around Mom's birthday Dad liked to pull it out and sit and stare when he didn't think Colin was looking. Colin loved looking at it too, because his mom was so pretty.

But different than Del. Del was beautiful in an awesome kind of way. The best lady—not his grandma—he'd ever known, even better than Abby and Maddie and Vanessa put together. He thought his mom would have liked Del, because he had a warm feeling about her, the same kind he got when he thought about his mom.

Someone knocked hard on the door. "Hey, Colin. You coming out?"

"I'm going number two!" he shouted, glad he'd locked the door.

"Okay," Noah yelled back.

"Dude. TMI," J.T. muttered.

"What? Oh, sorry. That was Noah at the door."

"Right. Go on back and keep your cover. Remember, Operation Sampson needs you on this. We can do it."

Colin stared at his reflection in the bathroom mirror and gave himself a smart salute. "Yes, sir."

"Good kid. Now I've gotta get back to Del. Keep it real, bro. I'll talk to you soon. In fact, I'll try to swing by to grab you in a week or so. We'll hang at the garage or something while Brody helps with the plan. So make sure to pay close attention to everything your dad or grandparents say about Del, Grace, or anything you think is important."

"Right." Colin swelled with pride, so excited to be involved in a deep-cover assignment. Just like his alien super spy figures.

"Gotta motor."

"Roger. Over and out." He disconnected the call, then pocketed the phone. Knowing he had to make it look good, he flushed the toilet and pulled out the smelly spray from under the sink. He let loose a lot of flower smell to cover the fact that he hadn't done anything.

After hiding the spray under the sink, he opened the door and nearly ran into his grandfather.

"Boy, did you go overboard again?" Grandpa chuckled and shook his head. "Don't tell your grandmother. She thinks you're on the verge of inhaling more toxins to go with your developing food allergies."

"What?"

"First sugar and gluten, then aerosol spray. Trust me, you don't want to get her started on the evils of processed foods. I still have to hide my cheese puffs."

Colin nodded and tried to pass his grandfather, except before he could, the big man fished his own cell phone out of Colin's back pocket.

Shoot. No. *Damn.* Better.

"Now why do you have my cell phone?"

"Um, I was, well—"

"Video games again, boy? What did I tell you last time?"

Bowing his head in perceived shame, Colin prayed his grandpa bought the act, because he hadn't had time to clear the call history, the way Ubie had shown him.

"Next time, you ask."

"Sorry, Grandpa." Inspiration struck. "It's just that Noah is such a pain."

Grandpa nodded. "I know. You're a good boy for being nice to him. Just do your best to get along, and your dad should be home shortly." *If he's got a brain in that fat head,* he could have sworn his grandpa added under his breath. Then Colin was shoved clear of the door, and Grandpa shut it behind him to use the bathroom.

Colin trudged back to the living room, where his grandma and Mrs. Meadows sat talking. Noah waited for him with some stupid paper airplanes and more instructions on how to do *everything*. Colin would have just ignored Noah, the way he'd been trying to since Mrs. Meadows had come over, but by sitting close to the ladies, he might learn a few things. Especially if it appeared he wasn't paying them any attention.

"I tell you, Nadine. I think it's wonderful your girl came out here to help you."

Mrs. Meadows nodded. "She's been a godsend. I just worry that she's too housebound with me. With her new job and helping me and Noah, I was worried she wouldn't find time to have fun. I'm so glad Mike offered to show her around."

"Yes. Mike's a good boy."

More like an alien sacrifice if he had to hang around Mousy Meadows—that's what Vanessa called her. Uncle Cam had seen him listening in on her conversation and shut her up. But not before Colin learned that Vanessa didn't like her either.

Now to convince his dad to stop messing around and get back to dealing with Del.

Colin could all but see his future puppy in his arms, could feel Del's kiss on his forehead before his dad wished him a good night's sleep in his deep voice. Two parents—a mom and a dad—and a puppy. If all went well, he might start adding that little brother to the fantasy too.

Just as soon as his dad got his head out of his ass— one of J.T.'s and Uncle Flynn's often-used expressions. He rolled the phrase around inside and realized it applied. He liked it. He'd have to tell Brian how well it worked, just as soon as he could get his dad to stop goofing off and call Del again.

Mike cursed his own stubbornness. She'd given him an out earlier, but he'd refused to surrender to his need to see Del again, resolving to break his fascination by this outing with Grace…that wasn't working.

"I'm so glad your mom is okay with Noah and my mom hanging with her. Mom's having a bad night with her bursitis."

"No problem." No problem? Why then had he been miserable since he'd picked her up?

He caught a bit more of her conversation about how pleased she'd been to go out on a Sunday night. He'd made sure to show her around Queen Ann and his favorite spots. He especially liked the popular spot Betty for their beer and burgers. Grace, however, had frowned at his food and asked for a salad. In a bar.

He swallowed a sigh. Del would have gobbled down the burger faster than him, turning it into a competition.

"Did your mom talk to you about Del?" Grace asked, as if reading his mind.

He finished off his fries, wondering if he should order more. "Del?"

Grace blushed. "About the awful things I said, and how I didn't mean any of them? Del is so nice, but kind of aggressive. I was intimidated. Then everything I tried to say came out wrong. I feel terrible for hurting her feelings."

He felt better about being out with her, knowing Grace hadn't meant what she'd said. She'd just been clumsy.

"I'm sure Del will be fine." He could only imagine, because instead of sharing a meal with her and Colin, he was suffering through what felt like an eternity of *nice* with Grace.

"Good. So you and her… You're not an item, are you?"

Mike immediately rejected the idea—because he liked the sound of it too much for comfort. "I'm happily single. The way I plan to be for the foreseeable future," he added, in case she got the wrong idea.

Grace nodded. "Same way I felt after I left my husband. It takes a while to ease past it."

He didn't point out the fact that she knew shit about losing a soul mate. Instead, he smiled, ordered another soda, and waited for her to pick at her food.

"This is nice, us being out," Grace said softly. "We could do this again. Just as friends," she hurried to tack on before he could reject the idea.

His mother had warned him to be pleasant. Del didn't seem too bothered by the fact that he was with Grace anyway, and at least she made a nice buffer—she kept his mind off Del. Mostly. So he nodded. "Sure, when I get the time. Been really busy lately."

"I know." She frowned. "I like being here for my mom, but it's not easy. Noah's in a weird phase where he doesn't listen to me, and the new job is an adjustment."

"Congrats on getting work."

They clinked glasses. "Thanks." She blushed and smiled.

When she didn't look away from him, he subtly broke eye contact and stared at the couple toasting to something celebratory across the bar. Was he reading her all wrong? For all that Grace said she didn't want anything more than friendship, he sensed some weird vibes. But then, he'd thought he and Del had something a lot more special than they did, so what the hell did he know?

He sighed. "We should head back."

"Oh, right." She sipped at some frou-frou drink that remained half unfinished, then smiled at him. The bill lay on the counter, and she reached for it.

He grabbed it first. "It's on me."

"Are you sure?" she asked with big eyes.

"No problem. Consider it your welcome-to-the-neighborhood meal."

She slid off her barstool and stood on tiptoe to kiss him on the cheek.

He froze.

"Thanks."

A kiss on the cheek. No big deal, right? Flustered but not showing it, he paid the tab and ushered her out to his truck, nonplussed when she wrapped a hand around his arm. Nothing too forward, yet… It felt a lot like a subtle claiming he didn't appreciate.

Relieved to set her in the truck and get her hands off him, he drove them to his mother's in record time. Had they not been touring the city, they could have walked the short distance.

"That was really fun, Mike." Grace smiled and seemed to lean toward him.

Shit. She wasn't trying to kiss him again, was she? He darted out of the truck and came around to open the door for her.

She let him, then followed him to his mom and dad's. He didn't bother knocking, just entered and found Colin and Noah playing in the living room in front of his mother and Nadine.

"Oh, you're home early." His mother gave him an odd look. "Everything all right?"

"Yeah. Just wanted to get back for Colin. School tomorrow, you know." Thank God for his kid.

Colin glanced up at him, gave Grace a look that didn't say much about any softening feelings for the woman, then rose quickly. He kissed his grandmother on the cheek then latched on to Mike's hand. "Come on, Dad. Time to go. Bye, Mrs. Meadows," he directed to Nadine.

"He's eager to get home," Nadine mused. "Noah, say good-bye to Colin."

Noah shrugged and continued to play.

"Noah." Grace frowned.

"I'm playing." He fiddled with crayons over what looked like a mangled airplane.

Colin tugged on his hand. "Dad, let's go."

While Grace gently reprimanded her son, who seemed not to hear her, James walked into the room.

"So. How was the date?" he boomed into a room that suddenly went silent.

"It wasn't a date, Dad. Just two friends seeing the town," Mike corrected in his most polite voice.

Colin beamed up at him.

His mother scowled.

Nadine looked back and forth from him to Grace.

But thankfully, Grace nodded. "Yes, Mr. McCauley. It was a fine time between friends."

"Now call me James, honey. None of that Mr. McCauley nonsense."

Grace blushed.

She did that a lot, and for some reason it annoyed him. Del would have shrugged and said something snarky. None of that shy crap. Del would have—

He interrupted the thought and forced himself to seem relaxed, not tense because he kept comparing poor Grace Meadows to larger-than-life Del. Since when did other women have to measure up to Del, and not Lea— *his wife*?

"You okay, boy?" his father asked, looking at him closely.

"Fine, why?" He unclenched his jaw and smiled.

"Ah, no reason."

"You know, this was great. But I need to get Colin

home. Thanks for keeping him, Mom. Great seeing you, Nadine." He turned to Grace, uncomfortable to see her watching him like a hawk. "Grace, Noah." *You mouthy little snot.*

"You know, Mike," Grace said softly, "maybe next weekend we could—"

"Oh boy. I promised Flynn I'd call him back on a job. Shoot. I'm late. See you. Bye." Mike dragged Colin out of the living room and into the truck. Then he hotfooted himself out of there in case Grace had thought to ask him out in front of his family. Again, he had the feeling he'd misread things. Hadn't he explained they were just friends? She'd agreed with him, in front of his mother, that there was nothing intimate between them. But then to ask him about next weekend…?

"Did you have fun, Dad?"

"No," he growled, then noticed Colin studying him. "I mean, it was okay. Grace is nice."

Colin didn't seem bothered. His broad smile said otherwise. "No, Dad. She's not. But it's okay. 'Cause Noah was a pain in my ass too."

"Colin." But he couldn't stop his laughter. After the night he'd had, the humor hit him right where it needed to. He laughed so hard he cried, and Colin laughed with him.

Pulling into the driveway of his house, he finally stopped and had to wipe his eyes. "Shoot, boy. Don't repeat that, okay?"

"Yeah. But I bet Grace bugged you, didn't she?"

"You want the truth? Yeah, she did. God, what a night." He rubbed his eyes. "Come on, let's get you ready for bed."

"Uh, Dad? It's only seven o'clock. Maybe we could watch TV and have a snack before bedtime?"

Which was at eight-thirty.

No wonder his mother had given him that odd look.

Hell. He'd have to hear about this tomorrow. If not from his mother, then relayed through his father on the jobsite. Well, at least he didn't have to deal with Grace anymore. Her sweetness had begun to sour about five minutes into their non-date. No way he'd be following up his asinine offer with another outing. No way, no how.

He blew out a breath and pasted a smile on his face that turned genuine as he and Colin spent the evening together. Then, as he tucked Colin into bed, taken by the smell of little boy and minty toothpaste, he leaned down to kiss him on the forehead when Colin stopped him.

"Dad?"

"Yeah?"

"What was your favorite thing about Mom?"

The tiny pang of sorrow hurt less and less with each of Colin's questions. Mike knew it meant he was finally hurdling the agony of her passing, but he couldn't help missing that ache, the part of Lea he could hold on to.

"That's a tough one, buddy. I loved so many things about your mom."

"Well, what didn't you like?"

Mike blinked. "Huh. That's… I guess I'd say your mom was too nice sometimes." After tonight, he could easily classify it as the top of his dislike list. "Nice is good, but people had a habit of taking advantage of your mom sometimes, so I'd have to step on them." He made a fist and shook it in front of Colin. "But then, that's why I'm so big and strong. So I can protect the people I care about."

"Like puny Uncle Flynn and Uncle Cam, and Ubie's big mouth?" An insult he'd often heard his father say.

"Exactly."

They smiled at each other, then Colin sat up and hugged Mike tightly. "I love you, Daddy."

Colin never called him "Daddy" anymore. His six-year-old had stuck with *Dad* for the past year, trying to be a big boy.

Mike blinked away the moisture in his eyes. "You too, Colin. Now go to sleep."

Colin let him go and snuggled under the covers. Mike turned on the night-light and left the room. He walked back into the kitchen, where he'd left his phone. He stared at it, tossing it around in his hand. No reason to call anyone, not at this hour. Quarter to nine on a Sunday night, when most people he knew readied for jobs the next morning. He walked back to his room and stared at his bed, then at the top drawer in his dresser. He'd put Lea's picture in the closet.

Without thinking, he dialed Del's number. His stomach flipped and his palms sweated as he waited for her to answer. Instead, he heard her sexy voice telling him to leave a message.

Not sure what to say, he hung up, then tossed down his phone and headed into the garage for some work on the heavy bag. It was going to be a long night.

Chapter 13

"SO I HOPE YOUR DINNER WENT WELL. COLIN CAN'T stand Noah, and Grace was a pain in my ass. So yeah, you can say 'I told you so' and feel good about yourself." Mike's voice sounded gravelly on her voice mail. "Anyway, call me if you can get your head out from under the hood of a car in that death trap you work in. *Delilah*."

She sat in the office and replayed the message again, the way she'd been replaying the others. It was her favorite of the half dozen or so he'd left. He'd left this one early yesterday morning, the day after his crappy date with Grace. Del gave a nasty grin, glad he'd had a miserable time. Couldn't have been any worse than dealing with her annoying family who still wouldn't leave her the hell alone about her supposedly bad mood. She felt just fine. Pissed at the world and too busy to give a shit.

Putting her phone aside, she got down to business straightening out work orders and dealing with Sam's absence. Poor guy had the flu. Or at least, he'd better. She swore under her breath and went into the garage to take care of a few oil changes and some carburetor work. The sound of heavy metal music, swearing, and male laughter echoed through the place, and she let the familiar comfort of home and work take her mind away from all things McCauley.

Hours later, someone kicked her feet. She hated that.

"You'd better have a damn good reason for fucking with me," she growled.

"Nice mouth, daughter."

Hell. Her father.

She rolled out from under a jacked-up Chevy and stared up at her dad. "Liam."

"Delilah."

Behind him, someone chuckled and drawled, "De-li-lah."

She fumed. "I know that's you, Johnny."

"Nuh-uh. That was Foley."

"Dickhead," Foley swore. "Was not."

While they bickered, her father reached down and hauled her to her feet, ignoring her greasy fingers.

"What's up, Dad?"

He tugged her with him. "We need to talk."

She groaned. "I'm busy. Sam's out sick, Lou's doing some paint work and can't cover, and Dale has the week off for finals. Or so he says, because if he's screwing off, I'm gonna—"

"She's on break," he yelled to the guys.

"Thank God," someone muttered.

"Now that was Foley!"

They continued arguing while her dad muscled her into the office and shut the door behind him. Then he closed the hall door as well.

"I can't see if we get customers," she warned him and sat at her desk. With Dale out, she had to man the front.

"It'll keep." Her dad rested his butt against her desk and stared at her. "So."

"So." She reached for the wipes nearby and tried to get at least the surface gunk off her hands.

"What crawled up your ass and died?"

"And you get on me about *my* language?"

"Delilah."

She hated that now whenever someone said her full name, Mike came to mind. She thought about him all the time. Even though she'd decided not to like him anymore, it was as if her heart hadn't gotten the memo.

"What, Dad? Seriously, I'm busy. Tomorrow I have to meet with Gil about some bigwig with money he wants to throw our way. Wants to commission two total rebuilds because he liked Foley's work on the Chevelle and Lou's paint on that Camaro."

"J.T. did the mock-up for the Camaro. You going to tell him?"

"His ego doesn't need the help, but yeah. I'll tell him."

"When? Because from what I hear, you're ducking his calls, Rena's calls, and even mine."

"I'm busy."

"Honey, you're full of shit. You can't lie to your old man."

"Really? Then you were okay with all the stuff I got up to in my high school years?" She smirked at him. "'Cause I was lying like a rug back then, and you never caught on."

He frowned and crossed his big arms over his chest. "Mouthy little witch. Maybe if I hadn't been so busy keeping your brother out of jail and your cousin from getting her ass handed to her by her fuckhead of a stepdaddy, I would have seen you up to no good. But now that everyone—but you—has matured, I have the time and energy to devote to helping my little girl."

She rolled her eyes. "I'm fine. Yes, I was annoyed everyone made fun of my chicken. So what?"

He just watched her, and she had to fight not to squirm.

"Delilah."

"Geez, Dad. Back off. I'm fine."

"When are you seeing Mike again?"

She hadn't figured he'd actually bring Mike's name into the conversation. "What does he have to do with anything?"

"Nothing really." But her dad's satisfaction was hard to miss. "I was talking to James the other day, and he mentioned firing up the grill for a family barbecue."

"*You* got an invite?" The man who tried to romance James's wife?

"Nah, but he did mention there will be other parties before their big Fourth of July celebration. Apparently that's the one I'm not allowed to miss. Nice to be invited. I think he's finally accepting that Beth and I are just friends."

"I'm probably not invited."

"Yeah, you are. For this weekend, as a matter of fact. James made sure to let me know. You're invited to their *family* barbecue."

"Too bad. I'm busy."

"Doing what?"

"Girl stuff."

He didn't even try to hide his laughter.

"Hey, I'm girly." Del glared. "Kind of."

"In what universe?"

It irked to know he was right. Especially since no one would bat an eye at Grace Meadows being girly.

Or Maddie or Abby. Then again, Vanessa would probably rather gnaw off an arm than be associated with anything foofy.

"I'm getting a massage."

"Where?"

She tried to come up with a fake name, couldn't, and stood in a rush. "Okay, it's not girly. I need to work on the house and run errands, boring stuff I don't have time for during the week."

"Oh, you poor thing." Her father hugged her, squeezing the breath out of her, then pulled back. "Tell you what. I'll fill in for Sam and Dale. You go take care of stuff today, so you're free tomorrow and this weekend."

"But I—"

The cell phone on her desk rang, and before she could reach it, her father did.

"Hello?" His expression turned into one of pure delight, and her heart sank. "Why, Mike McCauley. Del and I were just talking about you."

She groaned.

"What's that? Yeah, I was just telling Del about your dad's invite on the Fourth. With this much lead time, I'll make sure to clear my schedule. We'll be there. All of us, including J.T. and Rena, if that's okay. Oh, good. Yeah, I agree. The more the merrier."

She started to slip toward the door when her father caught her by the back pocket of her jeans.

"Del? She's right here. Oh, I'm sure you had a hard time getting through. But don't take it personally. She's been busy with work lately."

She glared at her father, who smiled back pleasantly while thrusting the phone into her hand.

"Yeah?" she barked.

"Delilah. What a pleasure."

Her entire body lit at that deep, husky voice. "What's up, McCauley? I'm busy."

Her father frowned at her, but she ignored him.

"I was calling to invite you to our barbecue this weekend. I need a plus-one and you're it. Oh, and something else. It's kind of an imposition, and I hate to bother you, but—"

She hadn't made up her mind about being his plus-one yet. "You're all about being an imposition. This phone call is an imposition. Get to it already. Before I turn forty."

Her father grinned.

"Okay, sweetness." She heard Mike's humor and gritted her teeth. "Thing is, Colin has a field trip Thursday. I'm busting my hump with a new remodel for the client from hell. My brothers are all busy, and I know he's going to be super disappointed if I'm not there. But I know how much he likes you, so I thought…"

"That I'd take your kid on a field trip?" She stared at her father, who raised a brow.

"You don't take him. You just kind of help supervise. You show up and help the teacher, but basically it's really to hang with Colin for the day. Probably stupid to ask. Sorry. I'll talk to my mom, I guess."

"No, hold on." She liked Colin a lot. Dumb for a nearly-thirty-year-old woman to like spending time with a little kid, but his sweet innocence reminded her of what fun and youth should be like. To her father, she asked, "Can you fill in for me Thursday so I can hang with Colin at some field trip?"

Her father nodded. "No problem. It'll give me a chance to remind the slackers out there to stop skating anyway."

"Yeah, like I don't know how to work the guys." She snorted, then before she could think too hard on how good she felt that Mike had asked her to go, she answered him. "Yeah. I'll hang with your kid."

"You're the best, Del. We'll call the bet even. I'll make you dinner this time."

"Wait. The bet?"

"You know, the one you never made good on?"

She couldn't believe he'd bring that up. "Excuse me. I had a meal waiting on your sorry ass, but you never showed up because you were too busy showing your girlfriend around."

"She's not my girlfriend. I told you." Mike sounded calm, and his refusal to engage in debate infuriated her. "I took her around for my mother's sake, to get her off my case after the damage *you* did at book club."

"*I* did? So you're saying *I'm* responsible for you blowing me off the other night? Really?"

"Hey. I didn't call to argue."

"The hell you didn't. I can't believe—"

"I appreciate you taking Colin. Look, I'll spring for a greasy pizza to make peace, okay? Thursday night, after the field trip. I promise."

She looked away from her father's shit-eating grin and double thumbs-up. Only for Colin would she tolerate his jackass father's attitude. "A really big pizza," she snarled. "With pepperoni. And I want a big fat chocolate cake for dessert. For me *and* Colin."

He sighed. "Yeah, yeah, fine. Now quit ducking my

calls. I'll text you details for Thursday. If you aren't
there, Colin will cry for days on end. Just sayin'."

He disconnected, and she stared at the phone, wondering how she'd been manipulated into not only talking
to Mike again, but going with his son on a school field
trip *and* spending another dinner at Mike's.

Expecting her father to make some smart remark, she
was nonplussed to see him nod and shove her out the
door. He picked up her keys and backpack and tossed
them to her. "Go. Take care of your errands so you can
get back here tomorrow to deal with Gil. And for God's
sake, don't screw around on Thursday, or Beth will be
upset. She loves her grandson."

"I'm not going to mess with Colin just because his
dad's a jerk."

"You're a good girl, Del. No wonder you're my favorite." Her dad pulled her close for another hug, this
one gentler than the last, and kissed her cheek.

"You know, you'd be much more convincing if you
hadn't called J.T. your favorite on Sunday night. With
me standing right behind you."

"Yes, honey. But he needs the reinforcement. Boy is
self-conscious and shy."

"How you can lie with a straight face I'll never know."

Her dad winked and nudged her out the door again.
"My secret. Now quit your whining about shit. Get
gone. I don't want to see you here before nine tomorrow morning."

"Hard-ass," she muttered and left, a smile curling
her lips.

She spent the remainder of the day taking care of the
annoying shopping, laundry, and cleaning she'd been

meaning to do last week but hadn't. That evening she ate dinner with Rena and did her best not to jump across the table and choke her cousin.

"I mean, from what Abby and Maddie say, Mike is totally hot for you. Why would you not give the man another chance? So he went out with Grace on Sunday. From what I hear, he was miserable the whole time. He practically flew out of his mother's house when he left Grace…at seven o'clock. I mean, how romantic could their date have been? Or do you think they had a quickie while his mom watched Colin?"

"Would you shut up about Mike McCauley?" She stabbed a fork at her cousin as she enunciated each word. "And for that matter, you're a blabbermouth!"

"Am not."

"Are too. You wouldn't shut up at Abby's book thing. Then at dinner Sunday night, you kept talking about Mike and Grace—*in front of Dad and J.T.*—and how I shouldn't be upset. As if I have a thing for him."

"Oh? So you didn't screw all night and into the wee hours? Yes, Jenny told me all about it. Our town house has thin walls, cuz."

Del flushed.

"Aha! You did bang his brains out. I knew it!" Rena laughed. "So easy. A big, handsome, muscular, sexy, kick-ass man enters your world, and you become a mattress. Way to go."

"God."

Rena continued to laugh. "Oh, man. It's about time. I was worried you were going to turn into a house hag. Wearing your robe all day, watching soaps, in slippers…"

Del groaned.

"From what I've heard of his brothers, you go, girl. Get some for me while you're at it. I'm so freaking in no-man's land it's sad. I think my vagina has forgotten what it's there for."

"*Gag*. Rena, I'm eating."

"Anyway, so what are you going to wear for the field trip?"

Del just stared at her cousin.

"What?"

"It's a field trip. For kids. I don't think what I wear matters."

"No, but afterward, when you head to Mike's for dinner and a good wall banging, you need to be lookin' good."

"I'm not screwing him after dinner. I'm simply going to let him apologize and be thankful I helped Colin. Besides, I like the kid. He makes me laugh."

"He's so cute." Rena sighed. "Doesn't it make you wish you had some?"

Oddly, it did. So she denied it. "Hell no. I'm too young. Got too much to do before I have to change diapers."

"Like what? Yell at Foley and order wrenches by the bazillion?"

"You have no idea what I do every day, do you?"

"Nope. Just like you have no idea what you're missing by not giving true love a chance."

"Oh no. Not this again." Del sighed, loudly.

"Say what you want. My books might be fiction, but they're all about finding love. Relationships are hard. Between *all* people. My mom's a peach, her ex-husband a dick from hell. But you don't see me shying away from romance."

"Please. You work all the time. When's the last time you went on a date?"

"I'm working toward a goal, to own my own business. That's the difference. If a Mike McCauley fell into my lap tomorrow, I'd make time for him. You're just scared and stupid."

"Stupid?"

Rena nodded, but her eyes were kind. "Because your mom was such a bitch, you think everyone will treat you the same way. Come on, your dad and J.T. love you. I love you. And all the guys who know you want to do you."

"So romantic," she mumbled. "None of that's true anyway. I know I'm lovable."

"Do you?" Rena glanced at her forearm at the scar there that had gone so much deeper than skin level. "Then why haven't you gone out with anyone seriously in years?"

"I date."

"I said seriously." Rena gave her the look.

"Maybe because I want someone worthy of my time."

"Mike is."

"Maybe. Maybe not. He sure the hell didn't have any problem bagging last weekend."

"I knew it." Rena pointed at her. "You were hurt by him not coming over."

"No, I wasn't."

"Liar."

"You know, this whole conversation is ruining my appetite. I will date, screw, or enjoy anyone I feel like. Because yes, I am lovable. And cute, and sexy, and smart, and—"

"You accuse *me* of being the one with the huge ego?"

"—in shape, fast, clever, intelligent—"

"Clever is the same as smart."

"Amazingly   organized.   A   good   cook. Multitalented—"

"Ack! Enough. I give. You win. Now shut up about your awesomeness and just be straight with me about Mike. Be honest, sweetie. I swear I won't tell anyone, and you'll feel better admitting the plain facts. Do you like him or not?"

Del knew she couldn't avoid the truth forever. Lord, it felt like ripping her fingernails out one by one to confess that, "Yes, I like him."

"Does he scare you?"

Deep breath, then let it out. "Yes."

"Do you think he likes you right back?"

A tough question. "In bed, yes. The rest, I'm not sure."

"Fair enough. Now the final question, and you don't have to tell me, just think about it. If he does like you right back but, being a man, makes bad choices and hurts your feelings, your ego, and your pride before he remembers how wonderful you are, will you fight through all that to make him yours?"

The question remained with Del all through dinner, that night, and into the next day. She continued to dwell on it even when she arrived at Colin's school and signed in, under the suspicious stares from the secretaries in the main office. After showing them her driver's license and wondering if she'd need to offer a DNA sample to walk through the halls, they let her go through the school to the back. She passed a lot of happy kids playing and lining up in the hallways to go places. As usual, they all stared at her, though she'd done her best to appear presentable.

Today she wore a pair of jeans, unscuffed boots, a long-sleeve tee, and had her hair in a regular ponytail. More PTA, less grunge. She reached the back lot, where a travel bus waited. Nice. Back when she'd been in school, they'd carpooled to get anywhere.

She saw Colin waiting in a cluster of small children. Man, they were tiny. He saw her and waved wildly.

"Del. Del. Over here!"

Seemed like half the crowd turned to stare at her. Fortunately, the teacher standing near Colin didn't pat her down the way the office chicks had clearly wanted to.

The woman smiled. "Thank goodness. Colin's been going on and on about you, and I was afraid if you didn't get here in time for our bus ride, he'd have a meltdown. He's been so excited for you to come with us. I'm Marci Sheffer, by the way."

Del shook the woman's hand. "Del Webster."

"Mike told us you'd be here. Thanks so much for offering to come. We didn't get as many volunteers today as I'd hoped." Marci waved to the two men and one woman standing with their kids. "Not too many moms fond of reptiles."

Colin's hand wormed into hers, and he gripped her tight.

Pleasure filled her, especially when she glanced down to see him smiling at her with such joy.

She winked at him and said to his teacher, "Well, I had a pet snake as a kid, so reptiles don't really bother me."

"Good." Marci seemed relieved. She gathered

everyone together, explained the rules, and before Del knew it, they'd boarded the bus for the Reptile Pit.

Colin sat next to her on the bus. "I'm so glad you came, Del."

"Me too. I'm playing hooky from work." She put a finger to her lips. "Don't tell. My dad has to work for me today."

"Ha." Colin held up his hand. "Pinky promise it'll stay a secret."

They hooked pinky fingers, and then he started asking questions. "Did you really have a pet snake?"

"Yep. Her name was Salmissra, after a character in a book I once read. Then I found out she was a he and named her Roger."

"Oh. Neat. Did she try to eat you?"

"Nah. He was a corn snake, about four feet long and really pretty. He was orange and just the nicest snake you'd ever meet."

Across the aisle, a little boy with red hair leaned toward them. He looked familiar. Oh right, Brian. Colin's best friend. "What did he eat?"

"Little kids," she teased. "Totally kidding. He ate feeder mice. You can buy them already frozen at a pet store. Hey, snake's gotta eat."

"Oh wow." Colin continued to pepper her with questions. She enjoyed his inquisitive mind, the quick way he processed her answers. Their time at the Reptile Pit went smoothly, and the attitude she'd expected to have to deal with from the other parents didn't happen.

Instead, she talked with the adults, enjoying them as much as the kids. When it came to holding the snakes,

Colin volunteered to be first. Except he grabbed her to go with him.

Rob, Mr. Reptile, gently explained the proper way to hold the python.

"Del will go first," Colin so helpfully offered.

"Sure thing." She said to Colin in a lower voice, "I'll get you later for this."

He snickered.

"Alice is a ten-year-old royal python, also known as a ball python. She's somewhat large for her species at seven feet in length. She weighs close to nine pounds," Rob was saying. "She's very gentle though, and has a slow metabolism. So I feed her once every two weeks, mostly rats or mice."

Behind him the class *oohed* and *ahhed* as Del accepted the cool coils around her arm without flinching. She wondered if she could get J.T. to give her a new tat on her shoulder, something with coils winding up and onto her back. Then she wondered what Mike would think of the idea, if he'd trace the pattern with his tongue the way he had her other tattoos not so long ago.

Her entire body tensed, remembering their intimacy, and she deliberately relaxed and winked at Colin, putting his annoyingly sexy dad out of her mind. "Your turn."

After they progressed to other reptiles and a few amphibians, Marci crossed to her. They'd talked a good bit, and seeing that Marci wasn't a stuck-up educator like the many teachers Del had once had, she'd warmed to the woman quite a bit.

"You're a pro at this, aren't you?" Marci asked.

"Come again?"

"You're so good with Colin. He was adamant with

quite a few of the other students that you wouldn't freak out over anything you came into contact with here on the field trip. He also brags about you whenever the other kids talk about their moms."

Del started. "Oh?"

"Mike's a great dad. His brothers are wonderful too. We've met the entire clan over the course of the year." Marci grinned. "If I wasn't married…"

Del chuckled. "The McCauleys can be a little overwhelming." Especially Beth.

"Yes. And though Beth comes in to help out, Colin is different with you. Don't get me wrong, I mean, I'm not saying Beth isn't a terrific influence…"

"I get you." She did. Del had spent her childhood with only her dad and brother for company. Liam Webster had been there for her through everything. Gruff and rough around the edges, yet he had a heart of gold and could be counted on when it mattered. Still, Del had always felt as if she missed out by not having a mother in her life.

"I'm probably putting my foot in my mouth, but I just wanted to let you know how pleased I am to meet you. Colin's such a wonderful boy, and it's great to know he's got even more solid female influence in his life now."

Mike hadn't offered any of his past girlfriends the opportunity to hang out with Colin at school? That, or none of them had wanted to. *Quit overthinking this. It's just a stupid field trip.*

So she kept telling herself.

The rest of the day passed without incident. Even the nasty PBJ lunch she'd gotten for accompanying the class tasted better than she'd thought. Plus, chocolate milk? Cha-ching. When she arrived back at the school in time for Colin to have one final recess before reading time, she hunkered down to see him eye-to-eye and accepted his tight little hug.

"Bye, Del. See you tonight." He grinned, and that missing front tooth just killed her.

"Man, you are too cute. Are you sure you don't have any girlfriends?"

She saw an adorable blond behind him pointing at herself and mouthing *"Me."* But when Colin turned around to see who Del was looking at, the girl shrieked and raced to the playground.

"Yuck. Girls are gross. Not you," Colin said as he turned to pat her shoulder.

She rose from her crouch and watched him dart away to play with his friends. As she turned to walk back to her car, she bumped into one of the dads. "Sorry."

"My fault." The guy wasn't bad-looking. Tall with dark hair, but without that charisma the McCauleys seemed to have in spades. "I'm Mitch, Crystal's dad." He pointed to the blond girl with a crush on Colin.

She grinned. "Right. We met earlier. I'm Del. Colin's friend."

"I know all about Colin McCauley." Mitch held the door for her as they walked inside and down the hallway toward the front of the school. "Crystal lives with me every other week when she's not with her mom. And I swear, my girl thinks the sun rises and sets on that boy. He's a nice kid. Didn't realize he had a mom, though. Crystal only ever mentioned his dad."

"Oh, I'm not his mom. Just a friend of the family since his dad couldn't make it today."

"Yeah?" Mitch sounded interested. "Too bad. So…are you and his dad dating?"

She had to admit, it boosted her ego to know the guy—a decent-looking suburban dude—liked the look of her. "Nah, just friends."

"Great. I mean, well, that came out wrong."

She laughed with him as they walked to the parking lot. "Nice meeting you, Mitch."

"You too. Maybe we could go out sometime? Grab coffee or a drink?" Before she could respond, he reached into his pocket and pulled out a business card. "That's my number. If you'd like to meet up or something, give me a call. But no pressure. I promise not to have Crystal hound Colin for your number."

She smiled and waved good-bye. After she got into her car, she looked down at the business card. Mitch was an attorney. She chuckled to herself, wondering what a guy like him would think of her past misdeeds. Nothing more serious than shoplifting and possession of a joint during her junior year of high school. But it could have gone much, much worse if her father hadn't stepped into her ass.

Her dad and his psycho kid versus great guy Mike and his sweet boy.

With that in mind, she used the next few hours to relax and think good and hard about where this thing with Mike might be going. The all-American stand-up dad and the tattooed mechanic who felt more at home at Ray's than an elementary school. What kind of future would they—*could* they—have? More importantly, why did she keep wondering about the R-word with a man still in love with his dead wife?

Chapter 14

MIKE REFUSED TO FEEL NERVOUS. HE WAS SIMPLY thanking Del—with pizza—for making his life bearable with the boy. Colin hadn't stopped talking about newts, pythons, or Del since Mike had picked him up from his grandma's half an hour ago. What surprised him, though, was the fact that his mother hadn't seemed disapproving or made any comments about Del's presence at the field trip, or that Del had been invited to dinner.

"So Grandma said nothing when you told her Del was coming over?"

"Nope." Colin bounced on the couch. "When's the pizza coming, Dad? I'm hungry. I held a snake today."

"So you told me. Fifteen times."

"I held a snake today. Sixteen." Colin snickered then jumped from the couch and ran to his room to get his snake-like alien action figures. He returned, making shooting and hissing noises as they toppled over one another under his nimble fingers.

Mike continued to spruce up the house, not that it needed too much help. He'd done a major cleaning last night. Now he only had to clean himself. Man, talk about ripe.

"Keep an eye out for Del while I take a quick shower."

"Okay." Colin turned on the television and the dreaded Cartoon Network appeared. "And, Dad?"

"Yeah?" Mike ripped off his shirt and toed off his boots. The things were coming apart at the seams, but they were his favorite. He hated to part with them.

"Wear something nice."

"What?"

"Die, newt scum." Colin slammed one minion into another, and Mike left him to play, needing the time to clean up.

He finished showering and heard the doorbell ring. Damn. He still had to go next door and grab their dessert—an amazing chocolate cake Abby had promised him. After toweling himself and his hair dry, he slapped some cologne on his chest, going for understated. He looked for a pair of clean underwear and found nothing. Figured. So he put on his clean, non-ripped jeans, found an equally clean henley, his last hanging in the closet, and without looking, knew he didn't have a clean pair of socks left either, so he left his room in bare feet. When he entered the living room, he noted Del and Colin kneeling by the couch discussing Colin's alien figurines.

The sight of one blond head next to a smaller, darker head made him smile. Especially because they looked up at him at the same time and grinned in sync.

"Well, the snake lady arrives."

"Yeah, you owe me."

"Do I?"

He loved her sneer. God, she got him hard. Not good without an extra barrier of underwear to mask his arousal. He walked to the kitchen, his back to her, and thought about his mother and father and Grace. Yep. That killed the mood.

He rummaged in the fridge. "Beer, water, or lemonade? Oh, and apparently I have some leftover wine. Must be Cam's." He pulled out the corked bottle.

"You really have to ask?"

He grinned and put the wine back, then withdrew a beer. He handed it to her, and their fingers brushed. As always, the tingle that started from their contact made its way through his body.

She had to feel the same, because her eyes narrowed and she whipped her hand back.

"Chicken," he taunted and turned to grab himself a beer as well. He opened it and drank a good bit before turning to find her in his space.

She poked his chest good and hard.

"Ow."

"You're calling *me* chicken? You're the one who bailed on Sunday because you're afraid of your mom."

"I am not." So close, he could see the slender band of steel gray around her light gray irises. She had the longest eyelashes, so thick and dark over that creamy skin. She wore no makeup that he could see, and her fresh face only made her that much more appealing.

"Yeah, you are." She turned her head to the side and drank a sip, then turned back to him and smiled. A mean grin that turned him inside-out. "So scared you hid behind Grace's skirt instead of dealing with how crazy you are about me."

He opened his mouth and closed it with a snap. "What the hell are you talking about?" Wow. That hit too close to the mark for comfort.

"Yep. You're hot for me, but you're feeling all that guilt because you'd rather wallow in the loss of your wife. No offense, because I get that you loved her, but dude, it's been six years."

He leaned close to her, nose to nose. "Repeat. That."

She stepped back but not any farther away, as if not worried about his growing temper. "Sure thing. You're afraid you like me more than you should. I've been thinking about it, and I realized something today." She glanced over her shoulder and, not seeing Colin, continued, "You're a good guy. Really good. You love your mom, your dad, your annoying brothers, and your kid. You loved your wife. So losing her messed you up. You can't move on, because a good man doesn't stop loving his people. Except now you're wanting more, having sex that isn't just a one-time deal."

"Of course I want more than a one-time bang. I'm not a fucking dog," he growled, conscious to keep his voice low so Colin wouldn't overhear.

"No, you're a man who found someone way cool that he likes—me. But you're not supposed to ever do more than fuck. I understand," she said gently, and to his surprise, he thought she did. "So I'm not going to put pressure on you or demand anything. We're friends, Mike. Nothing more."

"Please. Even I don't believe that. Friends don't go down on each other."

She snorted. "So okay, yeah, we screwed and it was good."

"Try great."

She shrugged. Nothing like killing a man's ego with some sexy shoulders. "Whatever. Point is, it's done. So why not remain friends and quit with all the feeling bullshit?"

"Someone's got an ego, and it ain't me." He crossed his arms over his chest. "You're telling me I'm in love with you, but I'm still mourning my wife and can't get over the guilt."

"Don't know that I said *love*, but I'll work with it."

"Bull. I think *you* like *me*, and you're planting this misplaced anxiety at my door. But really it's you who doesn't know how to feel." Getting into the spirit of the argument, he ignored the ringing doorbell and crooked a brow. "Who was it that got her feelings hurt when I missed a casual dinner Sunday? So much she wouldn't take my calls until her father bullied her into it?"

"That's crap."

"Ha. I think you're *way* into me. You know I'm an honest guy, and you've probably had your share of losers, because if your friends make Ray's their home away from home, I'm guessing they're not running for president any time soon."

"If that isn't stereotyping, I don't know—"

Loving the way she got his blood pumping, he continued, "I have a great job, a nice family, and I made a cute kid."

"About the only thing you have going for you," she cut in.

In a lower voice, still looking out for Colin, he added, "I have a big cock. One that made you beg and scream for more. Oh yeah, there go those hard little nipples. Ones I sucked until you came."

"Shut up. The kid's in there." She flushed, and that red over her cheeks reminded him of how hot she'd been when he'd spanked that glorious red into her delectable ass.

"Say what you want, but you and I are magic in bed. Trouble is, we're probably magic out of it too." That hurt to say, but the truth kind of set him free. Clichéd, but there all the same. He let out a frustrated breath, missing her and the way she'd felt beneath him, and ran a finger down her cheek, risking her wrath.

Her pupils dilated, and her breathing grew raspy. "Yeah? You think?"

"I—"

"Dad. Pizza guy. Can I open the door or not?" Colin paused at the kitchen and stared at them with wide eyes. "Oh boy. Are you gonna kiss?"

"Hell." Mike walked around her, praying his erection wasn't noticeable, and hurried to the front door, where he took out his wallet. He paid the guy, grabbed the pizzas, and put them on the dining table. Then, as if he hadn't started a wicked war of words with Del, he smiled. "Hungry, *friend*?"

Del stared at him, wanting nothing more than to get back to their argument. The man got her blood racing. Yes, her nipples had grown hard. Because what woman wouldn't react when Mike McCauley reminded her of that amazing sex while standing almost on top of her smelling so damn good?

Still, she thought she'd hit on something when she'd accused him of being into her. A gamble, considering she didn't exactly believe her own bullshit, but he'd grown pale, then flushed and slapped that challenge right back at her.

What was it about him that made arguing so much

fun? She loved talking to him, almost as much as she liked fucking him. And yeah, she hadn't missed that giant pole in his pants. All for her.

She wanted to take a picture and send it to Grace. *"See, Mouse? This is all mine."* Immature, and nothing she'd ever stoop so low to doing, but it pleased her to think about it just the same.

She liked the glint of challenge in Mike's dark blue gaze. He didn't back down, except when it came to broaching his emotions, apparently. The more she thought about it, and the more she remembered what Rena had kicked around the other night, the more she considered the notion Mike was running. From her.

Baring her teeth at him in a smile before sinking into some mouthwateringly cheesy pizza, she listened to him and Colin, entertained by Mike and his little clone. They looked so much alike, had so many of the same mannerisms. Yet Colin also had that sly charm not present in his dad. With Mike, it was *what you see is what you get*. A big dude with a big heart buried under bluster and sex appeal.

Del found herself wanting a real relationship for the first time in a long time.

"Another slice?" Mike asked, looking down at her nearly finished piece.

"Heck yeah."

"Me too." Colin glanced from her to Mike and grinned, a little too widely for her peace of mind.

Mike must have seen the look too, because he frowned. "What's in that head of yours, boy?"

"Nothing but rocks, according to Grandpa."

She laughed. "Your grandpa is funny."

"Do you have a granddad?" Colin asked her.

"Well, my dad's parents are dead. And I never new my mom's parents, so no."

"She died when you were little." Colin nodded. "You can have mine if you want."

Mike blinked. "Ah, what's that?"

"Del needs a grandma and grandpa. She can use mine."

Del coughed, choking on her crust. She could just imagine Beth's face if Del called her *Grandma*. Hmm. Might be worth it to see the woman speechless.

Mike started laughing, apparently thinking something similar. "Seriously. Fifty bucks if you call her Grandma to her face."

Del grinned. "No way. I like living without artificial lung support."

Mike shook his head. "Colin, you sure can make your old man laugh."

"Yep. I'm a funny guy, just like Ubie and Uncle Flynn."

"But not your Uncle Cam?" Del asked.

"Nope. Uncle Cam is more serious and almost never curses. He's not as much fun as Ubie and Uncle Flynn. And Vanessa is kind of scary. But I like her."

"We all feel that way, son." Mike sighed. "My poor little brother, taking on that viper."

"Mike." Del didn't want to laugh and encourage him. Minutes ago she'd wanted to strangle him, yet right now she didn't want to be anywhere else but with him and Colin. It was like the man had hexed her into some serious crushing.

"I'm telling Vanessa you said that," Colin said.

"Narc."

Colin frowned. "I'm telling her you called me that too."

Del couldn't help it. She chuckled.

Mike laughed with her, and she felt an instant of true communion, two adults laughing over the innocence of a child. With humor and affection, never the condescension her mother had once shown.

Mike's gaze met hers, and she was astonished at the warmth there.

Confused, aroused, and alarmed, because maybe he was right about her being the one doing all the falling, she shored up her sarcasm and let the insults fly.

"So, Colin, do you think your wussy dad would have run screaming if he'd held Alice today? Because I think that's why he didn't make the field trip."

"Oh." Colin regarded his dad with a crafty sneer. "Wussy man."

"Colin. Del," Mike tried to growl but couldn't stop himself from grinning. "Wussy? Wussy is your Uncle Flynn when I gave him his first swirly. Or Ubie when I pantsed him in fourth grade in front of Suzie Belcher."

"Oh wow. And I thought I was a delinquent." She listened to him recount all his misdeeds as a kid, wondering if he realized the many bad ideas he was planting in his son's head but too captivated to care. "Mike, you did not try to shave all Cam's hair off."

"No. I was trying to give him a mohawk, because one of my sports heroes had one and I thought it would toughen him up."

Colin nodded. "Yes, Uncle Cam was not a tough kid."

"Mike. You can't be talking about your brother like that to Colin."

Mike frowned. "Why not? Colin knows. Hell, you've met Cam. I love him, but he's a little, ah, sensitive."

"A Nancy," Colin corrected.

"Colin," Del chastised.

"What? That's what Grandpa called him. Dad too."

Mike coughed and focused on his pizza when Del glared at him.

"Calling a boy a girl's name as an insult is, well, insulting."

"Huh?" Colin looked puzzled.

"It's like, if there was this dorky boy at school, and no one liked him, and we all called him a Colin."

"Dorky? Not great?" Colin asked.

"No. Quit calling people a Nancy. Call them something else. Like a knucklehead. Or a dork."

"Okay." Colin didn't even need to mull it over. He returned to his pizza.

Mike smirked. "What if she's really cool and has big muscles and scares boys? Can we call her a Del?"

"Oh, that's good, Dad. Yes, let's call the good ones Dels."

Touched that Colin thought of her as one of the good ones, Del tried not to grin and encourage him. "Never mind that, goofy. Tell your dad about Brian and how he scared your teacher with the iguana."

Colin launched into more stories about his field trip. Before Del knew it, the pizza had all but disappeared. Good Lord, but Mike could eat. Colin had shocked her too by putting away so much food.

"Maybe next time you should get three pizzas." She stared at the remaining two slices in shock.

"Maybe." He winked at her. "You have a healthy appetite."

"What? I'm supposed to nibble at the edges and pretend I'm full? Please. I work for a living."

Mike laughed. "Exactly."

He seemed inordinately happy over her pizza consumption, but whatever. He wasn't making fun, that she could tell.

"So where's the cake?"

"Cake?" Colin perked up. "There's cake?"

"I was running behind before you arrived or I'd have picked it up already. I'll be right back."

"You provided pizza. I figure I can pick it up if you want," she offered.

"Awesome. It's next door. You offered, no takebacks." He blew out a breath. "Whew. Now I don't have to answer twenty questions from Abby."

"Great." So much for being nice.

Del walked next door and knocked. She'd barely put her hand on the wood before the door opened. Abby and Maddie crowded the doorway. Then Abby's smile split wide.

"Come on in, Del."

"Said the spider to the fly," Maddie intoned, then laughed. "So how's the date?"

Del entered and closed the door behind her. "It's not a date. I'm just here to get the cake I was promised."

"The one I baked because Mike finally answered some questions for me for my book." Abby smiled. "It's coming along great, by the way. My characters feel so alive."

"I am *not* in it. Promise me."

"Of course not." Abby sniffed. "It's fiction."

"Hey! I saw that wink."

The one Maddie returned.

"You should see the Mike character. So strong and handsome. So...sexy." Maddie gently shoved Del toward the kitchen. "So was he good in bed? We're all dying to know."

"Maddie." Abby frowned. "Forgive her, Del." Abby grabbed a Tupperware container housing the cake and handed it to Del, but she didn't let go. "Well? Is he?"

Del had to laugh. "You two are ridiculous. You've seen him. Of course he was good in bed."

"I knew it. No way he's a dud. Just still lingering over Lea," Abby muttered. At the silence that settled, she shook her head. "Del knows what I'm saying, don't you? Maddie and I have talked about Mike and his solitude for months. The man needs to stop living in the past and move toward the future. Apparently his other lady friends are way on the periphery. No one meets his parents, and he has sex to sate an itch. But not with you, Del."

Maddie grinned. "Yeah. You're like a major case of poison ivy he can't stop scratching."

"Lovely." Del tried to pull the cake away, understanding why Mike hadn't wanted to be the one to get it. "Can I have my dessert?"

"I assume you'll be getting it soon enough." Maddie laughed at her own joke. "Sorry. Too easy."

"That's what he said!" Abby joined her laughter. She let go of the cake, and Del made a beeline for the back door. "Hold on, Del."

"I'm in hell."

"With chocolate cake. Things could be worse." Abby's laughter faded. "Look, we're pulling for you. Grace is not invited to any more book clubs."

"Thanks, Abby. I'm touched you're ostracizing neighbors for me."

"I don't like her on principle," Maddie added.

"Don't let Beth hear that. She's in love with the woman," Del cautioned, trying not to smile.

"I don't think so." Abby opened the door for her. "Not from the reports I'm getting."

"Wait. Reports?" This sounded interesting.

Maddie pushed her out the door. "Bye, Del. Do everything we would, and then some."

Del returned to the house, mulling over what to do with the rest of the evening. After dessert, then what? Colin would go to bed soon. Then it would just be her and Mike. They hadn't had sex since last week. Granted, she'd gone for much longer stretches of celibacy, but she'd never been so hot for a guy before.

And she'd have him all to herself in an hour.

Still… He'd been obnoxious about acting like *she* was the one with all the emotional issues. Should she ignore him or confront him about feelings he'd buried? Leave after cake and put Mike back into a platonic pocket? Or should she try to get the man naked again?

Decisions, decisions.

She entered the back door without knocking and found Colin sitting at the kitchen table in his cartoony alien pajamas. He grinned at her, his focus quickly centering on the cake. "My favorite."

Mike joined them, and just like Colin, he lit up when

he spotted the Tupperware in her hands. "Oh, chocolate cake. Yum."

"I thought you hated sweets." Del calmed her racing heart, and the ball of affection inside her swelled into an uncomfortable longing as she watched the pair of them.

"I do, but if I have to have something bad for me, I go for cake."

"You know, beer isn't exactly its own food group, despite you treating it like it is. Matter of fact, it's fattening."

He frowned. "Beer doesn't count. It's a beverage."

"Man, you sure do like to make your own rules about things, don't you?" she asked, referring to more than just the beer.

By his narrowing eyes, he understood what she hadn't said. Funny, but it had been like that between them since their first conversation. She understood him, and he her, on another level she didn't know how to describe.

"You going to put the food down or what, sweetness?"

Colin guffawed. "Get it? You're just like the cake, Del. Sweet and chocolaty."

"Chocolaty?" She frowned. "That I don't get."

"Well, it's my favorite and Dad's favorite, and you're our favorite."

Mike gave her a wicked grin as he withdrew plates, forks, and a knife to cut the cake. He set them down on the table before musing, "I bet she tastes good too, son."

She blushed. The jerk. He well knew what she tasted like. And wow, but she could say the same about him. "Oh, I don't know, Mike. I'm probably not nearly as…tasty…as you are."

To her delight, his cheeks reddened and he quickly

sat next to Colin. To hide a mouthwatering erection, maybe?

She rounded the table to lean next to him and put the cake on the table. A glance down his front revealed his arousal. "Nice. That for me?" At Colin's questioning expression, she added, "The cake, I meant. Did Abby bake it for me?"

Colin nodded. "Dad told her it was for our dinner, and he said he wanted something extra good 'cause she was such a pain in the ass earlier." At Mike's glare, Colin shrugged. "What, Dad? That's what you said, isn't it?"

"You have big ears, you know that?"

Colin just smiled.

Del cleared her throat to hide another laugh. "So Abby was a pain, huh?"

As Mike cut the cake and set it on the plates, he nodded. "About her book, yeah. Woman asked so many questions I thought my head would explode. Especially because she kept making me stop so she could write, erase, and write again. She seems to take her research seriously." He set a piece of cake in front of Colin, then another across the table from him, where she supposed he meant for her to sit.

She sat across from him—only so she could see him while they talked. Not because he wanted her there. "She bugged me too. In a nice way, but man, she sure wants to know everything about everything."

"I do too." Colin licked the frosting from his fork and practically glowed with happiness.

"Yeah, you do ask a lot of questions." She remembered the first time she'd met him, when Abby had been taking him to his soccer practice and her tire had blown.

Del had been changing it while Colin bombarded her with questions.

"How come you don't have kids, Del?" Colin asked.

Mike stared at her, his knife poised above the cake.

Colin stared at her too, a carbon copy of his father.

"Gee, that's kind of personal, don't you think?" She waited for Mike to agree with her, but he said nothing.

"Do you like kids?" Colin asked.

"I like you. Then again, you seem more like a mutant than a kid."

Colin nodded. "I'm an alien. Dad is too."

"Now that I can believe."

"Funny," Mike snorted. "This from a woman covered in tattoos and piercings."

"Really? I was under the impression you liked my body art."

The heat in his gaze as he traced a lot more than her tattoos satisfied the sultry woman inside.

"I like 'em." Colin glared at his father. "Dad does too. He's teasing. Tell her, Dad."

Mike sighed and took a large bite of cake. After chewing then swallowing, and taking a hell of a long time to answer, he said, "I guess they're okay. If you like tattoos."

"I do. I'm gonna get one when I'm eighteen. Del said I could."

Mike lifted a brow.

"Hold on," Del corrected. "I said when you were eighteen, you could get a tattoo—*if* your dad said it was okay."

Colin's smile could be described as nothing short of devious. "Oh, *I know* it will be okay. He'll say yes."

"Yeah? How are you gonna make me, you little monster?" Mike taunted. For a guy who didn't like sweets, he'd polished off his cake pretty quick.

"I won't have to. My new mom will."

Silence descended while Colin finished his cake.

Mike studied him with narrowed eyes. "Ah, what's that? Your 'new mom'?"

Colin flashed her a subtle look that unnerved her. The kid couldn't be plotting to throw her and Mike under the matrimonial bus, could he? As if Del would ever marry a guy like Mike McCauley—who hadn't even asked, thank you very much.

"I just know you'll find a nice lady to be my new mom. Not for a while, but maybe when I'm ten or eleven. To settle me down, like Brian's mom did for his older brother."

Mike relaxed, but Del had seen the little con artist in action before. What was he up to?

"Mmm. That was good. Dad, can Del tuck me in with you tonight?"

Mike looked at her. "Well?"

"Sure. Why not? But when he's not so gooey."

Colin wore more brown icing than what was left on his plate.

"You are one messy eater, boy." Mike sighed. "Brush your fangs and go potty. Five minutes, tops."

"Yes, sir." Colin gave him a smart salute, then raced from the table, only to return and put his plate in the sink first. He darted away, waving at Del.

"Wow. You have him trained right."

"Thank my mother. I heard 'I'm not the maid' from that woman so many times I felt like I had her voice playing in my brain twenty-four-seven. But she did get me to start picking up my shit."

"Nice mouth."

Mike's grin slowly faded. "Come to think of it, my mom wasn't the one who got me to be cleaner. Actually, I was kind of messy all the time, despite Mom's Olympic nagging. It was when I met Lea, and I wanted to impress her." He sounded sad but fond of the memory, and she kept quiet. "So I'd hide all my dirty crap when she came over. But I still was never very clean." He chuckled at that.

His smile made the decision for her, and she was determined to take what she wanted. She moved closer, saw him tense, and leaned down to whisper in his ear, "You know, I hear that good pussy will whip a man into shape in no time."

A dare she *had* to offer. Now to see if he was man enough to take her up on it.

He stood and backed her against the kitchen counter, and she had her answer.

In a low voice, he countered, "I wouldn't know. Haven't had good pussy in six long fucking days. After the boy's in bed, you're mine. Problem with that?"

I'm already yours, you moron. And I don't know what to do about it. But all she said was, "No problem. But you have it backwards, McCauley. You're *mine*." She cupped him, feeling how long and hard he was under the denim.

He groaned and nipped her lips, surging against her. "Behave, Delilah. And think non-sexy thoughts while we tuck Colin in."

Together.

After taking a moment to compose themselves, she let him grab her hand and tug her with him out of the kitchen and down the hallway.

He didn't let go. She didn't pull free.

Colin saw their clasped hands and smiled so widely she worried his face might break in half.

Now what the hell to do about the little master manipulator and his sinister plans?

Chapter 15

MIKE LET GO OF DEL WHEN HE SAW COLIN REACHING out for her. She didn't resist as his son pulled her down into a big hug. The bliss on the boy's face worried him, though, on top of comments about a new mom.

It didn't take a rocket scientist to see that his son wanted Del in their lives—permanently. Mike supposed he should have seen this coming. Colin loved being around Del. He talked about her, emulated her, and spent way too much time with his devious uncles Brody and Flynn. If the boy wanted her, he was no doubt conniving to get her.

Knowing how much Abby and Maddie pestered him to date, and that both women were engaged to his brothers, another piece of the puzzle fell into place. Neither woman had been too surprised to know Del had been coming for dinner tonight. And his brothers had been pretty hands-off about his love life recently—the opposite of how they'd behaved not even a week ago. They had to be scheming with Colin.

They all thought him a big dumbass who couldn't think past construction, apparently. He'd been raised around the tricksters. Did they honestly think he wouldn't see right through them?

The problem was, the more time he spent with Del, the more he *wanted* to let their convoluted plans continue. Not good. He needed to sort out his conflicting feelings about the woman before long.

One thing he'd never been in denial about though—he wanted her with a fierceness that alarmed him. Simple sex would have been easy to have and forget. Except time with Del went from sexual to emotional to meaningful in a heartbeat, tying him up in knots. Yet he couldn't stay away.

If she hadn't agreed to tonight, he would have stolen his way into her house days ago. Taking Grace out Sunday night had been stupid because it had shown him how much he was missing by not being with Del.

"Okay already. I'm losing the ability to breathe," Del teased and freed herself from Colin's bear hug.

"A kiss?" his son asked.

Mike smiled, seeing his brothers in the sly gesture of supposed innocence.

Del snorted. "I'm not buying the act. It's lucky for you you're so cute."

She kissed him on the cheek, and his face flushed.

Colin stared at her, his blue eyes wide. "I love you, Del."

Mike saw her tense, knew his son had pushed a little too hard, and hurried to ease the emotional intensity in the room. "Quit hogging my kid." He nudged her out of the way with a gentle bump of his hip.

She collected herself fast enough. "Yeah, yeah. Don't get pushy, McCauley."

Mike leaned down and kissed Colin on the forehead, the scent of minty toothpaste and chocolate leaving an indelible imprint on his heart. His little boy, who was getting so big. "Okay, alien. Get to bed."

Colin smiled, and right then, Mike saw Lea so clearly in the genuine sharing of his heart. The loss still hurt, but the pain seemed easier to bear. His son had her best traits, and it made him proud and happy to see her there, always with him.

"I will, Father."

Mike coughed to hide the emotion making his voice thick. "Father? What happened to Dad?"

"Luke, I am your father." Colin made shooting noises. "I want a lightsaber for Christmas."

"Random change of subject, but okay. When did you see *Star Wars*?"

"With Brian last week. Del likes *Star Wars*."

"I do," she said from behind him. "How he knows that I'm not sure."

"Everyone loves it," Colin explained. "Even Dad."

"Yeah, great. We all like *Star Wars*. Now go to bed. I love you, dork." Mike set the night-light on, then left the room, closing the door behind him.

He stood in the hallway, staring at Del, who watched him with a weird look on her face. "What?" Had he seemed as vulnerable as he felt? Women didn't like weakness. For that matter, neither did he. His father might be a pain in the ass at times, but James had forged his oldest boy into a man, teaching Mike how to build more than houses, but to form strength from within.

Del didn't look pleased anymore. "Mike, we need to talk."

Shit. That didn't sound good. He followed her down the hall toward his bedroom. Only an idiot would assume she wanted to screw him there. More than likely, she wanted privacy to tell him all this family stuff had freaked her out. She was done. Panic set in. Colin would be devastated. Though Mike had no intention of making anything serious between them, he still wanted to be with her. To see her, laugh with her, kiss her…

In his bedroom, she quietly shut the door behind them.

How best to fix this? "Look, I'm sorry if Colin—"

She shoved him back against the door, yanked his neck down, and planted a kiss on his mouth that left him reeling.

"You are so sexy when you're being all good-dad-like." She moaned softly and kissed him again. When she came up for air, her busy hands were all over him, under his shirt, around his back, then…

Christ.

…down his pants. She gripped him hard.

"No underwear? I love it."

He tried to reach for her, but she shook her head and unbuttoned his jeans. "Uh-uh. This is my show. Sit back and enjoy the ride."

Relieved she had no intention of leaving—just the opposite—Mike couldn't speak, could only feel as she tweaked his nipples under his shirt and continued to fondle his dick with her other hand. The fire in her eyes lit his lust, and he forced himself not to take what she wanted to give, to simply accept it instead. He leaned his head back against the door as she lifted his shirt to suck his nipples.

"Del, baby," he whispered, still conscious of his son's room so close.

"You smell good." She nuzzled his chest, her fingers stroking his taut nipples before sliding through his chest hair.

Man, he *loved* that. He arched his cock into her palm, needing to come so badly he could taste it. "Come on, Del. Let me fuck you."

"Not make love?" she taunted and stroked him, sliding her thumb over his wet slit.

He moaned. "Make love, fuck, have sex. Whatever you want to call it. I can't think. I want you so much." He put his hand over hers, curled around his dick. "Need to come."

"Been a whole week for you, hmm?" She left his chest and used her hands to push his pants down to his thighs. Then she lowered to her knees, slowly.

"Oh fuck. Yeah, a whole damn week. I want inside you. Now. But I want your pussy, Delilah."

"Uh-uh. It's my show, remember?"

As if he could forget. When she grew all tough and aggressive, she turned him on as much as she did lying beneath him. He couldn't tell which part of her aroused him more, and at this moment, he didn't care.

Her hot mouth wrapped around him, and he nearly came while she sucked, hollowing her cheeks. The hoop in her eyebrow winked in the dim light of his room, and the stud in her nose and the colors bright and glaring on her forearms tripped his switch from aroused to desperate.

"You're so fucking sexy," he admitted on a gasp. "So hot seeing those pretty hands, that mouth, wrapped around my cock."

She moaned in agreement, and he feared coming way too fast. Right down her throat.

"No." He pushed her back, then dragged her to her feet and switched positions, planting her back against the door. After stripping out of his jeans, he went to his knees. He pulled down her pants and underwear, taken with the thin strip of blond hair over her mound.

He kissed her, then prodded her feet farther apart.

"Mike. This was my—" She broke off on a sigh while he clamped his mouth over her clit. She was wet, and the notion that his arousal increased hers was a fantasy come true. He licked and sucked, then added a finger inside her, imagining all that silken heat over his dick.

Her moans grew louder, and he knew he'd pushed as hard as he could without losing his own mind.

"Stay," he ordered, then hustled to grab a condom. He donned it in seconds and lifted Del into his arms. "Have I told you how much I love pounding into you against a wall? Or in this case, a door?"

She sunk her fingers into his hair and yanked him close for a kiss at the same time she wrapped her legs around his waist.

He didn't wait and positioned himself at her entrance. He shoved hard and deep inside her, and the damn woman cried into his mouth and came, her body like a vise grip.

He swallowed her moans and mounted his own climb toward ecstasy, fucking her faster, unable to stop himself from following her into perfection. Each brush of their bodies had him rubbing against her breasts, feeling her strong legs holding on to him. He pumped and came, so hard he saw stars.

He would have shouted but she returned the favor by muffling his cry with her kiss. He eased back from her mouth, breathing hard, as he continued to spend. Staring down at her slack face, he watched her eyes open and saw her watching him while he came.

She stroked his shoulders and dragged her nails over his skin, making him shudder. "You have a sexy O-face."

"Huh?" He thrust in and out a few more times, loving how incredible it felt to be inside her.

"Your orgasm face. Sexy. I like it."

"Well hell, I like everything about you. Especially the way you taste." He moaned and withdrew, still half hard and wanting to take her again. "I can't believe how long it's been since we were together. You have to stop avoiding me. I mean, I might die of blue balls. You have any idea how much come I just gave up, and all for your sexy body?"

"Mike."

He chuckled at her pink cheeks. "Yeah, not romantic. I know. But damn, girl. You about blew my mind."

He paused, and they both said at the same time, "Literally."

The humor of the moment caught them, and after laughing so hard he nearly dropped her, he eased her down the door and kissed her. She felt both soft and firm, and her size gave her an edge that fascinated him. She wasn't small, so tiny he feared crushing her. He loved knowing his roughness excited her.

She kissed him back, their embrace slow and sexy, not frantic as it had been moments ago.

"I want you again," he admitted, not shy about doing so. "I want to fuck you long and slow, and have you begging for more."

"Begging, hmm?" She kissed her way down his chin to his neck and sucked harder at his throat.

He jerked when she found a sweet spot, and her low laugh gave him the shivers. "I think you like control in all its forms, don't you, Mr. Nice?"

"Mr. Nice?" he growled. "Really? Is that how you see me?"

"Nah. But it's how everyone else sees you. This wounded widower with only his young son and brothers for companionship. So sad, those big blue eyes of yours."

"Bullshit." The snap of anger at her words was turning him on again.

"Oh yeah, it is." She chuckled. "You're a bad boy in the sack, aren't you?"

"If you say so." He liked her sensual lack of inhibition. She didn't seem to mind being half-naked—God knew he loved it. Her perception of him, though, could use some work.

"I do say so." She reached down and rolled the condom off him, then dropped it to the floor. Del being Del, she gripped him and started pumping. "Love to stay and fuck some more, but I have work in the morning."

He shouldn't have been ready to go again, not so soon, but she had him nearly there, almost fully erect, especially because he couldn't take his gaze away from her hand over him. "I have to work too."

"Yeah, but your job is easy. Mine is hard. I mean, I work with my father."

"So do I," he rasped, humping her palm, unable to stop himself.

"I work with a lot of men," she whispered. "With a lot of tools. Getting all greasy, all dirty." She dragged him closer, rubbing his cock against her naked belly. "You want to come inside me, don't you?"

"So bad." He stared at her, wondering how she could make him feel so much. "I want…"

"What, baby? What do you want?" She gripped him harder, painfully tight, and the sting jolted him into an unexpected crest of need.

"*Shit.* What are you doing to me?" He stared at her, knowing his desperation had to be plain to see.

"Mmm. Yeah. All over me."

"In you," he panted, then swore when she squeezed out an orgasm that shattered him.

He came all over her belly as she whispered naughty things in his ear. Finally easing her hand off, she brought a finger to her mouth.

"Do it," he whispered. "Lick it." He trembled, watching her take that pink tongue over her finger. Taking him into her mouth.

Sex shouldn't be so consuming. Normally he had no problem coming and leaving, an agreement that satisfied his partners as well. With Del, he wanted to…*cuddle*.

"You can't leave yet." He left her to pick up his shirt and wiped them both clean, then tossed it back to the floor and stepped into his jeans.

"Oh?"

He pulled her underwear and pants back up, aware she let him care for her. Such a small thing, yet it made everything right. He tugged her hair, bound up in a staid ponytail that didn't excite him half as much as her funky hairdos usually did. "Del, you do something to me."

"Do I make you itch?" The smirk on her face had an unexpected effect.

Mike felt it, that scary, horrifyingly intense emotion that punched him in the gut. Enough that he felt shaky and unsure and glorious all at once.

Her laughter faded. "Mike?"

He couldn't help it. He kissed her, with all the affection he felt for her wrapped into the embrace, and knew by her tension she felt the difference. Then he hugged

her, bringing her close. He didn't have the words to describe what he didn't understand. He loved Lea. But he
loved Del too. Two completely different women.

So what did he do about his new secret truth?

He pulled back and watched her, curious about the
tender look she gave him.

"A little sex makes you pliable. Have to remember
that," she said in a husky voice.

"Yeah. Good to know, eh?" He didn't let her go, even
when she tried to push him back.

"You're in my space."

A place I intend to be for a while. "So?"

"I have to leave," she reminded him.

"Not until we get something straightened out."

"Oh?" She tried to cross her arms over her chest and
gave up when he refused to budge.

He moved back just enough to focus on her face.
"Yeah. You still owe me a dinner."

"*What?* Don't go getting a big head just because you
got laid. Remember, you were the one who ditched me,
genius. Besides, you said the bet was over."

So. Apparently still not over him going out with
Grace. Good to know. "For the record, that trip
with Grace was nothing more than me being neighborly and giving her a tour of the city. Period. I was up
front with her about not wanting anything casual *or*
permanent. No fuck-buddy or girlfriend."

Del stiffened. "Yeah, I get that."

"No, dumbass. I meant with her."

She blinked at him. "Did you just call me a dumbass?"

"Hell yeah. How casual are we if we're way past a
one-night stand? That implies we fucked once. And it

was far more than that." He tried to remember how many times they'd had sex. To his glee, he realized they'd hit his new personal best that night at her place. Talk about never-ending enjoyment.

"Please don't tell me you're counting how many times we did it."

He grinned. "You know me so well."

She blushed, and he loved that she could be so tough yet sensitive. So incredibly sweet.

"Del, we have something good going. Why not hang out, have sex, have fun, and enjoy each other?" He said nothing about forever or marriage, because God knew he wasn't ready for that again, if ever. Lea had been his one. But this newness, this incredible connection with Del—he wanted it. More than he felt comfortable acknowledging. That he'd even suggest partnering up showed she meant something special to him.

"Gee, Mike. When you put it that way…" She pushed him again, and this time he gave her some space. "Dinner at my place Saturday night. Bring Colin." She gave him a mean grin. "My dad, brother, *and* Rena will be there. So don't think you're getting out of hanging with my family."

"Ouch. But hey, fine. On Sunday, you come to my mom and dad's for a family meal. And it'll be a big one."

"It's a picnic, I thought. I was already invited."

"Yep. But as my friend. This time you'll come as my *date*."

She tried to look nonchalant. Mike knew she dreaded the gathering as much as he dreaded her family night. But at least most of his family accepted her. She liked his brothers and the girls, and his dad was usually okay about

Mike's dates—not that Mike had brought anyone home in, well, years. His mother would be the tough nut to crack.

Her family, on the other hand… Rena he wanted to meet. Her brother and father he could do without, though Liam wasn't too bad a guy. Colin would be in heaven around the gruff Websters.

Mike sighed. "Any way you look at this, everyone is going to be on our cases to make a formal statement or something. Might as well get our status out of the way."

"Our status?"

He shrugged, trying to keep it light. The few attempts he'd made to try to see if anyone else could come close to his wife had failed. Dismally. Hence his decision to fuck and fly. But Del…

"Our status," he repeated, reinforcing the notion of "our."

"That we're fucking, you mean?" Del asked.

He slapped a hand over her mouth. "Shh. Colin."

When he let go, she punched him in the gut.

"Ow."

"Don't muffle me like that. Next time I'll lick your hand."

"Which reminds me of you licking my dick. Now *that* was hot."

"You just came twice. Don't tell me you're still horny?"

He smiled. "Only for you, sweetness."

She groaned. "Quit calling me that."

"I will if you agree to be my *girlfriend*." Saying the word after being unattached for so long gave him hives…and a primitive satisfaction that she would belong to him, if only temporarily.

"Hmm. Girlfriend, huh?" She tapped a finger against her lips as she thought, and Mike wondered how she'd react if he grabbed her, dragged her down with him to the bed, and just kept her with him all night. Sleeping together.

"Yes or no? I don't have all night, Delilah. I have to work tomorrow," he mocked.

"Fine. You can be my *boyfriend*—and I use that term loosely. I figure we get some mutual kick-ass sex out of the deal." She paused. "And I can help you with your shitty truck."

"Hey."

"Don't kill the messenger. The thing needs an overhaul, and you know it."

"Fine. You save my truck, I'll help you with those pathetic flower boxes and the minor damage in your town house. Like the bookcases and some of the wainscoting. Even if you're renting, it needs to be fixed."

"I bought the place, jackass." She planted her hands on her hips and leaned toward him, his aggressive girlfriend at her finest. "I'm not poor, you know."

"Ah, what are you talking about?"

She sniffed. "Just because you live large on the hill and I don't doesn't mean I'm without means."

"O-kay, Ms. Sensitive." He shook his head. "I don't even want to know how I'm insulting you without trying. The girls next door are renting. I don't see that as making them poor."

"Yeah, but…"

"But what?"

"That house is nice."

"So's yours." He meant it. "It's got an eclectic charm.

And yeah, I know exactly what that means because my mother makes me watch the stupid home garden network with her, and my aunt is a big-time real estate agent and always going on and on about house shit."

"Oh." She nodded. "Good then."

"Fine."

A long pause settled between them before she said, "So I'll see you at my house, Saturday night. And bring some beer."

"I will, so long as you serve something healthy and *green*. And I don't mean pistachio ice cream."

She grinned. "You're so cute when you try to be healthy. Pushy, but cute."

"Del..."

"Whatever. I'll make something you and the kid will enjoy. Okay?"

"One more thing. No swearing at the table. My son will not be 'passing the fucking potatoes' again."

She laughed and opened the bedroom door, being very quiet as she walked down the hall while Mike followed her. She grabbed her keys from the console table in the living room, then went to the front door.

"Ahem." Mike crossed his arms.

She paused with her hand on the doorknob and turned to face him. "What now?"

He bit back a grin. "A kiss before you leave, *girlfriend*."

She rolled her eyes. "I can tell you're going to be a demanding kind of guy. My pain-in-the-ass *boyfriend*." She sneered. Yet she gave him a kiss all the same, one that sent fireworks through his system, despite coming twice in the span of an hour. "Later, McCauley."

"Sweetness." At her scowl, he corrected, "Sorry. Delilah."

She groaned. "Better, but not by much. So Saturday, don't be late."

"I won't. Oh, and I won't be hanging out with Grace anymore, either. Wouldn't want to make you too jealous."

She glared at him. "Don't be more of a dick than you usually are." Then her scowl cleared, and a smile broke out over her face, a rainbow of devious joy brightening her expression. "Although, maybe while you're showing Grace around, I can call my new friend Mitch, the one who asked me out to coffee today. I'm sure he and I could get along just fine while you're chilling with the neighbor."

"Mitch? Who the fuck is Mitch?" He instinctively stepped forward, needing to stake his claim again, to remind the woman she belonged to him.

"See ya, sucker." She left before he could demand answers.

Annoyed because he had a feeling she hadn't made Mitch up, he at least felt a measure of peace that he'd come to an internal resolution about her. They'd date, officially. Boyfriend and girlfriend. And that would be enough.

Because it had to be.

Chapter 16

J.T. watched his sister with the giant all evening. She laughed, smiled, and seemed to enjoy herself more than he could remember her ever acting with a date. He tried to catch his cousin's gaze, curious that Rena couldn't seem to stop staring at McCauley. He sure the hell hoped she wasn't developing some crush, because Del had finally found a guy *he* liked for her. Drama and family jealousy wouldn't help anyone.

He cleared his throat, loudly, and finally caught Rena's attention.

"What's up?" She sidled next to him. "You keep giving me a look."

Seeing his sister, her new *boyfriend*, Colin, and his dad occupied at the table, he nodded for Rena to come with him.

She frowned but turned to Del and said, "Be right back."

Del barely acknowledged her, still bragging about how she'd landed them some big account with some gearheads he'd never heard of.

Rena met him out on the front porch. "What's up?"

"What's with you and Mike? Why all the looks, Rena?"

She seemed confused. "What are you talking about?"

"You've been eyeing Del's new *boyfriend* all night. You realize Del hasn't been this excited about a guy since she found Lou to be her new paint man at the shop."

"Sad, I know." Rena grinned. "Oh relax, J.T. If I'm staring at Mike, it's because he looks so familiar. I can't place him, and it's killing me, because I know I've seen him before."

Relieved she wasn't trying to take Del's man away—and Lord help them all, but when Rena set her sights on a guy, look out world—he pulled her in a for a hug and squeezed the breath out of her. "Good."

"You're…killing…me."

He laughed and let her go. "So what do you think?" He nodded to the house. "They look solid together, right? Colin too." It had surprised him, though it shouldn't have, how happy his sister seemed when Colin was around. Colin clearly adored Del, and he thought J.T. was cool too, which made J.T. feel good.

He liked Mike more than he'd thought he would. The guys his sister had brought home in the past had been users or losers. One or two decent but boring guys had made it past an introduction before she'd dumped them for being too dull. McCauley had to have some mean buried beneath that nice-guy front, though, to hold Del's interest. He'd been threatening enough that one day in the shop a few weeks ago.

"What do I think?" Rena asked and peered through the window next to the door. "I think he sits really close to her because he likes her. *A lot*. He's not just fronting. Mike smiles when she's near. He seems to laugh at her dry humor, even encourages her to be rude to her favorite cousin." She sniffed, then smiled. "I can see how much he loves his son, and he'd never do anything to hurt Colin. So he must *really* like Del if he's calling her his girlfriend in front of him. Did you see how she blushes when Mike calls her that, by the way? It's beyond cute."

"It's alarming."

"No romance in you, is there?"

"I'm just saying I think she's falling for this guy, and if he fucks her over, she's going to be really hurt. Not like Brad and Jonesy, those assholes. They dicked her over, she was pissed, maybe hurt, she moved on. But she digs Mike a lot. I can tell."

"Yeah, there is that." Rena chewed her lower lip. "But it's so sweet how she is around him. I mean, she softens. I live with her. I know Del-the-hard-ass, Del-the-stacker—you did see all the neat piles of crap around the house, didn't you?—Del-the-mechanic and office jockey. Del-the-woman wants someone to love, though she'll never in a million years admit it. Mike's not a bad guy, you know. Abby and I talk, and we've discussed getting them together." Her tone implied she hadn't said all of it.

"But…?"

She sighed. "But he's still not quite over his dead wife, and that could be a problem. Especially because she's been gone for six years."

"Yeah. That's a problem." J.T. didn't like it, but he understood that kind of devotion. His father had never gotten over J.T.'s mom, her cancer a sudden thing that had taken her too soon. Del's mom had been a rebound chick, and a huge mistake—with the exception of Del.

On the one hand, J.T. admired that kind of loyalty. On the other, it worried him, because his old man had been burned once and still hadn't found a woman to spend his nights with. Well, one who didn't use a pole as a method of income.

"I'll keep an eye on her," Rena said. "And him." At his glare, she corrected with a scowl, "Not for the reason you're thinking. I am dying to know where I've seen him before, that's all. Now let's get in there before they know we're talking about them."

J.T. followed her inside and smiled when Colin patted the empty seat next to him.

"Sit with me, J.T."

He sat and frowned at the empty dessert plate in front of him. "Where is it?"

"Where's what?" Del asked from the kitchen.

"My dessert."

"I don't know. What did you bring?"

He frowned, especially because Mike smirked at him. "What are you looking at?" he asked the guy.

Mike shrugged. "An idiot who doesn't know how to say please, I'm thinking."

He opened his mouth to retort when he caught Colin's big eyes watching. J.T. swallowed the nasty rejoinder he'd been about to make, and saw his father and cousin grinning big as well. Del, he noted, wore a smirk identical to Mike's. "Hel—ah, heck. Can I *please* have that amazing pie you wouldn't let me touch earlier? You know, because I'm your favorite brother and all?"

Colin beamed at him. "You're so polite, J.T. Did you get gold stars in school?"

His father choked.

J.T. turned his back on the traitor. "You know, I think maybe in kindergarten I did."

"Or was that juvie?" Del muttered, to which Mike didn't bother to hide a laugh.

Rena just had to chime in. "Actually, Colin, J.T. used

to get in a lot of trouble for not listening to his teacher and goofing off. But if you asked him now, he'd tell you how important it is to do well in school." Del was right. Their cousin did like to over-share.

Mike gave her a wide smile, and Rena gaped.

Mike's smile faded. "What's wrong?"

"Don't move." Rena darted from the table.

Mike and Del exchanged glances.

"What is that girl's problem?" Liam asked. He shook his head. "Anyway, Del, honey, you were bringing in the dessert?"

"Now I see where you get your sweet tooth," Mike said to her.

She stuck her tongue out at him, then turned to grab the pie plate sitting in the kitchen. She returned at the same time Rena did, clutching a book.

"It's you," she said dreamily and handed the book to Mike.

J.T. wanted to laugh her off. Rena and her freaky romance books. The girl had stacks of them in bookcases in her room. Thus her fascination with Del's new friend Abby.

Del glanced from the book cover to Mike, equally fascinated. "Oh my God. That's you!"

"You saying he's on the cover?" J.T. snorted. "Yeah, right." Yet the flush on Mike's face said otherwise. "You're shitting me."

"J.T.," Liam warned, nodding to Colin.

But the boy paid him no mind, looking curiously at the book Mike tried to pull away from Del, who'd reached for it. "Dad?"

Sounded like Mike said, "Fuck me."

Though he'd sworn under his breath, J.T. heard it all the same. "Now that's just embarrassing."

"That's not me. Some other guy who looks like me."

Del snorted. "Uh-huh. Who just happens to have the same jaw line, neck, chest, abs, and thighs."

When everyone looked at her, she shrugged. "I mean, I *imagine* they're the same."

Rena chuckled. "Yeah, right." To Mike, she pushed the book and a pen. "Look, just sign it. I won't tell anyone."

"I will," J.T. said with delight. "He was a romance cover model. Jesus, you can't make this shi—stuff up." His laughter made Mike's frown deepen.

Colin bounced with excitement. "Wow, Dad. That's so neat. You could be the guy on Abby's books." Then he added with overdone innocence, "And Del could be the lady. They're hugging, Dad. You two could hug. Maybe kiss."

J.T. rolled his eyes. "Real subtle, Colin."

Mike looked like he'd rather be anywhere but at the table with Rena shoving her pen at him. "Rena, I'm not confirming anything. But you know what? I'll sign your book…if everyone at the table"—he glared at J.T.— "promises *never* to speak of this again. To anyone."

Liam shrugged. "Fine with me. I'd rather my friends didn't know my daughter is dating a model anyway. Ruins the street cred, you know?"

"Dad." Del couldn't seem to take her gaze from the cover, comparing it to Mike, then staring at it again. "Man, you fill out a kilt pretty well, McCauley."

Mike groaned. "You have to promise. All of you."

"Not even Uncle Flynn, Ubie, or Uncle Cam?" Colin asked. His eyes took on a mercenary gleam. "How much, Dad?"

"Ten bucks. Take it or leave it."

Colin whooped. "Yeah!"

Rena gave J.T. The Look. Her big brown eyes grew impossibly large, sweeter than honey, and mesmerizing.

"Damn, girl. Fine. I swear. I won't tell anyone Del's new squeeze is a cover model. For love books," he added in a sneer.

She leaned over to whap him in the head. "Hey. Those books are mine. I love them. Watch your mouth."

"Whatever."

Del managed to wrestle the book away, then opened the front cover, and Mike reluctantly signed it.

"You have no idea how much this is worth." Rena danced with glee. "No one ever knew who Mr. Sexy was ten years ago. They still don't know. My friends online talk about you—him," she corrected for Mike's benefit, "to this day. And I have his signature. You have to sign the other ones too."

Mike dropped his head to the table and groaned.

"There are more?" Del asked.

"Yes," he mumbled.

J.T. started laughing and couldn't stop. His sister and the model. Classic.

Mike lifted his head and fixed on J.T. "You ever tell anyone about this, I will rip your head off and use it as my own personal bowling ball."

Colin nodded. "Dad's a great bowler."

"Then I'll bury your body in cement under a building. They'll never find the body," Mike continued. "Don't test me, J.T. I can do it. I know people."

Liam cut in before J.T. could answer. "Don't worry, Mike. J.T. has his own secrets."

Now things best kept buried weren't so funny. "Dad…"

"Oh?" Mike perked up.

"Sad to say, back in the day, I was partial to music's influence. Well, that and some funny little pills."

"What color were they?" Colin asked.

Liam hurriedly continued, "J.T. was born back when I had just gotten into really good classic rock. 'Aqualung' was my favorite song, so…"

Mike gaped at J.T.

"Dad. That's not right," J.T. grumbled.

"Wait. J.T. *Jethro Tull?*" Mike started laughing. "So your name is really Jethro. God, that's just…"

"I know," J.T. said glumly.

His father slapped him on the back. "Aw, come on, son. J.T. has a ring to it. And I haven't called you Jethro since you turned eight, now have I?"

"Yeah, Jethro. It's not such a bad name," Mike teased.

"Keep your mouth shut about me, I'm quiet about you. *Jethro.*"

"Okay, okay. Cut it out."

Colin stared at him. "Jethro Tull?"

While his father explained about the band, J.T. ate the pie Del kindly handed him.

She didn't say a word, even tried to wipe the smirk from her face. The same one sitting on Mike's fat mouth.

"More pie, Mike?" she asked McCauley—her stupid, romance-cover boyfriend.

A friggin' model. J.T. could have had a field day with that. But leave it to his father to ruin things. What the hell good was blackmail material if he couldn't use it?

Then his father handed his cell phone to Colin, and

the beginning of "Thick as a Brick" began to play. J.T. buried his head in his hands while his cousin, his sister, and her *boyfriend* laughed.

———

Mike hadn't had so much fun in a long time. With the exception of Rena's discovery, the night had gone surprisingly well.

After the dinner ended and he'd left Del with a kiss on the cheek, he drove Colin home. From the backseat of the truck, Colin asked, "Did you like kissing Del, Dad?"

"I did." Before they'd left for dinner at Del's he'd given his son a simple explanation—that he and Del were dating. The boy hadn't batted an eye, but Mike had been waiting for the eventual questions.

"So are you going to get me a little brother now that I have a new mom?"

Mike gripped the steering wheel tight and watched the road. "Colin, Del and I are dating. She's not your mom."

"I know. But she *could be* my new mom."

How to answer that?

"Dad, Brian didn't have a dad for a long time. Then he got a new dad, but he still sees his old dad sometimes. I saw Mom with you at the cemetery, but she's not really there. You and Grandma told me that. So why can't I have a new mom?"

Mike didn't want to have this discussion. Not now, not later. How the hell did he describe a soul mate to a six-year-old? How to explain why he couldn't settle for a cheap imitation when he'd known true love all too briefly? Not that he could classify Del as anything remotely cheap. An image of her smiling face and laughing eyes filled his mind, and he hurriedly wiped her from his concentration. Del… She wasn't a forever kind of girl. She made him happy now. But she wasn't Lea. Could never be Lea.

And part of him hated how much fun he'd had tonight, and how often he thought about Del instead of his wife.

He said nothing while he figured out how to talk to his son about the sensitive subject.

"Well, if I can't have a new mom yet, can I at least have a puppy?"

Relieved Colin wasn't dwelling on the idea of a new mom, Mike answered, "You know, you're getting older. Maybe we could see about getting a dog."

Colin cheered.

"But you have to show you can handle that kind of responsibility. I'm not going to be cleaning up its mess all the time. That'll be your thing. Dog poop, walking him, feeding him. That's a lot to handle, boy."

"I know, Dad. I can do it. I swear."

Hearing himself agree to a dog made him want to smash his head against the dash. But it was too late now. "Well… How about if you watch Hyde for a month? If you prove you can be responsible with Ubie's dog, then we'll talk about getting you your own."

Colin might last a day or two, but a whole month cleaning up Hyde's massive dog piles? No way. He didn't consider himself cruel for crushing his son's hopes for a canine. Teaching his kid to be a good dog owner made more sense than giving him a living, breathing creature to look after.

Colin didn't stop talking about the kind of dog he wanted the whole way home. Nor had it escaped Mike's notice how often Del's name came up in the conversation.

Of what kind of dog she wanted, or how she said she'd find one she could take to the garage with her.

He put Colin to bed with relief, cranky yet amused his son had somehow managed to make him commit to a possible pet.

"More like Brody than I'd thought," he muttered.

Someone knocked on the back door. He walked into the kitchen and looked through the door window. Speak of the devil...

He opened the door and found all three of his brothers standing on the back porch.

"Hey." Flynn smiled. "We were slumming and thought we'd give you a pity drive-by."

"Funny." Mike stepped back, waiting for them to enter.

Cam nodded, the serious-seeming one of the bunch. If you overlooked his laughing eyes. "We know it's safe to be over since it's not a school night."

"Smart-ass."

The others snickered. He let them enter, waiting for the third degree. That they'd waited this long to probe into his relationship with Del surprised him.

"So," Flynn started.

Brody dug into the refrigerator for some leftover cake. Then he shared with the others.

"Sure, help yourself."

Brody grinned. "Thanks."

"How did things go with Del?" Cam asked, his tone casual, nonthreatening.

"Is this the voice you use with Vanessa, to keep the monster at bay?"

Flynn chuckled.

Cam took the teasing in stride. Hell, they all knew Vanessa was a handful. Personally, Mike didn't think anyone else could suit his youngest brother better. A mega-brain for a mega-brain.

Cam smirked. "Say what you want, guys, but my kid will be doing circles around yours in school."

"True." Brody nodded. "But mine will be fleecing yours for milk money before he can talk."

"No doubt," Flynn agreed.

"You know, it's getting late…" Mike tried. A mistake, because all attention focused on him again.

"So," Brody started. "I hear you and Del are now a couple."

"Couple of what?" Flynn asked, frowning. "I didn't hear that."

"Probably because Rena isn't obsessed with Maddie. Not like she is with your accomplice, Abigail D. Chatterly," Mike drawled, pleased to see the flash of guilt that darted in and out of Brody's eyes. "Yeah. I might be big and look dumb, but I'm not. Did you really think you guys could conspire to set me up with Del and I wouldn't catch on?"

"Conspire? What the hell?" Flynn looked honestly confused…for a split second. He'd always been tight with Brody, and the flash of smugness that passed over his face didn't do him any favors.

"*Ha.* I knew you were in on it too. Cam, I'm not sure."

"Oh, I knew they were setting you up," Cam agreed. Flynn snarled, "Narc."

"Seriously, bro. No secrets with you, are there?" Brody frowned in annoyance. "And you wonder why we never clued you in on shit when we were growing up."

Now Cam frowned. "Yeah, about that, why did—"

"This has been a *long* day," Mike interrupted.

"I heard." Cam cleared his throat. "So your date… What's going on with you and Del?"

"Nothing serious. We like each other and we're hanging out."

"You having sex?" Flynn asked bluntly.

"No, moron. We like to paint watercolors together." He snorted, amused when Brody shook his head, and even Cam rolled his eyes. "Of course we're having sex. What's the point of having a hot girlfriend if we're platonic? And before you go all women's lib on me, Cam, I enjoy her company too. Okay?"

"Fine." Cam grinned. "So you *like*-like her."

Brody laughed. "Classic."

Flynn slapped Mike on the back. "She's kinda scary, but in an 'I'll kick your ass if you play me' kind of way. You're good with that?"

Mike grinned. "Hell yeah."

"Oh." Brody nodded. "Big guy likes being handled, I see." He paused. "A lot different from Lea though, isn't she?"

They all grew quiet, and Mike tried to stem his annoyance. "Um, guys? I know Lea's dead. We can move on."

Cam studied him. "Normally you get all emotionally shut down when someone talks about Lea. I think Del is good for you."

Flynn groaned. "Please don't go all touchy-feely on us, Cam. Leave the therapy to Dr. Rosenthal." Their parents' shrink.

"Maybe you could talk to her," Brody suggested. When everyone stared at him, he flushed. "What? Abby made me go to her once, and it helped. You know, after Seth passed." At their amazement, he murmured, "It was just one time. Assholes."

"No, man. That's great." Flynn smiled. "Your head was never on straight to begin with. I think you should use any help you can get."

"Dick." Brody sneered.

"*Anyway*," Flynn continued. "I just meant Del wants more than the typical sex all your other 'girlfriends' wanted. You slept with them and that was it. Del's probably more of a relationship, knock-your-socks-off-with-sex girl."

"Uh-huh." Amused at Flynn, Mike waited to hear more.

Brody added, "Yeah, what numbnuts said. Like when I was with Abby, I was finally in a good headspace. You look good with Del. Not that we've seen you guys together or anything. Well, not since that one time we went bowling and you couldn't stop staring at her ass."

"There was that," Flynn agreed with a smirk.

"This might be a good time to ask if Colin's in bed," Cam reminded them.

"Oh, er, right." Brody looked around. "He is, isn't he?"

"Yes." Mike sighed. "Look. I like her. A lot. She's funny, mean, sexy. All of it. And yeah, she's way different from Lea." He mused, more to himself than them, "Never thought I'd like that, but I do."

"She's a good person too." Flynn nodded. "Maddie and the girls love her. Grace…not so much."

Curious, Mike asked, "Do any of you like Grace?"

As one, they all frowned.

"No." Brody first.

"Hell no. She's too nice—and I don't trust anyone who smiles all the time." Cam second.

Flynn snorted. "You're kidding, right? Watching her play my big brother at Abby's party was embarrassing. She led you by the nose, man."

"I was trying to be polite, like Mom asked me to be," Mike growled, not appreciating Flynn's comments.

"We all know how polite you are." Brody took a huge bite of cake and talked with his mouth full. "But there's such a thing as too nice."

"You really think I'm nice?" A four-letter word no man liked to be associated with. It was the kiss of death with women. Though Del seemed to think he had more going for him than manners.

Flynn answered, "You're kidding, right? How many times growing up have I heard—have *we* heard—to follow your example? Because Mike always holds the door for the ladies. He always says please and thank you. He always washes his hands after he takes a piss."

"It was hell for Cam growing up with you," Brody said sadly.

Flynn laughed. "True. Bro, you were Mr. Perfect. Not as smart as Poindexter," he paused and thumbed at Cam, who gave him the finger, "but you were like the perfect son. It was even hard for Brody to keep up."

Brody swore. "Fuck you. I was the golden boy. *You* were always in his shadow. And that's also why Cam turned, sadly, to book learnin'," he said in a Southern accent. "So our littlest could stand out among his nerdy peers. Not the beefiest McCauley, but the bookwormiest."

Mike laughed, because his brothers were idiots. "You guys are so weird. So you paled in my glorious shadow." He struck a pose, outlining his muscular biceps. "I understand it can be difficult being raised around so much excellence, but you tried. I give you credit for that."

Flynn gagged. "I think I'm going to be sick."

"Figures. Weakest link and all." Cam buffed his hands against what was probably an expensive sweater. Brody and Flynn were dressed in T-shirts.

Mike glanced down at the button-down shirt he'd washed so he'd look decent at Del's. It had been important that her family like him. So… "Mom is having this barbecue tomorrow."

"No, it's next week," Cam corrected. "It's supposed to rain tomorrow, so she moved it. She texted me earlier, so you should have that on your phone by now."

"So no barbecue tomorrow, but next week," Mike said after checking his phone. "Fine. I need your help though. Be on your best behavior with Del." He smacked Brody, then Flynn, in the head.

"Hey." Flynn glared.

Brody shot him the finger.

He didn't worry about Cam, who knew how to behave. "Look, Del likes the girls. You two, don't be obnoxious. Cam, maybe you can help with Mom. She doesn't seem to like Del much." He'd noticed. And he didn't like it.

"Sure. But I don't think it's that she dislikes Del, so much as she's worried about you," Cam offered.

"How's that?"

Cam shook his head. "Nothing that can't keep. Come on, guys," he said to Brody and Flynn. "It's late. Let's let Mike off the hook."

"For now," Flynn warned. "Poker, Friday night. Brody's place. Come see how great it looks now that we're helping him fix it up."

Brody scowled. "I resent that."

"Dude, you know it's true." Flynn sighed. "It's a good thing Maddie's taking pity on you and Abby and helping design your place. Because, sadly, Abby's taste sucks."

"Ass." Brody glared.

Cam, wisely, said nothing. Now living with Vanessa full-time, he seemed to be taking impending fatherhood and life with Van-zilla in stride.

"Okay. So Friday night at Brody's."

"Brody's and Abby's, as soon as she moves in," Brody corrected with pride. "And Hyde's if you want to get technical."

Mike groaned. "Oh, about your demon dog. I need to borrow him." He explained the deal he'd made with Colin, leaving out the reason behind it, and accepted the laughter and *sucker* insults thrown his way. He knew he deserved it.

"That kid." Brody wiped away an imaginary tear. "What a manipulator. I'm so proud."

"Figures." Mike herded the three of them out the back door. "Remember, be nice to Del when you see her. And get Mom off her ass," he directed to Cam, who was right about being her favorite. Considering he was most like her, Mike figured Cam had earned his due.

"I'll do my best." Cam smiled, and Mike had to admit his brother looked good wearing happiness like a second skin. "Mike, I like Del. She suits you."

Mike nodded. "Yeah, yeah. Now all of you, go home to your women. And you call me a sucker?"

They laughed at him knowingly. Because he'd just joined their ranks, still not sure how he'd become so enamored of a woman he had no idea what to do with. His *girlfriend*.

He savored her image as he settled into bed. Not even Lea's memory could keep him from dreaming about Del and what he planned for them the next day.

Chapter 17

DEL GLARED AT FOLEY WHO WOULDN'T STOP SMIRKING at her. "What?" she snapped.

"Nothing, boss. You're looking pretty good today is all. Pretty…satisfied."

Across the garage, Lou coughed to no doubt muffle laughter. Then Johnny entered, giving her a telling once-over, and whistled "Here Comes the Bride."

Her stupid brother must have talked, because she couldn't see her dad spreading rumors about her love life.

"The next one of you assholes who thinks he's funny—before I've had my coffee—goes on desk duty."

The garage grew silent in a heartbeat.

"Yeah, that's what I thought."

Her father entered, took a good look around, and sighed. "Bullying the guys again? Really, honey. That's no way to treat valued employees. Even Foley."

"Thanks a lot," Foley muttered and disappeared under the hood of a '69 Mustang coupe.

"You're hilarious, Dad." She stormed back into her office and settled in for a few phone calls.

Some time later, her father brought her a steaming cup of coffee from a local shop down the street, and she finished her call and guzzled it, sighing with pleasure as the perfect amount of creamer and sugar lit her up from the inside. "Thanks. Gino was in this morning, wasn't he?"

"You can tell?"

"He always makes my coffee perfect. Nell adds too much sugar."

Her father shrugged and sipped from his own cup. "Take it black, like me, and it never matters who's serving." He studied her while she typed up a few back invoices she'd been meaning to get to last week but hadn't. "So. We missed you last night at dinner. Rena made lasagna."

She nodded, focusing on the monitor and not her dad's shit-eating grin.

"Expect you were with Mike and Colin."

"Yeah."

"What did you do?"

The rain had in fact made the barbecue a wash, so it was a good thing it had been canceled.

"You really want to know?"

"I'm curious."

"I met Mike at his place for dinner, then spent the evening getting my ass handed to me at Chutes and Ladders, Candy Land, and Monopoly, though I'm pretty sure they cheated. I ended up landing in jail an awful lot. Pass Go and collect two hundred dollars, my ass."

Her father choked on his coffee.

"What?"

"Just surprised you spent the evening playing board games."

"Well, it's not like we could have sex with Colin watching."

Her father cringed, and she allowed herself a mean smile. Nosy bastard. "Do you hound J.T. each time *he* goes out on a date?"

"No, but only because your brother's a pig."

"True."

"I'm glad to see you with Mike. But…"

"But?"

"Is the kid too much? Colin's cute, but it can't be easy dating a guy with baggage."

Mike's baggage had less to do with the living. She didn't tell her father that, though. "Colin's great. I like him. I think it would be harder dating a guy whose kid wasn't so well behaved. Like Jenny's brood." She shuddered. She loved her neighbor, but her children were undisciplined monsters. She couldn't see Mike ever letting Colin get away with so much.

Her father nodded. "Yeah, you have a point." He glanced at the stacks on her desk. "Need help?"

She frowned. Her father avoided paperwork like the plague. "Why are you being so agreeable this morning?" She noted his sleepy satisfaction, the telltale pleasantness, the fairly clean fingernails—and God knew it was a bitch to get the grease out when you worked day in and day out with motor oil and lube.

She stared at him with wide eyes. "You got laid!"

"Delilah Webster." Her father turned three shades of red. "Watch your mouth."

"Sorry. But, Dad, who is she? Do I know her?" She frowned. "It's not slutty Sheila from Cat's Kitty Kat House, is it?" The popular strip club had been a point of contention between Del and her dad for years. The man might find someone special if he stopped shoving bills down G-strings.

He mumbled about something he'd forgotten and took off.

"Well, that's one way to get rid of them." She sighed and got back to her to-do stack, but while she worked, she thought about how much fun she'd had last night. None of it had involved sex. They'd spent the evening, all three of them, playing games. After Colin had gone to sleep, Mike had cuddled with her on the couch, the two of them watching a detective movie together. Hugging and occasionally kissing.

Curiously, he hadn't done anything about the erection in his pants. No making a move. And for the life of her, she couldn't explain why that meant so much to her.

She liked sex. Actually, she *loved* sex with him. She'd never had so many orgasms from a man in such a short period of time. Del knew Mike felt the same. Yet he'd abstained last night, enjoying her company. So odd, and so…romantic. In a weird kind of way.

Even Rena had agreed. After staying up late to give Del the third degree, she'd sighed and lamented the fact that Del had landed Mr. Sexy while Rena, a die-hard romantic, had to make do with plastic toys.

Too much information, but Rena had shrugged away Del's discomfiture and demanded Del go over every detail of the evening.

To hear her cousin tell it, Mike was smitten.

Del didn't believe it. Sure they liked each other. The chemistry between them was off-the-charts amazing. They fit each other, seemed to like the same things, or at least, making fun of the same things. Mike a nice guy? Yeah right.

She smirked at her spreadsheet. The guy had bad things to say about reality TV stars, rival construction companies, cartoons inappropriate for kids—which she found hilarious—and self-help books. She imagined he'd been deluged with them when he'd lost his wife, because he had a real stick in his craw about any expert who might try to tell him how to feel about anything.

Yes, watching television with Mike had been an eye-opener. It had also showed her another side to him. When he asked her a question, he waited for an answer. If she even thought about caging an answer, he'd catch her hemming and hawing and demand the truth. The guy liked her warped sense of humor. For that alone she wanted to reward him.

Finding out he was a closet hard-ass who liked to sneer, taunt, and jab at others—mostly those deserving of it—skewed her image of him as a nice guy. Except in bed. Not to say Mike couldn't be a genuinely kind man. Far from it. He loved his family, could be generous to a fault, and had half the neighborhood in love with him, according to Rena, who'd heard it from Abby.

A great source of intel, her cousin. Rena and Abby had grown tight lately. Personally, Del liked the thought of her cousin hanging with her new friends. Rena could have done a lot worse in the friendship department.

Kind of like Del with her past boyfriends.

She sighed at the dark cloud settling over her day, one even coffee couldn't seem to dispel. Last night had been almost magical. Too good to be true. It made sense she and Mike would bond over great sex and lighthearted fun. She knew they'd never go the distance, and that unfortunately had less to do with his deceased wife than with her inability to hold another's affection for long.

Though she normally broke off her relationships, she did it when she sensed her boyfriends getting ready to pull the plug. Her mother hadn't been that wrong all those years ago. Del was a spoiled, willful brat more concerned with her own feelings than with others.

"Am I gonna be half full or half empty?" She mulled over the idea for as long as she could stand it. Finally determined not to dwell on the negative, Del decided to enjoy her time with Mike for as long as she could. She just hoped Colin wouldn't suffer when her pairing with Mike eventually went south.

Another sip of coffee, and she tasted only the bitterness under the sweet. Typical, and so very real. Best to remember dreams were called that for a reason. She'd be smart not to fall for the charming side of Mike, or she'd be flattened when he eventually grew bored with her.

As they always did.

The week passed swiftly. She met with Mike for a movie on Wednesday, and again on Thursday to just hang out after Colin went to bed. By Friday night, she'd had enough. This girlfriend business was nice. Okay, she liked it. Holding hands, kissing, hugging, all the crappy sentimental stuff that Rena would have died for gave Del a warm feeling inside. God forbid she confess to her cousin how much it made her feel good to just *be* with Mike and even Colin.

But no sex? What the hell was that all about?

She pulled into Mike's driveway, remembering she needed to schedule his truck into the shop, and parked. Before when she'd arrive, Colin or Mike would usually open the door and race out to hug her before she reached the landing. Colin seemed to love when Mike touched her or kissed her, and the little guy made sure to shove her into his father's clutches whenever possible. But tonight, no Colin. And no Mike.

Frowning, she walked to the door and rang the bell.

Still nothing. She raised her hand to knock when she noticed a slip of paper at her feet. She bent down and read instructions to enter. Mike's chicken scratch. Intrigued, she opened the door and found candles all over the place. A gooey part inside her liked the ambience. Not something Mike would normally do.

"Hello?" No one answered, and she closed the door behind her. "Colin? Mike?"

Still no answer. Weird. She walked through the living room, not surprised to see everything as neat as a pin. Mike had a thing for organization, and she knew he'd eyed the stacks at her house and in her office with misgiving. Too bad. She was neat too, just in her own way.

She looked into the kitchen and saw a bottle of chocolate syrup, some gummy bears, and an ice cream scoop. Were they making sundaes? Frowning, because no one had come out to greet her yet, she wondered if she'd mistaken the time. If Mike had set up the night for a seduction, his absence sure the hell wouldn't put her in the mood.

"Hey, Mike," she yelled. Annoyed, she stomped out of the kitchen and down the hallway. She found nothing in the spare bedroom or Colin's room. Mike's door was shut.

She opened it, expecting to find him in nothing but a rose between his teeth. But when she pushed through, she found an empty room, just one candle lit on the nightstand. It smelled like lavender, her favorite scent, the only thing going for Mike right about now.

"What the hell?" The bathroom remained dark, so she doubted he was in there.

She started to worry. Lit candles in an unoccupied house, no kid or guy in sight?

She crossed to the nightstand to blow out the flame. Just as the room turned dark, the only illumination some dim candlelight out in the hall, large arms wrapped around her waist and picked her up off her feet. At first she panicked. Then she recognized the strong arms and the cologne Mike wore when he wanted to impress her.

"Don't try to fight back, slave. You're mine tonight," he promised in a low voice. "I have no problem punishing naughty girls who don't obey."

Playing into the role he'd assigned, she fought him. "Damn it. Get off." She tried to kick back and got nowhere. Instead, she found herself gagged and trussed up like a turkey in no time. Excited as hell but unwilling to show it, she waited for her "captor" to set her down. She dangled over his back, her belly uncomfortably braced on powerful shoulders. The lights came on, and she stared down at a familiar tight ass.

"Asshole," came out muffled, but she did her best to flail and beat his lower back with her bound wrists.

"Now, now, Delilah." Mike chuckled, his deep voice giving her shivers. "We talked about this. Remember that fantasy about being dominated? You're due."

She wanted to ask what had brought all this on, when it came back to her. *Hell.* She'd made a crack about him not being man enough to handle her, that he'd need to tie her down if he ever thought he could take charge again. But that had been late at night, after beating him at cribbage, a game she loathed yet always won.

Apparently Mr. Good Loser, who'd taken his defeat with humor, wasn't so forgiving.

How sick was she that she grew wet thinking about how he'd make her pay?

"Colin's sleeping over at Brody and Abby's, taking care of Hyde. It's just you and me, sweetness." He slapped her ass hard, and she bit back a moan. "Go ahead, let it out. I know how much you like a good spanking."

Oh boy. Maybe taunting him when she'd skunked him at the game hadn't been her smartest move. Then again, if it finally got him to have sex with her again, she'd play along. She wanted to say something, but the gag prevented anything but muffled moans.

"Yep. I frustrated the hell out of you this week, didn't I? We had some amazing sex before." Mike dropped her onto his bed and shoved her arms above her head before she could wriggle free. He latched the silk binding around her wrists to a lead on the bed. God. He'd prepared for this.

He wore a pair of unfastened jeans. She didn't see any underwear where they parted, just dark hair and the skin God had given him. Oh boy. Commando. Her favorite. His muscles rippled under the light, and she watched him smirk at her before he relit the lavender candle, turned off the overhead light, then returned to her.

"This scent reminds me of you." He cupped himself and showcased a handsome erection. "Gets me hard every time."

Removing her shoes, socks, pants, and underwear took little time. She didn't fight him when he fastened her ankles wide apart to more restraints at the edge of the bed.

He slid his hands up her legs, massaging her muscles until she moaned with relaxed—and aroused—pleasure. Boneless yet tingly all over, she wanted him to take her, to own her responses and overwhelm her with pleasure.

His lips soon followed his fingers, and before she knew it, he was sucking her clit, shoving his fingers in and out of her, and stroking her to a climax that might just break her.

Then the jerk stopped.

"I can't hear you, baby. Do you like what I'm doing to you?"

Take off the gag and eat me, she wanted to demand. Instead, she glared at him.

"Oh, right. Sorry. My bad. It's supposed to be a blindfold." His wicked grin thrilled her. Kinky, sexy, creative Mike. *Wow.* This wasn't at all how she'd imagined she'd spend her Friday night. She'd thought she'd have to set him straight on how things needed to change.

Instead, he'd fulfilled another desire of hers without her even having to tell him what she wanted. They really were on the same wavelength.

Mike stood and took off his jeans, showing her his long, thick cock. "I am really hard right now. You have no idea how much I wanted to tie you up. When you took that spanking like a champ…" He shivered. "Oh yeah. I couldn't stop thinking about this. With you," he murmured.

She pondered the meaning behind his desire and growing closeness.

"Now, now. I can see you thinking too hard." He pinched her nipple through her shirt and bra, and she arched off the mattress, lost in lust. "Hmm. I should have taken the shirt and bra off first, hmm?" He leaned closer and cupped his ear. "What's that?"

She glared at him, not deigning to speak around the gag.

"Oh, right." He winked and removed the gag.

"You ass."

He kissed her, and she lost the rest of what she wanted to say under the heady sensation of being taken. His tongue penetrated, his lips seduced, and she was left reaching for him with her body, incapacitated and aroused beyond thought.

"That is so fucking sexy." He breathed hard, staring down at her, and massaged her breasts. "But I need you naked. Don't move when I take the ropes off."

"Ropes?" More like scarves. Nothing to bite her skin.

"Pretend, would you?"

She grinned. "Sure thing, my kinky lover." She glanced down his superbly conditioned body, lingering on his cock. Loving the shine at his tip, the detail that showed her how much he wanted her, she licked her lips. "I think you need some release, hmm?"

"You're damn right." He untied her, gripped her wrists tight, and stripped off her shirt and bra. Then he settled over her, bracing on his elbows while the lower half of him ground against her. "Shit. You feel so soft."

"Yeah, all soft against that hard cock."

He moaned. "Shut up."

"Why? You gonna come all over my belly? Let me see." She rubbed against him.

He firmed his hold on her wrists and lowered his mouth to her breast. Taking the nipple in his mouth, he teased and rolled the bud, licking her until she couldn't stop begging him to fuck her.

"Not yet." He moved so that he positioned himself between her legs, her arousal coating him though he took pains not to angle for penetration. Yet every slide against him engorged her already sensitive clit.

"Come on, Mike. Inside me."

"Without a condom?" He switched to her other nipple, licking her into a state of dire need.

"Fuck. I don't care. Just do me."

He tensed and leaned up. "Look at me. I want to come inside you. No diseases, no babies. Understand?"

"I'm not stupid. Just pent-up. And it's your fault," she barked.

"Delilah…?"

"Hell. I'm on the Pill. Have been for years. I mean, you never know. Besides that, it's a safe time of the month."

He closed his eyes and swore. When he opened them, the dark blue of his irises looked black. "You sure it's okay? I'll wear a condom if you want, though God knows I'm dying to feel you over me, skin to skin."

She looked into his face, seeing the handsome cheekbones, the sultry mouth, the warmth in his gaze. Her protection, her desire, came first with him. So unexpected yet addictive to be with someone who put her first for once.

"Come on, sexy. Yes or no?" He tightened his fingers around her wrists and ground his hips against hers, rubbing her again.

"Yes, yes, now."

He didn't smile, didn't laugh, but she read the mirth

in his face. "You giving orders, Delilah? Tsk. Naughty girl. Time for some real punishment."

"Mike…" she whined.

He laughed, a dark sound that fired her blood. Then he took her to another plane entirely. He retied her hands and fastened them over her head, to the restraints on the bed. The gag turned into a blindfold as he smoothed it over her eyes.

"Oh yeah. This is how I pictured it. So fucking sweet."

He let her go, moving off her. She couldn't see him, and the loss of one of her senses amplified the others.

"Let's see how many times I can make you come before I lose my mind…"

Chapter 18

MIKE WANTED THIS NIGHT TO BE PERFECT. CANDLES, chocolate syrup—his fantasy to lick it off her breasts—and tying her down. Jesus, she looked like a painting. Bound, open, and aroused. All for him.

He had to touch her, committing each stroke to memory.

"I love how you feel."

She'd already come twice from his mouth and his fingers. Fuck if she didn't taste so sweet, and she still smelled like lavender. That or the candle had gone straight to his head. She moaned as he felt her from her ankles to her thighs, lingering between her legs. He rubbed her folds, sliding through the slick need pooling there.

"Your clit is so full. You need to come, baby?"

"*Mike.* I can't. Twice is too much."

"You can never come too much." He smiled at her.

His breathy name on her lips made everything right. This past week had been brutal, but he'd wanted to make it clear that he wanted to be with her even without the sex. Saying it didn't matter. Proving it did. Plus, he had to admit it gratified him to see mirrored frustration in her face after each date. The woman wanted him as much as he wanted her.

He continued to touch her, grazing her sharp hip bones, over her flat belly, lingering over the muscle there. "You're as ripped as I am."

"Please. You're huge. I'm just in shape." Her breath hitched when he moved over her ribs. Oh yeah, she liked that.

Grazing the soft skin under her breasts, he rubbed his knuckles under her firm mounds, wondering what they might look like plumped together. Why not see? He pushed her breasts together, making them look bigger. Her rosy nipples stood tall, and he couldn't help himself when he took each one in his mouth and sucked.

Her raspy moans and cries for more tore at his own discipline. Especially knowing she trusted him enough to let him take her without a condom.

Mike straddled her body, resting his cock on her belly, and played with her breasts, watching her face for her reactions. She had the most beautiful expressions. Her lips parted, shiny from his kisses. Her increased arousal showed everywhere, in her tight nipples, the goose bumps on her skin, the play of constricting muscle wherever he touched her. And the throaty moans as she surrendered herself to him...

"Open your mouth wider, Delilah." He gripped himself. "I have a treat for you."

"Oh yeah." She parted her lips, and he scooted forward to rest the tip of his cock at her mouth.

"Suck me, baby. Yeah."

She licked him, and he fought the urge to shove himself in her and come. He was so ready, so on edge. Yet he wanted to last, to make it good for her first. And fuck, watching her blow him was a thing of beauty.

Careful, he angled so that he could push deeper, but not too deep. He gave her short, shallow thrusts while she sucked him, unable to do more than obey...

"Shit, Del. I wish you could see this. You're amazing. So hot."

She moaned around him, and he knew if he didn't do something fast, he'd come down her throat.

He withdrew in a hurry and settled over her. Then he removed her blindfold and her wrist restraints, but held on to her wrists, wanting to reinforce that he was on top. "Watch me while I enter you."

She stared into his eyes, her diamond-bright gaze glowing in the shadows. "Do it."

With one hand, he positioned himself at her entrance, then pushed forward.

They stared at each other while he moved, and the slick glide inside her felt like heaven.

"Mike, you feel so good."

"Yeah, honey. So fucking good." He thrust all the way inside, sweat beading on his forehead, fighting the urge to hammer inside her until he climaxed.

"God. You're so big." She squirmed, and he swore, gripping her wrists tightly. Her breasts mashed against his chest, her sultry mouth needing to be filled, her scent…

Lightheaded with lust and no longer able to wait, he withdrew and slammed home.

She cried out, begging for more, and he did it again.

And again. Fucking her, loving her, while they moved in harmony. He'd never experienced such erotic bliss—especially when he took her mouth and ground against her clit. She clamped down on him, and he felt her orgasm like an electric glove around his cock.

He pulled back from the kiss to finish, watching her climax while he rode through it.

"Fuck, Del. Oh fuck," he groaned as he thrust once more and lost it. He shattered, his climax incredibly powerful. Knowing he filled her and not a condom increased his excitement, and it took him a while before he had the capacity to think.

Finally finished, he let go of her wrists and leaned up on his elbows, then bent down to kiss the smile from her lips.

Passionate yet comforting, the kiss summed up exactly how he felt about Del. He wanted to fuck her, make love to her, argue with and comfort her. All in the same breath. But he didn't want to think about the future or emotional nonsense. Not right now, when he could bask in the feel of her. Loving being a part of her.

"That was amazing," she said on a sigh and she put her arms around him, her small but rough hands stroking his back.

"Yeah, amazing." He kissed her again. "I should spank you for making me use condoms before. Holy fuck. Now I know where the term 'bust a nut' comes from."

Del snickered, the mean little laugh stroking love and lust from him in equal measures. "That's what I love about being with you, Mike. The incredibly romantic pillow talk."

"Hey, I lit candles for you."

"You did." She ran her jagged little nails up his spine, and he moaned with contentment. "So what's with the gummy bears?"

"Oh. Well, those were for Colin's sleepover but he forgot them. The ice cream spoon too."

"And the chocolate."

He smiled. "No, baby. That's for us. I have this fantasy about drizzling it all over your tits and licking it off, slowly."

"My tits, huh?" She licked her lips, and he wished he wasn't so drained that he couldn't make love to her all over again right now. "I was thinking more like your cock. You know I have a sweet tooth."

"Hell." He closed his eyes and pressed his forehead to hers for a moment. "Now I'll never get that image out of my head until we do it. I'm gonna need some time to recover though. I mean, I kind of lost my head with you."

"You made me beg, you big jerk. I came so hard I'll be walking funny tomorrow." She dug her hands into his hair and pulled his head back, then nipped his throat.

Damn if his cock didn't stir.

"Del, be nice."

"You want nice from me?"

"Well, only if your mouth is around my cock. Remember, it's not a chew toy."

She grinned. "I'll do my best."

He forced himself to move off her and removed her ankle restraints. "Best night ever. Just sayin'."

She crooked her finger and he joined her again on the bed, cleaning her up with a rag he'd set on the bed stand. After he finished, she rolled them over and slid down his body.

"Del, seriously. I'm spent. I need a little rest…" He just stared as she took his limp cock in her mouth and started bringing him back to life.

She paused with a wicked grin. "You can dish it out but can't take it, hmm? Three for me? The least you can do is two." Orgasms.

And damn if his body wasn't willing to work with her. Especially when she left him and came back with the chocolate syrup.

—∿∿—

Sunday's barbecue looked like something out of a magazine, Beth thought with pride as she surveyed the festivities. Her sons had arrived with their fiancées. Brian attended solo, waiting for Colin, while his parents took his older brother to a baseball game. Nadine and Grace smiled and laughed with Noah, who stuck close to his mother. And her husband tended the grill with that blustery sense of humor that had captivated her over thirty-six years ago and still made her laugh.

She joined him, pleased when her boys tossed around a football, including Noah and Brian.

James shook his head at her. "Woman, why can't you leave well enough alone?"

Surprised at the criticism, because since their marital troubles and counseling, James had been beyond considerate, she stared. "What?"

He nodded to Grace. "That. You know Mike isn't having her. He found someone else. Accept it, honey."

"Why? Because he's infatuated with someone different from his usual type? I admit, the fact that he's openly admitting he has a girlfriend is a step in the right direction. But Del Webster?"

"So is it that she's a mechanic, has tats, or that she's the first woman Mike's been truly interested in since Lea that has your back up?" He flipped a few burgers and watched her, his dark blue gaze unblinking.

Beth thought about it. "A little of all three, I think.

Del comes from a good man. I love Liam." At her husband's growl, she amended, "I mean, I love him as a *friend*. Oh hush. He's a kind man, and I know you've talked to him a few times."

"Maybe I have. Your car was making some odd sounds, and I figured I'd ask him what he thought."

"And?"

His lips quirked. "The brake pads need replacing, and he's not in love with you. We're good."

"Yes, *we* are." She kissed him. "Best thing that man ever did for me was agree to go to coffee. Got you to see what an ass you were making of yourself."

"We were talking about Del…"

She shoved down her laughter. Her husband's jealousy had shown her he still cared, and it had shown him that his wife was attractive enough to get another man's attention. "Maybe I want to see how Del reacts if Grace is around."

"Beth." He sounded disappointed. "You've never been one to play games. What are you doing?"

"Nothing. James, I like Nadine."

"I know you do. I like her too. She's a great neighbor."

"Yes, and her daughter is a nice person needing a fresh start. What's so wrong with her and Mike going out?"

"Nothing, as long as you discount the fact that Mike doesn't love her. Hell, I don't even think he likes her."

"And he loves Del?" She huffed. "That boy is stubborn, like his father. He has it in his head that McCauleys only love once. Bullshit."

"I love when you swear."

"You'll be hearing it a lot then, because it's time your son and I had a talk. He can't avoid me forever." Though he'd been trying. "I only want him to be happy."

"Then stop trying to set him up with another Lea. Let him make his choice."

Mike, Colin, and Del arrived together. To her bemusement, they looked like a family. Colin held Del's hand, his face turned up to her while he spoke and she smiled down at his answer. To Beth's surprise and discerning eye, Del seemed to honestly enjoy Colin's company. She'd seen her share of women try to charm her grandson to get into Mike's good graces.

Her gaze drifted back to Nadine and Grace, wondering if what the girls had mentioned was true. They'd filled her ear with nonsense about Grace being a passive-aggressive minx. Well, Vanessa had used the term *bitch*, but Beth didn't like the word.

Beth didn't know what to do anymore. She liked Grace, mostly because the girl reminded her of Lea. Soft-spoken, sweet, pretty. And a wonderful mother to Noah...who again tried to smack Brody's dog with a stick. Might want to use that stick against his backside. She looked to Nadine, who spoke sharply with the boy. Then Grace was there, hugging him.

Frowning, Beth watched Grace take in the scene of Mike with Del. She didn't seem pleased.

"Look alive. Boy's coming this way," James murmured and rotated the hot dogs.

Colin darted away from Del to join the football toss. Del seemed to stiffen as they drew closer. That attitude would need to go, Beth thought as she deliberately relaxed and offered a wide smile.

Mike reached her first and hugged her.

"Put me down," she squeaked as her once-little boy, now a huge man, pulled her off her feet.

He laughed. "Hi, Mom. Dad." He took the soft blow James gave to his back without flinching. "You guys know Del." He paused and put an arm around her shoulders. "My girlfriend."

James grinned. "And a pretty one at that. We McCauleys sure know how to pick 'em, eh?"

Beth noted Del's shy smile with astonishment. *Never would have imagined the girl had a quiet side to her.* Thinking maybe she'd be better off to observe and shelve her assumptions, she did her best to welcome the girl. "Hello, Del. Glad you could come. How's your dad?" A safe enough subject.

Del smiled. She wore a small silver loop in her eyebrow and a diamond stud in her nose, had a short-sleeved purple T-shirt that showcased her colorful arms, and wore jeans and black boots. She'd done her ash-blond hair in a set of tight braids and looped them together in what should have been a mess but on Del looked fashionable. "Dad's just fine. I think he's got a new girlfriend."

"Thank God," James muttered.

"Dad." Mike frowned.

Del laughed. "Don't worry, James. Dad's too busy with work and his new lady friend to cause you any trouble."

"What's he got going at work?"

Del discussed a new client and some engine for a classic car they were rebuilding. Mike, Beth noted, smiled and looked on proudly. He wasn't putting on a show either. He genuinely liked the girl. Beth grew a little worried. It was one thing for Mike to fool around with someone she wasn't sure suited him, but another if he started falling for her.

Then Grace approached.

"Oh boy," James said under his breath.

Mike nudged Del. "Why don't you go say hey to Vanessa before her arm breaks off. She's waving."

"I see that." Del sounded amused. "Fine. Don't worry. I won't rip her head off. No blood in front of the boys."

Del walked away, and Beth realized she'd been talking about ripping off Grace's head. "Mike, really."

"What, Mom?"

"Beth," James cautioned.

He had a point. But she'd darn well talk to her son later, in private.

"Nothing. Enjoy. I'm going to get the pie out. Hey, Grace, why don't you come help me?"

"Sure, Beth." Grace smiled. Such a nice girl.

Beth went into the house, prepared to wait to talk to her son. She was determined to get to the bottom of Mike's fixation with that Del Webster once and for all.

Mike let out a breath. "Thanks, Dad."

"No, son. Thank *you*. About time you dealt with your mother about this bullshit so *I* don't have to hear about it anymore."

He groaned. "Throw me to the wolves why don't you?"

James chuckled. "Boy, I know when to fight the battles that matter. Sticking up for your sorry ass is ridiculous. You're thirty-four. Act like it. Talk to your mother." He paused. "You know, I never did think you and Grace would be a match. No way my boy could be attracted to a girl like that. Sure she's pretty. But way too agreeable."

They stood together over the grill while Mike thought about what his father had said. An odd notion struck him. "I thought she was a little like Lea."

"Well, a little, I guess. But Lea wasn't all that agreeable, was she? I remember you two had some whoppers of fights."

Mike smiled. "We did at that." He and Lea hadn't been perfect. They'd been in love.

They watched Flynn toss a football that hit Colin in the head. Good thing they were using a foam ball.

"Now that's just sad," his father said loudly. "Boy has hands like Cam."

"I heard that, old man," Cam shouted. "And it's more like he's a chip off the old block."

It took a minute for that to sink in. "Hey." Mike glared at his brothers. "I played linebacker, not receiver. Want me to show you?"

"Yeah, Cam. Let him show you," Brody taunted, then went down when Cam tackled him. Colin and Brian piled on, and the game devolved into a tickle fest when Flynn joined in.

"Boys." His father grinned.

Mike noted Del hanging with the girls but didn't like the fact that his mother had once again taken Grace under her wing. He had a feeling he'd have to have a sit-down with her before too long. This need to fix him up with Grace Meadows had gotten on his last friggin' nerve.

"Grab me that plate." His father nodded to the large platter on the table near the grill. "I like your new girl-friend, by the way." He laid hamburger patties on the plate, then followed with hot dogs. "She won't take your shit."

"I know."

His father nodded. "How serious are you two?"

"We're not. Just having fun together. No biggie."

"Son, for you, a declaration *is* a biggie. You've pretty much announced that she belongs to you, and you to her. Don't fuck it up."

"Great advice, Dad. Thanks."

Before his father could smack him in the head, Mike took the platter and set it on the center picnic table next to the potato salad, the beans, mac n' cheese, and salad. One thing he could say for his parents—they knew how to throw a backyard picnic like nobody's business.

A glance at Del showed her laughing at something Maddie was saying, and he smiled, liking the way she fit in to his family.

"Hey, Dad. Think quick."

He looked up in time to duck the ball aimed directly at his head. "Colin."

"It was Uncle Flynn, Dad. You said he throws like a girl."

When Del glared over at the boy, he shrugged. "Sorry, but that's what he said."

"Nice, Mike." Del gave him a disgusted look. "Hell. Even I can throw better than you idiots."

"Yeah? Put your money where your mouth is, Nancy," Brody sneered.

When Del stood, he hid behind Flynn. "Help, Abby! The mean lady is coming to get me."

Abby laughed. "Put up or shut up, Brody."

Del rubbed her hands together with glee. "Okay. Let's have a contest. Girls against the boys."

Half an hour later, while everyone waited for Mike to take the last throw, aiming for the old throw pocket net his father had dragged out of the garage, he readied to win.

Del approached from the side.

"Hey, no tampering with our guy," Flynn complained.

"Shh. She's allowed," Maddie argued. "You did it to me."

"That was nothing. I was scared for you to break a nail. You did just get them done, honey."

"True."

"Hey," Mike barked. "I'm trying to throw here."

He saw Nadine laughing with his mother. His father waited next to them, his arms crossed, and nodded to the net. "You don't win, you're no longer a McCauley."

"Come on, Dad." Colin seemed anxious. "You have to win."

"Thanks *so* much." Mike glared at his father. Then he lowered his throwing arm and dragged Del closer. "What?"

"Just going to wish you good luck...*Nancy*."

James laughed. "Oh, nicely played."

Mike looked into her laughing eyes. "Oh yeah?"

"Yeah." She smirked at him.

So he did the only thing he could think of to shut her up. He kissed her. Not an innocent, quick peck, but a deep kiss with tongue and fire.

Whistles and shouts sounded behind them, and Del finally pushed him away.

"Good luck," she rasped. "Doubt your arm's steady

after that." Damn if she didn't saunter back to the girls' table looking smug.

Vanessa high-fived her. "That's the way you play. To win."

It had been *his* idea to kiss her. Whatever. He calmed himself, took aim, and threw right through the center hole into the net.

That's when Cam started singing Queen's "We Are the Champions." Brody and Flynn chimed in, and his father couldn't stop pumping his hand in the air in victory.

Del laughed along with them. "Lucky throw. You want my take, it was my kiss that saved him."

He noted Grace and Noah coming back out of the house. They'd been gone for a while, and he assumed the kid had a bellyache from all the cupcakes he'd been wolfing down when his mother and grandmother hadn't been looking.

"What did I miss?" she asked.

"My son is the new champion of backyard football, apparently," Beth said while rolling her eyes. "Hurray."

Grace blinked. "Oh?"

"It's time all you women bowed to me and all the men in this yard. For we *are* the champions." He started singing with them, and Grace just watched him in confusion. Del flipped him the bird when the kids weren't watching.

And that is why I'm with her. That finger...and that kiss.

Chapter 19

AS THE PARTY WOUND DOWN, MIKE HELPED HIS FATHER clean up. Colin and Brian had had a blast. Noah, as usual, hadn't listened to Grace or Nadine. So after vomiting up his cupcakes after his bellyache, he'd gone home with his mother and grandmother to feel better.

The girls—and Del—helped his mother. To Mike's pleasant surprise, his mom treated Del like she did the others. It gave him hope for the future—the immediate future, he quickly amended, but not quick enough, because a few daydreams about joint vacations and playing house started to take up residence in his mind.

Then Beth McCauley ruined his day.

"Mike? I need to talk to you, sweetie."

"Oh boy," Flynn muttered next to him. "You know she's been waiting to get you alone. Away from the pack."

"Like a mountain lion cornering its prey," Brody intoned. "Separating the weak from the group."

"Shut it, you two."

Brody laughed. "Your funeral." He rejoined Abby and swung her into a kiss, then grabbed his dog. "Hey, Colin. You going to watch him or what? I hear you have to pass a few tests to get your own dog."

Great. Brody hadn't forgotten that favor from last week. Mike wished he had.

"Michael?"

Everyone stopped and looked at him. His mother had pulled out the big guns, using his full name.

"Ah, how about I take Colin back to your place and wait for you there?" Del offered.

"You have to take the dog too." Brody handed her the leash.

She stared at the dog, and he sat, all docile-like, waiting for her while she slipped the leash on him.

"See, Brody? That's how to be the alpha. Del has presence." Abby nodded.

"Shit—ah, shoot." Brody saw Colin staring at Del in awe. "Dude, I'm alpha too."

"No, Ubie. You're not. I'm sorry. Bye, Dad." Colin took Del's other hand, and the pair left with Hyde.

"Turned against by the kid." Brody sighed. "My life is so sad. Abby, make me feel better."

"Come on, slacker. I'll soothe you."

He whispered something into her ear, and she laughed.

At his mother's look, Mike moved. "Coming."

She entered the house ahead of him, and his feet seemed to slow of their own accord as he neared the steps to the back porch.

"Good luck," Vanessa said, shaking her head.

"You're going to need it," Cam finished, then grinned at him.

His father shook his head. "Boy, better make your point loud and clear. That woman has a hard head. I love her, but..."

"I know." Mike blew out a breath, then joined her in the living room. "Well, Mom? I'm here."

"Sit."

He sat next to her on the couch, feeling hemmed in

by a woman he towered over when standing. His mother had always seemed larger than life, the way she did now.

"I'm not going to apologize for setting you up with Grace."

"Ah, okay."

"She's perfect for you."

"You mean she's perfect for *you*. I'm partial to Del."

"A woman with tattoos and a mouth like a sailor."

It annoyed him she wasn't going to give Del a shot. "She's a lot more than that. She's nice. She genuinely likes Colin. She's a hard worker."

"So's Ms. Sheffer, Colin's teacher. I don't see you dating her."

"That's not fair." He glared at her but did his best not to raise his voice. She was his mother, after all. "Del's a great person. You won't give her a chance."

"A chance at what, Mike?" his mom asked softly. "At being your wife?"

"No." Yet his answer felt weak. "I told you we're dating. Taking it slow."

"You've been taking it slow for six long years. No." She held up a hand to stave off his response. "I know it hurt losing Lea. Well, guess what? It hurt me too."

To his shock, her voice quavered. "Mom."

"We need to talk about this. For too long you've clammed up about her, so we all had to. But damn it, Mike. I lost a daughter." His mother's eyes filled. "I loved that girl to pieces. My own daughter. After four sons, I wanted to try again for a little girl. But your father thought four was enough, and I reluctantly agreed. Then you brought her home. She was so beautiful. Twenty-two and fresh and innocent and she adored you."

All the feelings came rushing back. "I know. I married her, Mom."

"We all lost her when she passed. You, Colin, me, the family. I never wanted that for you, to be widowed so young. But life happens. She died, and you locked your heart away."

"Mom, do we have to do this?"

"Yes!" She stood and started pacing, keeping her gaze on him. "You refused to go out for three long years. Then when you did date, you kept them all at arm's length. You think I couldn't tell you were using them for sex?"

"Mom." He flushed.

"I know you have needs. We all do. But you just refused to open up to anyone."

"Lea is irreplaceable. What's the point? McCauleys love—"

"—only once. I've heard it all before. And it's crap."

"It's true."

"Then explain to me the joy in your eyes when you look at Del."

"What?"

"Tell me why you're so happy. Why you seem to walk on air lately. I know you, son. This isn't a game. You aren't the type to play with a woman's feelings. She looks at you a certain way. The way Lea used to. The way you look back at her."

"It's not like that."

"So much denial." She shook her head. "That's partly why I worry for you. You won't be honest with yourself. Well, I'm being honest enough for you. I don't know if Del is good enough for you. How's that?"

Rage boiled, turning the hurt inside into something he could handle. "That's crap. She's a wonderful person, and if you weren't trying to get another Lea you can have tea with and knit beside, you'd see that. You want a best friend? *You* go out with Lea."

"Lea?"

"Grace," he yelled, fucked up that he'd called *her* Lea's name. "I know who Grace is. She's *your* idea of the perfect woman for me. But she's not my idea."

"Well, what is it then? A woman the complete opposite of the woman you once loved? The one you've apparently forgotten?"

"How the hell can you say that to me?" He stood, clenching his fists. Angry, hurt, and scared at how out of control he felt. "I loved her so much I wanted to die when she left us. But I had Colin and all of you to take care of."

"All of us?"

"Yeah, you. Everyone waited for me to snap, so I had to be strong. Had to take care of my son, had to find a way to keep moving when I wanted to curl up and die with her." His eyes burned, but he wanted her to know what he'd been keeping inside for so long. "My perfect family with their perfect lives. Everything isn't rainbows and hearts, Mom. Something you finally saw when you and Dad had issues. I'm glad you got back together. But gladder you finally stopped looking at the world through friggin' rose-colored glasses.

"Loss happens. Shit happens. Then we have to pick up the pieces and somehow live, even when we don't want to. So yeah, I had sex. And yeah, I dated women who knew the score, who wanted nothing but something physical. I have Colin and I have all of you. What the hell else do I need?"

"Someone to love, honey. Someone to—"

"Get ripped away again? Get taken from me so that I can't function anymore? I did that once. I really don't want to do it again." The thought of something happening to Del was unfathomable, and he wanted to suppress it, burying it like he normally did anything that bothered him. But this conversation with his mother... He had to let it out. "Del... I have something with her, something special. I don't know where it's going, and frankly, I don't care. I just want to live in the now. Is that so wrong? To want to be happy for a change?"

She wiped her eyes. To his embarrassment, he had to wipe his as well. Time to put it back, all that messy emotion. God, he hated this shit.

"Oh Mike. Are you sure?"

"Yes, damn it. Have you not been listening to me? I love Del." He said it out loud, and they both froze. "I mean, I like her a lot. We have chemistry, we like the same things. She's great." *I love Del.* His heart threatened to burst from his chest, and he panicked at the gravity of his declaration. "I don't want to talk about this anymore. Life is good. We're friends dating casually. No weddings, no happily-ever-afters. It is what it is. Please don't mess this thing up for me with Del. She deserves better than what you've been giving her. We're together now, Mom. Just accept that. I gotta go."

He left before she could stop him. But on the way back to his kid and his girlfriend, he wondered what the hell he was playing at.

—◊◊◊—

Del met him at the door with a smile on her face. Seeing his stark expression, she lost her smile and let him inside.

"Colin's in the back with Hyde. He's in love."

Was it her imagination, or did Mike flinch?

"You okay?" she asked softly.

"Yeah."

He didn't sound okay, but she didn't want to press. She well knew how rough mothers could be.

When Mike went onto the back porch and sat on a chair to watch Colin and the dog, she followed. "I can leave if you—"

He tugged her into his lap and held her there, burying his face in her hair.

She froze, wanting to help heal the pain she could feel radiating from his heavy heart, but she didn't want to make anything worse. So she sat in his arms, hugging him back, and they watched Colin play with the dog.

When Mike finally roused some time later, she stood with him. "I should go."

"Okay." He watched her say good-bye to Colin, accepting his enthusiastic and sloppy kiss. When she reached him again, he took her in his arms. "Maybe I could come over tomorrow with the boy. We could fix your window boxes."

"Oh." On a school night, she thought, biting back a smile. "Okay."

He grinned back at her, no longer seeming so strained. "You okay now?"

He nodded, his gaze searching as it roamed her face.

"Yeah." Then he kissed her, and the slow, bone-melting sensation never failed to entice her to lean into him.

"God, you get to me," he muttered and hugged her tight. "Go home, and I'll see you tomorrow."

"Yeah. Bye." She left him, going home to an empty house. Rena had left a note indicating she planned to be at her mother's for a week, taking care of the place while Aunt Caroline went on vacation.

Del puttered around the house, then made herself a quick dinner and took an early night's sleep. The day had messed with her head, big-time. She'd felt included in the McCauley embrace. Even Beth had been pleasant, to her at least. Del wondered what the woman had said to get into Mike's loop like that.

She didn't think she'd ever seen him so lost, or so needing an anchor. Providing him that stability meant more than it should. She'd felt needed, wanted, a part of him.

A part of a man who'd made it clear he wasn't looking for marriage or a long-term commitment. She'd stupidly agreed with him then. But now... She wanted more. She wanted what Maddie, Abby, and Vanessa had. What Beth and James had. What Rena's favorite books plotted out—true love forever. Del was tired of being so undeserving of her own perfect *The End*.

She rubbed her scar, feeling the burn all over again. *"You're nothing. A pathetic excuse of a girl always greedy for what she can't have. You're worthless."*

Annoyed at letting that witch into her thoughts, she turned on her side in bed and remembered Mike's kisses. How he'd tied her up and pleasured her until she couldn't think. Then she recalled his warm smile, the way he'd held one of her hands while Colin held the other. Keeping her tight. Keeping her…

The next morning and the rest of the day passed swiftly. Her father did his job and did it well, bustling with an energy that had all the guys wondering about how he'd spent his weekend. She ended up getting more done than she'd hoped, so that she managed to find a slot in her schedule for Mike's truck.

That evening, he and Colin popped over and set to work on her house. She fixed them an easy dinner of cold-cut sandwiches and iced tea, followed of course by ice cream. While Colin watched cartoons inside, waiting for his chance to help stain the window boxes, she watched Mike work on the front landing.

He intrigued her. Yet another side to her *model* boyfriend. She grinned. "So. Mr. Sexy."

He whirled with his drill raised. "*What* did you call me?"

"You heard me."

He advanced on her, backing her against the brick wall. "We were never to speak of that again."

"Come on. You won't put a kilt on for me, ever?"

He shut her up with a kiss that had her panting in seconds. "Now shut up. I'm working."

"You're working me, that's for sure." She slid a hand between them, feeling the growing bulge in his jeans.

"Dad. You done yet?" Colin yelled from inside.

"No," Mike yelled back. "Cock-blocker," he whispered to Del, then kissed her again. "Part of the joys of dating me."

She laughed, hugging his neck closer for another kiss. "Yeah, well, I like him. Better than you, actually."

"Hmm. I'd better remind you of what you're missing." He kissed her, then stepped back with a grimace. "Man, you make life uncomfortable."

"Part of the joys of dating *me*."

His smile turned her insides to mush. "How about you sleep over tomorrow night?"

She froze. "Sleep over?" She glanced at the front door, knowing Colin sat so close by. "At your house?"

"In my bed." He cleared his throat, trying to come off as casual but not cutting it. She saw his nerves, and his insecurity charmed her. "You know. You're my girlfriend. It's no biggie."

"So Colin's used to strange women sleeping over?"

Mike scowled. "Fuck no."

"I'm flattered."

He turned back to the window box. "You should be." He screwed it back together, then put it up again and fixed it to the wall. "So? Yes or no?"

"Hmm. Do I get S-E-X if I do?"

"Duh. Why else would I ask you to come over?" He crossed his eyes at her.

She grinned, not calling him on it. She could easily make love to him, then leave. The big guy wanted her to stay. Wow. "I guess. Might as well."

"Good." He went back to working on the other damaged box. "Don't wear panties."

"Mike. Little ears?" She nodded to the house.

He laughed. "Send him out. We're ready to stain. Then I'm taking a look at that bookcase inside. It's pathetic."

She didn't argue. She'd found the thing at a thrift shop, and beggars couldn't be choosey. Entering the house, she found Colin glued to the TV. "You're up. Grab your brush."

"It's gonna look great, Del." He whooped, picked up his paintbrush, and left to help his dad.

Del stared after him, and her heart opened a little more for the big guy and his little boy.

—∿∿—

The next night should have been a no-brainer, but she couldn't wrap her mind around the fact that Colin knew she was sleeping over. With his dad.

"Is it just me? Or does Colin seem inordinately happy about us together?" She sat next to Mike in his bed. Colin had been asleep for a few hours. Good thing the kid went to bed early.

Mike shrugged, his biceps bulging with his hands laced behind his head, his back against the headboard. "He likes you. No accounting for taste."

"Dick."

"Yeah, about that..." Mike nodded at the erection straining his boxer briefs. "I need help, honeybunches."

"You sure do. Mental help."

He grimaced. "Please. After last weekend..."

"Yeah, about that," she said, deliberately repeating him.

He groaned. "Not now. I swear, you do me, I'll more than do you."

"Good point. You're a screamer. I think it would be best if we kept your mouth occupied."

He sat up straight. "Oh?"

She took off her clothes, then locked the door, keeping the lights on. "I want to see this."

"Shit, yeah."

Mike and his potty mouth. How ironic he'd once jumped her case for cursing in front of Colin, when anytime he grew the littlest bit—or *biggest* bit, considering the state of his underwear—excited, he swore up and down.

He pushed down his briefs, showing off his thick shaft. "Suck me and I'll do you. Hel-lo, sixty-nine."

She laughed. "Sweet talker." She joined him on the bed, lying over him in the sixty-nine position he clearly wanted, and aligned her head with his groin. She stared down at his very aroused body. Before she could say something else smart, he dragged her pussy down to his mouth and started licking.

"Damn." Not planning to come before he did, she got to work.

All the moaning and groaning and sweating amounted to some fast, satisfying orgasms for them both. Good thing they'd been muted, because she for sure would have cried out at the mouth and fingers working their magic on her lady parts. *Dear God, he's good.*

"Del." Mike pulled her around to hug her. When he kissed her, she tasted herself on his lips and knew he had to taste himself as well. A lot of guys didn't like that. Mike wasn't most guys. "Fuck, that's sexy."

"Yeah. But you get off light. I had to swallow *a lot*."

He gave her a smug grin. "I'm a big guy. Blame yourself, though. You get me that way."

"Full of it?"

"If by *it*, you mean lust, then yeah." He leered at her, then kissed her again and curled her into his body. "I swear, I have a healthy sex drive. But around you, I always want it."

"Good to know."

"Not with anyone else," he continued, and she frowned, because she hadn't considered he meant that. "With you. Just you."

"So you're not this horny with everyone you know."

"Just you. That smart mouth, those blond dreads—"

"Braids."

"Whatever. You always do some funky thing with your hair, and every day I want to see what it looks like. I like it down though too. Especially when it's over my chest." He played with her hair, running his thick fingers through it. "Or over my thighs like it was earlier."

She blushed. "Stop."

"You turning red? Lemme see." He looked down and grinned. "You're so cute when you're embarrassed, Delilah."

"Jackass."

"Ah, the love words. How I bask in your affection."

She pulled his chest hair, and he flinched. "You're a funny guy."

"I try." He stroked her hair, then her back, and she started falling asleep. "I'm so glad you're here," he whispered.

"Me too," she admitted before dozing off.

———————

The slap on her ass didn't amuse her.

"Wake up."

"Dad. I don't have socks," Colin bellowed from outside the room.

"Yeah, you do. Look in the laundry basket in the laundry room."

"Okay." The pounding of little feet sounded overly loud.

She pulled a pillow over her head.

Another slap on her bare ass.

"Much as I'd like nothing more than to fuck you senseless, you really need to move that fine ass. I don't think Colin's ready for sex ed in first grade."

That got her moving.

She dressed and met the pair at the kitchen table. Colin talked and talked and talked, while Mike grunted occasionally and sipped coffee while he scrambled some eggs. He nodded to the cup sitting next to the coffeepot.

She poured herself some then sat down, uncomfortably aware of the domestic vibe around her. But Mike didn't make it weird, and Colin acted as if she'd always been there, including her in his ramblings.

"Did you like the bed, Del? It's big, isn't it?" he asked.

Mike turned to raise a brow. "Isn't it?"

She choked on her coffee and laughter. "Yeah, it's okay." Then to Colin, she whispered, "But your dad is a bed hog. Next time, I'm moving in with you."

"Okay." He grinned, looking so happy she didn't have the nerve to tell him she was teasing.

"No way. Get your own girl, Colin." Mike set some eggs down in front of Del and a glass of milk for the boy. "She's mine."

"Whatever, Dad." He gave Mike the McCauley trademark sneer, then guzzled his milk. "Ah. Faster than Ubie can drink a Coke."

"Nice." Del nodded. "I like to sip at mine. *Slowly.*"

Behind her, Mike swore and dropped a pan. She grinned.

Mike left her to bundle Colin off to the school bus, and he returned seeming satisfied. He wore his stained jeans, a scruffy T-shirt, and those nasty boots she envied. Well-worn and stinky, they were the perfect blend of comfort and function.

Seeing where her gaze had landed, he looked down at hers. "I like yours too. You got a thing for black, eh, Delilah?"

"I have a thing for what works. Black works." She stood from the table and dragged him by the shirt to her. "You work."

"You better believe it." He kissed her, and those freaky little butterflies still swirled low in her belly. "Damn. How do you keep doing this to me?" He ground into her belly...hard. "It should have worn off by now."

"What's that?"

"Whatever magic is in that pussy," he said bluntly.

"Real nice." She frowned. "You don't see me equating your big dick to how I feel about you."

He froze. "Yeah? How do you feel about me?"

"Well, I don't hate you...anymore."

He grinned. "And?"

"And I like fucking you."

He put her hand between them and closed it over him. "You see it's mutual."

"But I almost, no, I think..." She gave him her best innocent, confused, longing face and saw his expression sober.

"Del, honey? Tell me." So tender and soft. So gentle and caring.

"Yes. I...*like* you. Whew. *That* was tough to say." She sneered. "Dumbass."

"Witch." Yet the humor—and relief—was telling. He wasn't ready to hear what she wasn't ready to say. That she loved the giant jerk and had no idea what to do about it.

"Time to get to work. Let's go." She clapped her hands.

"Fine."

"Oh, and you need to bring your truck to the shop later today. I'll work on it tonight and tomorrow, so have another ride through Friday."

"Okay. Just tell me how much I owe you and I'll—"

"Fuck that. You fixed my window boxes."

He stepped back from her and glared. "That was nothing."

"What about the bookcase and the cabinets? And the trim work you promised? You reneging?"

"Hell no. Fine. Fix my damn truck." He grabbed a travel mug and poured coffee into it, adding sugar and creamer. Then he handed it to her. "I want it to purr. Oh, and the door squeaks. Fix that too."

Feeling better that he'd acquiesced, so she could show him just what she could do with a vehicle, she nodded and took the mug. "I will. So tonight I can't sleep over."

"Fine. But tomorrow night, your ass is here."

"But—"

"No buts, unless we're talking about your ass. And my hand. And some spankings for talking back." He wiggled his brows, their tiny argument gone before it could start.

"Quit distracting me. I have to go. If I'm late, I'll never hear the end of it."

He looked at the microwave clock and groaned. "Oh yeah. My father is a huge pain in the ass. Gotta go." He walked with her to the front door, then gave her a quick kiss. "Oh, and I put a key on your key ring, so you can come and go whenever. Lock up, will you, sweetness?"

With that, he left. She watched him leave with a wave, stunned at how fast they seemed to be moving. Family picnics? Sleepovers? *His key?* She stared down at it, seeing the dirty metal, and seeing the possibility of so much more as well. She gripped it tight, then locked the door behind her.

Chapter 20

MIKE HATED TO ADMIT IT, BUT HIS TRUCK DROVE LIKE a dream. No more clinks and clanks, the brakes were solid, and the door no longer squeaked. Friday night he sat on the couch with Del while Colin and Brian goofed off with Hyde in Colin's bedroom. Colin's turn to host the sleepover, and the little guys were planning something, because he kept hearing his name mentioned in whispers between soft woofs from the dog. That and they gave him odd looks when he checked on them.

"So." Del waited with her arms crossed, her eyes narrowed at him.

"So you did a good job. You happy now?"

"Excuse me?"

She really didn't tolerate his crap. Or his crappy attitude. He'd growled at her earlier after dealing with yet another budget change with the homeowners on his project. Not to mention his father had been a huge distraction during the process, because he agreed with the changes Mike had begged the wife not to make. Sure it extended MCC's work and gave them added income, but Mike thought the tile detracted from the clean look she'd been trying to achieve. Artist and expert James McCauley had disagreed.

So Mike hadn't been in the best mood when he'd nearly stepped in the dog crap Colin hadn't cleaned up outside before slaving over the stove to make dinner.

He'd barely chewed out Colin for it before Del snapped at him to get his head out of his ass and chill the F—not *fuck*, but *F*—out. All said in front of Colin, who'd stared open-mouthed at them.

Like that, Del had stolen his mood, and Mike had laughingly apologized.

"Still waiting, Michael."

He winced. "Okay, sorry. The truck is amazing. You're a goddess. I worship humbly at your feet."

"Better." She sniffed.

They sat watching some stupid mystery, when he wanted to take her into the back and have his wicked way with her. Aside from Lea, he'd never been so into a woman as he was with Del, and he wanted to take advantage of it. This kind of lust and affection couldn't be duplicated.

What it meant that Del gave him the same rush, lack of appetite, and need to please as his wife once had, he didn't want to think about.

After a while of holding hands and watching in silence, Del spoke again. "Your mom left you another message."

Mike had a landline for Colin, and with it, an answering machine. He would have scrapped it, but sometimes he needed to use it to find his cell phone. "Okay."

"Mike, what's up with you and your mom? Sounds like you haven't talked since the picnic. And before you tell me it's none of my business, I just blew you last night, and that's about as intimate as it gets for me, so don't even try telling me to butt out. Spill."

He sighed. "I'm not ducking her calls."

She snorted.

"Not exactly. I was busy when I got home."

"You were playing with the dog."

"He needed me."

"Your mother needs you."

"I thought you didn't like her." *There, answer that.*

"She's okay. I like her."

"Really?"

"I'd like her more if she liked me."

"Yeah, well. That's kind of what we argued about." She wanted to know, he'd tell her. "My mom and I finally had it out about Grace. I'm tired of her setting me up, and she tore into me about grieving for Lea. As if sorrow has a time limit. Like, *Damn, son. It's been ten minutes. Why aren't you married again?*"

Del turned to fully face him, her features unreadable. He *hated* when she pulled that face. "So you told her we aren't getting married. Ever. And she backed off."

"Yes. No."

"Which is it?"

"Why the fuck are you so calm?" he asked in a low voice, annoyed by her lack of reaction and still aware they had small children in the house.

"Why wouldn't I be? You and I said from the start we're about having fun without drama. Hello? No drama."

He frowned. "So you're never getting married? Why not?"

"I consider it a personal choice."

He didn't think she realized that whenever she grew stressed, she rubbed her arm. An obvious tell and one he wanted to know more about. "Okay. You want the details between me and my mother?"

"Yeah."

"Explain the scar." He nodded to her tattoo.

She tensed, and he almost felt bad for prodding her. Almost.

"Del, you want to be open, right? Guess what, baby? Not only did I go down on you, I gave you a key to my house." *My heart.* "So I'm thinking that entitles me to some answers too."

He didn't think she'd answer when she started talking in a soft voice, her gaze darting between him and the hallway. "I was five and my mom had come to visit."

"Visit?"

Del sighed. "This is ugly. You sure you want to hear it?"

"Yes." *I want to know everything about you.* He lowered the volume on the TV and waited.

"Fine. I told you my dad was married to J.T.'s mom, and they were happy. She died of cancer, and it was really sad. My dad totally loved her. Ends of the earth kind of love." *Like you had with Lea* went unsaid.

"I get you."

"I know." She sighed again, but before he could say anything, she continued, "To hear J.T. tell it, Dad was lost. He kind of did his best, taking care of J.T. and the garage, which he'd just started. Then a few years after he lost Bridget, he met Penelope Light, my mom. And yeah, her last name really was Light."

"Suits you," he mused, stroking her hair.

"About the only thing that does when it comes to her. Penny was a shallow, spoiled, self-centered bitch. But she was pretty. And she liked Dad a lot. Until she had him and realized he wasn't going to be rolling in money with the garage. Just because he worked on fancy cars didn't mean he actually owned them.

"She came from a poor family, and she traded on her looks to move up in the world. Trust me when I say my dad was a huge step up."

"Huh." Mike held her hand, rubbing her fingers, which, like the rest of her, had gone tense.

"Anyway, not to bore you with details, but Dad fell for her looks, knocked her up, and before she realized he wasn't a rich fat cat, they married. Needless to say, she didn't like being locked down, and he knew he'd made a mistake as soon as they said 'I do.' So he agreed to stay married and financially support her if she wouldn't abort me."

"Shit."

"He'd pay for her, care for her, but he'd keep custody of me. I'd stay with him and J.T. if she wanted to float around, which she usually did."

"That sucks."

"Yep. I was this little kid, thinking she was an angel or something. I mean, Mike, she was really pretty. I can totally see why Dad fell for her." Del looked so earnest, trying to convince him why her dad had made his decision.

"If she looked anything like you, I can see why you'd think she's beautiful." He raised her hand to his lips and kissed it, hating the shine in her eyes. She didn't cry. She wouldn't let herself cry, and he saw himself in her restraint. "You don't have to tell me anymore if you—"

"It's fine. I'm over her."

Yeah, like I'm over Lea. "So that scar…?"

"Right. So she's beautiful, I'm in love with her. Whenever she comes to visit, I'm gaga to see her. And she visits when she needs love. Penny is depressed, having a rough day, she comes back to a stupid kid who thinks she can do no wrong. Insta-love."

"Kinda like Hyde," Mike said to shock her out of her mood.

She blinked. "Did you just compare me to a dog?"

"But you're much better-looking." He nodded, and she slapped his chest. But at least the sadness in her eyes faded.

"You really are an ass, aren't you?"

"Hey, I'm trying to reform. I'm with you, aren't I?" He gave her a quick kiss, and she squeezed his hand.

"Lucky, is what you are," she grumbled. "Anyway, to make a long, pathetic story short, she came back for some love and attention. I thought. I raced to hug her, expecting the needy hug back she normally gave me. But I was covered in grease and dirt, playing with Dad's grease gun. I wasn't kidding about that. He wasn't the neat guy you are."

"None of them are."

She snorted. "Yeah, well, Penny was less than pleased. She'd been in the process of doing up her hair and wearing some designer gown from some dude she'd been sleeping with at the time. See, Penny slept with the highest bidder. It fed her drug and dress habit. In her defense, I was dirty and I think she was half high. She shoved me hard away from her, and I fell onto her curling iron. Problem was, she held me down on top of it for a while, not realizing I was burning."

She held up her arm. "It fucking hurt. I was five, and I still remember the sting. J.T. rushed in and helped me get away from her, because she started raving and ranting, throwing shit, basically having a meltdown because of her ruined dress."

"Sorry, but what a bitch."

She gave him a sad smile. "Yeah. J.T. called Aunt Caroline to contain Penny, then got Dad home. Dad kicked Penny's ass out and rushed me to the emergency room, because he was afraid of infection. I think it was a second-degree burn." She rubbed her arm. "We don't talk about it. Dad still blames himself for letting me be with her. He knew she was losing it, but it kept her happy and she'd been nice to me until that point."

"Damn. That's harsh."

"Yeah. To be honest, I kind of forgot about it as I got older, but when I was in high school, I found some letters of hers she'd written to Dad. They were…ugly. Then J.T. filled in the blanks for me. Dad used to lie about her, said she was just sick and had to go away, and that she died in a car crash on the way to the hospital. Truth was, she was higher than a kite and blowing some rich guy when they crashed into a semi going eighty miles an hour down I-5."

Mike sat with her, not sure what to say.

"Ugly, I told you."

She put her arm down, but he picked it up to study the scar. "You know, J.T. did some nice work covering it up. When did you get this?"

"My bitchin' ass?" she said with a smirk, and he knew she'd be okay. "When I was sixteen. Dad was livid, but what could he say? It covered a mark none of us wanted to see."

"I like it. The dragon. But the scar… I won't lie. I like

my women pretty and perfect. No scars, tats, piercings, or imperfections. I'm making *huge* allowances for you."

She pinched his arm and leaned in to kiss him. "Thanks."

"For making allowances?"

She pinched him again.

"*Ow.*"

"For listening." She soothed the pinch by rubbing her fingers over him, and he squirmed, because he didn't want to be getting aroused when he should be providing comfort. Her mother had been a total scumbag. Anyone who would hurt a child deserved death, in Mike's opinion. A few months ago, when he'd learned what Brody had suffered as a kid, he'd wanted to find Brody's dad and rearrange the guy's body parts. Flynn had talked him down though. A good thing, because Mike really needed to stay out of jail for Colin's sake.

"So your mom…?" Del prodded.

He groaned. "You did that on purpose. Sharing all that crap so I have no choice but to tell you what Mom said."

"Yeah. I'm all about emotional scars and sharing."

He frowned. "I'm sensing that."

"Mike."

"Okay, okay." He didn't want to delve into Lea and his mother and his confusing feelings about Del, but she'd asked. "I told Mom to quit throwing Grace at me. Told her she's not my type." This would be uncomfortable. "But Mom said she kind of is. I've always dated smaller chicks. Quiet, kind of shy, a lot like Lea."

Del nodded. "And?"

"So Mom wanted to know why not Grace? She said maybe I'm into you because you're different."

"Maybe you are."

He frowned. "Can you *not* agree with my mother please?"

"Oh, sorry."

He tensed, but she kept her hand on his, squeezing for support. "Then my mom started crying. I hate tears."

"Oh."

"Yeah. She said she lost a daughter as much as I lost a wife. And that it hasn't been easy watching me…watching me bury myself. I mean, hell, I lost the woman I loved. I think three years before dating again is acceptable."

"Wow. No sex for three years. Didn't think you had it in you."

"Well, I was kind of numb for a long time. Numb and tired. Colin was a little pain in the ass for years. Never slept through the night, and when he was teething, forget it." He smiled, recalling his son as a baby. "But so cute."

"Braggart." She smiled with him. "So finish."

"Anyway, Mom cried, made me feel awful, like I was a loser because I wanted to be with you and not Grace. I set her straight." He abridged most of the conversation. "Told her we were great friends, dating, and that was that."

"In summation, you told her we're fuck-buddies and she needs to deal."

I love Del, he'd said. Oh man. He did. He totally loved her. "No, not 'fuck-buddies,'" he corrected in a lowered voice. "You know I hate when you use that word."

"Because we're girlfriend and boyfriend."

"Yeah."

She sighed. "Okay, I guess. You can't blame your mom for wanting something good for you. Six years is a long time to mourn. Trust me, I know. I've watched my dad do it for even longer."

"It's hard." He felt her fingers stroking his. "Especially because the pain keeps it fresh."

"What fresh?"

"The feeling." He wanted her to understand. "After a while, memories blur. It's hard to see Lea's face unless I look at her picture. When I see her, I feel her. The way I used to feel her. She died giving birth to Colin. She never got to see him grow. To watch him hold snakes and sleep over with Brian." He gripped her fingers. "I feel so guilty I have that and she doesn't. I couldn't do anything to help her at the end, and it still hurts."

"It would with you," she murmured. "You're a protector. And you loved her."

My soul mate. Yet as he saw Del's sympathy, shared in their truths and pain, he wondered… Did McCauleys only truly love once? Because what he felt for Del far surpassed simple affection or mind-blowing lust.

"You know, it's okay to put her picture where you can see it all the time. Maybe not in the bedroom though, cause that would be creepy, me kissing you while that picture is watching."

He blinked at her. "Huh?"

"Reminding yourself that you loved her isn't wrong, Mike. It's only my opinion, but I've found that avoiding pain doesn't make it go away. Not dealing with it only makes it worse." She paused. "Did you ever learn to deal with it? Therapy or anything?"

"Hell no." He'd thrown out more books on therapy than he could count. His mother, aunts, uncles, brothers, hell, even his father had tried to get him to see someone. As if Mike needed to cry in front of a stranger to make his broken world all better. "I just needed time. What about you?"

"Nah. We didn't have money for a shrink. My excuse is more valid. We were poor."

He shook his head. "So time to heal isn't a good excuse?"

"It's been six years and you're still messed up. What do you think?" Trust Del not to sugarcoat anything.

Yet he loved—liked—her so much for that brutal honesty. He glanced at the TV again, wanting to stop feeling so confused about her. "You know, all this caring and sharing is nice, but if you're done playing a shrink, can we find out who murdered the rich guy?"

She frowned at him. "Hey, you're the one who wanted to know the secret behind my heinous scarring."

"I never called it heinous. Ugly and off-putting sure. But heinous?"

She tried not to smile.

"Ha! I see that grin. Now shut up and watch with me. But after you check on the boys. I did it last time, and trust me, silence is not golden. Usually means they're up to no good."

"Fine." She stood and stopped by the hallway.

"What?"

"You aren't going to be all weepy since we just talked about Lea, are you? I find grown men crying to be kind of pathetic."

"Back at ya, Scarface."

"It's my arm, buttwipe." She flipped him the bird and patted her forearm bearing the scar, then went searching for trouble.

By her shocked, "What the hell did you do to Hyde?" in addition to the barking and screaming of small boys, she'd found some.

Mike didn't know how the hell she'd done it, but Del had convinced him to hang a picture of Lea in the hallway, at Colin's height. Delighted to see his mother anytime he wanted, and no longer limited to his nightstand to see her picture, Colin danced around and proclaimed Del his favorite person. Not Mike, but Del, as if the kid knew she'd had influence.

They decided to go to Green Lake for a kid festival on Sunday, and Del drove them in her GTO, now not so cool with the booster seat in the back, which he'd helpfully pointed out.

"Shut it. The car is cool with or without a booster seat."

"*With*, Del. I'm cool," Colin added.

"Yes, you are. Because you're not a backseat driver, like your dad."

"He's in the front seat," Colin corrected with confusion.

"And not driving," she said with relish. "You know, Mike, now I get your thing with keeping your house clean. Like always having to drive or have the clicker. It's a control thing."

"What? Because I like to drive and appreciate a clean house?" He leaned closer to her, wishing she had a bench and not bucket seats. "I'm not always controlling." He grinned at her blush, recalling exactly how she'd ridden him last night. "Am I?"

"We're here." She pulled into a lucky available spot in one of the park's lots and they got out.

"Okay, Colin. Stay close. It's crowded here."

They spent the afternoon having fun. Colin played on the playground for a while, had his face painted to match Del's, with matching paw prints, and ate cotton candy like it was going out of style. He shared it with Del, his partner in crime.

They looked so damn cute together, Del and Colin, sharing blue death on a stick, walking together hand in hand. He took a few photos on his phone when Del wasn't watching. Then he carried Colin on his shoulders while he and Del walked around the park, taking in the gorgeous spring day and the ducks quacking for bread crumbs.

The day came to a close as vendors shut down and the evening brought a light indigo blanket of color, interspersed with reds and purples, not a cloud in sight.

"Look, Dad, like cotton candy in the sky. I wish it was real. Then I'd eat it all."

"You and Del." Mike squeezed her sticky hand in his. He lifted her fingers to his mouth and sucked, then grinned when he heard her breathing speed up. "Hmm. Sugar."

She laughed.

"Dad? A few more swings, please?"

Most of the cars had cleared out, and Mike had to use the facilities. So he left the boy with Del while he took care of things.

He returned to the playground, looking for Del and

Colin. He didn't see them, until he looked at the parking lot, where Colin was bent over something he couldn't make out.

Del yelled at him, "Colin, come back here. There are too many cars around."

The main lot had enough movement to be troublesome. Not everyone had gone home yet, and the darkening shadows made visibility poorer.

"Colin, move," he yelled as he drew closer. And then it happened.

A car moving too fast too far away zoomed toward Colin.

Mike started running, but he could only watch in slow motion as Del shoved Colin away and took a hit. Hard. The car screeched to a stop, but not before it knocked her back. She fell and hit her head. And didn't move.

Colin lay crying near a tiny puppy, mewing for its mother.

People swarmed as Mike reached the accident. He gathered Colin in his arms, wanting to get to Del but unable to ignore his son.

"Daddy," he sobbed. "Daddy, I'm scared."

"Shh, it's all right. I'm here." Colin seemed okay except for a bent wrist that was either broken or sprained. He had to get to Del. He lifted Colin and quickly moved to her, then set his boy down.

Someone had called an ambulance, he heard that. But he couldn't take his gaze from her. She lay unmoving, blood on her temple. The rest of her looked at peace, as if sleeping. But…

"Del?" He moved closer, trying to see if she'd broken anything. "Del, honey, wake up." She didn't move.

"I'm a nurse, let me through." Someone joined him on the ground by her and took Del's limp wrist her hand. "She's a little thready. What happened?"

"Car hit her." Mike glanced from Del to Colin, completely freaked. "She saved my son."

"She did," another guy said. "Pushed the kid away when the car would have hit him."

"I didn't see her." A teenage girl stood by them, shaky and crying. "I'm so sorry. I didn't see her *or* him. I was going home and I didn't see them."

While someone comforted the girl, Mike knelt by Del's side with Colin, praying she'd wake up. Out of his mind with worry that she wouldn't.

Oh God. What if she didn't?

Chapter 21

"I TOLD YOU LIKE SIXTEEN BILLION TIMES. I'M FINE."
Del winced as her head throbbed.

"Yeah, I can see that." Her father and brother stood by the hospital bed, neither listening in the slightest. "You have a concussion. You're staying until they release you."

She groaned. For four hours she'd been dealing with this crap. She had work to do. And tomorrow would suck without her at the garage. Mondays were the worst. "But that's like two days."

"Or three," J.T. corrected, "if the nurse thinks you need it. So relax and kick back. And no funny stuff."

"What?"

"With Romeo. Mike's wearing a hole in the hallway. Been pacing like crazy."

"At least Colin's okay." The boy had a sprained wrist from the way he'd landed, but better that than a blasted headache that wouldn't go away. "From what I gather, he and I scared that teenager more than she scared us."

"Poor kid." Liam shook his head. "Oh, and that scrawny mutt Colin nearly died over? Mike grabbed it. Colin wouldn't stop crying, so he took it with him when they followed the ambulance over." Liam paused. "He's really shaken up."

"He should be. That shit hurt." She touched the bandage on her forehead and winced. "Well? Get him."

"They said they didn't want too many people in here because you—" At her glare, J.T. sighed. "But I'll go get him for you right now."

J.T. left to fetch Mike, and Liam watched her with concern. "You sure you're okay?"

"I'll be better once this headache goes away. What did they give me?"

"I heard Vicodin. Lucky lucky."

She grinned, tried to sit up, and moved too fast. Not good.

"Guess you pulled a few muscles getting banged up, too. But nothing broken. Just contusions," her father clarified.

She'd been awake since the ambulance ride, fully conscious of everything. No memory loss, and her CT scans looked fine. Yet she had to stay in this death trap for another two days.

The door opened, and a withdrawn Mike entered. Liam waved J.T. out and followed him, leaving her with Mike, alone.

"You okay? I heard everything's good except for some bruising and that hard head of yours." He tried to smile, but he looked grim.

"Relax, Mike. It's just a headache."

He walked toward her, reached out to touch her, then pulled back. "You look like shit."

"Gee, thanks."

He blew out a breath and rubbed his eyes. "You went down so hard, so fast. I was too far away."

She'd had a split second to make the decision. She hadn't needed even that. Colin had been in danger. She'd done her utmost to save him, no question.

Her time spent reflecting after the accident had made an impression. It could have gone so very wrong. A life she wanted slipping away in a heartbeat. A life with Mike and Colin.

She took a deep breath and let it out slowly. "Colin heard something, went to investigate, and found a lost puppy. You know your kid. He had to console it even though I told him to wait for me. The little animal lover."

Mike still wasn't smiling. Oh boy.

"When's the last time you were in a hospital?" she asked.

"Guess."

Lea. "Ah. Right."

"Damn it," he swore. "You could have been killed!"

"I know. I was there."

"You saved Colin. I can never thank you enough for that."

She frowned. He sounded…distant.

"Mike, relax. It's over."

"You shouldn't have done that."

"Saved Colin?" He was acting really weird. Maybe he'd been hit in the head too. "What are you talking about?"

"I mean, he's not even yours. Imagine dying for somebody else's kid." He paced. "It was a fun weekend. Just the three of us having a great time. And then that stupid dog…"

"It wasn't the dog." *Somebody else's kid.* She had to remember that.

Once again, reality came crashing down and she landed…hard. Colin didn't belong to her. And it seemed that perhaps Mike didn't either.

"Mike, look at me." She waited for him to make eye contact. The pain in his gaze hurt her. "I could have died."

He grew still. "I know." A whisper, and so much anguish in those two words.

"But I didn't," she added gently. "It makes you think, you know? Getting that close to the edge. Makes you realize what's important." After what had happened, she knew she needed to take a big step. Life was too short not to take a risk, right? She'd been burned so many times before, this had to work, if just by the probability of her finally getting lucky. "I think *we're* important. I love you, Mike."

He looked shell-shocked. "I... I..."

"Do you love me?"

He stared at her, seeming so lost, so hopeless. "Del, this isn't the time. You're hurt, Colin's hurt. I should have been there."

A *no* then. Why was she always surprised? "God, this guilt complex is giving me a headache." That and the concussion. "Lea's dead. I'm alive. So are you." She'd try just once more. Let him tell her no to her face. Confronting problems head-on—the Webster way. "What's it going to be, Mike?"

"What's it going to be? What's *what* going to be?" He threw up his hands, playing stupid. "Are the pain meds messing with your head? You could have *died*, Delilah. They won't let you go home in case you have a brain bleed the CT scan missed! It's not like you bumped your knee. You almost fucking *died*."

Did he think repeating it would give her dire situation any greater impact? Angry at him, and at herself for pushing too hard when neither of them were ready for the truth, she answered with bite, "Yeah, I did. But you've been dead for the past six years, just pretending to live in some giant pity party because Lea's gone. Buddy, open your eyes. You have a shot at happiness right now."

"Of course, that happiness is *you*," he scoffed. "Del, this is stupid. We can talk about this when you're better."

The rejection hit her where the pain meds didn't. So dismissive. So *insulting* for her to think she could ever fill a part of him his precious Lea had once satisfied. "You know what? You're right. This is stupid. Go home to Colin, Mike."

He frowned and took a step forward. "You okay? You don't look good."

"I know. I look like shit. Just go. I'm tired and my head hurts." She closed her eyes, then slit one open a fraction to see him dithering, unsure of whether to stay or go. He put his hand on the bed, so close to her foot but not touching. Then he pulled back and left without a word.

She didn't want to cry, because God knew she'd had messier breakups than this. But after how amazing her life had become, she had a hard time knowing she'd barely scratched the surface with Mike, and it was over. But better now than months down the line, when he realized he could do so much better than a mechanic without a tenth of the class of a McCauley.

Hell, she should have told him from the get-go they could be fuck-buddies or no buddies—with no room for in-between.

Tired and aching and wounded deep, where the scar

had never healed, she let the tears fall and surrendered to sleep.

Mike spent the next few days aware of Del's progress but far away from her side. She didn't want to see him, her cousin had insisted, though Del had given Colin a brief visit as soon as she'd left the hospital. She'd exclaimed over his "war wound" and showed him her bandaged head. To Mike, she remained cool, and he couldn't blame her. She probably needed as much space as he did. She could have been killed while saving *his* son, something *he* should have done.

He worked like a dog to exorcise his demons that refused to go away. The way he normally handled the troublesome times in his life. Colin, taken care of by his doting grandma and new aunts, thrived with his puppy. The raggedy thing pulled as much sympathy as Colin's wrist brace. And Colin was playing up the pity card for as much as he could. He'd done Brody proud.

Mike couldn't feel much of anything but relief that Del and Colin remained alive and well. It was as if his mind had gone into shutdown mode to cope, the way it had with Lea. He could function, working hard, feigning that he felt fine to his family and Colin, caring for the boy when Colin came home for the night. He'd let Colin sleep with him the past few evenings, but he'd sent the boy to Grandma's for the weekend, needing some time to recover.

He left a message for his mother to call his cell if she needed him and went out. Time to get a workout in, because the job hadn't given him the release he needed.

He was strung out. He couldn't eat. Couldn't sleep. He missed Del so much he ached, but he couldn't get over her near brush with death. Couldn't see himself going down that road again, knowing he'd never recover from losing her.

A catch-22, and he had no way to deal. So he tossed his gym bag in the truck and drove to therapy.

An hour and a half later, he and one other guy remained in the gym. Earlier, Mike had gone a few rounds on the mat with a new mixed martial arts guy, one who had a chip on his shoulder.

Not such a big chip now that Mike had knocked it off. He'd planted the guy's face into the mat so many times he'd earned a standing ovation from the regulars.

The guy jumping rope finally stopped, took the tape off his hands, grabbed his bag, and left.

Finally. Mike had the place to himself.

Almost. Sal entered.

"Yo, Mike. I'm going into the back office to work. You good out front?" Sal, the owner, usually knocked off early on Friday. Eight o'clock and he started in on bookkeeping.

"No problem. I'm just going to hit the bag for a while."

"Whatever you need. Work it off, man. You got a rage burning."

Mike grunted and ripped off his sweat-soaked shirt. Then he wrapped his hands and put on some gloves, needing the protection. Now alone, he gave in to the need to destroy and whaled on the heavy bag in the corner. For every hit, he wiped away the image of Del darting in front of that car. Of Colin crying out as he scraped himself on the pavement, busting his wrist. Of Del lying unconscious, bloodied, unmoving. Of Lea, reaching out a hand to him before closing her eyes and just fading away…

"Heard I'd find you here."

He glanced up to see Liam Webster standing by the raised boxing ring. Behind him in the shadows stood someone else. J.T. most likely. Terrific. Mike continued to punch, frustrated, angry, and…lost. "Yeah?"

Lights dimmed near the entrance, a sure sign Sal planned to close soon. But Mike could see well enough. Sal left the lights on near his end of the gym. Good man. He pounded a few more times, then Liam took the bag and held it steady.

"Keep going. I'll wait."

"For what?" Mike abused the bag, hitting hard enough he should have punched his rage away, yet it lingered. He kept his balance, grounded his feet, and didn't pause between punches like a newbie. Four shots, a pause, four more shots. Until finally, he needed a break.

Breathing hard, he took the water bottle Liam handed him. "Thanks."

"What's going on with you, Mike?"

"What do you mean?" Time to start hitting again.

"You dumped my daughter."

Mike blinked. "What the fuck are you talking about? I'm giving her space."

"No. You broke it off with her in the hospital."

"That's horse shit. I didn't break off anything. She wants me to give her space, I'm giving it to her. Ask Rena if you don't believe me. I've tried talking to her all week, but Rena's the one returning my messages." Mike tossed the water and started hitting again. Liam, brave man that that he was, stood close.

"She saved your son."

"You think I don't know that?" Mike knocked the bag so hard Liam jolted back. Stepping back in disgust, not as tired or as sore as he wanted to be, Mike rid himself of the gloves. "Why are you here?"

"Just tell me something. Do you love my daughter at all?"

Mike wanted to tell the man to shove off. It was none of his business how Mike felt.

"Because if you've been using her, just getting off while she nearly died trying to—"

"*Fuck off.* It's not your concern."

"It is."

"I love her, okay?" he yelled, needing to say it. "I was too late. She shoved Colin to safety, and the car knocked her hard. She landed on the pavement, smacking her head, just lying there. Bleeding." He paced, not caring, not knowing half of what he said, reliving that awful memory. "She didn't move. She was dead for all I knew."

"Mike, she's okay—"

"But she could have died! Again. And I couldn't do anything. Don't you fucking get it?"

"I do." Liam's quiet words didn't help.

"I love her so much it eats me inside. I didn't want to. Didn't want this again." He stopped, breathing hard.

Liam put a hand on his shoulder, and he shrugged it off. He heard J.T. shuffling behind him.

"Don't touch me."

"Mike, calm down—"

"You calm down! They all want me to get over it. To stop and deal. Well, I've been fucking dealing! Then your hard-ass daughter busts her way into my life, and I can't stop dealing, because I'm laughing and loving and she's fucking lying there, bleeding…" Mike wanted to stop, to make the pain go away. "She was bleeding out. All that blood everywhere."

He saw Del, then Lea. Lea's slack face, blood soaking the sheets, the table, while he stood by helplessly.

"They handed him to me while they tried to save her." Holding Colin while Del lay there, not moving. His son crying. A baby's wail, a little boy's tears. He looked at Liam, shocked to see the man's image blurring. "She just wouldn't wake up," he cracked on the word, breaking down. He sank to his knees, sobbing, unable to differentiate his losses. "I can't. Not again. I can't do this."

"Oh son, it's okay." Then his father was there, hugging him, holding him. "It's all right. It's okay, Mike. Let it out."

"Y-you don't… She was so quiet. So beautiful." He couldn't stop crying and found it hard to breathe. "She didn't move, and all the blood just kept coming. On her head…"

"They are, aren't they? So beautiful, even in that final stillness," Liam said quietly, and something about his tone got through to Mike. He looked up to see Liam standing there, a strong man with tears in his eyes. "My Bridget was like that. So beautiful, even through the cancer that ravaged her face, her body. But she just lit up whatever room she was in. That last day in bed, not breathing, not moving, she was fucking gorgeous. And gone."

"They don't get it," Mike whispered, wishing he could make everyone understand how difficult moving on could be.

"No, they don't. You're a strong man, Mike. A man who's known loss and moved on. But like me, you've never *really* moved on, have you?" Liam crouched to look Mike in the eye. "You buried your pain so deep it's never gotten a chance to heal. You pretend, so everyone will leave you the fuck alone."

His father hugged him tighter, suffocating him. Mike fought, but his dad wouldn't let go, and that somehow made everything worse.

"But then you find someone who makes your heart race and the world seem brighter," Liam murmured. "You don't want to fall for her, because you know how painful it can be if they leave you too soon. Do you die with her, or do you go on living?" Liam didn't bother hiding his own pain. "I had six short years with my Bridget, and I wouldn't trade any of them. But you know what? I wish to hell I could go back and undo the last thirty years of my life, because I've been a scared shit not letting myself deal.

"I fell into a nightmare with Del's mom. Only good thing that came of it was that precious girl. And she deserves the best life can give her."

Liam jerked Mike's chin up, holding tight to his jaw. "That girl loves you. And she's earned one of those happy endings her cousin's always reading about. Life sucks, son, especially when you're dealt the hand we've been. But you've got to take a chance, or you might as well have bled out with 'em."

He let Mike go. "I'm sorry for all you've lost, much as

I'm sorry for me. But I'm tired of living alone, of holding on to the grief. It'll only drag you down. If you love my daughter the way I think you do, you won't want that for her." Liam brushed his tears away, then winked. "Sac up, boy. Don't let her go too long, because my girl can rebound faster than you can say *boo*. And she's not known for being the wisest about a broken heart. She got into more trouble in high school than you ever want to know." Liam stared at him. "It's up to you, Mike. But whatever you decide to do, don't take her down with you." He walked away.

Mike's voice was hoarse when he answered to Liam's back, "I won't."

He tried to stand but couldn't with his father wrapped around him like a vine. Realization dawned. "Shit. You heard all that."

"Every fucking word. Lea's dead, Mike. Del almost joined her. How do you feel about that?" When he remained silent, his father shook him. "Answer me, you little shit. You never would have seen her again. Just like Lea. Do you really want Del gone?"

Mike wanted to tell his father to go to hell.

Then he imagined Del dead, as lost to him as Lea. And he cried. He cried as he'd never been able to before. He lost sense of everything but the massive grief for his wife, for the son who would never know her, for Del, and most of all for himself. *His* loss. *His* pain.

He unearthed it and let the festering rot go.

When he could reason again, he saw darkness all around him.

"D-dad?"

His father let him go and stood. "Sal told me to let him know when we were done. No problem."

Mike groaned. So Sal had seen him sobbing like a little girl. Terrific. He recalled what his father had said to him. "I'm not a little shit."

"More like a big one."

Mike glanced up at the roughness in his father's voice, shocked to see James McCauley's eyes as red as his must have been. "Dad?"

"I'm so sorry, Mike. We all knew it had been hard for you, but you bucked up so quickly. Then you didn't want to talk about her anymore. I guess we all wanted you to be better so much that we kind of didn't let you feel for her."

Mike sighed, feeling stupid, yet incredibly lighter as well. "It was my fault. No one else's."

"No. You needed to grieve. Your mother and I should have forced you to see someone." At his grimace, his father sympathized. "I know. It sucks. Don't tell your mother this, but it helps a lot. That couples therapist has made your mother see I'm not such an asshole either."

"Real magic, eh?" His throat felt scratchy.

"Come on. Let's get you home. I think you about beat that bag enough, don't you?"

Mike glanced around. "You were here the whole time?" So it had been his dad and not J.T. with Liam.

"Yeah. Liam was worried about Del and about you. Since your mother and I were worried as well, we decided I should check on you."

"Don't tell Mom about this."

"Oh hell no. Trust me. She finds out I punked a few tears, I'll never hear the end of it." His father coughed to clear his throat. "But, ah, I'm glad you let go about Lea. It's been a long time coming, son."

"I guess."

His father helped him to his feet. "So."

"What?" Mike walked toward the locker room, his dad trailing behind him. He grabbed his things, yelled a good-bye to Sal, then left through the front door. "Dad?"

"So…Del. You said you're in love with her. The real deal."

"I am."

"Well, correct me if I'm wrong. But didn't Liam just say Del and you broke up?"

Mike frowned. "He did, didn't he? What's that all about?"

"Sounds to me like you're not the only one having problems. Think you should talk to Del, maybe?"

"Don't act meek. It doesn't become you." He sounded like he'd just chewed gravel, and his eyes burned from so many tears. Walking felt like he moved through sand, taking forever.

"So I should say what I think? Fine. You haven't been eating. I think you've lost weight. You had a huge drama tonight, and you need to sleep it off. See the girl soon, make things right, and try to do better than your bumbling brothers did with their women. I mean, of the four of you, you're the one who takes after me most. Try not to fuck it up."

"Why is that always your soundest piece of advice?"

They got into the car, with his father driving him home since Liam had driven James to the gym. On the way, his father asked, "Do you have a plan?"

"Beyond going to bed and sleeping off a crying jag? No."

"Well, when you're looking better and have eaten

something, figure it out before you see her. And remember, she's more fragile than she looks. Be easy on the girl. She has feelings, you know."

"Yeah, just like you," Mike sneered.

"Get off it, Nancy. You cried a river," his father teased back. "You do realize Cam would be royally pissed to know he missed so much emotional sharing."

Mike leaned his head back against the seat and closed his eyes. "So we'll never ever tell him."

"You got that right. What goes on at the gym stays at the gym."

"Amen."

They drove for a while. His father broke the silence. "You know, this truck is driving a lot better than I remember. You have some work done?"

Mike sighed. *By the best mechanic in the world. Now I just need to get her to work on me.*

Chapter 22

SUNDAY MORNING, DEL SAT ON HER BED AND WINCED as her cousin opened the shades and tiptoed around the room. "What the hell are you doing?"

Rena shrieked. "Oh man. You nearly gave me a heart attack!"

"You're the one skulking around my room."

Rena looked around her and grimaced. "It's like you built shrines to *Popular Mechanic* and Marvel. What is going on in here?" She tried stepping around the stacks Del had carefully placed around the room.

"I'm cleaning. Since my father all but booted me out of the garage this past week, I had to do something or go stark raving insane. I'm cleaning out five years' worth of magazines."

"Where were they before now?" Rena gaped, mystified.

"Under my bed."

"In horizontal stacks, I'm sure."

"Don't judge, Ms. Romance."

"Hey. Books make you smart. Magazines... Maybe *Omni* or *The New Yorker*. But She-Hulk?"

"That attitude will not get you any classic copies of my comics."

Rena wiped her forehead. "Whew. Thank goodness. I was worried I'd have to pretend to accept them, then hoof it down to the recycle center."

"And you wonder why nobody likes you."

Rena laughed and opened more blinds.

"The light. It burns." It actually did exacerbate her headache.

"Easy, Golem. I'm just trying to bring some light into your life…" Pause, and here it came, "…since you've refused to see Mike, that golden god of sexiness, *again*." Rena sat next to her on the bed and nearly knocked over a new stack.

"Careful."

"To hell with the magazines. Why are you not taking Mike's calls? Because his son nearly killed you?"

"*Rena*. What are you talking about?"

"Colin. I'm thinking you blame Mike because you had to save Colin's life. Right?"

"First of all, I don't think Colin would have died. The girl stomped on the brakes pretty quick. Second, it had nothing to do with Mike. I was watching the kid when Mike needed a bathroom stop. It was really my fault he was in danger." She still felt terrible about that, even though Colin had darted into the lot despite being told not to. "Anyway, Mike and I broke up. Your blame game is stupid."

"So are you if you think you two are over. He stopped calling only because I told him you didn't want to talk to him. He loves you."

"Actually, he doesn't. I flat out told him I loved him and he said nothing."

Rena's eyes widened. "You did not."

"I did. Right there in the hospital, hooked up to tubes and in that nasty hospital gown. I told him I loved him. He told me we'd talk about it later."

"And?"

"And what? He doesn't love me. We're through. He also mentioned that I don't make him happy."

Rena gasped. "He said that?"

"Not in so many words, but I know what he meant. He doesn't love me." *None of them do, not the ones who matter.* At the pathetic—though true—thought, she realized her pity party had no place in the World of Del Webster. She'd finished that need-to-please phase by doing every swinging dick in high school. Threesomes, girls, boys, whatever and whenever to get people to like her. The drugs and shoplifting had been the icing on the cake, and had shown her that no matter how hard she worked or what she did to please others, they'd never give her what she wanted. Del had to love herself. And she did. She just wished others would as well.

She didn't count her dad or J.T. or Rena, who'd inherited her. They *had* to deal with her. Only those with a choice turned their backs, consistently.

Colin didn't. Her stupid conscience forced her to be honest with herself. So she ignored it. "I thought you had a date today."

"With a client, but I did him." Rena leaned closer and gave a mock shiver. "Oh baby, I did him *so good.*" She chuckled and pretended her fingers were scissors. "A nice surfer cut. Dude looks hot on the arm of his biker boyfriend. The pair went over to J.T.'s for matching love tattoos when I finished with him."

"Fuck true love," she muttered.

"Oh boy. It's gonna be a long day at the Webster household."

⁓

A long night, and a long couple of days after. Her father refused to let her leave the office except to take a piss. The guys at the shop treated her like spun glass. Even when she glared and roared about deadlines and cleanliness in the shop, they yessed her to death, not giving her the fight she wanted. Mike, that huge asshole, had taken their breakup to heart. Rena was so full of it. The guy hadn't called. Period.

The only bright spots in her convalescence were the cute get-well cards from Colin and Brian, and the visits from the girls—Abby, Maddie, and Vanessa. They cheered her up, talked about their men and the move-ins getting ready to take place, and in general made fun of Brody's nervousness about living with Abby, which Abby found delightful.

"He's scared of me." She'd grinned over a margarita last night while Del had been forced to drink lemonade because of her painkillers. Her headaches had mostly gone away, but the bruises and occasional neck pain still hit.

"That's because he's in love," Maddie said.

Abby smiled. "Yep. That big lout knows he has it good. He's afraid I'll bolt. Me. Plain old, ten pounds overweight—"

"I thought it was fifteen?" Vanessa frowned.

"—Abby Dunn," Abby finished through gritted teeth. "So you see, Del? Miracles do happen." Then she gave Del a sly grin and a thumbs-up. "Good for you for making Mike work for you. You're worth it."

Yet as Del sat staring at the clock, wishing she could be sliding under the shiny red Corvette in the bay, she felt anything but worthy. When Dale popped in the doorway, she nearly bit his head off.

"What?" she snapped.

"Uh, the guys say, um… They want you to…"

"Just spit it out." Figured they'd send in the weak one, the youngest, so she wouldn't send him back out minus his ass.

He said in a rush, "The hostile work environment is killing production."

"They want *hostile*? I'll give them hostile." She went into the garage and chewed some major ass. The slackers gave her a lot of glares, scowls, and attitude, but they turned-to on the vehicles. She slammed back into her office and went through accounting, calling in the guys when she had questions on some of the orders. In the garage she heard a lot of clanging and swearing and, though she couldn't be certain, she suspected several unflattering comments about her leadership style.

An hour and a half later, Dale knocked on the door again.

"What?" she barked, buried nose-deep in invoices.

"Um, Del, they, uh…"

"Spit it out."

"They want you to leave. They say your bad attitude is killing morale."

"Foley," she yelled.

She heard nothing from the bay.

"Fuck it. *Fine.* I'm going to Ray's. You all can kiss my ass. And be prepared to work even harder tomorrow," she shouted.

Not even a groan. She more than needed to leave. It neared five anyway. She'd definitely overstayed another desk day's welcome.

———m———

J.T. frowned at his cell. He was in the middle of a sit-down with a new client, and they needed to talk about design detail, the lowdown on the hows and procedure of the tat, and proper hygiene to prevent infection.

He knew the ringtone, though, so he excused himself from his client and took the call in the other room. "Hello?"

"Hey, man, it's Foley. Look, your demon of a sister just took off for Ray's. Call the big guy, get his ass over there, and fix this. Or we're all quitting."

J.T. swore. "Shit. Okay, okay. Calm down, drama queen."

He heard mumbling before Foley came back on. "Oh, and twenty says they don't get back together until next week. Sam and Lou bet on two weeks. But my money's on Mike. By the middle of next week, latest."

"How do you even know he wants to get back with her?" Considering what a bitch his sister had been lately, even Satan's mistress had to be looking good in comparison.

"Liam talks. We're all family here. Besides, she was really happy with the dude. Just get him back so she's off her period twenty-four seven."

"If she heard you say that, she'd skin you alive."

"You mean kill me, torture me, then kill me again. Seriously. At least you work away from hell. We're living it, and it ain't pretty. Fix this."

J.T. disconnected, then made a call. One he'd been meaning to make, except his father had told him to let things work themselves out. Well, screw that.

"Hello?"

"Mike, it's J.T. She's at Ray's. And she's in a mood."

"Aren't we all." Mike paused. "Thanks." Then he hung up.

J.T. grinned, then he called Rena and filled her in. She wanted in on the action, so he called Foley back with his bet, doubling his cousin's. McCauley might be a pain in the ass, but the guy had skills. He'd tamed J.T.'s little sister for a bit, hadn't he? And according to Liam, the guy was head over heels in love with Del. "You know what, Foley? Make it fifty. And add a proposal in there for me too."

"An *I Do* from Miss *I Don't*? Hell, man. You're on."

J.T. smiled. He'd be there for the wedding. With any luck, he'd convince the groom-to-be to accept a signature Webster tattoo as a wedding gift. With arms like Mike's, it'd be a walking billboard for business.

J.T. couldn't wait.

Mike parked his truck at Ray's, got out, and searched out the biggest-looking asshole he could find. Near the front of the lot, toward the bar, he found what he'd been searching for.

"What the fuck are you looking at?" a guy looking like Mr. Clean on steroids asked him, leaning against a dirty blue Blazer with monster wheels. He recognized the guy as Earl's bouncer friend from the last time he'd been by. Perfect.

"You work here, right?"

"What if I do?"

"You're a bouncer?"

"I'm security." He crossed his arms over his chest.

"Oh right. You're the prick that hit Jim."

The others around him watched with narrowed eyes. No friends here.

Not in the mood to play nice, Mike leaned close. "I want my truck in one piece when I get out. That's your job, right? So do it."

Mr. Clean stepped closer. "Yeah? What's it worth?"

In Mike's mood, he had no urge to play nice. "Your nuts." Mike waited, dying for a fight.

Fortunately, Mr. Clean's friends didn't like his attitude and attacked. He made short work of them, then waited for Mr. Clean to say something.

The fucker put up his hands. "Easy, guy. I'll make sure it's watched over—like every other car in the lot."

"Fine. But if my truck has even one scratch on it, I'm coming for you." Annoyed at not getting the real fight he needed, Mike grunted and walked past him.

Wishing he felt more bad-ass for handling two dirtbags, Mike did his best to pump himself up to deal with the *real* threat at Ray's. He put his shoulders back and walked past the clusters of groupies toward the entrance. He'd come straight from work, wearing his nasty jeans and a ripped T-shirt stained with teak oil. He had dirt under his fingernails, probably smelled like hell, but had no problem dealing with his princess while looking less than refined.

If she loved him the way she said she did, she'd take him, warts and all.

He'd never been so nervous in his freakin' life.

Pushing through the doors, he noted a few patrons sitting nearby whom he recognized from the night he'd visited. Unfortunately, the place had filled up. Earl stopped him with a hand on his chest.

Mike glanced down at the hand, then up at Earl, who smiled at him.

"Nice moves in the lot. Come on in. She's in the corner." Earl lowered his hand. "Word of warning—she's majorly pissed."

"Great. Thanks." He wound through a bunch of folks dressed much like himself and spotted Lara behind the bar. Tonight she wore a shirt that read *Bartender*. Obviously not waitressing this evening.

"Hey, handsome." She crooked a finger at him, and he leaned across the bar. She kissed him on the cheek. "Want a beer?"

"I'd love one." Before he could ask, she fetched him a Heineken. "On the house if you turn her frown upside down." She nodded to Del.

"I'll do my best. But if she starts throwing shit at me, you might want to clear the room."

"Oh honey. Don't you worry. Rena told us all about your situation with Del. God, you are so sweet." Lara gave a sad sigh.

Mike frowned. "Wait. What exactly did Rena tell you?"

"Go, go. Before she sees me talking to you and tries to punch me out. She's been a bitch lately. And God knows I don't want to have to handle her in a mood."

"Ah, okay." He had no idea what the hell Lara had been told, but he made his way to Del regardless. Seeing her put everything right. She looked thinner and in pain. Annoyed with the world, yet still so beautiful. And alive.

Thanks to his talk with Liam, he knew he had to get his head on straight before dealing with Del. After many days of soul-searching, he knew what he needed. And what she needed. But getting her to talk to him had proven difficult. She had a head injury he didn't want to further, and according to Rena and J.T., the woman still wanted nothing to do with him.

Too fucking bad.

"Hey, sweetness. Mind if I sit?" He didn't wait for her to answer and sat, pleased to see her wide eyes.

"What the hell are you doing here?"

"I'd say slumming, but we both know how that turned out when Jim said it." He took a swig of his beer. "You're looking better than last time. How's the head?"

She shrugged, keeping a wary eye on him.

"I'm here to talk."

"Really? I thought you were here for the ambience."

A few tables down, a man spilled his beer onto another guy. The girl with him dumped a pitcher over his head, adding to his sopping clothes. Then the three laughed like loons at each other and took turns grabbing drinks to douse over themselves.

"There is that."

Earl and another bouncer dragged the happy drunks away before they flooded the bar.

Mike glanced at Del again, secretly pleased at how intently she studied him.

"I'm busy. What do you want?"

"Busy and angry, I'd say. Okay. Rumor has it we broke up. That true?" He kept his voice even, pleasant, and waited.

She toyed with her glass, and he readied to duck.

"You would know."

"You'd think." He finished his beer and held up the bottle so Lara, who hadn't stopped watching him, could see he needed another. "And fries," he yelled.

"For God's sake." Del hunched lower in her seat.

He looked at her, then back at the bar and yelled, "Make that two."

Lara nodded.

"You're always yelling," Del griped.

"How else can people hear you? Especially in here?" Instead of the alternative music he expected, a funky rendition of "Viva Las Vegas" jammed from the overhead speakers. "Okay, I'll bite. How did I break up with you? Because I don't remember."

"Too busy wallowing in guilt."

"That's true. I felt awful you'd been hurt saving Colin, when I should have been there protecting you both."

She frowned. "How's that? You went to the bathroom. I told you I'd watch him, then he nearly got run over. It was my fault."

"Right. Now who's got a bad case of the guilts?"

She flushed.

"You losing weight? Your hair looks bigger than your face."

She snorted. "Compliments will get you nowhere."

"I saw your dad."

"Yeah?" She pretended not to care, but he could see her listening intently to everything he said.

"Bastard had me crying like a baby." He hadn't intended to admit that, but he wanted her to know.

"He—*what*? He did?" She sat up straight. "Did he hit you?" She looked him over.

"No. Well, kind of. We talked about J.T.'s mom…and about Lea."

"With *my dad*?" her voice rose. "He won't even talk about her to me or J.T."

"He talked to me because he knew I'd understand. When you love someone the way I loved Lea, the way your dad loved Bridget, it leaves a hole in your heart when they leave you." *A hole in his heart.* Such an apt way to describe how he'd felt without Del.

Del blinked and looked away. "I know."

"Your mom left you a long time ago, way before she died. I'm sorry for what she did. For what I did, though I didn't mean to." Mike sighed. "You have the worst damn timing."

"For being honest? Screw you." She angrily wiped her eyes, and he felt awful—and glad. If she hadn't cared, she wouldn't cry.

"My hole has been huge and ignored for six long years. Then you came into my life, and you started filling it up. Your snarky attitude. Those grubby fingernails. That sexy ring in your brow. Your bitchin' ass, and I don't mean the one on your arm."

He reached for her hand and pulled it close, despite her protest. Over her shoulder in the distance, Earl gave him a nod and looked over the crowd, ignoring an objecting Del. With the noise in the bar, only someone close could hear them in the corner. He just hoped she didn't start swinging at him before he could finish saying what he needed to.

"What do you want from me?" she snarled. "I put it all on the line for you and you told me—"

"That we should talk about it later. Jesus, Del. I'd just

watched my son and the woman I love nearly die. You'd think you could cut me some slack."

She tensed and blinked at him. "What?"

"Seeing you on the pavement, just lying there, bleeding… It took me back to a very dark place. Then having to visit you in the hospital… Seriously, the last time I was there before this accident, Lea bled out after giving birth. So yes, I was way fucked up when we talked."

She didn't try to jerk her hand free. "And maybe scared?"

"No maybe about it. I haven't felt so deeply for anyone since Lea. Then you came along, flaunting that ass, feeding my boy sugar, kissing me with that mouth that always makes me burn. I mean, come on. How could I not love you?" He smiled.

She teared up. "Don't lie. I know you don't really—"

"Love you? I do. And not because you can tolerate my brothers' odd girlfriends."

"They're not odd."

"And my hyper son."

"He's not h-hyper." She grabbed a napkin and blew her nose with her free hand.

"Or that you can swallow me like a boa downing an ostrich egg. I know, the visual's not the best, but Colin has gone on and on about snakes since the field trip, and I know more than I'd like to about their dietary habits."

She snorted.

"He misses you, you know."

She wiped her eyes. "That is so low, playing the kid card."

"I know. I'm a desperate guy." Feeling as if he'd gained some ground, he waved away Lara with the tray

of food and moved around the table to Del. He picked
her up and seated her sideways across his lap, praying
the chair wouldn't give way. "Del, I'm not the only one
with baggage. Your mom did a number on you." He
stroked her scar. "I won't lie and say I expected this,
because I didn't. It's been a long time since I've said this
to a special woman. And I didn't think she existed out
there for me anymore. But she does. You do.

"I love you. And I want to marry you."

She stared at him with huge eyes. "Wait. *Marriage?*"

"Sweetness, I want it all. But you have to know, if
you take me, you have to agree to getting not only a kid,
but a puppy too. Colin wanted me to tell you that."

"He did?"

"You're not going to faint, are you?"

"Shut up. I don't faint." There, her voice sounded
stronger. He'd been worried for a moment. "So Colin's
good with us being, uh, together?"

"Uh, yeah."

When she smacked him on the shoulder, he knew
they'd be all right.

"I'm not done," he continued. "You get my stellar
family, and we really know how to barbecue. You get
my brown house with my brown furniture, and you
get to fend off Maddie when she tries to get you to
change that brown furniture. Because I'm not dealing
with the diva designer anymore. That's part of your
job description."

"What's wrong with brown?"

He grinned. "Exactly. I love you so much. We're
so alike."

"We are?"

"Who else gets your jokes?"

She settled her arms around his neck. "There is that."

"And who else can make you come like crazy?" he said on a whisper and kissed her, as he'd been aching to do for days. "Del, I miss you so much. Come home with me. With us." He looked into her shining eyes. "Colin's a part of this. I won't lie. He's bugging the crap out of me about a little brother. The puppy was pushing it, but I'll let you deal with the brother issue."

She bit her lip. "Mike, are you sure? I just… When you didn't say it back in the hospital, it about crushed me."

"It's hard to admit a feeling you're scared shitless to have. You have no idea what almost losing you in that parking lot felt like. I never want to feel it again. I'm scared as hell I might have to, but I can't stand the idea of never living with you and finding out if you're as amazing as I think you are. And if you think about it, I've seen your morning face and still want to be with you. That's magic right there."

"You're an ass." She kissed him.

"*Your* ass. Well, you know what I mean."

She laughed softly. "I do."

"That's what I want you to say when we walk up the aisle together. I want it all, Delilah. With you." When she said nothing, he blurted, "I even promise to like your brother. I already like your dad and Rena, but I'll throw in Jethro as a bonus."

She stared into his eyes, and then she smiled. "Shh. That name's a family secret."

"Then marry me or I'll tell everyone I know, and I know a lot of people."

"Blackmail, huh? I guess I'd better then, to save my poor brother."

"Yep. Marriage, babies, dogs, the works."

Her bright smile teetered.

He frowned. "What? What's wrong?"

"Your mom hates me."

"Oh, that."

"Yes, that." She scowled. "Mothers-in-law can be vicious, so I've heard. And you are clearly a momma's boy."

"Hey."

"Well? You took Grace out when she said to."

"Oh." He flushed. "Okay, I might have stretched the truth about that. Grace and me that night? That was actually me being totally afraid I was falling for you. So *I* asked her out to stop thinking about you. Not my mom. And no, it didn't work."

Instead of being angry, she looked pleased. "Really? I scared you back then?"

"Yeah. You scare me now. Say yes, honey. I love you. My family loves you. Even my mother loves you."

"Let's not get carried away."

"Well, okay." He laughed. "But honestly, she was worried *for me*, not *against you*. There's a difference."

"If you say so."

"Here." He handed her his cell phone, having anticipated the problem.

"What's this?"

"A message for you."

She read it and gaped. "Is this for real?"

"Read it out loud." He nodded.

She stared down at it. "'Del. I'm sorry for behaving

abominably toward you, but I worry about my boy. Mike has a stubborn streak like his father.'" She stopped and glanced at him. "Like his *father*?"

"Read on."

"It stopped there."

"Hell, next message. Read that."

She scrolled down. "Oh. Ahem. 'I want him to be happy, and you make him so happy, Del. Please ignore a cranky old woman. Give him a chance. He puts the toilet seat down and doesn't move his lips when he reads.'" Del started laughing so hard she cried.

But these tears made him happy. "You finished?"

"Wait." She finally stopped laughing. "Okay, she's funny. Where was I? Hmm… 'when he reads…and he told me he loves you.'" She stared at him. "When was this?"

"When she and I had that argument two weeks ago."

"Really?"

"Really." He tried to take the phone back.

"Wait. There's one more part. 'Welcome to the family, Del. We'd be proud to have you'." Del cleared her throat. "Oh my gosh. That was the best text message *ever*." She narrowed her eyes. "Are you sure you didn't write that from your mother?"

"You'll see this weekend when you come to your own engagement party. Now you have to say yes. I can't take back all the food my mom bought. Oh, and about Grace…"

"You're not convincing me to say yes."

"I was thinking maybe you could give her Mitch's card. He is a single attorney, and she's a single paralegal."

"How do you know he's an attorney?"

"Rena gave me an earful." He had no problem diming

out her cousin. She'd outted him as Mr. Sexy. She deserved to be thrown under the bus.

"You know, that's not a bad idea."

"Exactly. Don't worry about Grace anymore, Delilah. Only one woman can handle my monster cock. And we both know that's you."

Lara returned with their food and overheard that last bit. "Oh wow. Monster cock, hmm? Don't suppose you'd be willing to show us? Consider it my tip."

Del growled, "Here's a tip. My fiancé isn't showing anything to anyone but me for the next eighty years," she shouted to the bar.

Lara set down the food and clapped, along with everyone close by. "Hey, everyone. Del got herself engaged to the guy who decked Jim and scared John!"

"John?" Del frowned at him.

"Ah, does he look like Mr. Clean?"

She blinked. "Actually, yeah. Something you want to tell me, MC?"

"Later. If my truck's not in the lot in one piece when we leave, I'll visit John again, and this time we'll *really* talk."

"Talk, hmm? The way you 'talked' to Jim?"

"More or less. I went easy on Jim."

"Oh. Now I'm all tingly."

He grinned. "What say we skip this place and let you handle my M.C.?"

"You're on, McCauley. Let's go home."

Chapter 23

COLIN RACED AROUND HIS GRANDPARENTS' BACKYARD. They had the best parties. Hyde followed him with Jekyll. Since Abby had told him the story of how she'd named hers and Ubie's dog, he'd decided on Jekyll for his puppy. And it totally fit, because Jekyll liked to play with Hyde as much as Colin liked to play with Hyde.

"Dog is going to be big," Uncle Flynn said and bent down to pet him. "Look at those paws, Maddie."

Maddie scrunched up her nose. "He seems to have a fetish for licking my feet, just like Hyde."

"We all do, sweet thing."

She laughed at Uncle Flynn, who made little sense, and Colin continued through the crowd, leading Jekyll and Hyde. Searching for Brian, he bumped into Ubie and Abby standing with Uncle Cam and Vanessa. They were arguing about Abby getting a tattoo. Vanessa and Uncle Cam were against it, but Abby and Ubie wanted her to get it.

"Come on, guys," Ubie said with his most charming grin. "A little honeypot right…*there*."

Colin frowned, not sure what "there" meant.

"Brody, really." Abby turned pink, so Colin knew his uncle was saying stuff he wasn't supposed to hear. "Oh, Colin. Hi." She leaned down to pet Hyde, who cozied up to her.

Not to be ignored, Jekyll yipped and pawed at her leg.

"He is so cute. He almost looks like Hyde's baby boy."

"Oh man, that dog is gonna be huge. And ugly," Vanessa said in a low voice.

"Hey." Colin frowned at her. "Jekyll's not ugly."

"Of course not," Uncle Cam agreed. Behind Vanessa, he mouthed, "*Ignore her. Pregnant lady,*" and made the sign of a bump over his belly.

"Oh. Um, sorry." He'd once overheard Dad talking about how pregnant ladies could get scary, and Vanessa was scary to begin with. Time to find Brian, and fast.

"What did you say?" he heard Vanessa ask Uncle Cam, but Colin was on the move.

He found Del and his grandma and hid behind a bush. Del seemed a little afraid of Grandma, even though Dad had told her it would be okay. Sometimes Grandma could be bossy, and Del could be bossy, so he wondered who would win in a cage match. Then he wondered if Del had tights, and if she'd mind if he entered her in that drawing on TV to join that reality wrestling show. Brian would probably have an idea how to make that happen.

"Your text meant a lot to me, Beth," Del said in a quiet voice.

"Oh honey. I'm only sorry I had to say it with letters instead of in person." To Colin's shock, Grandma hugged Del. "You're more than a part of this family. You saved Colin for one." Grandma wiped away tears. Gah. Girls. Always crying. Then Del blinked a lot, and he worried, because his eyes felt funny too. She really had saved him. "More than that, you saved Mike. He loves you so much, you know."

"I do." Del smiled. "But not as much as I love him and the kid trying to hide behind those bushes."

"Darn." How did she do it? He could never sneak up on her. Ever. It was like she had super powers.

Grandma grew stern. "Colin McCauley…"

"Colin," Brian yelled as he entered the backyard. "I'm *heerree*."

Colin raced to join his friend and pulled him away, with the dogs still following him. "Hey, Mr. and Mrs. Daniels. Come on, Brian."

Brian followed him, and they ran into Great-Aunt Sophie, Grandma's younger sister. "Hey, Aunt Sophie."

"Well, Colin, who's your friend? Is this *The* Brian?"

Brian puffed out his chest. "Yep. I'm Brian." He grinned and pointed to a new missing tooth.

"Oh, cool." Colin peered closer then turned to his aunt and opened his mouth wide. "Me too, Aunt Sophie." He stared up and up at the man next to her. "Liam?" Del's dad. He had a hand on Aunt Sophie's arm. Oh no. Not another pair of kissing people.

"Hey there, Colin." Liam smiled wide and hugged Aunt Sophie close. "Where's your grandma and grandpa? I want to say hi."

"Back in the house. Grandma's crying with Del." He sighed. "Too many girls crying all the time."

"Blech." Brian agreed.

"Are they okay?" Sophie asked Liam.

"Happy tears, I'll bet." He turned to Colin. "Did Del cry?"

"No. She was thanking Grandma for a test or something. Does Del have super powers? 'Cause she always knows where I am."

Liam laughed loudly. "She's good like that. Always spotted J.T. too."

"Is he here?" Colin looked around for him.

"He is."

"He's the guy I was telling you about," Colin said to Brian. "Looks just like him, and he gives tattoos."

"Oh, cool."

Liam lifted Jekyll in his big hand and held him high. "So. This is the culprit. The little guy who had you darting in the way of a car. I trust you won't do that again."

Colin flushed. "No, sir."

"Good boy." Liam put Jekyll back into Colin's hands and ruffled his hair. "We'll be back." He and Aunt Sophie walked in the direction of the house.

"Come on." Colin ran with Brian and the dogs to the back of the yard, near Colin's fort—a bunch of cardboard boxes he'd decorated with alien drawings. "Whew. Now we're safe."

He and Brian fit without a problem, and Jekyll too. But Hyde whined from outside the small cutout.

"Soon, Hyde. Go find Ubie."

The dog huffed and left.

"He's smart." Brian petted Jekyll, who quivered with joy under his hands.

"Yeah. So's Jekyll."

They sat together, looking down at Colin's toys clustered in the corner.

"So it worked?" Brian asked.

Colin nodded. "Yep. First the puppy, then the new mom. Now I just need the little brother."

Brian frowned. "Well, be careful. I tried for that and am getting a little sister." He sighed. "But at least I won't be the baby anymore."

"I'll be careful. I don't know how to do it, but if I ask

Del real nice, I bet she'll get me one. She loves me." He had tingles of good feeling running through him. Del was a keeper. He'd known as soon as he met her that she was special.

"*Aha*. There you are."

The boys yelled with fright when Colin's dad reached down from above and lifted Colin out.

"Dad. Brian and me are playing."

"Not now, you little monster. We have to do the thing with the proposal, remember?"

"Oh. I'll be back, Brian. I have to ask Del to marry us first. Hold Jekyll for me, okay?"

"Okay." Brian grinned. Man, he'd lost *two* teeth now. Colin was one behind.

He wiggled his loose one while his dad dragged him toward the front of the gathered crowd. Where Del—his new mom—waited. She looked so cool. Her hair had loops and braids. She wore a tank top, and her dragon seemed to wink at him. He planned on getting a dragon just like it as soon as his dad and Del said he could. J.T. had already promised he'd do the ink himself. He spotted J.T. and waved, happy when his new uncle waved back.

"Everyone," Dad said. "Thanks for coming."

"About time you did this," Uncle Flynn said. "I had money on last week, but okay."

The crowd laughed. All his family smiled back at him. Aunt Sophie and Liam, his uncles and new aunts, J.T., Rena, Great-Aunt Linda and Great-Uncle Van and their kids—who were Daddy's cousins and his too, once-removed or something like that. Brian, even Jekyll and Hyde. It was the best day *ever*.

His dad cleared his throat, and everyone grew quiet. "Thank you all for coming. Today's a special day, when I get to celebrate Del Webster agreeing to be my wife."

Colin's cue. "And my new mom."

Everybody cheered.

"Did she really agree? Are you sure?" J.T. teased.

"I did, brother." Del smirked. "I'm gonna be a McCauley."

"Darned straight," Dad said with a grin.

"Hell yeah," Colin added, and his father said something cross under his breath Colin probably shouldn't have heard.

"Boy…"

J.T. thought that was really funny, and so did Liam, his soon-to-be granddad. Man, Colin was getting an extra uncle and Aunt Rena too! Christmas would be super special this year. He wondered when Del would let him use those power tools Liam let him try in private.

"She's mine. End of story." Dad kissed her right on the lips. *Whooee.*

When he finished, both he and Del looked kind of goofy. Then she turned to him.

"Aw, Del." In love with her anyway, even if she was a girl, he closed his eyes and turned his cheek, prepared to take it.

The big kiss turned into a hug, and he squealed when she lifted him up in her strong arms and squeezed.

"I love you, Colin," she whispered, holding him close.

Now how was a guy supposed to deal with that? So he did what felt right. He hugged her back and kissed her cheek. "I love you too…Mom."

Then he lifted his head and saw his dad staring at him with a big grin and love in his eyes. His dad looked at

Del, then back at him. "A real family for you, Delilah. Kid and all. Can you handle it?"

She sniffed. "In the immortal words of Colin McCauley, hell yeah."

Laughter abounded and cheers rang out.

Del waved them away. "All right. Show's over. Now get back to eating and drinking, guys."

The crowd dispersed, and Brian waved him over while Hyde danced around him and Jekyll nipped at Hyde's feet.

Colin looked at his father, content to stay in Del's arms forever. "Dad?"

"Yes, son?" His dad kissed his hand, then kissed Del again.

Colin knew he'd never get a better chance. "So, well, I have Jekyll, and he's great and all, but…" He turned in Del's arms and saw Brian giving him a thumbs-up, so he forged onward. *Less is more. Keep it simple.* Mantras from Ubie he'd been raised hearing. "So if I can't get a snake…"

"No." His dad refused.

"Or a tattoo or work in Del's garage…"

Del—*Mom,* he reminded himself—chuckled. "Colin, we talked about this."

"Then I guess a little brother would be okay instead."

His new mom and his dad looked at each other before she grinned and said, "Oh, he's good."

"How do you think he hoodwinked me into a puppy? Con man tried to get hit by a car to soften me up." His dad plucked him from his mom's arms and hugged him tight, then whispered, "Nice. We'll keep working on her. She's getting there. Trust me."

"I do, Dad," he whispered back.

He turned back to his mom, smiled, and said, "I love you, Mom. But about that baby…boys only. No Nancys allowed."

Read on for an excerpt from

The Troublemaker Next Door

"But Uncle Flynn, you promised."

Flynn McCauley shook his head, his eyes glued to the television, where the Mariners played out the top of the ninth inning. "Just let me see the highlights from last night's game. I promise I'll turn it back in a minute."

"But, but…" Colin tapered off, and Flynn watched the next few minutes in disbelief. He hadn't thought the Mariners could pull off the win. Damn, he owed Brody twenty bucks.

The frightening sound of a child's tears tore Flynn from the game. He stared at his nephew in shock. "*Colin?*"

Five-and-a-half-year-old Colin McCauley didn't cry when he skinned his knees, when he'd suffered a black eye from a wild pitch, or when his father had mistakenly thrown away his favorite T-shirt just last week, thinking the holey thing a rag. The kid was tougher than a lot of grown men Flynn knew, a mirror image of Mike in too many ways.

"Colin, what's wrong, dude?" Panicked when Colin continued to cry, Flynn hurried to change the channel. Then he offered him some of the soda Colin had been asking for earlier but wasn't allowed to have. Anything to dry up Colin's tears. "It's okay, buddy. Don't cry."

He crossed the couch to hug him, concerned there might be something really wrong.

After a few moments, Colin stopped his tears and squirmed to get free so he could see the television. His grief dried up as if it had never been, not even a hiccup to indicate emotional trauma.

A remarkable recovery. "Are you, or are you not, upset about something?"

Colin took a long drag of soda and laughed at the screen. "Not now." He beamed, looking exactly like Mike—smug and annoying.

"Scammed by a kid. This is embarrassing."

"Ubie told me it would work, but I didn't believe him."

"Uncle Brody, right. Now why am I not surprised?" He had his best friend and business partner to thank for Colin's ability to lie with a straight face. "When did he teach you that?"

"At dinner last Sunday. Oh, watch this, Uncle Flynn. See how the monster eats the school? Awesome." Colin dissolved into boyish laughter.

Flynn sighed and sank into the couch. Babysitting duty wasn't so bad, or at least it hadn't been when the kid attended preschool. But if Colin was mastering Brody's tricks now, imagine what he'd be like at eight, ten... hell, as a teenager. Flynn resolved to have a firm talk with good old Ubie. No point in encouraging Colin to scam people if Flynn wasn't allowed to be in on the joke.

Flynn sat next to Colin, enjoying the cartoon despite himself. He rubbed the kid's head. Colin McCauley, future heartbreaker. He had good looks, a great sense of humor, and a quick mind, one that would keep them all on their toes for years to come. Mike had done pretty damn good with the kid, but Flynn liked to think he'd had a hand in Colin's greatness. At least the part of him that kicked ass at sports.

Just as the back door opened and heavy footsteps signaled Mike's return—*thank God*—the phone rang. And rang and rang.

"Flynn, answer the frigging phone, would you?" Mike yelled from the other room.

"What, are his hands broken?" Flynn asked the boy as he reached for the phone. "Can't he tell I' m busy watching you?"

Colin ignored him in favor of a cartoon sponge. Like father like son.

Into the phone, Flynn barked, "Yeah?"

"Um, hello?" A woman's voice. She sounded soft, sexy. Interesting.

Flynn straightened on the couch. "McCauley residence. How can I help you?"

Colin turned to look at him with interest. Flynn never used the good voice on anyone but customers or women.

"Is this Mike?"

"No, but I can get him for you."

"That would be great."

"Hold on." Flynn sought his brother and found him struggling with a tool belt and muddied boots in the kitchen. "Yo, Mike. Phone call."

"Take a message, Einstein. I'm busy here." Mike struggled with dirt-caked knots on his work boots, the scowl on his face enough to black out the sun.

Flynn flipped him the finger while he spoke to the

angel on the phone again. "Sorry, but he's busy right now. Can I take a message?"

Silence, and then a long, drawn-out sigh. "Can you just tell him that we're having a problem with the sink? I hate to bother, but my roommate threatened to cut all my hair off if I don't get this fixed soon. The problem has been going on for a week."

"Ah, hold on." He covered the phone. To his brother, he asked, "Why is some hot-sounding chick asking you to fix her sink?"

Mike groaned. "Hell. That's probably one of the tenants next door."

"Mom and Dad have new renters already? Since when?"

"Been four months now. You aren't that observant, are you? Didn't get the family looks or brains, apparently." Mike's sneer set Flynn's teeth on edge. Arrogant bastard. His brother glanced at the phone and sighed. "Tell her I'll be right over."

Flynn passed the message, then hung up. "I don't remember Mom telling us about renting the house again. All I knew is they had some renovations done since the last bunch trashed the garage. I thought the cars I'd seen in the drive belonged to her fix-it crew."

"Well, in case it's escaped your notice, the garage has been fixed for a while now. She rented the place out to three women who moved in around the middle of February. I think you and Brody were doing that job in the San Juans then. They aren't bad neighbors. Keep to themselves, really quiet, and I think one of them has been working on the flower beds in the front, because they've really taken off this year."

Trust Mike not to come to the heart of the matter. "Any of them hot?"

"And this is why Mom didn't mention them."

Acknowledgments

Much appreciation to Jess O'Brien for his valuable knowledge in all things construction. It's no wonder your business is so successful, Jess. Thanks for taking the time out of your busy schedule for me.

To my beta readers, Angi, Rox, Kim, Eniko, April, and Charity, you help more than you know. I truly thank you for your input.

To the wonderful people at Sourcebooks. My editor Cat C., the line editors, proofers, cover artists, PR folks. I appreciate all your hard work. This truly is a team effort, and it shows.

And to Jake, for giving me the chance to get all this started so many years ago.

About the Author

Caffeine addict, boy referee, and romance aficionado, *USA Today* bestselling author Marie Harte is a confessed bibliophile and devotee of action movies. Whether hiking in Central Oregon, biking around town, or hanging at the local tea shop, she's constantly plotting to give everyone a happily ever after. Visit marieharte.com and fall in love.

The Troublemaker Next Door

The McCauley Brothers—Book 1

by Marie Harte

USA Today and *New York Times* Bestselling Author

She's sworn off men

It's been the day from hell for Maddie. Instead of offering a promotion, her boss made a pass. She quit, then got dumped by her lukewarm boyfriend. As the fiery redhead has a foulmouthed meltdown, her green-eyed neighbor Flynn McCauley stands in her kitchen…completely captivated.

Until he throws a wrench into her plans

He was just there to fix the sink as a favor. He's not into relationships. She's done with idiots. But where there are friends…sometimes there are benefits. And sometimes the boy next door might be just what you need at the end of every day.

Introducing…the McCauley brothers

Welcome to the rough-and-tumble McCauley family, a tight-knit band of four bachelor brothers who work hard, drink beer, and relentlessly tease each other. When three independent women move in next door, all hell breaks loose.

For more Marie Harte, visit:

www.sourcebooks.com

How to Handle a Heartbreaker

The McCauley Brothers
by Marie Harte

USA Today and *New York Times* Bestselling Author

—⁓—

He can't get her out of his head

It's lust at first sight when Brody Singer lays eyes on Abby Dunn. The dark-haired beauty looks a lot like a woman he once knew, who died years ago. At first Brody fears his attraction is a holdover from that secret crush, but Abby's definitely different. She's a lot shyer, a lot sexier and, despite her attempts to dissuade his interest, absolutely mesmerizing.

She can't get him out of her books

Abby isn't having it. She's still trying to put her last disastrous relationship behind her and overcome the flaws her ex wouldn't let her forget. But somehow Brody isn't getting the hint. It doesn't help that when writing her steamy novels, she keeps casting Brody as the hero.

Brody is more than happy to serve as her muse and eager to help make sure her "research" is authentic. But when their research turns into something real…will she choose her own happily ever after?

For more Marie Harte, visit:

www.sourcebooks.com

Ruining Mr. Perfect

The McCauley Brothers
by Marie Harte

USA Today and *New York Times* Bestselling Author

It's tough always being right

Vanessa Campbell is a CPA by day and a perfectionist by night. She's fit, smart, healthy…and decidedly lonely. She can't stop thinking about the youngest McCauley brother, Cameron. He's just like her: smart, beautiful, and usually right—except when dealing with her.

…But someone's got to do it

Cameron McCauley likes Vanessa a little too much. She's a blond goddess and she knows it. She hates to be wrong, just like him. They tend to rub each other the wrong way, which is unfortunate considering how well they could fit. He's dying to shake Vanessa up—get her to let loose. But if he succeeds, can his heart handle it?

Praise for Marie Harte:

"Off the charts scorching hot. Ms. Harte wows with sex scenes that will make your heart pump." —*Long and Short Reviews*

For more Marie Harte, visit:

www.sourcebooks.com

Find My Way Home

Harmony Homecomings
by Michele Summers

She's just the kind of drama

Interior designer Bertie Anderson has big dreams for her career, and they don't include being stuck in her hometown of Harmony, North Carolina. After one last client, Bertie is packing up her high heels and heading for her dream job in Atlanta. But her plans are derailed by the gorgeous new owner of that big old Victorian she's always wanted to renovate…

He's vowed to avoid

For retired tennis pro Keith Morgan, Harmony is a far cry from fast-paced Miami—which is exactly the point. Keith is starting a new life for himself and his daughter Maddie, and he's left the bright lights and hot women far behind. Bertie's exactly the kind of curvaceous temptation he doesn't need, and Keith refuses to let their sizzling attraction distract him from his goals. Keith and Bertie both have to learn that there's more than one kind of escape, and it takes more than wallpaper to turn a house into a home.

For more Michele Summers, visit:

www.sourcebooks.com